HAVENSTAR

V I R G I N
W O R L D S

meet the future

Virgin Worlds is a new imprint. Its aim is to showcase the best in British SF and fantasy, and in particular to discover new talent. This is one of the three launch titles. Here is the complete list.

MIRRORMAN
By Trevor Hoyle

Frank Kersh is a convicted killer on death row. When the Messengers offer him eternal life, he's not going to turn them down. All he has to do is commit one more crime for them: one final murder.

Cawdor and his family live in present-day New York. He's also a British settler bound for the New World several centuries ago. In all his incarnations, he stands between the Messengers and their plans to inherit the world.

Kersh sets about rubbing Cawdor out — again and again and again.

ISBN 0 7535 0385 9

MNEMOSYNE'S KISS
By Peter J Evans

In the near future, the world isn't an ecological disaster area. Quite the reverse. But human beings still have the capacity to make the worst nightmares come true. Addicts such as Rayanne Gatita consume new drugs to erase the memories of life on the streets; an entrepreneur such as Cassandra Lannigan can still end up with half her brain shot away when a deal goes wrong.

Lannigan wakes up in hospital, unable to remember more than a whisper of her past. But someone's out to assassinate her — again — and her only ally is the street-girl Rayanne.

ISBN 0 7535 0380 8

HAVENSTAR

Glenda Noramly

V I R G I N
W O R L D S

First published in 1999 by
Virgin Worlds
an imprint of
Virgin Publishing Ltd
Thames Wharf Studios
Rainville Road
London W6 9HT

ISBN 0 7535 0390 5

Cover illustration by Jon Sullivan
Map illustration by P. Phillips

Typeset by Galleon Typesetting, Ipswich
Printed and bound in Great Britain by
Mackays of Chatham PLC

To my mother
JEAN LARKE
who taught me how to read

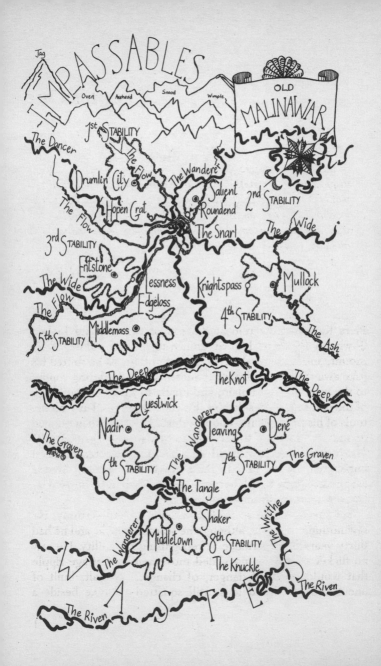

Chapter One

In the beginning there was only Chaos — but this was displeasing to the Maker, so He took the matter of Chaos and moulded it to form the firmament and the stars, which was more pleasing to Him. But the Unmaker Lord looked on His work and was unhappy, for Chaos is Lord Carasma's Realm, and only in the Unstable does he find joy.

Creation, Book I: Passage 1, Phrases 2 & 3

Piers Kaylen drew rein at the top of the rise and looked down on the halt. He sat unmoving in the saddle of his mount, and his emerald eyes missed nothing as he shifted his gaze away from the distant mountains and bordering roughs to the tree-spattered plain, and finally to the stolid buildings of the halt below. Beside him, his packhorse — laden with the tools of his profession — shook a dusty head and then nudged its master's leg as if to tell him to get moving again. It was a crossings-horse, with all the habitual bad temper and impatience of its breed. Piers Kaylen, however, Master Mapmaker from Kibbleberry, was not a man to be hurried by his pack animal's irascible temperament.

He surveyed the scene below with careful scrutiny. He saw nothing unstable, although he searched for it, and he had thirty years of experience at recognising instability. He saw no flicker of colour, no veiled movement or mirage-ripple that would speak of danger, of change. The halt, built of uncut and undressed logs, still squatted toadlike beside a

1

soak, shedding bark from shingles and walls like scales of unwanted skin – exactly as it had done when Piers had passed this way on his outward journey. The spiked poles of the stockade surrounding the buildings were still level, one with another, their tips as even as a ruled compass heading; no signs of Unstable attack there either.

Your luck holds, Pickle, my friend, he thought. Three years in one spot, and not a hint of ley. You chose well.

He knew enough not to be complacent. There were no paths to and from the halt; no tracks leading to the building; no trace of the passage of man or animal. The blue-grey grasses and the scrubby prickle bushes around the stockade looked as if nothing had disturbed them for a generation – which was all the indication needed for Piers to know that instability was as powerful here as ever. This was no place of Order, for all that the buildings still stood, untouched and untainted, three years after they had been built. Here, nothing could be taken for granted. This was the Unstable after all.

Piers urged his mount down the gentle slope and the packhorse followed obediently. Where the feet of the two beasts had crushed the grass a moment before, the grey leaves sprang back into shape as the plants quivered and shook off the effects of their violation the way an animal shakes water from its coat. Where the weight of the horses had impacted the soil, sand grains stirred and loosened themselves, their irritation shivering the ground like a heat mirage.

Piers took no notice. In the Unstable, that was normal.

The jangle of the bell pull brought Pickle himself out to swing open the gate of the stockade. Piers knew the halt-keeper well enough not to be fazed by the fact that he seemed more a nightmarish personification of a troll than a man, and grinned. 'Greetings, Pickle. Still here, I see.'

'How goes it?' Pickle asked in return, using the ritual words of greeting to all ley-lit, and he accompanied the phrase with a kinesis of welcome to a friend: right hand moving from heart to diaphragm, extended palm outward.

The words and gesture may have been ritual, but Piers knew a full answer was expected. 'Ah, you're secure enough this night,' he said as he rode into the safety of the enclosed courtyard and swung himself down from his mount. 'There's no change I can see, not within twenty leagues east, anyway.'

'The Wanderer?'

'The Bitch travels east this season, moving fast, and the emanations from the Snarled Fist are even nastier than usual with a number of new offshoots, all as mean as Chaos, but none of it's coming this way. Your halt will stand a little longer, with the Maker's grace. How's the company?'

'Building up. Still a little early in the season for much in the way of pilgrims, but there are one or two small fellowships in, with a devotions-chantor among 'em too. There'll be a kinesis session in the common room after supper.'

Piers grimaced. 'Thanks for the warning. I'll stay in my room. You do have a vacancy?' He began to unsaddle his mount without even waiting for an answer: there was always a place for a mapmaker to lay his bedroll, even when the beds were all taken.

'Oh, aye. No worries there. You can take the room you had last time.' Pickle signalled a reluctant stable boy to come and help unstrap the bundles from the packhorse. The horse curled its lip back and displayed its discoloured teeth in an evil grin.

'Stop that,' Piers growled and pulled in warning at the stiff hairs of the animal's striped mane.

'Join me for supper,' Pickle said.

Piers nodded his thanks, knowing his meal and his lodging would be free; no ley-lit mapmaker ever paid a reckoning in a halt. It was their knowledge that helped haltkeepers stay alive, after all.

Pickle stomped off on thickened legs, the hide of his bare feet hitting the beaten earth of the yard like battering rams. The haltkeeper weighed three hundred pounds, and every pound was solid flesh and muscle. Pity that his hide is that colour, Piers reflected, not for the first time. Green made people think of creatures such as wart-toads or jowled water monitors, which was a shame, because Pickle was very much a man for all that he looked like something that lurked in the dark of age-old slime beneath a bridge.

Keeping an eye on the snapping teeth of the pack animal, the stable boy led the two horses away. In the gathering dusk their stripes blended into the perpendicular lines of the stockade wall behind them. Piers, staff in his hand, watched for a moment, then headed for his room and a much-needed wash.

Supper was a stew, overladen with yams and onions and heavily spiced in a vain attempt to hide the stringiness of the dried meat it contained. Meat in the halts of the Unstable was never fresh.

As usual, the conversation in the common room centred around the latest peregrinations of ley lines. Pickle was not the only person interested in what Piers had to say: two couriers, a guide and a trader – all ley-lit themselves – wandered over to exchange a word with the mapmaker and to learn what they could of the changes. With none of them was Piers particularly forthcoming, even though he was acquainted with them all.

'My information is for sale,' he told them, 'as usual. I have old maps of every area north of the Wide, including the best Wide crossings. I can sketch in the latest changes now as well, or you can have properly updated maps within a couple of weeks from my shop. You all know my place in –'

'– in Kibbleberry on the South Drumlin Road in the First Stab,' one of the couriers finished for him, grinning. He turned to the others, saying, 'Come on, you load of misbegotten Unstabler carrion-eaters – you ought to know by now you'll get nothing out of Piers Kaylen without paying for it.'

'Bloody freeloaders,' Piers said without rancour once they

were gone. 'They want the best information to save their hides, but they hate to have to pay for it. They forget I've been out there in the Unstable for three months, risking my neck half a dozen times a day. I was attacked by Minions near the Fist, nearly lost my life fording the Flow, got bitten by a snake-devil within a leyflame's throw of the Wanderer – do they think I do it all for nothing?'

Pickle laughed. 'A normal trip, eh? By all that's dark in Chaos, Piers, I reckon you must be the toughest bit of leather ever to roam the Unstable. There's not many can say they've lasted as long as you have. And often alone, what's more.'

'True.' There was quiet pride there, rather than boasting. 'Thirty years I've been at it. And I reckon it may well die with me too – that damn son of mine'll never make a decent surveyor. Maker knows what sort of maps he'll turn out, left to himself.'

'Seemed tough enough to me the few times you've brought him here.'

'Nah – all bluster. He's about as tough as melting sugar-cakes.' Piers stuck out his left leg and waved a hand at it. Flesh and bone ended just below the knee; the stump nestled inside a leather cup attached to a wooden peg leg. 'This happened twenty years back, and it never stopped me. I saw my own foot disappear down the gullet of one of the Wild and I still survived – yet that son of mine winces when his hipbone nudges a pebble under his bedroll.' He sopped up the last of the stew with a piece of bread and shrugged. 'He'll run the business into the ground when I'm gone. My girl's got twice his gumption and it's a jiggin' shame she's the wrong sex. Jiggin' shame, too, that Chantry took the other son we had, the over-encoloured bastards. Still, why worry, eh? I don't suppose I'll be around to see what happens to Kaylen the Mapmaker's twenty years from now.' He paused suddenly, head cocked in disbelief as he listened. 'Chaos-damn, Pickle – you've never got a *baby* in here?'

From somewhere above the unmistakable sound of a

hungry infant wailed down into the common room.

Pickle gave a grimace that made deep green furrows in his face. 'What's the Halt coming to, eh? Yep, it's a babe right enough.' He lowered his voice. 'The parents are a young couple, making the Long Pilgrimage, so they say. But the babe's Unbred, or I'll be pink and white myself. They are certainly keeping it away from yon chantor.' He nodded at the man who had appropriated the room's most comfortable chair by the fire. He was dressed in the scarlet and mauve robes of Chantry and was reading the text of a book with the aid of a gold, wire-rimmed lorgnette. Every now and then he shook his yellow silk stole to emphasise the importance and holiness of what he read, and the bells along the stole's hem tinkled.

'So what are they doing dragging a baby all the way across the Unstable?' Piers asked.

'Looking for sanctuary in Havenstar, or I've missed my guess.'

Piers shook his head in disbelief. 'Poor souls! Ah, Pickle, when will people stop believing in miracles? They'll get themselves and their babe tainted, and all for a dream that doesn't exist.'

Pickle gave the mapmaker an embarrassed look. 'Maybe it's a dream worth having.'

'Ley-life! Not you too! Next you'll be telling me there are winged fire-elementals sitting on your kitchen hearth.' He yawned. 'My friend, I'm for my room before that chantist kinesis-maker over there gets going. Just listening to his bloody bells is bad enough.'

Pickle regarded the red and mauve figure pensively. 'Don't knock 'em, Piers. Kinesis devotions stave off the predations of instability and I'm damned sure they keep the Wild at bay, too.'

'So they reckon. I wonder myself if they don't just make the Wild flipping wilder. Anyway, I'm off.'

He limped away, his wiry frame all muscle and sinew, only his swinging walk betraying his lack of a foot. The polished black staff he carried seemed more ornament than necessity.

And in the eyes of those in the room who watched him go there was both envy and respect. Piers Kaylen was a legend: an Unstabler who had survived thirty years of crossings, a mapmaker who often travelled alone in places most men would not go without an armed escort. He possessed all the instincts of a hunted animal and yet had the talents of a hunter – it was said that even the worst of the Minions of Chaos slunk away rather than face the throwing knives Piers wore strapped to his chest, at his hip and, it was said, in his single boot.

Piers was halfway undressed, stripped to the waist with his knives lying on his bed, when there was a knock at the door. Habit made him pluck up one of the knives as he went to answer it; he expected no attack and scented no danger, but you did not stay alive in the Unstable by being careless about anything.

'Who is it?' he asked. He laid his face against the door and was immediately aware of the faint vibrations of wrongness given off by one of the Unbound. 'They call me the Mantis,' came the reply. 'You probably noticed me down in the common room – I want to talk to you about a map.'

Piers unbarred the door with a fair idea of who it was he would see. The man standing there was, like Pickle, one of the Unbound – or an Untouchable as they were sometimes called – and the Mantis was an appropriate name. Piers had indeed noticed him in the common room: he had been hard to miss. He was at least seven feet tall, with limbs and body as elongated and as thin as the insect whose name he bore. He had to fold himself up to enter the room, and there was no way he could stand erect once inside: the ceiling was too low.

Piers put his knives away and waved a hand at the bed. 'Sit down. You want a map? Are you buying on your own account?'

'Well, no. I mean, I don't want to buy at all, really. I want to sell.' He shoved a hand inside his shirt as he sat and withdrew a mapskin wrapped around a rod of wood.

'I don't buy maps,' Piers said. 'I make 'em.' But he reached out a hand to take the skin nevertheless. One could always learn something from another man's chart.

He had spent a lifetime dreaming about this moment: the wonderful second when his hands would unroll a trompleri map and he would feast his eyes on magic. Yet, as he opened up the skin and the dream became reality, he could not believe the moment had arrived. He stared at the map in his hands, felt his jaw dropping – and still could not believe it. *A trompleri map*. One of the legendary wonders that he had only half believed existed but which was now unfolded before him in all its glory . . .

'Where – where did you get this?' he stammered finally. His knees gave out and he sat down heavily on the bed next to the Mantis.

'What does it matter? What I want to know is, do you want it?' The man poked his lean features into Piers's face. His nose and chin and jaw were all sharp-edged, insect-like. A long-fingered hand seized Piers's arm, circling it. There was surprising power there, even though his wrist was scarcely wider than a broom handle, and each finger as slim as a pipe stem. 'Do you want to buy it?'

Piers strove to regain both his native caution and to avoid shuddering. He hated to be touched by one of the Unbound, even though the man was careful not to cause him pain by brushing against his bare skin. 'Well, it's not really of that much value to me,' he said. 'I deal with the land north of the Wide; this appears to be some place south of the Graven. Who in heaven's ordering wants to go there? That's even beyond the Eighth Stab!'

'Don't fool with me, mapmaker! I know the value of a trompleri map to one of your ilk. You'd sell your soul to have one of these, in the hope that you could find out its secret so that you yourself could produce the like. How much will you give me for it?'

'I don't carry much money with me. What need have I of money in the Unstable? I keep what meagre wealth I have at home in the First.'

'And you know very well that I can't go that far into a stability. Quite apart from the fact that stability makes me as sick as a cat with worms, I've no wish to challenge Chantry. How much do you have on you?'

'Hardly more than a handful of coppers. Just enough to tip a stable boy or two and buy me a meal or two between the kinesis chain and home. Nothing more.'

'Come now — no one of your experience travels without a little fund for an emergency. Don't take me for some newly tainted kid who doesn't know his way about the Unstable and who's never met a mapmaker. I know what's what. You have more than a few coppers hidden about you.'

'Well — three silvers and a gold. That's all. And, yes, I'd part with them to own a trompleri map, but you must know that it's worth more than that.'

'I'll take the coins and your horse for it.'

'My packhorse?'

'No, your mount.'

Piers was genuinely dismayed. 'That mare and I have been together a long time. We've been through a lot. Besides, it's a crossings-horse. Ley-lit Unstablers don't take kindly to other folk having them.'

'There's no law against it. That's my deal. And it's a generous one. Take it or leave it.'

'I ask myself the reason for your — er — generosity.'

'Don't be daft. You don't need me to spell it out. I'm in need of cash and a mount. My animal took a tumble and is as lame as an old man's pecker. I'll give her to you, if you want.'

Piers was silent, thinking. The map was obviously stolen. He'd never be able to admit to ownership of it, or resell it. The fact that the Mantis was in a hurry to rid himself of it also seemed to indicate that the real owner was only a step behind him.

But Piers's hands itched to hold it, his mind begged

to analyse it, his mapmaker's soul longed to solve its mysteries . . .

'All right,' he said. 'I'll buy it. And I'll take your lame nag. Come back in half an hour and I'll have the money and the papers ready for you.'

By the time the Mantis returned, Piers had retrieved his money from its hiding place and had the horse's ownership scrip ready. He handed them over wordlessly and received the map and another horse scrip in return. As he checked the skin to make sure it was the same one he had first seen, he said casually, 'Don't think to divert your followers to me, Mantis. I'm too wily to be taken like that. This map disappears the moment you leave this room. They wouldn't find it on me, and then they'd still be after you, madder than before.'

'I don't have the dribbling tongue of a betrayer,' the Mantis said indignantly. 'No one'll ever hear aught from me, even if they ask.'

'Look after my horse,' Piers returned, imperturbable. 'If ever you want to sell her back to me, send word to Kibbleberry. Her name's Ygraine.'

'A highfalutin handle, that.' Legend – or was it history? – said that there had once been a great Margravine of Malinawar called Ygraine. She was said to have led an invasion into Yedron with particularly nasty results for the Yedronese monarch of the time, simply because she had thought herself insulted. The Mantis evidently did not think much of the choice of name, but he said, 'I'll take care of her. She's my passage out of here.' He tucked away the paper and the money, nodded briefly, and let himself out.

Piers hardly noticed his going. Instead he pored over his acquisition, revelling in the beauty and workmanship, touching it with reverent fingers, already looking forward to the moment when he would share his awe, his joy, with Keris. And Thirl, of course.

Then, reluctantly, he secreted it away in the hiding place

he used for valuables when travelling. He was hoping that he would have another one or two visitors, people wanting to buy his maps this time, and he did not want anyone to see this purchase.

Within the next hour he made four sales of maps roughly updated with the latest information. Then – just as he was about to spread his bedroll out on the straw mattress and turn in for the night – there was another knock at the door. As before, the habit of a lifetime made him pick up one of his knives and caution made him ask the visitor to identify himself, but he was tired and he did not notice the emanations that might have warned him what waited for him on the other side of the door.

The name given in reply meant nothing, but he thought he recognised the voice of one of the chambermaids and unbarred the door anyway. After all, no one really expected to be attacked inside a halt. Certainly no one expected to confront one of the Minions of Chaos within its walls, especially not when there were kinesis devotions being performed in the common room to ward off just such evils. And, most of all, no one would have dreamt of seeing one of the Wild . . .

Yet no sooner had Piers lifted the bar than the door was flung open with immense force, catching him across the chest and arm. His knife went flying and before he could utter a sound he was flattened by his attacker and two clawed hands the size of dinner plates were around his throat, squeezing, crushing his windpipe. It happened so fast – and his assailant was so unnaturally strong – that he never had a chance.

Even as he struggled, even as he battered at the thickened nose, gouged at the yellow eyes, he glimpsed the Minion standing with folded arms behind her Pet, he saw her blood-soaked nails tapping impatiently on her bloodied forearms, and knew he was going to die. His only thought was one of surprise that it was all going to end this way, in the relative safety of a halt, and not out there in the Unstable some-where, as he had always thought.

Chapter Two

*And no more did the lands beyond the sea send their sailors;
nor yet did the Margravate of Malinawar see its own sails
return on the wind, decks piled high with the fragrant oils of
Premantra and the golden cloth of Brazis. No more did the
caravans come from Yedron and Bellisthron and the lands
behind Beyond. All about was Ley. All about was unstable,
and Humankind feared to cross. Malinawar was as eight rafts
afloat on a storm-soaked ocean, and none knew the way to
swim.*

The Rending I: 7: 8—11

On the outskirts of Kibbleberry village a party of Tricians
rode past the mapmaker's shop at a brisk trot: six women
and five men, guarded by twenty of the Defenders and
followed by a baggage train of servants and kinesis-chantors.
The Tricians might have been clad in the normal brown and
grey of the unencoloured, but their clothes were of the finest
deer leathers, soft linens and plush goat wool; the domain
symbols they wore around their necks were of gold, some
even studded with jewelstones, although it was doubtful that
Chantry would have approved of that. The Defenders — all
of them as noble as those they guarded — were lavishly
accoutred and armed.

In the shop, Keris Kaylen laid her work aside to watch
them pass. *Even the servants are better dressed and mounted
than anyone in Kibbleberry,* she thought. She felt no envy.
Tricians and their servants were as remote from her as the

forests of the Eighth Stability, even though fellowships such as this one passed along the road often enough. She had never spoken to one of their number and had no reason to think that she ever would; none of them ever stopped. If they had needed a map, the purchase would have been done long since through an intermediary. Tricians rarely made commercial transactions themselves.

These were bound for the Unstable, yet they seemed happy, laughing and joking and flirting and never thinking about the dangers ahead once they crossed the kinesis chain. They were young, they were beautiful, they seemed carefree – yet Keris would not have changed places with any of them. Too many of these same young men would lose their lives one day as Defenders; too many of those young women would raise their children alone – only to see their sons die or be tainted in the Unstable just as their husbands had been. The very word 'Trician' was derived from some longer and more ancient expression supposed to have meant 'of my father's arming'. Tricians were born to bear arms, or to marry those who did, just as their parents had; it was not a life Keris envied.

Better, she thought, to be a canny ley-lit mapmaker like her father, who was scornful of noisy young Tricians and their arms and their delicately bred horses. 'In the Unstable they and their chantors just attract trouble,' he had snorted once. 'Better to be solitary. Wiser to be quietly elusive than to be challenging. Never take your pilgrimage with a guide that hires Defenders, Keri. It means the fellow doesn't know his job.'

One of the young men saw her looking out of the shop door and winked. The girl next to him giggled and said something that made him laugh – then they were all gone from her sight. With a shrug, Keris lowered her eyes once more to her work. None of them mattered.

And then her head jerked up again as she realised what she had just seen – beyond the road, beyond the fields and the wood. Or rather what she had *not* seen.

There was a line of mountains beyond the stab, and on a clear day it was possible to see the whole range from the shop. Keris had been able to name all the main peaks since she was just four years old: the Jag, the Oven, the Shadow . . . the Axe Head . . . the Snood and the Wimple. All told, they were the Impassables. And now the Axe Head was missing. For three days they had all been hidden by cloud, and now that the weather had cleared —

In a daze she slipped off her stool and went to stand in the doorway, to stare. It was true: it really had gone. There was the range; there were all the other peaks — but the Axe Head had simply vanished. There was a space on the skyline that gaped vacantly like the cavity left by a pulled tooth.

She whirled from the door, wanting to run inside to tell someone — and then stopped. There was only her mother, and it would be better if she was not bothered. Not now. Keris sighed. Not for the first time, she wished her father was home.

And then she remembered the roof-mender at work returfing part of the barn roof. He wasn't a learned or particularly knowledgeable man, but at least he was *somebody* to tell. She left the shop to go to the barn, walking around the outside of the house so as not to disturb her mother. She found Articus Medrop arranging cut turf on his hod at the foot of his ladder.

'Master Medrop —' she began, but he did not let her finish.

'Good turf I've got you,' he said. He showed her some, waggling it at her with a muscled arm extended in her direction. He was all lean muscle: arms, shanks and calves; even his face seemed tautly sinewed. 'You tell your dad when he comes home. This came from Jeckitt's top field, and it's full of snow bells and mauves. Your roof'll be a picture next spring. Had Carasma's own job trying to persuade the Rule Office to let me cut it, I can tell you —'

She interrupted. 'Master Medrop, have you seen the Axe Head?'

He looked at her imperturbably. 'Oh aye. That I have. Or not seen it, more like. It's gone.' He bent to stack more turf on the hod. 'Best forgotten now, lass.'

'*Forgotten?* How can you forget a mountain?'

'Easy – it's gone, hasn't it? It was far away, and never did concern us, even when it was there. Beyond Order, the Impassables. As long as stability lives – and it will if we live right – why worry your head about it? Lass, it's better you concern yourself with that there roof beam in the barn. Won't last more than another year or two, and all my returfing ain't going to repair a beam that's about to crumble.'

She allowed herself to be diverted. 'We did plant a replacement tree about five years back, but the Rule Office says we have to wait until that one's been growing ten years before we can cut another for the beam. And we have had our name down for a lightning-struck tree, or a wind-felled one – but the list of people waiting is an ell long. It'll be *years* before we get a beam.' It was a sore point with her father, who thought the Rule Office ought to be more flexible about allowing wood to be imported from the Unstable.

Articus grunted. 'They won't like it if the roof of your barn falls in,' he said. 'That'd make a change to the landscape, and what then? I'll mention the state of the beam to the Office. Mayhap they'll reconsider.'

She thanked him and went back to the shop, but could not resist another glance up at the snow-dredged peaks of the mountains. They had always seemed so unchangeable, so impervious to everything – even time. She could not recall ever seeing any alterations to their outlines, yet perhaps it had been an unreal expectation to assume that they would never change. After all, they no longer seemed to resemble the objects they were named after. Snoods were the accepted way for a married woman to contain her hair at the back of her head, but no snood Keris had ever seen resembled the Snood Mountain of the Impassables. If anything, it looked more like a chantor's tricorn. And the Wimple bore no

15

resemblance to the obligatory headgear of widows, either.

For the first time, she wondered just how many changes there had been in the thousand years since the Rending, but it was not an idea that she wanted to dwell on.

With one last lingering glance at the new silhouette of the Impassables, she returned to her stool and her work.

It was warm for the first day of summer. Sometimes, there in the First Stability in the shadow of the mountains, the season's warmth came late, but that year it promised to be otherwise. Sunlight shafted in through the open door of the shop to warm the cat where it dozed in a furry ball on the floor near a pile of vellum squares; the breeze that nudged a scroll of parchment along the counter top was pleasantly balmy.

Keris, lightly dressed, with her arms bare and her skirt immodestly hitched up (a habit that might have prompted the Trician's wink), enjoyed the feel of the sun on her legs as she laboured over a master chart.

She dipped a fine-haired brush into a pot of paint and hesitated briefly before dabbing colour on to the oblong sheet of parchment pinned to the mapboard in front of her. The hesitation was an ingrained ritual, something she did without real thought, in deference to her father. He disliked her adding colour to maps, and had accepted the idea only after she had shown that they did sell better that way. His acceptance had not stopped him from muttering things about newfangled ideas and silly feminine frivolities, utterances that had induced a sense of guilt in Keris every time she loaded her brush with vegetable dye – hence her pause.

Yet, when her brush did move on to tinge the trees of Taggart's Wood with green, the colour added life to the ink work already done. Under the strokes the map began to live, and she was careful not to allow her desire to turn a chart into a work of art interfere with the map's technical accuracy. She was not a mapmaker's daughter for nothing.

The cat near the door snuffled and stirred uneasily. Keris worked on, thinking often of that awful gap in the mountains, more occasionally of her mother and her brother – unhappy, worrying thoughts – but with most of her being concentrated on the picture taking shape in front of her. The First Stability, nestling in the foothills of the Impassables (darn it, she would have to blank out the Axe Head later), oval in shape with its numerous towns and villages and one large city, Drumlin. On the other side of the River Flow, the Second Stability, smaller, perfectly round and much flatter. And, somewhere in between, the Wanderer – but she would not put that in yet. Not until her father came home with the Bitch's new coordinates.

Her brush moved on to the Third Stability, the border chaotic where it followed the contours of a more rugged landscape . . .

It was the cat that broke her concentration. It raised its head from the flagstoned floor, ears pricked, and miaowed. Outside, Keris heard the sounds of riders coming up to the shop from the road that passed by the front door. She began to clean her brush – she had made it herself from cat hair, and was not about to leave it to dry stiff with paint while she attended to customers.

The cat – named Yerrie for reasons long since forgotten – stood, stretched elegantly and jumped up on to the counter top. Keris patted its head absently and moved the map she had been working on to the shelf out of sight. A moment later four horses, stolid plough animals with two riders between them, stopped in front of the shop door. Quickly she pulled her skirt down and ran her fingers through her hair in an attempt to tidy it. She was pilgrimage age that summer and she thought herself grown, but she was ruefully aware that to those who visited the shop she probably seemed more girl than woman, even though she had reached the age of full majority. Her figure was still more boyish than womanly and she had resigned herself to the knowledge that it would probably stay that way until she had borne children. Worse still, she had nondescript brown hair that streaked unevenly into half a dozen indeterminate shades, and a skin that freckled in the sun, a combination that made her seem more hoydenish than mature.

There was nothing pretty about her face. Her pale-grey eyes were unremarkable, although they could tinge blue on bright days, or darken to slate in winter when they could seem as leaden as snow-laden skies. Her nose was too long, her mouth too wide and her chin too solid for beauty, while her hands were too large and her feet too long for grace – but, for all that, she was more ordinary than ugly. She was, in fact, the kind of woman men passed in the street without giving a second glance, failing to note any possibility of passion or intelligence or character simply because the face and the figure promised only banality.

She regretted the lack of beauty, but never dwelt on it; she had never had any reason to do so. Her entire sexual experience consisted of deterring one or two pimply village youths from thrusting a hand down her blouse on the odd occasion when they had detained her hurrying home in the cold dark of a winter's afternoon; if this was what being a woman meant, she saw little advantage in possessing an attractiveness that would only give her more such problems.

However, as she watched the young woman of about her own age slide down from her horse into the waiting hold of her companion, she did wish she looked a little older. People listened more when they thought a person was old enough to have experience.

Newly weds, she thought, wanting to get their pilgrimage over and done with before they settle down to raise a family. She had seen many such.

They came into the shop together, more than a little anxious, tired and dusty and in need of a bath and rest.

'Greetings,' the man said, making an appropriate kinesis with his hand moving from forehead to mouth. 'We were advised that we'd need a map of the First Stability, and that this was the place to come. Is the mapmaker here?'

She shook her head as she returned the kinesis, hiding a momentary irritation. 'I'm sorry – no.' And his son's not here either, as he should be, she thought. But I am, and what's the matter with me? 'Can I help? You are pilgrims?'

'Yes, from the Second Stability,' the woman said with an anguished sigh that came from somewhere deep inside her.

Keris was immediately sympathetic. 'A bad crossing?'

'Terrible,' she said. 'There were two who were tainted — *two*! And six separate ley lines to cross, four of them uncharted. The guide said he hadn't had such a trip in years.'

'My wife doesn't want to go back,' the man said bleakly.

'The guide'll have new maps by the time you are due to return, and you're unlikely to be tainted on a return journey anyway,' Keris said. 'It usually happens the first time you cross a ley line, or not at all.'

'That's what they say,' the woman said. 'But I've heard it can happen.'

'It can. Just not very often.'

'I don't want to go back. And it doesn't matter if we don't, does it? I mean, the pilgrimage is still valid, isn't it?'

'Now Cosey,' the man said with patronising patience, 'you know you would be hankering after your ma and sister within a few weeks. We got to go back.' He turned to Keris. 'We need a map of Drumlin City, maid.'

Keris indicated a map pinned to the wall behind her. 'We have ones like that. They show all the hostelries for pilgrims, and all the holy sites you are supposed to visit within the city. And we have this one too.' She spread out another map on the counter. 'This one is of the whole of the First Stab, showing the most convenient route from shrine to shrine. See? They are numbered, and the paths are marked. The obligatory shrines are shown in red; the minor ones in blue. The names are written beside them.'

Cosey looked at it doubtfully. 'I dunno that we can understand maps. We're just farming folk —' Her husband gave an embarrassed nod of agreement.

'There's nothing to it, really,' Keris said. 'Imagine you're a bird, flying up in the air, and you're looking down on the ground. Well, this is what it would look like. Everything tiny, looking a bit odd because you are looking at it from above. See here: that's a wood, and this is a road. And there you have a village. See the houses? And here's a stream —'

'Oh! And look, Jax, there's a water mill!'

'That's right. So, if you were on this path and wanted to go to this shrine here, you would turn right at the crossroads where the water mill is.'

'Why, that's easy! Jax, do you see? If we had a map, we really don't have to pay a guide.'

'It's certainly cheaper,' Keris agreed. 'And you can always ask the way as well, once you have studied the map and decided where you want to go.'

'How much is it?' Jax asked.

'A silver for a vellum one. A parchment one is cheaper, only half a silver. But then you really need a leather map case for it, and that costs twenty coppers.'

'A silver doesn't sound much for a chart,' Cosey said, surprised. 'I thought maps were very expensive. We were wondering if maybe a guide would be cheaper.'

'Charts of the Unstable *are* expensive. Mapmakers like my father risk their lives six months in every year to map the Unstable. But these stability maps hardly need much updating because of the Rule. Look, if you'd like some advice, I'll tell you what I think. Don't go direct to Drumlin. Go to Kte Marlede's Shrine first. That's just about an hour's walk off the main road, and you turn off just forty minutes or so from Kibbleberry.' Keris pointed to the shrine on the map. 'Here, see? It's an obligatory one. There's a chantist hostelry there if you want it, or you can camp in the field for a small fee. It's where the Knighte begged forgiveness from the Maker for her previous disbelief. She wasn't a sworn Knighte of Chantry then of course. You can still see the melted rocks where the Maker sent down His warning. It's a beautiful place with a river — just the place to rest after your journey, to make your peace with the Maker for your past sins. What better way to start a pilgrimage?'

Cosey sighed. 'It sounds lovely. I'm so tired.'

'Drumlin, on the other hand, is a day and a half's ride from Kibbleberry,' Keris added. 'If you go to Kte Marlede's instead, then you can go on to the second obligatory shrine, here. That's Kt Gallico's. And then the third here. After that you have to decide whether to take this route here –' her finger traced a pathway across the map '– which takes in five minor shrines, all in Taggart's Wood, or stay on the main route to Kte Felmina's. The deviation rejoins the main path here. There are several other detours like that further on. Eventually you will arrive in Drumlin from the north. It's the route most pilgrims take.'

Cosey turned to her husband. 'Jax – let's.'

He squared his shoulders. 'All right. We'll take this map. I dunno about the other, though –'

Keris smiled. 'Look, I shouldn't say this, but you'll be able to buy a used one in the city for a few coppers from a pilgrim about to return to his or her own stability. You may even be able to sell this one just before you leave, although that may be more difficult because most people will already have bought it here on their way into the stab.'

The man began to look happier. 'That's a good idea.' He dug into the pouch around his neck and produced a silver.

Keris rolled up the map and fastened it with its attached ribbon. 'There you go. May the peace of Creation be yours on your journey.' She signed a kinesis of farewell.

'Thank you,' Cosey said, as her hands fluttered the reply. 'You are nice – I feel better about being on pilgrimage already.'

Keris watched them from the doorway while they re-mounted and rode away, then turned to pick up the coin from the counter. She hesitated a moment, then slipped the silver into her apron pocket.

From the next room a weak voice asked, 'Have they gone?'

'Yes, Mama, they've gone,' she answered. She went into the main room of the house, the kitchen, where her mother was lying on a bed under the window, well wrapped in spite of the day's warmth. Only her face, tired and pale, and her thin white hands, moving restlessly on the much-patched cover, were visible.

21

'Your father would say you threw away the sale of the second map.'

Keris nodded, unrepentant. 'They were farming people without much money. We don't need their silver.' She made an impatient gesture with one hand. 'Riding their plough horses, poor souls. They probably won't get their knees together for a year once they've got home. And – obedient to the Rule – the wife has already changed back into a skirt, which can't be comfortable to wear while riding such a beast.'

'Now, Keris –'

She didn't let her mother finish. 'It's nonsense that they are here anyway, risking their lives crossing the Unstable – and for what?'

'For the good of their souls, Keris, dear.'

'But *why* should it be good for their souls? What's the matter with devotions at shrines in their own stability? Why should we all have to make this truly ridiculous journey once in our lifetimes, or risk dying unhallowed and destined for the Hell of Disorder no matter how knightly a life we have led? The whole thing is just a way Chantry has of fleecing the population –'

'Nonsense, dear, and you know it. They could fleece us quite adequately at our local shrines if need be. We do this because the Maker requires it of us, to show that at least once in our lives we put Him first before our personal desires and indeed before our personal safety.'

'Is He so – so – *petty*? It's not right, Mother. People *die* out there in the Unstable. Or are terribly tainted and then excluded, unable to ever return – is this fair?'

Her mother's expression was that of someone who had heard it all before from the same source – and often. She said quietly, 'Those who die are received directly into Heaven's Order. You would be more tolerant of your faith and the Rule if you were older and closer to death, child.'

Keris winced. The words struck too close to home: her mother's illness was worsening. The strange lump that grew inside Sheyli Kaylen was sucking her life away as it swelled and groped its way through her body. She was frail now. Even her hair, once luxuriantly abundant, seemed as fragile as the delicate lacework woven on to the neck of her nightdress. (An illegal frippery, that; but it showed that once Sheyli had been a woman of spirit prepared to defy the Rule, even if she did keep the rebellion hidden on her nightwear.) Keris said with unaccustomed gentleness, 'Father will be home soon. Perhaps even today.'

'Perhaps. But Keris, you heard what that Cosey woman just said: four uncharted ley lines on their route. Your father will have had much to do. Did you put their silver in the till?'

Keris shook her head and took the money out of her pocket. 'For Thirl to drink or gamble away? No. This will buy you some more sleeping medicine for a start, and still leave more than enough to pay what we owe to Master Ferit for the yams and onions he bought us at the Daltoner Market last week. Thirl needn't know about it.'

Her mother sighed. 'I don't –' she began, but whatever she was going to say was obliterated by the sudden desperate howling of a cat.

'Yerrie?' Keris looked up in astonishment and went back into the shop to see whatever was alarming the normally placid animal.

It was another customer, a man just dismounting out in the yard.

'Hush up,' Keris hissed at the cat. It backed over into a corner, lashing its tail angrily. Keris stared out of the door, thinking the visitor must have had a dog, but she couldn't see one. He did have a pair of matched crossings-horses that could have been twins, they were so alike. Short, with stumpy necks, stiff manes and thick legs, striped all over with brown and black and dirty grey, crossings-horses were unprepossessing beasts, much ridiculed by those who did not ride them. Their value lay in their stamina – they could run for hours carrying heavy loads – and their ability to leap, not heights, but widths. They had hindquarters and back legs that had the hidden power of coiled springs, yet they had narrow backs, well padded with fat, which made them comfortable to ride, even though they were bad-tempered and impatient. Unstablers — those ley-lit who lived in stabilities, yet worked the Unstable for a living — would ride nothing else, and traditionally resented anyone else owning or using one.

Even if she had not seen the horses, Keris would have soon known that their owner was an Unstabler. He had the aura of assurance and the lack of conformity that was commonplace among those who chose to work outside the stabilities. Couriers, guides, mapmakers, traders, tinkers, peddlers — such men, leading dangerous and often solitary lives, rarely followed convention, and, while some were gauche and tongue-tied in any kind of town society, most displayed the same sort of quiet confidence this man had. He was dressed all in brown and his clothes were of Trician quality, but they seemed to conform only loosely to the dictates of the Rule. At a guess, she would have said he was dressed more for comfort than any desire to please rule-chantors. His age she thought to be about thirty-five or forty. When he swung himself out of the saddle with an easy animal grace she saw that there was a long whip coiled at the side of his saddle. She had seen such before: the plaited hide of it would be impregnated with slivers of glass. It was not a weapon for the squeamish and her immediate thought was: a tough man. His eyes were chips of black obsidian; the gaze he gave her as he crossed the yard to the shop door was one of total disinterest. He had looked and seen nothing that merited the slightest curiosity on his part and his gaze ranged on to look past her into the shop.

She turned away, humbled and riled, and went to stand behind the counter top.

He stopped in the doorway for a moment to look around. Even as he made the greeting kinesis he scarcely seemed to notice her. When he spoke, he was looking at the maps on the wall, not at her, and he had a voice like a slide of gravel down a hillslope, all rough edges and conflict. 'Is Piers around?' he asked. The tone was polite enough; it was just the voice that was extraordinary. The cat backed up against the wall in the far corner, its whole body shivering with fear, all its fur on end, its teeth bared. Keris blinked in surprise; she had never seen the animal in such a state before. Whoever this man was, he had reduced Yerrie to a mass of trembling terror just by his presence.

'I'm sorry,' she said, eyes still on the cat. 'He's not here. How can I help you?' She wrenched her gaze away from Yerrie to look at the man. He wore throwing knives, she noted; she had never seen anyone but her father wear throwing knives – to use them required a skill not many bothered to master.

'I need to see Piers. It is important. Where is he?' He looked at her then, still without much interest. He obviously did not intend to explain any further.

'He's away on a surveying trip. He is expected back any day now.'

'Ah. Then I shall have to come again.' He sketched a farewell kinesis and swivelled on his heel.

'Can I give him a message?' she asked, coldly polite. Some perverse part of her wanted to detain him; wanted to have him really see her as a person, instead of having his eyes flick over her as if she was part of the furnishing, and a rather shabby part at that.

He turned back in the doorway. 'If it's up-to-date maps I want, child, you can hardly give me those if Piers is still out on his surveying trip.' The tone was still mild, but the 'child' rankled.

Bastard, she thought. In her mind she savoured the word forbidden by convention to her tongue. In the corner, Yerrie spat.

He heard and turned his gaze on the cat, noticing it for the first time. The animal's back rose, fur hackled, and it snarled, a low growling in the back of the throat.

The effect on the man was extraordinary. He stood stock-still while a slow flush spread from the back of his neck to his face, suffusing his sun-tanned skin with colour. It wasn't embarrassment, Keris realised — it was shame. *The man was ashamed*, like a lad caught peeping in a girl's bedroom window as she undressed. For a moment he seemed at a loss. Twice he made as if to speak, but closed his mouth each time as if he could not trust himself. She gaped at him as he turned his look back to her. A competent, whip-wielding, knife-throwing Unstabler who blushed like a schoolboy? It was incongruous.

'Has anyone else been asking for Piers lately?' he asked finally. The gravel-slide voice seemed explosively harsh and Keris almost jumped.

'Everyone asks for Piers,' she replied tartly. 'They don't seem to think I know enough about maps to sell one.'

'I mean *specifically* for him. Someone not interested in buying a map.'

'You mean someone like you?' She shook her head. 'No, I can't say there's anyone like that been here lately.' She stared at him full in the face, and for the first time he really appeared to see her.

He nodded his thanks, sketched another farewell, and was gone. Yerrie took the opportunity to flee into the kitchen.

Keris remained standing where she was, unaccountably afraid.

She thought back, trying to place the man. Over the years she had come to know the ley-lit who regularly worked the crossings to and from the First Stability; they all needed maps and Piers Kaylen was the best mapmaker who charted the land north of the Wide. As a young child she had spent hours hidden beneath the counter listening to her father talk to his customers, hearing the tales of their encounters with the Wild and the Minions of Chaos; hearing their experiences with ley lines told and retold. Sometimes she thought she knew as much about the fickle character of the Wanderer as her father did; or she would see in her mind the brooding expanse of the Wide or the knotted upheaval that was the Snarled Fist, and she would dream of the day when she would ride out with Piers: Keris Kaylen, apprentice map-maker.

But she could not remember ever hearing or seeing before this man with obsidian eyes and a voice that would scour burnt stew pots. A man who was ashamed because he terrified a cat halfway to Chaos . . .

Perhaps he had only recently come north of the Wide. Perhaps he came only infrequently and she had happened to miss his visits – for, of course, as she had grown older, there had been less opportunity to eavesdrop and she had grown too big to fit unnoticed under the counter, although for a while she had continued to cling to the fanciful notion that she would one day be her father's apprentice. It had seemed so logical, after all. Thirl was not interested in mapmaking; she was. She loved everything about maps and charts; her brother did not. She loved poring over them, was fascinated by the changes one season to the next; he was bored stupid. She was always begging Piers – when he was at home – to show her how the theodolite worked, how to use a compass, how to translate surveying angles into features drawn on a chart and how to read map coordinates. Thirl could hardly contain his impatience when such things were mentioned. Surely, then, it was obvious she would be the one to follow in her father's footsteps.

She had worried miserably about whether she was one of the ley-lit or not, because only someone who was ley-lit could possibly map the Unstable, but it had never occurred to her that the Rule did not encourage women to be Unstablers. Still less did she dream that her father did not want her to be a mapmaker. She was so sure he would that she had never mentioned the subject; she just took his approval for granted. Then, on the day that a chance remark of hers indicated to Piers the way she was thinking, he had thrown back his head and roared with laughter until tears ran down his face. She had been standing there in the shop, dressed in her grey pinafore, her hands locked behind her back, and she had listened to that laughter ending all her dreams, the hurt of the knowledge crushing something inside her with a pain she would remember for ever. *Thirl would be the mapmaker.* Thirl who had no wish to see the Unstable, who never dreamt of crossing the Graven or the Riven.

Worse still was the reason. The stupid, horrible, unbelievable reason that had nothing to do with ability or interest or skill. *Because she was a girl and Thirl was a boy.* Because she was born to be for ever without any vocation or trade except that of wife. Because of the *Rule*.

The bitter seeds sown deep inside her that day had rooted and grown. Never again would she wholly believe that there was some innate goodness to Order and the Rule. How could there be goodness when she was condemned to marriage, housework and raising babies, simply because she was born the daughter of a mapmaker?

And yet even then she had not rebelled. How could one rebel when there was nowhere to rebel to? Every other stability obeyed the same Rule, had the same prejudices. And love created its own ties, anyway, even stronger than those of convention. She loved her parents. Both of them. She respected them. Love made it impossible to rebel.

'Keris? Sorry to bother you, dear, but could I have a cup of water?'

Her mother again.

Keris went through into the kitchen, thinking how hard it must be for a woman like Sheyli Kaylen to come to this, unable even to get herself something to drink with any ease. She and Keris had often clashed: they were both too strong-willed for it ever to be otherwise, but there was also respect there between them. Sheyli had spent six months in every year alone, as was the fate of a mapmaker's wife; it had been she who had run the shop every autumn and every spring and raised two children while doing it, knowing there was a good likelihood that one day her husband would not return from one of his trips. It was she who had softened Piers's rough edges with her gentleness, who had given the children something beyond the outlook of an Unstabler to think about. It was seeing her father's courage that had taught Keris to be strong; it was her mother's lively curiosity that had taught her to question. Sheyli had never intended that her example should stir rebellion and an unhealthy desire to experiment, but that was what had happened. She had encouraged her daughter's development, realising too late that she had nurtured a bird too big for the nest. 'Stubborn,' Piers had growled in the direction of his daughter. 'Stubborn as a dung beetle trying to get too large a ball of dung into his hole.'

Keris handed her mother the water she had pulled from the kitchen pump. 'There you are. Is there anything else I can get you?'

'No – Ah, is that Thirl I can hear?'

'That's him,' Keris agreed, hearing the sound of her brother's boots crossing the back yard to the door.

He came in as he always did, full of bonhomie and expecting to be the centre of the world. He washed under the pump at the sink, splashing water and discarding the towel on to the floor, dispensing village gossip all the while.

Thirl Kaylen was a small man who compensated for his small size and the ordinariness of his features with an overpowering personality; people always knew when Thirl Kaylen entered a room just as they were always aware of when he left it. He was listened to with deference, not because he was particularly astute or wise, but because, when he spoke, such was his assurance, the sheer vigour of his character, that it was difficult *not* to listen.

'Mistress Pottle was asking after you, Ma,' he was saying. 'She said she'd look in on you later. I met Harin down in the square; he's asked me to join him over in Upper Kibble this evening. I'll need some money, Keris. Have you made any sales so far today?' He gave her a peck on the cheek, and smiled.

It was a fond smile, the smile of a man for a loved younger sister, and it almost swayed her. Almost. 'No,' she lied, shaking off the temptation to trust that smile, to bend before him, as wheat before the wind. Harin's father owned the

29

tavern in Upper Kibbleberry and she didn't want Thirl spending all they had on drink. 'It's too early in the season to be expecting many pilgrims, and the Unstablers won't come until they know the new maps are ready; you know that.'

'Damn. Then give me a silver out of the caddy, Sis. I need it.'

'That's the housekeeping money.'

'So? I shan't be in for dinner. You will save the price of a meal.'

'A home-cooked meal doesn't cost a silver – and nor does a tavern one,' she said sourly, even though she knew her mother would nod her acquiescence – as indeed she did. Keris hid a sigh. 'You can have a quarter-silver, Thirl. That's all we can spare.' She went to get it. The caddy, black with age and made of a metal that no one could identify, stood on the mantel over the fireplace. It had been the repository of Kaylen housekeeping money for as long as anyone could remember. Keris handled it carefully: family legend said that it dated back to the days before the Rending, that it had come from lands across the sea. Brazis, perhaps. Or the isles of Quay Linden. She didn't know that she believed that, and she was rather vague as to what a sea was anyway, but she did not want to be the one who dropped and dented so ancient an heirloom.

'Harin was asking about you,' Thirl said to her. 'He said he might drop by this week.'

'Tell him not to bother.'

'I'll do no such thing.' He took the money from her. 'Don't be impolite. Thanks, Sis. I'll see you both later.'

'You're going already?' Sheyli asked, disappointed and trying not to show it.

'Yeah, why not? Nothing to do around here, is there? As Keris said, it's too early in the season for much business yet and we all know Keris drafts better maps than I do – and enjoys it more.' He bent to kiss his mother on the cheek and was gone before either of them could protest further.

Keris gritted her teeth. 'He didn't ask after you,' she muttered, picking up the towel.

Sheyli smiled gently. 'Come, now, perhaps he wanted to take my mind off my ill health. Anyway, you can hardly expect a healthy man like that to be wanting to talk about illness. Thirl's young, Keris. He wants to enjoy himself – and why not?'

I'm young too, she thought resentfully. And why the Chaos should we always be excusing him because he's a male?

Piers had not taken his son into the Unstable this trip because of Sheyli's illness; Thirl had been supposed to stay at home and help out. But he only ever comes back to the house when he is hungry, or sleepy, or in need of money, thought Keris. He would breeze in, cheer Sheyli with ten minutes of gossip and jokes, and then breeze out again. He had not touched ink and map pen in three months and he had hardly even taken a turn in the shop either. But what's the use of saying any of it? Keris thought. It never makes any difference and it never will. He could make Sheyli laugh and forget her illness; she could not. He was Sheyli's son and she forgave him everything; Keris was her daughter and, as much as Sheyli might have loved her, she also took her for granted.

'Is Harin Markle interested in you?' Sheyli asked suddenly.

Keris was diverted. 'Ley-life! I hope not. He's a gutter-minded sharpster, just like his father.' She went to stir the hotpot that had been slowly cooking on the hob all day.

'Is he? He's always seemed polite and attentive when I've spoken to him.'

'Attentive? Oily's the word you're looking for. Slippery, like greased pork just lifted from the pan.'

Sheyli gave the faintest of shrugs and stirred uncomfortably on the couch. 'Perhaps. But you ought to be looking over the young men, Keris. You have to marry soon.'

Keris turned to her but the sharp words on her tongue died unspoken. Her mother was worried about her daughter's future only because she was – Keris stopped the thought right there. It was hard to admit, even inside the privacy of her mind, that her mother was dying. 'Not Harin,' she said at last. 'Anyone but Harin.'

'Then perhaps a mapmaker, or a courier or a trader or a guide — it's not such a bad life for an independent woman,' Sheyli continued tentatively. 'An Unstabler, Keris. Chantry likes the children of an Unstabler to marry one.'

'Is that why you married Father?' Keris asked. 'Because he wasn't around all that much to curb your independence?'

Sheyli did not get a chance to reply. The bell on the shop door tinkled, indicating another customer. 'Business is brisk today,' she said with mild surprise.

Keris replaced the pot lid and turned to go back into the shop.

'Shut the door, dear,' Sheyli said, suddenly losing interest. 'I think I will sleep for a while.'

Keris walked through into the shop and pulled the door to after her. There was no one there but she could hear sounds outside at the hitching rail and someone had propped the door open. She looked out into the yard.

And her heart skittered.

Two of the crossings-horses there were undoubtedly her father's, but of Piers Kaylen there was no sign. The man now untying packs from the back of one of them was a courier; she had known him for years.

Blue Ketter came twice a year to Kaylen the Mapmaker's to buy charts because he regularly worked the area north of the Wide. He was good at his job, known — as indeed most couriers were — for his reliability and honesty. He was an ugly man, short and squat with hands the size of fire bellows and a twist of blueish scar tissue across the centre of his face like some bizarre mask made by a child at play. A ley line had been responsible for that on his very first ley crossing; he had been known as Blue ever since.

Like most couriers, he preferred his own company to anyone else's, and spent as little time as possible within the boundaries of any stability. He appeared in the First every few months, where — with a minimum of conversation — he bought new supplies and perhaps a new map or two, made his deliveries within the Stability, collected new letters and packages for other stabilities, and then rode off back into the Unstable.

Keris stood stock-still, hand on the counter, and knew she was not going to like what she was about to hear.

He came into the shop slowly, refusing to meet her gaze. The kinesis he gave was one of subdued greeting, used rarely, for occasions of sorrow. 'Maid Kaylen,' he said. 'Your brother about?'

'No, Master Ketter, he's not. And my mother is very ill. You had better tell me what's happened.'

He untied his kerchief, mopped the back of his neck with it and then twisted it through his fingers, stalling for time while he decided what to say.

Sick in the pit of her stomach, unable to wait even to hear what she did not want to know, she helped him out. 'Is he . . .? He can't be – He's – he's dead, isn't he?'

Bleakly, Ketter nodded. 'Sorry.'

And even then part of her would not believe it. *Piers? Piers Kaylen? Never!* Not her father, with his slow smile and lightning-quick reflexes, not Piers Kaylen, with his rough tongue and decent heart. She did not move, but instinctively lowered her voice to be sure that her mother would not hear. 'What happened?'

'Pickle's Halt. He was attacked. Died right away.'

She stared at him, still unable to accept that Piers was dead, and certainly not comprehending what she was hearing. She had never been into the Unstable, but she knew enough to know that halts were generally the safest of places anywhere outside a stability. 'He died in a *halt*?'

He nodded. 'Sorry, lass,' he mumbled. 'Now, I got to go. Got deliveries to make. Brought back his horses. And his things, what was left of them. Pretty torn up, they were.'

Still stupefied, she repeated the words without understanding them. 'Torn up?'

He nodded. 'Got to go. Got packages for the Rule House

in Kt Beogor. And letters for Drumlin. Perfumes for the Margrave's daughter there from the son of the Domain Lord of Salient Meadows. Courting her, they say.'

She stared at him, unable to believe he was passing on gossip about Tricians when all she was interested in was what had happened to her father.

'Who killed him?' she asked. *Piers? Dead?*

'Uh – a Pet, I heard. Had to have been. The way he was ripped up, you see. Crushed. Never had a chance.'

A Pet? She did not want to hear – yet she said, 'Can't you be more – more specific? About how it came about, I mean.'

'Wasn't there,' he said simply. 'Lass, better not to ask. He's dead. Chaos got him in the end. Happens out there. Piers was one of the best, but even the best get caught sometimes. Got to go. I'll unload the horses and put them in the barn for you.' He left the room, scarcely concealing his relief.

None of it made sense. A Pet? Died in a halt? Pets did not enter halts. She took a deep breath, tried to control the enmeshing grief that threatened her calm – and failed. She cried noiselessly, helplessly; cried for a man who had been many things to her: mentor and inspiration; detractor and disparager; friend and adviser. Piers Kaylen, master map-maker, was dead. The best of fathers, sometimes. And an indifferent parent too, often. Always away, or too busy; skilled at leaving discipline problems to Sheyli, or ignoring what he did not want to see. But still her father. Living, he could have been more to her; dead, he could only be loved for being exactly what he had been.

By the time Blue Ketter returned carrying her father's packs, she was composed again, sitting quietly in the shop with her hands folded in her lap. The sun had retreated; her skirt covered her legs but still she felt cold.

'Thank you, Master Ketter,' she said politely. 'Doubtless we owe you something –'

'Nay, lass,' he said in deep embarrassment. 'Couldn't charge Piers's family for a service, not with him gone. Wouldn't be right. Besides, Pickle of the Halt gave me a bit for my trouble. Not that it was a trouble really,' he added hastily. 'Glad to do it. Good man, your dad.' He took a deep breath and plunged on. 'Best maps in the business, you know. Accurate. And clear. Last few years, well, they've been better than ever. Coloured, you know. Better than before. Easier to follow, better drawn. He was improving all the time. Not often you get a mapmaker like that. Best maps of all, Piers Kaylen's. Everyone knows them, you know.'

She looked up at him, and her tear-streaked face betrayed her doubt. He said, 'True. Wouldn't say that just 'cos he's dead. Piers Kaylen made the finest maps in all the stabs and it'll be a long time before we see his like again.'

Bitter laughter bubbled up from within her, coupling with an ambivalent grief. Piers Kaylen had not drawn a map in almost five years: *she* had been the draughtsman in the family. He had given her his sketches and his notes, the cross-staff and theodolite and compass readings, and from them she had created the maps to scale, even as he had concealed her talent. 'No one will buy a map if they know it was drawn by a woman,' he had said. 'Don't ever let anyone see you working at a chart, or we'll be out of business, there's a good girl.' They had been a good team, each complementing the other, but no one outside the Kaylen family knew the truth of it.

Now he was dead, and his daughter laughed and grieved and – in the deepest recesses of her heart – hated, just a little, the father she had also loved, because he had hidden her talent from the world, because he had used her but never publicly acknowledged his debt, because he had never truly admitted her potential even in private. He had been Piers Kaylen, Master Mapmaker.

Chapter Three

*And all this was displeasing to Lord Carasma, so he looked
for ways to unravel what the Maker had ravelled, until he
found what he sought: the imperfection of humankind's greed
was in the warp just as human goodness was in the weft.*

*And so it was that, when Goodperson prayed for an end to
the Chaos that ate Malinawar, the Maker replied, 'I gave you
choice, but some of you chose the Unstable. Therefore has
Chaos cut a hole in the fabric of my Creation and torn the
weave of your world asunder.'*

The Rending I: 1: 10—12

Two days later, when the immediate shock of Piers's death
had subsided to a vague awareness of loss, a sort of grum-
bling pain that would not ever quite go away, Keris was
sitting in the main room beside her mother's bed. She
had the cat sitting on her lap and was searching absently
through its fur for fleas; Yerrie submitted, unprotesting.
Thirl, polishing his boots on the other side of the room,
occasionally glanced at his sister with disapproving eyes.
Only the presence of an outsider, a village woman called
Helda Pottle, stopped him from telling Keris exactly what
bothered him.

Mistress Pottle was folding the washing, and prattling. The
first she did because she was paid to help with the housework
now that Sheyli was ill; the prattle was freely bestowed — and
habitual. 'Well, Sheyli, I must say I enjoy those frill flowers
you've got planted around your washhouse, but I shudder to

think what would happen if old Mistress Quint saw them! She'd be off to tell the Rule Office, sure as her face is as sour as a green plum. Mean-spirited old bag — she'd be sure to notice that you'd changed the garden there. 'S'posed to be cabbages along the washhouse, I remember. Oh, and that reminds me: Adarn Morl — you know him, Sheyli? — that hulking farm labourer who got himself wed to Chickee Oster? Well, their son's got himself tainted, they say. He's excluded, and Chickee was howling fit to bust her laces. Went for the Chantor at evening Prostration, saying it was all Chantry's fault.' She flapped creases out of a sheet and slapped it down on the table. The loose furls of fat on her upper arms wobbled in sympathy. 'Dunno what the world's coming to, myself. What with mountains disappearing and so many not coming back from the Unstable. Your Piers, Adarn and Chickee's son, that lass over Upper Kibble way . . .' She shook her head. "They say a live Wild turned up in the Flow last month near Drumlin city. A water monster. The Defenders slew it, but Chantry's none too popular for letting that one in, you can be sure. And then right here in Kibbleberry the rule-chantors came and took one of Maree's twins last week, just like they done to your Aurin, Sheyli, all those years back. 'Tain't right.'

Sheyli shivered and turned her face to the wall.

'Watch your tongue, Mistress Pottle,' Thirl said. 'That kind of talk doesn't do, you know.'

'Ah, bah — which one of you lot's going to tell on me? Chantor Nebuthnar knows what I think, anyways. I tell him to his face, the silly old chook. Let me tell you, Master Thirl, if Chantry wants us to follow the Rule, then they ought to make sure they give us summat in return. But mountains disappear from right on our doorstep, and lasses and lads get tainted, and they take our children, and monsters come down the river — what's the Stability coming to, eh? Things like that never used to happen when I was a girl, let me tell you.' She gave a self-satisfied grunt, as if her very youth had once been responsible for keeping the Unstable at bay. 'All

Chantry seems good for is spiriting away bairns, and making life difficult. Why, only last week they were telling my Nevvy that he can't put plain glass in his window, 'cos it's allus been bottle glass, and that even though the window was shattered by a runaway cart last week. And there was old Marcun the Cooper wanting to root up his apple tree 'cos it ain't had an apple on it for two seasons, and plant a pear instead, and they was saying the Rule won't allow it. Pah!' She took a breath and regarded the clean laundry. 'Anyways, there's the washing folded, and I'll be on my way for today.' She undid her pinafore and went to the door. 'Be seeing you all tomorrow, then.'

'Stupid old biddy,' Thirl said when she had gone. 'As if Chantry could ever have stopped the Axe Head from vanishing. Which reminds me,' he added, taking the opportunity to mention what was irritating him, 'you should be working on the maps, Keris.'

'You're the mapmaker,' she replied, knowing she sounded sullen, and not caring.

'You do a better job. Listen, Keri, it's got to be done. Why don't you do the master charts, using Father's notes and figures? And, once you have the first one ready, I'll start work on the copies. I'll do all the ink work and leave the final colours and artwork to you.'

Sheyli roused herself enough to endorse Thirl's suggestion. 'Your father gave his life to gather the necessary information,' she said, her fingers fluttering over the bed covers like the fragile wings of an injured butterfly. 'The maps must be made. Don't let his death be a waste, Keris. He gave his life to serve Unstablers – and the Pilgrimage.'

Not quite right, that, she thought. Her father had died not because he dreamt of a life of service, but because he could not keep away from the Unstable. It drew him to his death, just as it had drawn him to live dangerously for thirty years. The moth finally consumed by the flame.

Thirl nodded. 'The Unstablers will be coming in to buy the new maps as usual; they will expect them to have been done.'

She tried to maintain a stolid complacency. 'That's right. They will expect you to have done them.' Her faint emphasis on the word 'you' lingered on into the silence.

Thirl changed the angle of his argument. 'People will die out there if accurate maps are not available. From the gossip I've been hearing from pilgrims, there have been considerable changes in the ley lines since the autumn surveying.'

Mother's aged, Keris thought inconsequentially. She looks a hundred, yet she's only forty-four. Her illness, knowing father's dead — she looks desiccated, sucked dry of life — She dragged her thoughts back to mapmaking. Thirl was right, blast him. 'Yes, all right. I'll start on them.' And then, just so he knew that she saw through his righteous reasoning, 'Although I doubt if your motives, Thirl, are as pure as you would have me believe.'

'So we need the money,' he said. 'There, does that please you?' She gave him a level look. 'Have you found Father's notes?' he asked.

'I haven't unpacked his things yet.' *I haven't had the heart —*

'Do it today. Harin Markle is coming to see you later on, by the way.'

She bent back to her task. 'Whatever for?' She found a flea and chased it through Yerrie's fur with a dab of lard on her finger, ready to smother it.

Thirl waved an exasperated hand at her. 'Because he's interested in you, that's why. Disorder be damned, Keris, do I have to spell it out for you?'

'No.' She flattened the flea with grease then looked up at him. 'But maybe I have to spell it out for *you*, Thirl. I — am — not — interested — in — Harin — Markle.' She put the cat down on the floor and went to wash her hands under the sink pump.

'Well, you had better get interested,' he said harshly.

She turned to face him, expression blank. 'Pardon?'

'I am promoting his suit.'

'*Promoting his suit?* What is this? Your brains are tainted, Thirl Kaylen! Have you forgotten that I still have a living

39

parent? I may be legally under your protection in some respects, but Mother heads this family now. It is none of your business whom I choose to have court me and I can't imagine why you have developed this sudden interest in having me wed. Nor can I imagine why Harin is interested, anyway. He never used to even *like* me.'

Thirl flushed slightly under the intensity of her gaze.

'I'll be tainted,' she whispered finally. 'You've told him I have a proper dowry, haven't you?' Fifty golds, saved by her parents over the years, to provide for her. Sheyli had insisted on it, even though other girls in the village normally brought no more than the mandatory two golds to their marriage in addition to a trousseau of the practical items listed in the Rule.

Keris glanced at her mother, wishing this conversation was not taking place. Sheyli was tired and seemed swamped by her grief and the pain of her illness. That casual remark from Mistress Pottle about the baby she had been forced to surrender to Chantry had not helped, either. She was having to make an effort to listen and pearly drops of sweat glistened across her forehead.

Thirl was belligerent. 'So what if I have mentioned it to him?'

'What's *your* interest, Thirl?'

He shrugged. 'Harin needs capital.'

The conversation seemed to be slipping out of her grasp. 'Capital for what?'

He gave an uneasy look towards Sheyli. 'You may as well know. We are going to turn this place into a wayside tavern for pilgrims.'

Keris stared, slack-minded, unable even to consider the ramifications of what he had said.

Sheyli struggled to raise herself, saying in pained protest, 'But you're a mapmaker, Thirl.'

'No, I'm not. I hate maps. And I hate spending time in the Unstable. I'm not Dad. I'd be dead in my first three months out there. I'm going to be an innkeeper. And where better than this? A day's ride from Hopen Grat and the kinesis chain. I told Harin years ago that this would be a tavern if anything ever happened to Dad.'

'You are going to change your father's shop into a pilgrim's hostel?' his mother asked, incredulous.

'Not exactly. Into a tavern that also has rooms to rent. In partnership with Harin. Because he knows the business.'

Sheyli was appalled. 'A *public house*? You would try to seduce pilgrims away from the holy nature of their journey and into the licentiousness of a tavern?'

Keris added her own touch of acid bitterness. 'And my dowry is supposed to supply the capital for their seduction, it seems.'

Sheyli shook her head. 'It's just not possible. You are Piers's only son: you have to continue his trade. That's the Rule. There has been a mapmaker's shop on this site since — since — well, probably since the Rending. Chantry will *never* countenance such a change.'

Thirl smiled thinly. 'Mother, Mother — do you think that everyone follows the Rule to the letter? Nothing would ever get done! Anyway, this is one change Chantry will countenance because they don't like Unstablers and I'm offering to become a good solid citizen instead of a map-maker who spends half the year in the Unstable. I spoke to a chantor at the Rule Office of Order in Upper Kibble only today. And he is willing to grant me a dispensation for a — er — consideration.'

Sheyli almost choked. 'You *bribed* him?'

'I will, yes. Mother, don't worry — everybody does it.'

'I don't,' she said, with dignity. 'And your father didn't, either. Creation above all, Thirl — Order must be maintained. And, if some people pay others to thwart the Rule, then Order crumbles — and with it our safety.'

'My not being a mapmaker is hardly going to disintegrate Order, Mother, any more than your frill flowers are, planted where there should be cabbages.' He smiled at her. A smile of rueful charm. Keris didn't wait for the rest: she turned

41

and walked out of the room, clenching her hands in an effort to suppress her anger.

It wasn't fair! Anger tumbled towards tears. It just wasn't fair . . . she would have given anything to be a mapmaker. Anything.

She went to the stable, as she had always done when she was unhappy. There was something calming about the presence of the animals: the two crossings-horses standing sleepily in their stalls, the chickens scratching in the straw, the half-wild stable cat blinking as it woke briefly to contemplate if flight was necessary, then settling its nose back down into its fur. It was difficult to maintain a hot rage when Ygraine and her stable mate, the packhorse named Tousson, vied with one another for her attention, each hoping for some titbit from her pocket.

This time, however, she was not given the time to cool down. No sooner had she walked over to Ygraine than the sunlight through the door was blocked by Thirl appearing in the open doorway behind her; he must have followed her out of the house almost immediately.

She turned on him, all her tearful rage bubbling out. 'How could you do that to Mother? You didn't need to − not then, not now, not when she's so sick and not so soon after Dad's −' The stable cat, reacting to the anger in her voice, scuttled away behind the feed sacks.

He shrugged carelessly. 'You'd prefer me to live a lie? Keris the dreamer, who doesn't like to face the facts. I'm damned if I'll be a mapmaker, and I don't care who knows it. The shop is going to be a tavern. We'll continue to sell maps until the end of autumn, as usual. But I shan't be going off into the Unstable. Come winter, this place will be a public house. I shall be calling it the Mapmaker's Rest.'

She was so angry she was choking on it. 'But Mother −'

'− will be dead by then,' he said brutally. 'A fact which she knows full well.'

'Unstable take you, you're a heartless sod, Thirl.'

'Not particularly, I think. Just practical. And being practical means facing facts: I'll never make a mapmaker and I've never intended to be one. Mother will be dead within weeks, if not days, and you, Sis, have got to find a niche somewhere. If you want to hang around and be a housekeeper for me, well, you can – but bear in mind firstly that I intend to marry as soon as I find some pretty and willing maid, and secondly that I won't be paying your fifty golds in dowry to just anyone.'

'That money's mine!'

'No, it's not. It was intended to be your husband's. The moment Dad died it legally became mine, as long as I undertake to care for you and Mother. And I do. But I'm under no obligation to give you a dowry of more than two golds. I intend to have that money, Keris, to help pay for the expense of refurbishing the place as a tavern. And to pay the bribe – the rule-chantor is not going to accept this for anything less than ten golds. And so I shall take the money directly, or it can come to the business, indirectly, through your dowry to Harin. I thought to help you find a husband, that's all.'

'I don't want a husband – least of all someone like Harin!'

'There you go again, being impractical. What else can you do? You can't be a mapmaker because the Rule won't allow it, even if anyone would buy maps from a woman; and, anyway, a woman wouldn't last a handful of days out in the Unstable alone. Moreover, the Rule says you're supposed to marry, but you show no signs of even trying to find someone. Keris, a woman who looks like you will never do better than Harin.'

That hurt. Her fury poured out and Ygraine, unsettled, blew noisily down her nostrils. 'He's as slimy as a river flatworm! I wouldn't marry him if he was willing to pay me a hundred golds for the privilege.'

Thirl shrugged. 'That's your choice. I don't care. I reckon to win either way.'

His indifference deflated her. She took a deep breath, cocked her head on one side and considered him with all the

43

growing wonderment of making a bitter new discovery about a familiar object. 'Why, that's right, isn't it? You really don't care, do you? I wonder why I never saw that before. There's no feeling there inside you. You feel no grief about Dad, or Mother, do you?'

'Why should I? They never asked me how I felt about anything. It was always: "Do this, Thirl. Do that, Thirl. Learn how to draw maps, Thirl. Carry the theodolite, Thirl. Come with me into the Unstable, Thirl." Well, now I'm saying no. And I feel no grief that their time is over and mine has come. No grief, and no compunction. I'm no Minion, though, Keris. I'll do the decent thing by both of you – but no more than that. No more.'

She felt an odd fascination with his utter lack of feeling. 'And me? What did I ever do to have you dismiss me so lightly?'

'You really don't know, do you? Didn't it ever occur to you that a boy might resent the fact that his younger sister did just about anything one cares to name better than he did? Well, he did, Keris. He hated you when you drew more accurate maps, when you threw Piers's knives better, when you shot arrows straighter, when you beat him swimming across the river pool . . . Count yourself lucky, Sis. If you had been a boy, I might have killed you. I've got over that adolescent jealousy now, and I got good at turning on a show of fraternal affection, but don't ask me to go out of my way to help you, because I won't.' He smiled lightly, carelessly, and left her. There was no real hate for her in him, just a complete lack of interest, and she wondered if that was not worse.

She leant her head against Ygraine's neck and choked down the ache in her throat.

It wasn't really all her fault that he was like this, was it?

Harin Markle came as he had promised. Keris was alone, working in the shop, when he came to the door, traipsing in a trail of dirt from unwiped boots.

She tried to be detached in her assessment. He was not bad-looking, she supposed, even though there was a rather large spot developing right on the end of his nose at the moment. Still, she could hardly hold that against him. No, it was not his looks she did not like: it was his attitude. He was so cock-sure when he faced someone he considered his inferior – and so obsequious when in the company of those he considered his superiors. She came in the first category, she knew, while Thirl was one of the latter. With Thirl he was all smiles and flattery, couching his ideas as mere suggestions; with her he spoke with a heavy pompousness and treated her as though she were a recalcitrant horse to be persuaded out of wrongful behaviour.

'Keris,' he said, 'Thirl tells me he's told you of our plans for the tavern; what do you think of that, eh? Loads of money to be made because we're bound to catch the trade coming up from Hopen Grat. Great idea – but that's your brother all round. Always has bright ideas . . .'

She tried to freeze him with a look that would have stopped a rain shower, but he did not seem to notice. She said, 'I understand that the two of you have also had a bright idea about me.'

He did not seem in the least embarrassed. 'Why, yes – Thirl's idea, actually, but it seemed a good one. I mean, you and I could hook up together and everybody benefits –'

'Perhaps you'd be good enough to explain just what benefit I'd get from it?'

He looked taken aback. 'Why, you'd be married, of course! Otherwise you'll end up like Old Woman Raddles, with everyone saying you're a witch, too ugly ever to have found a man. Come on, now, Keris – it won't be so bad. You'd be a tavernkeeper's wife, lording it over the other women in the village. As for the other side of being married, well, I know you're a virgin, but we can get that out of the way quickly enough, and, once we've had a couple of kids, you won't have to worry about that sort of thing any more, I swear –'

She gaped at him, not knowing whether to laugh or be

angry. 'Harin Markle,' she said at last, 'get this into your insensitive skull: if I were to consider marrying anyone at all, you would be right at the bottom of my list of potential candidates. Is that understood?'

Unfortunately it did not seem to be understood at all. He laughed, made several condescending remarks about women having coy natures, and made it clear he believed that of course she was pretending modesty because that was the maidenly thing to do. He would, he said, be back again, naturally.

Keris gritted her teeth and refrained – with difficulty – from throwing something at his departing back when he finally left her.

Some time later, when she had calmed herself, she began to unstrap the packs belonging to Piers that Blue Ketter had left in the shop. The first things to fall out were the throwing knives, all five of them, still in their scabbards. She pulled one free and weighed it in her hand, feeling its balance. It was true: she could throw them more skilfully than Thirl, although even she had not quite perfected the knack of judging distance accurately enough to ensure that it was always the point of the blade – rather than some other part of the knife – that ended up hitting the target. Too often the weapon would spin out wrongly and clatter harmlessly to the ground as a consequence.

In exasperation at Thirl's even greater incompetence, Piers had told his son to concentrate on bow and arrow, but even there Keris had proved to have more innate ability than her brother, as well as a greater interest. She might not have been able to achieve the distances that Thirl, with his male strength, could manage, but she made up for that in accuracy. It was she who spent hours practising just because she enjoyed pitting her skills against the wind and a moving target. She had developed muscles in her arms and upper torso and calluses on her fingers that had horrified Sheyli when she had noticed them; Keris had just laughed and gone on practising.

When Piers had taught Thirl how to fletch his own arrows, it was Keris who had learnt; when Piers had shown Thirl how to select wood for a bow, how to season and fashion it, it had been she who had taken the lessons to heart and who had finally produced the better weapon. In the end Piers had bought a bowstave from the fletcher in Drumlin for Thirl, and he had taken that with him whenever he had gone into the Unstable with his father. In between times it hung on the wall, oiled and envied by Keris, unused and unwanted by Thirl.

She fingered Piers's knives, remembering the lessons, the first pathetic attempts to spin the blade through the air . . . The pang of those distant memories stung now, reminding her that Piers was dead, and Thirl lost to her for ever.

She laid the knives aside and delved deeper into the packs.

By the time she had spread all they contained out on the floor, her hands were shaking with shock. Someone, she noted with helpless pain, had even removed her father's wooden leg and sent that back, but her shock stemmed from the state of many of the items. Blue Ketter had not been exaggerating when he had said that Piers's things had been 'torn up': some of them were in shreds. Much was still blood-spattered, although an effort had been made to clean the worst before packing it up. She fought down the nausea and regarded the ripped clothing, the tattered notebooks, the slashed bedroll, and felt a total incomprehension. Whatever could possibly have prompted such wanton destruction?

She wanted to pack everything up again, forget – but her curiosity dominated. Why?

There was something odd about the destruction . . .

She sat back on her heels and let her eyes rove over all the items in front of her: clothes, surveying and mapping equipment, cooking utensils, canvas tent, fly and ground sheet. Some things – like the loose sheets of parchment – were untouched. Others – like the padding of the bedroll – had been so thoroughly pulled apart that the only possible reason there could have been to return them to Piers's heirs was to show that they had not been stolen.

As her eyes scanned the items, she began to see the pattern. Anything of thickness had been ripped apart. A fur-lined leather doublet, the heels to Piers's boots, the collar and double yoke of his best travelling shirt, the bedroll, the spines of his notebooks. Other things had suffered too: the telescope had been wrenched from its mounting on the theodolite, and then sliced open. The handle to the cooking pot had been similarly opened up. Only Piers's staff and his wooden leg had been left untouched, presumably because it was obvious that the former was a single piece of unjointed wood, and because he had still been wearing the latter when he was attacked.

She took up the telescope and examined it, feeling herself riven through with horror. She could not imagine what tool could have been used to do such a thing: the thick brass body of the instrument had been roughly cut in two lengthways. The edges were jaggedly scalloped and sharp. Not a tool, of course: claws – or teeth. And who would want to do that to a scope anyway? A telescope was one of the most valuable of all artefacts because the knowledge of how to grind the lenses had been lost after the Rending. Piers's instrument had been passed from father to son through generations of map-makers. Possibly the body may have been renewed and the lenses realigned several times, but there was little doubt that the lenses themselves dated back to the days of the Old Margravate, to Malinawar, before the world had been rent. They were priceless.

They were looking for something, she thought. Something small that could be hidden in the lining of a doublet or the spine of a book. Or flat, so that it could be folded up and put in the heel of a boot – or rolled up to fit inside a pot handle or a telescope. Precious stones? Money? A map? It seemed most unlikely. Mapmakers did not carry large sums of money and valuables, nor did they secrete their maps away from sight like hidden wealth. And what Piers's murderers had been looking for had to be something more precious than a telescope. Still, if Piers did have something valuable, she knew exactly where he would have put it, and it was apparently a place that the searchers had not thought of . . .

Reluctantly, with a sense that she was somehow about to violate her father, she reached out to take up the wooden leg. The padded cup made to hold the stump of Piers's amputation was cut from soft leather, which had then been lined with flannel and stuffed in between with tree-cotton. It was not the cup that interested Keris, however. She took the leg across to the shop counter, where she freed the several linchpins that attached the leather to the peg. She held the peg up to the light and peered into its hollow interior. There was money there as she had expected; but there was something else as well. Gently she upended it and shook out its contents into her other hand.

A rolled up mapskin.

She knew immediately that it was not one of her own or Piers's: the skin was the wrong colour. Carefully she unrolled it across the counter.

And stared. And stared.

Nothing had prepared her for this, nothing.

A trompleri map.

Her first thought was an incredulous — and joyous — *So they exist!* Then she felt the hot stab of prickling fear. There was magic in such a map.

And lastly the thought came: perhaps there were those who would feel a trompleri map was worth killing for . . .

49

Chapter Four

*And the map the Maker gave to Knight Weddon was such
that had never been seen before. The mountains stood high
before him and the Deep writhed across the mapskin, showing
its wickedness. Knight Weddon fled the Minions, following
the path the map showed him and was received safely . . .*

Pilgrims VIII: 5: 42—44

Keris worked hard on the master charts. She had decided
thirty-five such charts were needed that year and they were
among the hardest she had ever had to create, with more ley
lines than usual and some very odd manifestations along the
length of the Wanderer — the Bitch, as Piers had always
called it. In addition, his notes had been torn and muddled
out of sequence, so it was sometimes hard to tell which
figures corresponded to which ley lines. She worked fifteen
hours a day to create the master charts and then had to skimp
on the final artistic work of the copies, which was a blow to
her pride. She was only slightly mollified to hear the copied
maps praised by those who came in to buy them. The buyers
thought Thirl had drawn them, of course, and it rankled to
hear him praised when all he had done was the tracings and
repetitive work. It hurt, too, to have to send out most of the
maps uncoloured. Without Piers to help and with so much
more to do than usual, there simply was not time for the
extras that had made her work special in the past.

She worked in the kitchen where her mother now slept,
out of sight of the customers, keeping her mother company

and trying not to see how fast Sheyli's health was deteriorating, trying not to hear her restless tossing and moaning. The household chores and much of the nursing were now given over entirely to Mistress Pottle — even Thirl had acknowledged that Keris could not manage the house and the mapmaking, and he had been willing enough to pay to have Mistress Pottle work double her normal number of hours.

He himself went to the tavern in Upper Kibbleberry rather less and spent most of his time working on the copies in the shop or serving behind the counter. He raised the price of all maps of the Unstable, an action that drew instant protest from his Unstabler customers, but they were forced to pay. There was no one else in the First Stability who sold such good charts, and to try to cross the Unstable without the benefit of the latest maps would have been foolhardy for even the best of guides.

While she worked at the main table in the kitchen, Keris propped the door between the room and the shop ajar so that she could listen to what the customers had to say. It annoyed her that Thirl was not at all interested in the stories that people had to tell of their crossings; too often he would cut short a tale of adversity or adventure with a curt, 'Well, which map is it that you're wanting, then?'

Once, when Yerrie came tearing into the kitchen in total panic, she heard the gravelly tones of the man with the obsidian eyes as he bought a sequence of maps, asking for coloured ones. Thirl was impatient with his request and answered him rudely, but the man insisted — in steely tones — until he had bought the maps he wanted. Afterwards, when Thirl brusquely explained to him that there would be no more updated maps from the workrooms of Piers Kaylen next season, the man said, 'I'm not surprised. I had heard Piers had died and I have also heard that Thirl Kaylen couldn't match his sire.' The words were said politely enough, but Keris had the feeling that the man knew perfectly well that he was talking to Piers's son. She suspected that the remark was made merely to exact revenge for

Thirl's manner and his exorbitant prices.

Keris almost heard Thirl bristle. 'Who told you that?' he asked. But the man gave only a noncommittal answer, and Thirl, when he came through into the main room afterwards, looked strangely disconcerted.

Master Obsidian-eyes has that effect on people, it seems, Keris thought, wryly amused.

'Creation,' said Mistress Pottle, who had also heard the exchange, 'that one's got a voice like a mountain on the move. I wouldn't like to cross by *him* on a dark night.'

Harin Markle came several times in the evenings, ostensibly to see Thirl, more covertly to court Keris. He made a poor job of it. Lacking in imagination, he was puzzled by the absence of any enthusiasm for marriage on Keris's part. He just could not accept that she was simply not interested. The only way he knew of dealing with her indifference was to decide it was all an act — such a plain girl, he thought, *must* want to marry him and was therefore playing hard to get. Keris found his dogged attentions, so obviously inspired by greed rather than passion, both tedious and ludicrous.

Thirl merely shrugged in an uninterested fashion when he saw that she was not going to encourage his friend. 'You always were too stubborn for your own good,' he remarked.

Keris knew that Thirl was continuing with his plans for the tavern. Mistress Pottle told her he had ordered chairs and tables from the carpenter in the village. The blacksmith's wife, dropping in with some mutton-brain jelly one day, said that she had heard that Thirl had made a large order of wine from the vintner's up near Kt Weddon's; and Keris herself overheard Thirl talking to the brewer's man from Beckle East about ale and beer, and to Harin about purchasing some mead from Middle Kt Beogor.

Keris did not ask where Thirl was getting the money from to make the orders; she knew. He was raiding the coins behind the loose brick at the back of the sink; pipeweed money, Piers had called it, meaning money to buy the luxuries and necessities of his old age once he could no longer work – things like pipeweed, which was imported from the Eighth Stability.

Keris sighed. She knew the few gold coins would not last long the way Thirl was spending. And, after it was gone, there would only be her dowry money . . .

According to the Rule, all the money was now legally Thirl's as long as he undertook to look after his mother until her death, and his sister until she married. In fact, provided she was cared for, an unmarried woman had no rights to property unless her living male relatives – and the Rule Office – sanctioned the ownership. Keris had heard the village devotions-chantor, Nebuthnar, pontificate on the reasons for such laws: 'This Rule is designed to protect the interests of the weaker members of our community – the children and the women,' he had said. He was a pompous man who spluttered saliva everywhere when he talked.

'Who says women are weaker?' she had asked cheekily. She had been about fourteen at the time. 'All the oldest people in the village are women.'

He had not been able to give an answer that satisfied Keris; his spluttered, 'The Rule brings Order and should therefore not be questioned' was hardly an adequate explanation.

Order, all-important Order. Regularity was paramount, change was anathema. Order ruled, and the Rule brought Order. What nobody mentioned was that the Rule stifled, that Order suffocated.

Chantor Nebuthnar came several times to see Sheyli, to offer her solace and the usual homilies to the dying. He and Keris were old enemies: because Kibbleberry was so small, he was also responsible for seeing that the Rule was obeyed, and he'd had to double as mentor-chantor as well, which meant she had been in his winter reading classes as a child. She had stuck it out for four years, by which time she could read and figure as well as he could. A place the size of Kibbleberry was not thought to merit a chantor of quality; certainly Chantor Nebuthnar lacked learning, just as he lacked humility and half a dozen other virtues normally considered desirable in a chantor. What he did not lack was belief in the necessity of obedience to the Rule and a forthright officiousness in applying the law.

It did not help that he had an innate distrust of all the Kaylen family because Piers worked the Unstable, and, in Nebuthnar's rather simple mind, Unstablers were suspect: mapmakers and such lived outside of the Rule for the greater part of a year, after all. He kept a close watch on the Kaylens and pounced every time one of them made a mistake. He complained when Piers did not wear regulation clothing, fined Keris once when he caught her wearing trousers to ride Ygraine, railed against Thirl when he was caught climbing down from Mistress Verlan's window when Master Verlan was away – all transgressions against Order.

Still, Keris appreciated his visits to her mother; Sheyli needed the comfort of religion and he seemed able to offer her hope for an afterlife, which was more than all his teachings in winter school had done for Keris herself.

She might even have thought well of him, if he had not sought her out following one of these visits, to ask her what thought she had given to marriage.

She gave him a level look. 'My mother lies mortally sick, and you ask me such a question?'

'More reason now to ask it than ever. You will soon be an orphan and in need of a man's protection –'

'I have a brother.'

'And he shall have his own family soon. You must look to start your own. I understand that Harin Markle from –'

'I will not wed Harin!'

'Ah.' He considered that, obviously searching his mind for a possible reason, and not finding one. 'Ah, well then,' he said finally, 'if marriage doesn't appeal, then perhaps you should then consider a chanterie –'

'I didn't say marriage did not appeal,' she snapped. 'It is Harin that lacks appeal. And I have no intention of donning a chantora's habit!'

He shook his head sadly at her vehemence. The scarlet tassels on his brightly coloured hat danced in emphasis. 'Child, child, remember to whom you speak. You must find your own place within the Order of the Stability. Every person has his place, and every place is important in the pattern of stability. You just have to find yours.'

'I don't really have all that much choice, do I? No profession is open to me because my father's is not available to women and my mother had none that could be passed on to a daughter, save that of a married woman.'

'You would not want to do anything that would encourage instability or disorder by deviating from your ancestral lines, would you?' he asked gently. 'The safety of us all depends on the obedience to the Rule of every individual. And perhaps you have more choice than you know: if a cloistered life does not interest you, then perhaps you should give thought to joining the Knighten's Ordering. That also is open to one such as you.'

She gaped, speechless. 'Chantor,' she said at last, all her irritation vanishing in her surprise, 'can I have heard you aright? Me? A chantist holy *Knighte*?'

'Sometimes those children who give us the most trouble are those for whom the Maker has the greatest plans,' he said simply. She was sure they could not have been his words; he was parroting another. 'A Knight – male or female – has to have a character stronger than the ordinary. A female Knighte must be a woman who does not fit the normal mould of womanhood.'

She interrupted. 'Chantor, a Knighte must also be a woman of great piety, ready to dedicate her life to Chantry and the fighting of Chaos, the keeping of Order. Isn't there twenty years of training and study and kinesis and piety before a Knighte emerges from her novitiate and can begin her roving life? I heard once that of every thousand men and women who enter training, only one emerges fit to wear the knighten symbol.'

'An exaggeration. I believe there are at the moment one

55

woman and ten male Knights. Eleven if you count Knight Edion of Galman.'

Knight Edion, she knew, had been a man of great learning, revered for his scholarship and wisdom as much as for his charity. He had disappeared inside the Unstable ten or more years earlier. There had been an outrageous rumour hinting that he had joined forces with the Unmaker, becoming his personal assistant. Others said the opposite: he was actually fighting Lord Carasma in eternal battle somewhere or other. The most persistent rumour was that he had settled for a hermit's life somewhere in the Unstable; the most pernicious (as far as Chantry was concerned) was that he had been murdered by some of the more conservative of the Hedrin – the chantors of Chantry's ruling body, the Sanhedrin – because they thought he was preaching heresy.

All of that mattered little to Keris. Knights may have lived wandering unorthodox lives of adventure, at least after their training, but the price was far too high for her. 'I'd fail the first week of training!' she said. *And still be condemned to twenty years of toil, trying to attain the unattainable.*

He shrugged, obviously privately agreeing with her. 'If the Maker wants you, you will feel the call.'

She thought with annoyance: He's been told to look for suitable candidates, and he's decided it's one way of ridding the village of me. The one person who did not 'fit the normal mould of womankind'. Someone who disturbed his sense of Order. She smiled sweetly. 'I'll think about it. And doubtless, if it is my destiny, the Maker will tell me.'

The smile he gave back was uncertain; he did not know whether she mocked him.

Gradually, as the summer days lengthened, there was less work to do on mapmaking and Thirl was away from the shop more. Keris welcomed his absence. Sometimes, when there was no sign of customers and her mother was napping, she would take the trompleri map out of its hiding place and pore over it with a strange mixture of unease and euphoria.

She longed to speak to someone about it, but trusted no one enough to divulge such a secret. She had to content herself with remembering all that she had heard about such maps, with piecing together what Piers had told her, and the odd snippets of information she had heard from time to time from customers.

'Trompleri,' Piers had said once, 'is not the correct word. It was actually three words in the old language. Three words that have been run together to make one – and then hopelessly mispronounced. The original words meant "trick the eye".'

Trick the eye: it was true. That was what the map did. When she looked at it, she saw the world in miniature, shade and shadow, movement and motion, all of it real with depth and dimension and texture. Yet, if she ran a hand across it, it felt no different from any other mapskin; it was smooth to touch with just the slightest of bumps where the ink or paint was thick. How much better just to look at it! Then, it was *real*. She could see the hills projecting out of a rolling plain, jutting up out of the flatness of the vellum, so real that her mind could not understand why her fingers could not feel their roundness. She could see the twinkling shine of sun-shine on a stream, its moving waters flowing across the skin, skimming the stones drawn beneath. Yet, when her fingers dipped into the water, they felt nothing but the aridity of dried paint. Strange nodules – plants of some kind? – shaded the ground alongside, yet, when she touched nodules and ground, they were all on the same plane. An animal grazed on grass clumps, moving across the dry dust of a blighted landscape with dainty steps; a rocky outcrop cast a shadow that moved with the passage of the day; and once, just once, she saw a group of people ride across one corner, mounts and riders as real to her as the pilgrims who passed the shop would be to an eagle flying high over Kibbleberry village.

And there, in all its terrifying glory, was a ley line, snaking from north to south like a colourful, poisonous serpent, contaminating the land with its evil; worse still, inching its way sideways, sucking up colour and leaving behind a withered burn-scar of grey that the land struggled in vain to repair.

A trompleri map moved and changed as the landscape it portrayed altered. By showing the variations in light and shadow, a trompleri map recorded sunrise and sunset, daylight and dark – or even the passing of cloud, the falling of rain. A trompleri map showed the movement of people and animals, the passage of the tainted and the Wild, the trek of pilgrims and guides, couriers and traders; it showed all visible life – and the corpses of death. It was all there, momentarily etched on two-dimensional vellum with all the three dimensions of the real.

It was disquieting. And wonderful. It fascinated and it frightened.

A trompleri map was Magic.

'Imagine,' Piers had said several years earlier. 'Imagine, Keris. If I had such master charts, there would be no need to risk my life in the Unstable. When the ley lines moved, the change would be recorded there on the vellum. And, if an Unstabler had one, well – a glance at the map and he'd know where best to cross. And when. A trompleri map is the ultimate master chart: it keeps itself updated . . .'

'But do they exist?' she had asked, her youthful imagination stimulated by even the idea of such a wonder.

'Once upon a time they did. But the secret of making them was lost and gradually those that existed disintegrated with age. Maybe it's just as well.' He gave a wry laugh. 'I'd be out of a job otherwise.' He paused. 'And yet . . .'

'Yes?'

'I've heard tell just lately that someone has rediscovered the secret. Or is close to doing so.'

'Truly?'

'There have been rumours. But then there are always rumours about those who frequent the Unstable.' He sighed. 'It's the nature of the place and its people, I suppose. If I listened to rumours I'd believe in dragons spewing fire and fireflies that talk, in beautiful ladies imprisoned by the

Minions of Chaos and in heroes that rescue them, in a magic kingdom called Havenstar and wizards who live there and make trompleri maps –'

'*Wizards?*'

He had laughed and ruffled her hair. 'Ah, just tales, Keri. Nobody I know has ever been to Havenstar and nobody I know has ever seen a trompleri map. Or a wizard, or a dragon or an imprisoned maiden waiting to be rescued. And Havenstar is just a dream place, made up by the poor, wretched, tainted Untouchables who fantasise about a sanctuary where they will be safe and can lead normal lives, where wizards will miraculously cure their ills. Many set off to find it. They never come back.' He shook his head, touched suddenly by sadness. 'Pity them, Keris, the Unbound. Think about what the name means: Unbound, pulled asunder, unravelled. They have been partially unmade, just as our poor Margravate was partially unmade so long ago. Theirs is the saddest of all existences.'

Much more interested in talk of magic, she had hardly heard his sorrow. 'And the wizards make trompleri maps?'

'So it's said. Tales, Keri, lass, tales. Out there in the Unstable you hear a hundred such stories and no more than two or three are true.' He grinned. 'Usually the most incredible of all, at that. For that reason alone I'll keep dreaming of owning a trompleri master chart, but I won't believe in them until I have it in my hand.'

Well, two years later he had apparently held such a map in his hand. And a fat lot of good it did him, she thought. It probably killed him. Always supposing that whoever was searching his things was the one who murdered him, and it was the map that they had been looking for . . .

At first Keris had no idea what area the map represented. It was an abnormally large-scale chart – 1:5,000 – that covered only a small area. It portrayed no halt or houses or signs of settlement. It was signed with the name Kereven Deverli, and it was undated. According to the title at the top, it represented an area known as Draggle Flats West. It was certainly not a map of any place north of the Wide. The names written beside the features drawn there were unknown to Keris: Milkwaters, Gaggle Crag, Melldale Bushgrass, the Humps – she knew none of these places. Even the ley line had a name she did not recognise: the Writhe.

She searched through some of the old maps Piers had stored in the attic, looking for one that mentioned such names. These maps were not the ones that Piers had created – he had bought them from other mapmakers long ago, before he had been married, in the days when he had travelled widely in the Unstable, even as far as the Eighth Stability.

Eventually, after an hour or two of work, she found the Writhe – or the very beginnings of it – marked at the extreme edge of one of the charts. It was near the Graven, the ley line that separated the Eighth Stability from the Seventh and the Sixth. The most puzzling thing of all was that the Writhe angled south, beyond the Eighth Stability, into the Waste. Which meant that the trompleri map showed a portion of the Waste. But who would ever want to make a map of such a place? No one ever went even as far south as the Riven, the ley line that flowed beyond the southern edge of the Eighth, not any more; it was too dangerous. There were no stabilities there, no areas of Order at all, just endless instability and horror. Or so it was said by the few who had gone exploring in years gone by and managed to return.

According to legends, there had been other countries in the far south once: the twin nations of Yedron and Yefron; wicked Vedis where tyrants ruled; and fabulous Bellisthron, which floated on the lakes of Thron. The most ancient of the Holy Books spoke of such places, but, if they really had existed, they did no more, or were separated from what was left of the Margravate of Malinawar by too wide an expanse of Unstable.

No one searched for them any more, no one went that far south any more – and yet here was a map that evidently showed an area south of the Eighth Stability. It did not make sense.

Keris put the maps away with a sigh.

In the days that followed she spent a lot of time thinking about the riddle, but could come up with no answers — nor did she know whom to ask. She did speak about trompleri maps to several of the ley-lit Unstablers who came into the shop; they all dismissed them as something that may have existed once, but which were no longer to be found.

It was not enough for her. The map she had was not old, at least not so old that it was in danger of disintegration. Therefore, she reasoned, someone had indeed rediscovered the secret of making such a map. Someone called Kereven Deverli. And possibly someone else was so desperate to obtain it that they were willing to kill for it. (Because of what it portrayed, or just because it was a trompleri chart?)

As the days passed, the trompleri became an obsession. Its ever-changing beauty enticed her, intrigued her, fascinated her. She tried to discover the secret of its creation simply by looking at it, by examining it — but could reach no conclusions as to how it was made. Her fingers told her that it was just an ordinary map; her eyes told her it was no such thing. Touch told her it was flat; sight told her it was contoured — and time told her it changed. The inks and paints used to fashion it seemed similar to those she made herself from vegetable dyes, gums, resins, oils, lamp black, earth pigments and mineral salts. What, then, made it magic? She did not know and could not guess.

But, deep inside her, she knew that above all else she wanted to learn how to fashion such a map herself. It was the ultimate challenge to a mapmaker, and equally deep inside her she knew that she was indeed a mapmaker, not a woman destined to be just somebody's wife. Nor yet a woman destined to be a holy Knighte. *She was a mapmaker*.

She grew more and more restless and unhappy, knowing herself to be on the edge of a great change in her life, yet not knowing in which direction the change would take her. The trompleri map with its continually altering face seemed to symbolise the flux of her own existence. The mystery mirrored the mystery of her father's death and the unknown of her own future.

Her pragmatism told her there was no possibility that she could ever be a master mapmaker. True, she could use a theodolite, take readings and draft accurate maps. True, she could ride a horse and defend herself with a bow and arrow. True, she had accompanied her father on surveying trips within the First Stability and had learnt much of his skills on such trips. But she had never been into the Unstable and would not have known how to survive there. However often she heard its oddities and its dangers discussed, she was unfamiliar with them in practice. It was doubtful if a woman alone could have survived long at the best of times: brute strength counted for a lot when the Wild and the Minions of Chaos were abroad. And finally no one would have bought the maps of a woman anyway, because no one would have faith in them. Women were midwives and bakers, herbalists and tailors, barbers and weavers, but they were never blacksmiths or chantists or tavernkeepers or carpenters – or mapmakers. The Rule decided such things, and the Rule must be kept. A woman who tried a profession denied to her by the Rule would have been scorned and reviled, her business ignored, and that would have been enough. There would have been no need of other punishment: society had already devised a perfect one.

Order must be kept, and a woman who disobeyed the Rule threatened Order and would find no sympathy.

The most she could hope for was to do what she had done for her father and was now doing for Thirl: work at the creation of a map and step back to see a man take the praise. Perhaps she could find someone who would accept her talent and take her on as a copyist.

Better the dregs at the bottom of the glass than no drink at all.

Perhaps.

* * *

One evening, just at sunset, Keris was alerted by Yerrie to the coming of a visitor. She had already put up the shutters, but she opened the door and peered out. It was a strange time for a customer, or even a visitor, but she was more curious than frightened. They had no problems with thieves or bandits in Kibbleberry.

A man was standing beside the horse trough outside, looking at the water as if trying to make up his mind whether to drink it or not. He was middle-aged and tired; the face he turned to her sagged with weariness. He appeared to have no mount, and his clothes were shabby.

As he moved towards her she saw that his left cheek was scarred with the ritual disfigurement of the convicted criminal: two bars and a crescent moon. Two convictions, then, and the crescent moon meant a minor theft without violence. Her eyes dropped to his left hand. As if in answer he raised it for her to see: he had two fingers that had been broken and allowed to mend crookedly. Another mark of the thief. Anything worse than petty theft would have merited exclusion to the Unstable, of course, and thus a man who had been convicted of a greater crime would not have been standing before her.

She said, 'The nearest Chantry hostelry is at Kte Marlede's.'

'I've walked from Hopen Grat,' he said. 'Mistress, please, I can't get to Kte Marlede's tonight. I'm tired and hungry and thirsty.' His eyes dropped once more to the water trough.

'Don't drink that,' she said automatically. 'I'll get you clean water.'

'Food?' he pleaded. 'And a place in your barn for the night, maybe?'

'That's against the Rule,' she said. A criminal who had no property of his own was not permitted to sleep in inhabited areas, except at religious chanteries or Chantry-run hostels, and even then he was never permitted to stay more than two consecutive nights. It was also forbidden for unen-coloured people to give such a person food. He was supposed to be totally dependent on Chantry aid.

'The Rule says many things,' he said tiredly. 'And sometimes a man just doesn't have what it takes to obey the Rule.
I'm weary, maid.' He sat down on the edge of the trough,
and he did indeed look exhausted.

Damn the Rule, she thought. I'm sick of it too. 'All right,'
she told him. 'Come this way.' She led him around the side of
the house to the barn. 'But be careful – my brother will not
be charitable if he finds you. You had best hide yourself in
the hayloft. I'll bring you out some water and food and a
blanket.' He looked grateful. And relieved. 'Don't touch the
horses,' she warned.

'I won't steal them.'

'I know that,' she said. 'They'd never let you. I was
thinking more in terms of not going near them at all. They
are crossings-horses, apt to snap at strangers. And they have
sharp incisors, so be warned.' She left him then and went
back to the house.

Fortunately, Sheyli was asleep and Thirl had walked into
the village (she thought she knew why: he was courting
Fressie, the carpenter's daughter), so it was easy to take out
the water and the blankets, then to prepare a plate of food
without anyone wanting to know what she was doing.

The man fell on the meal as if he had not eaten for some
time and she had to refill the jug of water because he finished
it so quickly. They didn't talk much; he seemed disinclined to
chat and she was not sure she wanted to hear what he had to
say anyway. She could guess at the kind of life he lived and
she could guess at the bitterness he harboured inside himself.
If he did not want to lead the life of a wanderer, for ever
condemned by his facial scars and his crooked fingers, if he
did not want to be destined to live for ever on Chantry
charity, hassled by Defenders and upright citizens alike, then
he could be encoloured as a chantor himself – or he could
leave the Stability and live in the Unstable. Either way, it was
not much of a choice: encoloured he could only be a
kinesis-chantor, nothing else, condemned to spend most of

his waking hours performing kinesis devotions within the kinesis chain. As an inhabitant of the Unstable on the other hand, he would be condemned by the unwritten code that existed there to wander with other more vicious excluded criminals. His life expectancy would probably be short.

You don't have much more choice than I do, Keris thought, and pitied him.

She left him to finish his meal in peace.

Next morning he was gone before she went to the barn. There were suspiciously few eggs under the hens, but nothing else was missing.

She returned to the kitchen with the only egg she had found to discover that Sheyli was sitting up in bed, which should have been a good sign – but somehow she felt a lurch of fear just to look at her. Her mother's eyes glittered with an unnatural brightness; her skin was patchily flushed.

Keris sat on the edge of the bed and took her hand. 'Do you want something, Mother?'

She nodded. 'Yes. I've been thinking and thinking . . .' She was silent for a moment. 'About many things. About little Aurin, sometimes. Do you remember him, Keri?'

She nodded, although in truth her memory of her little brother was vague. She had been only four when he was born, and he had disappeared two days later.

'They shouldn't have taken him,' Sheyli whispered. 'Tessy kept her two sons and her daughter. And so did that drayman over in Upper Kibble. They make exceptions sometimes, but they wouldn't for us. It was because Piers was an Unstabler, you know, and they don't like Unstablers. Well, they'll pay for it now: there won't be a proper mapmaker in the First any more and they'll suffer for that. They shouldn't have taken him – it wasn't right. There's not been a day – not a single solitary day in the past twenty years – that I have not thought of him.'

The tragedy of her words caught in Keris's throat and she started guiltily, knowing that she had not cared much about Aurin and had hardly given him a thought.

'Ah, Keri,' Sheyli said finally, 'sometimes I think the whole world is falling apart around us.'

Keris was shaken. Sheyli had never criticised the basic *rightness* of the Rule and Chantry before, and in her shock Keris's protest lacked conviction: 'Nonsense, Mother. You're being fanciful, and that's not at all like you.'

'Keri, it's not going to be much longer. A day or two only. I can feel myself going.' Keris opened her mouth to protest again, but Sheyli rushed on feverishly, giving her no chance. 'Before I go, I want to know that you are looked after. Keri, I want you to take the dowry money and leave.'

'But – where would I go?'

'To my brother. Your Uncle Fergrand in the Second Stability. You could make your lifetime pilgrimage at the same time.'

'That money is not mine –'

'Your father worked hard for it. He did intend it for you, for your husband, that is; not for Thirl. Thirl was to have the business and the house, you were to have the money. I intend to see that Piers's wishes are carried out. Take the money, Keris, before Thirl spends it on his wretched tavern.'

Keris thought of the thief she had sheltered in the barn. Of a scarred face, crippled fingers, a vagabond's life. To take the dowry money would be to commit a crime. 'Mother – the Rule –'

'Firstly, you can only be charged with a crime in the same stab the crime was committed in. Once you are in the Second, you will be safe – it would be too much trouble to have you brought back over such a little thing. Secondly, I shall tell Thirl that, if he charges you, I will cloud the issue by denying that there was ever any dowry money to start with. It will be Thirl's word against the word of a dying woman. Who will be believed? I shall tell Mistress Pottle so that there will be someone else to stand witness.'

Keris swallowed. Crooked fingers, scarred face . . . It was as if she had been warned. As if the thief had been sent to her as a sign that she shouldn't put herself beyond the law. *Don't be ridiculous. It was just a coincidence, nothing more.* Aloud she said with certainty, 'Thirl will follow me to get the money back.'

'As long as he doesn't catch up with you before you reach the Unstable, you will be safe. Believe me, he's not going to follow you across the kinesis chain. He's made it quite clear how much he fears instability. And I don't think he'd turn you in to a Chantry Court or the Defenders anyway. He *is* your brother –'

'Mother –'

'Please, Keri. Please – so that I can die happy. Creation, child, you always were the hard-headed one, clinging to an idea and never giving up, arguing and kicking every inch of the way – but now's not the time to be stubborn. I'm asking you to do this for *me*. Do you understand? For *me*.'

'I don't know Uncle Fergrand and –'

'– and I haven't seen him for twenty years. Yes, I know. But he was always a good man. And your father met him from time to time in Salient. He was still alive in autumn of last year, and in good health. I'm sure he will give you a home and help you to find a husband.'

Keris opened her mouth to protest that she didn't know why everyone thought it was so necessary for her to have a husband, but thought better of the remark. Her mother needed to be reassured, not upset.

Sheyli continued, 'Thirl is going to Middle Kt Beogor tomorrow morning, in Harin's cart. Something about deliveries of mead or beer. He won't be back until after dark. You leave while he's away.'

Keris was horrified. 'I can't do that! Not before –' She stopped, flustered.

Sheyli gave the faintest of smiles. 'Not before I die? Keri, dearest, if you are gone I can die in peace. Please, dear, do as I ask. This is not the time to be contrary, not now.'

Sheyli was tempting her with a way out and Keris lacked the will to resist. She began to cry, not in noisy sobs, but with silent tears. She knew she was saying goodbye, not only to her mother but to the last remnants of her childhood and innocence, and the grief she felt for an impending loss was mingled with fear for her future, with guilt at the knowledge that she would leave while her mother still lived, with despair that Sheyli must die without her daughter by her bedside. Her mother desperately needed her now and yet also needed to know she had a future.

'Will you go?' her mother asked.

Keris nodded helplessly. She told herself she did it for her mother, but knew that the truth was she would do it just as much for herself. It was a selfish decision that shamed her, that would probably shame her all her life — yet it was a solution and she was not going to turn her back on it. She could not.

She prepared her packs that day while Thirl was gone. That night she dozed by her mother's bedside, Sheyli's hand held in her own. She left the next morning.

She did not look back. Her eyes were too tear-filled to see, anyway.

Chapter Five

*And great was the punishment inflicted on the world because
a few followed the ways of wickedness. Humankind asked in
despair, 'What barrier is there to Lord Carasma when ley
lends him strength, when Minions do his bidding? He will
take all the land that was the Margravate.'*

*Goodperson rose to find that his land, assaulted by ley,
was as coast shaped anew with each tide, and his animals
were as beasts of the forest. Yet he said, 'Fear not. Turn from
the Unmaker for before him you will grovel for all eternity.
Be of good cheer, for the Maker has handed down to you the
Rule that shall be your protection.'*

The Rending II: 6: 1—7

As luck would have it, Keris fell in with a chantor within
minutes of leaving Kibbleberry village. She was annoyed; she
had expected — *wanted* — to ride to the border alone.
Sheyli Kaylen lived still, but her daughter wanted solitude to
grieve. She wanted time to come to terms with her guilt at
leaving, yet she was denied the opportunity.

The chantor, a vision of red face and coloured silks,
was resting fanning himself beside the road not far outside
Kibbleberry when she rode past. He jumped up, waved his
jewelled fly switch in her direction, an action that sent his
bells chiming and his silks flapping in the sunshine, and
bade her wait for him. Obedient (this time at least) to the
upbringing that had taught her to heed those who represented Chantry, she waited, maintaining a bland expression

69

that reflected nothing of her irritation. He climbed on to his palfrey (he was a small man and had no need of a larger mount), grasped the leading rope of his pack-ass and joined her out on the road.

'Ah, lass,' he said in the lilting accent of the Eighth Stability, 'right glad it is I am of company. I was escorting several chantoras to Kte Marlede's, fine pious women off to a retreat at the chanterie there, but I've met no one going my way since, and Portron Bittle, rule-chantor of the Order of Kt Ladma – that's me – is not a man to be relishing a solitary life.'

'Then you shouldn't have chosen to be encoloured, Chantor,' she said, the words slipping out before she could reflect on their wisdom. She was thinking: Of all people, a chantor dedicated to the explanation and the enforcing of the Rule – hardly the sort of man I want to have as a travelling companion.

He paused in his flood of words and gave her a measured look, evidently unsure if she had intended the comment as a sly poke at his chantist celibacy, as indeed she had. His glance roved on to her bundles loaded on her packhorse's back (topped with Piers's blackwood staff and her bowstave), then to the single throwing knife she wore at her waist and the quiver slung on her back. Lastly he eyed her trousers and boots, her shirt and leather jerkin – clothes she had always risked wearing when on surveying trips with Piers in the countryside.

'You'll be off on your pilgrimage,' he said unnecessarily and straightened the cuffs on his bright-red and mauve gown. She nodded. 'You should be wearing your skirts, lass. I know even a chantor puts aside his robes to make a crossing because they may hamper movement at crucial moments, and the colour is not conducive to – er – camouflage either, but you're not in the Unstable yet. This is still the First Stability and you should be wearing your skirts. When we stop for a rest, you must be changing.'

'Into what? I brought no skirts with me,' she lied.

She thought he'd be shocked, but he seemed more interested than surprised. 'None? Well then, there's nothing much we can be doing about it, is there? I can hardly be lending you mine. Tell me, child, how is it you are unaccompanied?'

'My father and mother are – are dead and my brother has already made his pilgrimage.'

He shook his head sorrowfully. 'You should not be travelling alone. The Rule is quite clear: women should seek company for protection, lest they be a temptation to the unruly.'

It was the last straw. 'Then let the unruly conquer *their* lusts,' she said snappishly. 'The sin should be theirs, not mine. I'm willing to take the risk.'

He looked shocked. 'Lass, you don't have the right of it. Should you find trouble on your way, then Order is threatened and with it all humankind. Everybody should do their utmost to prevent disorder. For you to be taking a risk is selfish because more than just your own safety is threatened.'

She knew he was right, but it was still hard to accept. She took a deep breath and flexed fingers that had been holding reins too tightly. 'Never mind, Chantor,' she said, striving for lightness. 'Now I have met you and you can protect my virtue between here and Hopen Grat.'

She had never before dared to make fun, even obliquely, of a stranger, let alone one who was a chantor, and she felt a moment's amazement at her temerity. I feel like someone else, she thought, not Keris Kaylen, the mapmaker's meek daughter. I feel like – like a dog that's been let off the leash for the first time, ready to play, or fight. Free. She sat a little straighter in the saddle and felt good about herself. Darn you, Thirl Kaylen, she thought. I've got my dowry money and I've taken Father's – your – crossings-horses and your bowstave and your sleeping sack and your theodolite and your mapmaking tools and your master charts – and I don't give a damn. She had decided that, if she was going to be

71

hunted down as a thief, there was no point in being a modest one.

'Which crossing are you making, lass?' the chantor was asking. He had said several other things as well, but she had not been listening. 'To the closest stab, I suppose? The Second?'

'Yes. What about you, Chantor?'

'Oh, I'm not off on a pilgrimage. The Father-chantor of the Order of Kt Ladma has ordered me back for a spiritual retreat, that's all.' He stirred uneasily in his saddle as if there was something that bothered him about that. 'But you wouldn't be knowing where the chanterie is, would you, lass? It's in the Eighth Stab. I have to be trekking the Unstable from north to south in the months to come and it's a rough ride, I can tell you. Hard on one's rear.'

He shook his head sorrowfully and she almost laughed. He was perhaps fifty years old, and had round red cheeks, a rotund belly and large feet, none of which seemed to fit in well with his small frame. He had a bald patch in the middle of a white frizz of hair, but his face was unlined and glowed with a habitual expression of amiable goodwill. Which she found odd, seeing that most rule-chantors were hard men, ruthless in enforcing Order. 'I hate the Unstable,' he said suddenly. 'Ever made a crossing, lass?'

She shook her head.

He nodded reminiscently, his white hair flying about his ears. 'I hate it. It's an evil place that subverts the innocent and damages the pure. When I was a lad of your age – I was a butcher's second son, you know – I was setting off on my pilgrimage too. That was when I decided I wanted to be encoloured, when I came to see the chantist way was for me. I was looking about me, and seeing all that evil – nay, *feeling* it deep in my bones, contaminating – and that was when I knew that I had to be a chantor to fight its spread. Kinesis is the surest way to hold the Unstable at bay. Kinesis and the establishment of Order and obedience to the Rule. Up until then, I hadn't really been believing, not really, you know. I was young and scornful of Chantry and the rigidity of the Rule. But out there —' he waved a hand in the direction they were taking '— out there, you feel Chaos. You feel it corroding the very earth beneath your feet. You feel it unmaking what has been created, you feel it twisting the laws of life and growth. You feel the hand of the Unmaker trailing his fingers across your soul, wanting to make it his own. And then you know that the only bulwark against Chaos is Order, and where better to help in Order's maintenance than within Chantry?'

She looked at him curiously. 'You're ley-lit, then?'

He nodded again. 'Aye, for my sins, it's a hard thing to be ley-lit in the Unstable, lass. You *feel* more.' He sighed.

'Do you go through the other stabilities to get to the Eighth?' she asked. 'Or do you go direct?'

'The usual route is due south to the Fifth. Stock up there, and then on to the Eighth, straight as a mule to water. Of course, it'll be depending on the guide one has.'

'You'll go through Pickle's Halt, then.'

'Pickle's Halt? I don't know it. But it's a dozen years since Porton Bittle was leaving the First and the halts come and go like the seasons. It's a dangerous job to be a haltkeeper. May the Maker bless 'em. I remember once . . .' He started to reminisce, telling a story that, as far as Keris could tell, had nothing whatsoever to do with halts or haltkeepers. She stopped listening and occupied herself with her own thoughts instead. She was tempted to go to Pickle's Halt herself. The trouble was that it was not on the way to the Second Stability, and it was doubtful that anyone ever went from the Halt to the Second. If she visited the Halt, she would then have to return to the First Stability in order to reach the Second — a dangerous manoeuvre if Thirl was after her, and one that would cost money in guides. Yet she did so want to talk to Pickle. She wanted to know where the map had come from. She wanted to know who had murdered her father. And she wanted to know how he had been killed. Piers Kaylen, who was as wily as an old rat in a farmer's barn . . . He could not have been an easy man to murder.

'. . . and so there I was,' Chantor Portron was saying, 'covered in feathers from my pate to my toes, naked as a babe, with a beautiful lass in my arms and the hedrin-chantor coming in the door.'

She blinked, startled, and wondered what she had missed.

'And you, lass, haven't heard a word I've been saying.' He sighed. 'Few people listen to me after a while. I talk too much.'

'And what if you do?' she asked, amused, suspecting now that he had just tagged on that startling punch line to wake her out of her reverie. 'You like talking.'

He laughed. 'Aye, that I do. But a chantor should be listening more than he prattles. Here I am, telling you all about myself, and I don't know a cat's whisker about you. What's your name, lass?'

'Keris. Keris – Kereven.' She had not thought to lie until her name had already been trembling on her lips; then she'd had a blinding flash of memory of herself, kneeling on the floor with the tatters of her father's blood-spattered clothing in her hands and the thought was in her head that, if someone had murdered Piers Kaylen, perhaps Kaylen was not a good name to own – not in the Unstable. And, if Thirl was chasing her, it might not be a good name to have in the First, either.

With a momentary sense of wry bafflement, she considered herself. Where was the girl she had been, the obedient daughter? Since she had learnt of her father's death she had done a dozen things that ought to have shamed her deeply: she had hidden something that was not hers to hide, then hidden and fed a convicted thief; she had stolen from her brother, run away from home, left her dying mother – and now she had lied about her name. And she felt amazingly light-hearted about all of it – except leaving Sheyli. That did shame her, but she pushed the feeling deep inside her and let the other emotions dominate: joy in her new-found freedom, excitement at the thought of what lay ahead, contentment with the idea that she was controlling her own life.

A dog let off the leash? No: rather a butterfly shedding its chrysalis only to find it had wings . . .

As they rode on she was smiling to herself.

At her side the chantor noted the smile and envied the boundless confidence of the young. He at least was old enough to know that it was not so easy.

Maylie, he thought. Maker, how she looks like Maylie. And he felt a pain he had not felt for years.

They arrived at the border towards sunset. The cluster of shops and tents there at the end of the road had once been known as Hope and Gratitude. The hope was for those leaving on their crossing; the gratitude was that of those arriving from the Unstable, grateful their crossing was over. The name had long since been contracted down to Hopen Grat.

There was nothing permanent about Hopen Grat's appearance. No one lived there for very long; it was too close to the Unstable. As a consequence a sense of uneasy transience pervaded the ramshackle constructions that lined the rutted tracks. The shopkeepers operated out of shanties or tents, made quick money by selling goods at high prices, then moved back into the interior of the stability with relief. Chantry transferred kinesis-chantors (to maintain the chain) and devotions-chantors (to serve the needs of pilgrims) in and out of the town in quick succession. There were no Defenders posted here – perhaps because no Trician would have stayed – so there was no one to enforce the Rule. In fact, Order hardly existed. In Hopen Grat a moment's lack of watchfulness could mean being robbed penniless, raped or murdered.

And yet there was some commerce, some normality. You could buy the supplies you had forgotten to bring, or replenish those you had used up. You could have your mount shod – or have his wounds sewn up. You could hire a guide or send a letter via a courier. You could ask for information about relatives or friends who had ridden out and never returned. You could have a bath in the bath house if you were dirty enough, visit the doctor if your need was urgent enough, or purchase a horse if you had money enough. You could also buy the services of an overused whore, perform your kineses at the shrine, seek absolution from a chantor, buy a good-luck charm or pay for a ward against being tainted. But some things you could not do: you couldn't find a thatcher or a mason or a tailor – nothing that hinted at permanence or luxury was for sale in Hopen Grat – and you'd never find the scum who'd robbed you, raped one of your party or murdered your friend.

The main street was a diseased gut. It smelt, seethed, belched, grumbled. It twisted and turned, narrowed and swelled. It groaned with people and animals, shuddered with noise, heaved with activity. The buildings – if they could be called such – squatted along it like growths and exuded garbage like running sores. Hopen Grat resembled no other place in the First; it had its siblings elsewhere, on the edge of the other stabilities. Border settlements were all alike, contaminated towns, polluted by their proximity to the Unstable, muddied by the touch of Chaos, tainted by the gaze of the Unmaker.

As she rode into Hopen Grat with Chantor Portron, Keris felt overwhelmed: her earlier confidence had ebbed away. Everyone seemed to be shouting, pushing, shoving. All about her purses were being stolen, bottoms pinched, bargains made, wagers lost. Hopen Grat made her feel dirty.

'Watch your purse, lass,' Portron said unnecessarily under his breath.

'Is it always like this?' she asked and kicked away a hand that groped for Ygraine's bridle.

'Every time I've been here, anyways. Shall we be hunting out the guides before making camp, do you think?'

She nodded. 'I wouldn't want to leave our tents unattended in a place like this.' A blue-scaled hand brushed her boot and she flinched away in alarm. The owner of the arm scuttled away between a press of mounted men but not before she had an impression of webbed feet and a hairless head that was sunk directly on to bony shoulders. She turned wide-eyed to Portron. 'Chantor – the *Unbound* come here?'

'Aye,' he said and his voice was a mixture of distaste and distress. 'It's hard to stop them. They're coming for supplies, poor souls. The Defenders do patrol the length of the kineses chain sometimes, but you'll need hundreds of men to keep the tainted from crossing the border entirely.'

She was shocked. 'But the kinesis chain should keep them out –'

'It works better against the Wild and Minions. The Unbound aren't noticing it much, I'm thinking, at least not unless they have committed themselves to the Unmaker. It's more Order that repulses the tainted, and, as you may have noticed, there's not too much Order here. Alas, you can see many of the excluded here, too – not just the Unbound. Hopen Grat's a dangerous place, I'm always thinking, lass. Murders aplenty, and the corpses bear the mark of the tainted often enough. Keep your wits about you. Hey, you,' he called to a passing hawker of supposedly magical amulets, 'where do we find the guides?'

'First right and straight on! An amulet, maid? Guaranteed effective for ten days against ley tainting.'

The amulet, Keris knew, would be useless for all its guarantee. She nudged Ygraine after the chantor and Tousson, her packhorse, followed obediently. When a stranger put a hand to the packs, the crossings-horse turned to nip at him savagely and Keris grinned.

The guides were camped along a rise away from the worst of the town. She surveyed the neat row of canvas and tethered animals with approval; guides had the same orderliness to their camps as Piers had inculcated in her. 'Which go where?' she asked.

'Look at the numbers,' Portron said. Each camp had a number indicated somewhere, scrawled in charcoal on the canvas perhaps, or just indicated by a number of ribbons fluttering from a ridgepole. 'You'll be having a choice, Maid Kereven. There's five or six bound for the Second Stab. I'll just have to take this one.' He pointed his fly switch at a canvas strung between two trees. A man lay at his ease on a bed roll in the shade beneath, his head pillowed on a pack with a hat tilted over his eyes.

Yet she knew instantly who it was and repressed a feeling of vague unease. *Just because a cat didn't like him doesn't mean anything* . . .

She remained seated on Ygraine while Portron dismounted and went forward on foot. 'Um, begging your pardon for rousing you, Master Guide – but would your services be for hire to the Eighth Stab?' he asked.

The hat tilted back and the head raised itself a little. Black eyes – the same obsidian chips she had expected to see – scanned the chantor neutrally. Whatever it was that had been the cause of his shame back in Kibbleberry, it didn't seem to make him blush in the presence of a rule-chantor. 'They are,' he said in that voice like the scrape of a millstone. He sat up but did not bother to stand, or even make a kinesis of greeting. 'I'm leaving first light tomorrow. Ten golds each for the full journey, payable before we leave. You supply your own hard rations, enough to get as far as the Fifth. And I don't travel with Defenders. If you want an armed fellow-ship, you'll have to wait another three weeks for Mink Medrigan's.' His eyes flicked briefly to Keris. 'The child goes with you?'

'The *woman* does not,' Keris said with emphasis, and wondered if he would recognise her. His gaze returned to her – with awakening interest. His eyes lingered momentarily on her throwing knife, then on the quiver, then drifted down to her mount. The crossings-horse gave him pause and she saw him frown as he tried to place her. Then he appeared to lose interest again and looked back to Portron.

'Are you ley-lit?' he asked.

'I am.'

'What hard rations do you have?'

'A flour sack of biltong and a half of dried minnows. Two grand rounds of hard cheese. One of damper flour mixed with dried fruit. A mix of horse beans and fullen oats for the animals – just the one sack.'

'That should suffice. Be down by the pond over there –' he waved past his tent '– at sun-up. And no skirts or bells or bright silks, please.' He nodded a dismissal and lay down again. A hand tilted the hat over his eyes once more.

'Ah –' Portron cleared his throat. 'May I be asking your name, lad?'

Keris grinned at the thought of Master Obsidian-eyes being addressed as lad, but the man did not seem to react. 'Storre. Davron Storre. And yours, Chantor?'

'Portron Bittle, at your service, of the Order of Kt –'

The hard eyes emerged briefly once more from under the brim of the hat. 'Perform your devotions all you want on this journey, Chantor Portron, but don't bother me with them. Is that clear?'

'Ah – yes, as you wish, although devotions to the Maker can never be –' The eyes disappeared as the hat thunked down under a determined hand. Portron blinked and retreated.

'I think you just met your match, Chantor,' Keris remarked as they rode away. 'You won't get much conversation out of *him* on your journey.'

'Alas, I do believe you may be having the right of it.' He sighed. 'And the pilgrimage will be taking all of two or three months, too. I hope his heart is not as black as his eyes.' Then he shrugged. 'Ah, it's all on the palm of the good Maker, blessed be His name. If it's my fate to arrive at the Fatherhouse, then arrive I shall. Now what about you, lass? Which of these guides heading for the Second Stab will you take?'

'The one who leaves earliest,' she said promptly. She knew any one of them might recognise her, but the odds were against it: she had a face that was easily forgotten. As for Ygraine and Tousson – for all their good points, there was nothing remarkable about their appearance. It was unlikely that anyone would remember them as Piers's animals.

79

She visited all the guides who were bound for the Second Stability — there were six of them — and there was not one who showed that he found her familiar. Two chided her about her ownership of the crossings-horses, a third tried to buy them from her and a fourth told Portron it was a threat to stability to have a woman ride one, let alone own two of the beasts, and what was he going to do about it? The man closest to having the ten pilgrims he considered necessary to make the journey profitable estimated that he would be leaving the day after the next and didn't mention the crossings-horses at all, so she added the name Keris Kereven to his list, and then she and Portron rode off to find a place to pitch their tents.

That evening, while Portron was giving an impromptu sermon on the Rule to a group of fellow campers, Keris went off to find the Hopen Grat Chantry shrine. She was not so much interested in performing evening devotions as in buying the pilgrim's pass she needed, and also in making some ritual kineses for Sheyli. And perhaps for herself too — for forgiveness for her abandonment of her dying mother.

You did it for yourself, Keris Kaylen, she told herself. Admit it. Because you couldn't bear the idea of marrying anyone, least of all Harin Markle. Because you couldn't stomach the idea of living in Thirl's house for the rest of your life, either. Especially not if he was going to marry that fluffy little idiot, Fressie Leese. You let Sheyli persuade you to go because it was convenient . . .

She wriggled the end of her nose in an attempt to stop the tears that threatened her. Right then she did not like herself very much. And she did not feel very old, either.

She was not too sure that devotions would make her feel any better — her dislike of implicit obedience to the Maker's Rule made her regard all kineses and the value of the Maker's forgiveness with deep scepticism — but she went anyway.

She found the shrine without trouble, bought her pass in the Rule Office next door, and discovered that there were already devotions in progress in the shrine itself. Many worshippers knelt on the bare ground outside, as the building was full. Keris joined them, kneeling as they did in the attitude of reverent attention: both knees to the ground, back straight, hands flat to the front of the thighs. In a way it was better outside than inside: the ground was softer than the stone floor of the shrine, and she could look around if she was bored. There were people passing by, and there was the front of the shrine to look at as well. It was highly coloured, as were all chantist buildings; this one had murals of knights fighting off Minions, their hands outlined in colours as they made their ritual kinesis gestures at their enemies. Keris had doubts whether a few kinesis signs would really scare Minions, but the picture was interesting nonetheless.

A devotions chantor was reading the Phrases as she arrived and, predictably, they were from the Book of Pilgrims. A pleasant smell of jasmine oil drifted out of the shrine: jasmine was always used at the evening Prostration devotions.

'And so it was,' the chantor read, 'that the Maker turned to Knight Batose and said, "Go thou — and thine — once in thy life, to worship at my shrines and holy places across the Unstable, for only such a journey will entitle thee to come to the ordered Table of Paradise in the afterlife."

' "But," the Knight protested, "my life shall be endangered, and my children placed in jeopardy before the maws of the Unstable."

' "Thou hast the will to choose," the Maker said, "but this I say unto thee: no Man nor woman who comes not to worship at a distant shrine shall sup Order at my Tables after death, unless 'tis a child less than twenty summers —"'

Stupid convoluted language, Keris thought morosely. Why don't holy men ever say anything plainly? The answer supplied itself, unbidden: Maybe it's because if it was said clearly enough we'd know it was nonsense. And why do we have to risk our lives to save our souls? It doesn't make sense, and the Maker ought to be logical.

She sighed and tried not to think that maybe, just maybe, the Holy Books were not the inspired word of the Maker speaking through his holiest followers after all, but the ravings of some mad knight, ensconced in a cave somewhere and suffering the visions of the insane.

Still, when the time came for the congregation to perform kinesis, she joined in with the rest of the gathering, fingers and hands and arms making the ritual gestures, her body taking up the correct postures – first on this knee, then that, then both, forehead to the ground . . . She did it for her mother, for forgiveness – and finally she did it hoping that she would survive the crossing; survive – and remain untainted.

At least this is the service of Prostration, she thought, and not Abasement. Abasement entailed kineses performed mostly flat on one's stomach.

It was dark by the time the devotions were finished. She wondered if she had been foolish to leave it so late to return to camp. She and Portron had pitched their tents a little distance away from the bulk of the pilgrims, too – at her insistence. The smell from the public pit latrines at the back of the camping ground had been too much for her to stomach. Now the darkness of the unlit town and the rough paths that led to the tents was disturbing. Most people abroad moved in groups, with lanterns, and she had not thought to bring even a candle from her pack.

She set off from the shrine, walking fast, glad of her trousers and boots and regardless of the hardened ruts underfoot, trying not to think of the stories she had heard about the Unbound who served the Minions of Chaos. 'They like the dark,' Piers had said once. He had been trying at the time to convince her that the Unstable was no place for a woman Unstabler. 'They kill for pleasure, but never cleanly and never fast. The younger the victim the better, because to Carasma the death of the young is the greatest insult he can bestow on Creation. What they do to women, especially the young ones, is the worst. Sometimes they don't have human shape but that doesn't stop them taking what they want first . . .'

When she reached the foot of the rise where most of the pilgrims were camped, she saw a group of people ahead on the track. There were both men and women, with several lanterns among them, and they were standing talking. None of them looked her way, and without a light she knew she was almost invisible anyway. The scene looked ordinary enough; it was the voice she heard that stopped her dead. *Thirl*. Thirl giving her description, right down to the horses and the colour of her tent.

'No,' someone replied, 'we haven't seen anyone like that. A thief, you say? Fella, your chances of finding a particular thief in Hopen Grat are as slim as a flatworm.'

'Perhaps. Should you see her, don't tell her I'm looking, eh?'

Keris waited and watched in silence, shivering. The group moved off towards the tents; Thirl angled his way up the hill away from her, and – she was thankful to note – away from where she was camped with Portron. She hastened on her way.

'Ah, there you are,' the chantor greeted her cheerfully, reinforcing his relief with a kinesis. 'I was beginning to worry. This is not a place to be wandering about in at night, lass. You're a mite too confident for your own safety, you know.' He handed her a plate of stew. 'Fresh meat I bought from a hawker. I cooked enough for you, too.'

She accepted his rebuke with a nod, knowing he was right, and took the food with thanks. As she sat beside the fire to eat, she was glad of his presence and reflected wryly that she had never thought she would be grateful for the company of a rule-chantor. She did not think Thirl would be able to find her or the tent in the dark, but she was worried nonetheless. Come daylight he would find her fast enough, and, if he intended to charge her with theft, she was in trouble. At the very least, he could force her home.

'Chantor Portron,' she said, 'I think I've changed my mind. If Master Davron Storre will have me, I'm going to leave with you tomorrow.'

He gaped at her, face blank, white hair a halo lit by firelight. 'You want to go to the Eighth Stability?'

'No. No, just as far as Pickle's Halt. That's about a week into the Unstable. It's a — private matter. A pilgrimage of sorts, I suppose. My father died there, you see.'

Suddenly, she had an unbidden vision of Storre as she had seen him back in Kibbleberry: as hard as knotted ironwood, all muscle and toughness dressed in worn brown leather and coarse linen. A man who had done something so shameful it could make him flush like a chantora teased by the town rake. She had to remind herself that the Minions of Chaos could not survive in a stability. Could not, in fact, pass the kinesis chain. Davron Storre, therefore, could not belong to the Unmaker. Besides, she thought, no Minion would *blush*, for goodness' sake . . .

Portron had his own vision as he watched her. For a brief moment he was transported back more than twenty years . . . A face under the wimple of her Ordering: freckles across a straight nose, and frightened grey eyes looking into his. He had not been so very young then, but his fingers had trembled as he had loosened the wimple and seen her hair for the first time: soft and fine and long.

'I'll try not to hurt you, Maylie,' he'd said.

'I hope it takes a very long time to make a baby,' she had whispered, love shining through her fear. 'I want it to take forever.'

Chapter Six

*And Chantry shall guide us, and be our protection against
Lord Carasma the Unmaker. They have established the Rule,
and they shall oversee the establishment of Order in every
stability, devoting their lives to our well-being and the defeat
of Chaos. Honour them and give them their due.*

Knights X: 12: 2–3 (Melcom the Pious)

Rugriss Ruddleby was seated at his desk in the Anhedrin's
office of the Chantry Hall in Middleton, going through a pile
of reports. The Chantry Hall was the most impressive building in the whole of the Eighth Stability, possibly in all the
stabilities, and the Anhedrin's office was the most mag-
nificently appointed room in the building – as befitted the
head of the sixteen-member Sanhedrin, the ruling council of
Chantry. The ceiling and walls were heavy with gilt and
festooned with ornate tracery. Chandeliers dripped crystals,
chairs squatted on curled carvings, polished onyx gleamed
on table tops, inlaid wood parquetry was evidence of trees
slaughtered with scant attention to the Rule. (It did not
matter after all: this was only one room in one building, and
anyway it was dedicated to the greater glory of the Maker,
blessed be His name . . .)

The office had belonged to Rugriss Ruddleby for a year
past, and it would be his for another two years, before a strict
cycle of rotation passed the position of Anhedrin on to another
of the Sanhedrin. Rugriss had long coveted the post, but now
that it was his he was finding that the responsibility and the

decision-making that went along with the power was fraught with petty irritations – or worse. He was finding that not even the gilded luxury of his surroundings could make up for the major worries and aggravations of being Anhedrin.

Rugriss was a tall thin man with a lean face and, in spite of his anxieties, he was as sleek as a cat on the prowl. He carried no excess weight, his muscles were hard to the touch, his stomach as flat as a millstone and he did not look his age. He was a man who believed that a person should care for the body that the Maker had created for him: he exercised, he watched his diet, and, if taking care of himself also meant adding a little colour to greying hair, then he wasn't past doing that either.

Someone had once told him that frowning encouraged wrinkles, so he was careful not to frown as he read the report from a devotions-chantor that had happened to come across his desk – but he felt like frowning. The report disturbed him, although it took him a while to realise exactly why. After some thought, he took hold of his stole of office and shook it in an agitated fashion. The pure silver bells around the fringe at its end tinkled like wind-chimes; the nacre sewn to the gold satin of the stole flashed with kaleidoscopic colour.

A lowly novice-chantor hurried in to the office in answer to the summons.

Rugriss did not look up. 'Ask Hedrina Cylrie Mannertee if she would be so kind as to step into my office,' he said brusquely, and the novice hurried to obey, slippers slapping on the polished parquetry.

The hedrina, however, took her time in coming: it was a full half-hour before she appeared at the door. Cylrie, the sole female member of the Sanhedrin, did not believe in hurrying anywhere, least of all to a summons from Rugriss, who had once been her lover. When she did arrive, it was with languid ease. She was a tall, regal woman – like Rugriss, she had a certain stature that proclaimed itself without her ever having to open her mouth. She was greying over the temples and the first wrinkles of age were already lining her face, but she was still a beautiful woman.

Also like Rugriss, she was dressed in the robes of the Sanhedrin: the red gown of silk that reached her ankles, the gold stole of office that was draped around her neck with its bells tinkling below the knee, the heavily beaded belt of blue and gold around her waist. Over the top she had flung a fur-trimmed cope of shot-silk, embroidered with the Chantry motif at the front edges. She shrugged the cope off on to a chair as she crossed to sit in front of the Anhedrin.

She gave him a lazy wave of her hand in greeting; the precious stones in the rings she wore flashed gaudily. 'Well, Ru, what is it that merits a summons at this hour? You have interrupted my session with the cloth merchant. He was just showing me some new silks —'

He cut her short. 'A report I've just received.' He flung it across the desk. 'Here, you read this and see what you make of it. The man who wrote it is a devotions-chantor who was accompanying a fellowship that was on its way between the Third and the Fourth Stabs.'

She took the paper and read it carefully. Then she raised an arched eyebrow at Rugriss. 'So?' she drawled. 'A traumatic experience for the poor man, I'll grant you, but of what possible significance is the death of a mapmaker and a few pilgrims in a halt? Even if it did occur in a rather unusual and blood-thirsty fashion?'

'Firstly because it smacks of a certain desperation on the part of the Minion concerned, and therefore on the part of Carasma. And anything that prompts the Unmaker Lord to desperation is surely of interest to us. And, secondly, did you not note what the chantor said concerning the man who was asking about this same mapmaker several days earlier?'

Cylrie glanced back at the paper and then clicked her polished fingernails in recognition. 'Of course! It's Edion!'

Rugriss nodded. 'Yes. Our elusive ex-Knight has sur-faced. Now why do you think he would be so interested in a mapmaker — the same mapmaker that intrigued one of Lord Carasma's Minions so much that they ventured into a halt?'

Cylrie shook her head. 'I haven't the faintest idea.'

Rugriss ground his teeth. 'Unfortunately, neither have I. But it worries me. And Edion has vanished again, of course. He could be anywhere in the Unstable by now.'

'The rumours about this place called Havenstar continue?'

He nodded grimly. 'And often linked to a man who fits Edion's description. But the rumours are so – so grotesque. Impossible! How can one believe in such a place? One may as well believe in dragons!'

She looked at him shrewdly. 'Why, Ru, dear, I do believe you are worrying. That's not becoming in an Anhedrin.'

'Don't needle me, Cylrie. This is a worrying matter. There's a certain restlessness among the excluded of the Unstable that I don't like. There are rumours, there's an anti-Chantry sentiment – and there is evidence to suggest that Edion is behind it.' He grimaced. 'We made the biggest mistake of our lives when we excluded him. We should have kept him within Chantry where we could keep an eye on him. The man is dangerous.'

'Huh! You've changed your rhyme in mid-verse. You were the one who always had a compassionate word when we wiser souls railed against Edion of Galman.' She shook out a sleeve and admired the fall of the fabric.

'So, I was wrong. I admit it. The problem is: what do we do now?'

'That's obvious: chase him down and bring him in. Send a contingent of Defenders after him.'

'Not so easy. How do I justify that? The man was excluded! The Defenders are not going to be happy if I order a contingent to scour the Unstable to bring in a man we ourselves insisted on banning from stability.'

'You'll have to choose between upsetting the Defenders and letting Edion continue to do whatever it is he's doing,' she said impatiently. 'I can't see any alternative. Making difficult decisions is what being the Anhedrin is all about, Ru.'

He looked at her, frustrated. He had foolishly hoped she would be able to offer some miraculous advice that would solve the problem and of course she could not. Knight Edion of Galman had never been a man to be dealt with lightly.

'You're right of course,' he said. 'I'll compromise — I'll put out word to all Defenders and chantors making crossings to keep an ear and an eye out for him, and when he is found to either bring him in if possible, or to send for a force that can bring him in.' He fiddled with the papers on his desk. 'I'll admit Edion scares me. When we were boys together in the chanterie, he had a mind as sharp as a myrcat's fang, and about as devious. All of eleven years old, and he was ruthless. Not cruel, but as ruthless as only the really righteous can be. And that makes him a dangerous man. I keep on remembering that bit in Predictions, about a man cast out in the darkness, only to rise up and change the world —'

'You think that's Edion? Bah — you can't be serious! Haven't you noticed how predictions can always be twisted to fit what you want? Remember the tale of Wedlear the domain lord, who went to the witch to ask what would happen if he cheated his neighbour's widow and her son out of their inheritance? "There will be established the greatest domain in all the land," the witch promised. So Wedlear cheated the widow, but the lad put an arrow through him in revenge and then seized all *his* land. There was a great domain established, all right — but it wasn't Wedlear's! And that, in my opinion, sums it all up as far as predictions are concerned.'

'And the moral is: don't read the Holy Books?' he asked ironically.

'The moral is: read the Book of Predictions with a great deal of scepticism. Ley-fire, Ru, I never thought you would take one whit of notice of such superstitious nonsense.'

'Watch that tongue of yours,' he replied. 'That sounds perilously close to heresy.'

'Rubbish.' She began to buff her nails on her stole, but her gaze was thoughtful. 'Haven't you *any* ideas about the reason for this attack on the halt and the mapmaker?'

'I don't know what to make of it. The only thing I can think of is that Havenstar exists and that this mapmaker had a map of its location. Presumably Carasma doesn't like the idea of a Havenstar any more than we do . . . Perhaps he wants to find out where it is. And what it is.' He shrugged, a taut shrug of frustration. 'I don't know. The desperation I sense in the attack, Cylrie — it doesn't fit with what's happening elsewhere. Chaos is winning. Carasma is winning. You have only to look at how the stabilities grow smaller with each passing year to know he wins. A report I had last week says a whole mountain vanished from the Impassables. The week before, it was a ley line penetrating deep into the Sixth, crossing the kinesis chain as easily as it would a garden hedge. And there doesn't seem to be a thing we can do to stop the inroads. Order is no longer enough. The kinesis chain is no longer enough. All our devotions are no longer enough . . .' He looked up from his reports and there was real despair in his eyes. 'We're losing, Cylrie, and I don't know what to do about it.'

'And, if the presence of a mapmaker could somehow cause the Unmaker Lord to act precipitately even though he is winning, it would be interesting to know why,' she mused, nodding. 'The Minion could have easily waited until the mapmaker had left the halt before slaughtering him. Instead she confronted the Order of the halt, which can't have been a pleasant experience for her . . . Yes, I see your point.' She thought for a moment. 'Well, it seems to me that the only person who may just be able to throw some light on the matter is Edion. All the more reason to hunt him down.'

Rugriss sighed. 'The Unstable is a big place, and the excluded tend to look after their own.' He stood up restlessly, bells tinkling. 'May as well look for a particular grain of sand in a sand patch.'

Cylrie nodded. 'And Knight Edion,' she said softly, eyes glinting in memory, 'was always a very clever man.'

Rugriss did not reply, but he did forget himself enough to frown.

Chapter Seven

Go thou forth prayerfully and with good heart into the
Unstable and face the ley with courage, knowing that the
Maker has asked this of thee for thine own sake.

Pilgrims III: 6: 24

Keris glanced around the group gathered by the pond and
wondered if she was going to regret her decision to go to
Pickle's Halt.

The day had started well enough: Thirl had not found her,
and, although the Master Guide Davron Storre had been
clearly puzzled by her need to go only as far as the halt, he
had agreed to take her there for the sum of one gold. One
glance around the assembled travellers of Storre's fellowship
had, however, dissipated any feeling of complacency she
might have had: this was not going to be an easy crossing.

A typical pilgrim fellowship consisted of young people
embarking on the greatest adventure of their lives; Keris
had seen any number of them ride past the shop on the
South Drumlin Road: laughing, full of themselves, defiantly
excited to cover their nervousness at what lay ahead. At a
moment like this they would have been hiding the reality of
their fears beneath boisterous good humour and banter. But
the conventional pilgrim did not travel the length of the
Unstable from the First to the Eighth Stability; the people
gathered here to listen to Davron Storre's final orders were
no ordinary pilgrims. Certainly none of them appeared in the
least excited.

Apart from Portron Bittle and Keris, there were four men and one woman. The woman was close to sixty years old, and rode a battered mule that bared its teeth and flared its nostrils at anyone or anything that came too close; from the old woman's appearance, Keris half expected her to behave in a similar fashion. She was like old leather, chewed and tattered around the edges but still as tough as ever, and about as attractive. Shattered black teeth clamped down on the nicked end of a pipe stem; the bowl alternately glowed and belched forth an acrid black smoke. So reluctant was she to remove the pipe that she spoke out of the edge of her mouth rather than do so; as a disconcerting consequence, much of what she said was accompanied by what appeared to be a sneering leer. She told them all that her given name was Corrian and then glared as if daring someone to ask her to divulge her family name. No one did.

Of the men, one was about the same age as Corrian, and totally blind. He rode a crossings-horse and waited with calm ease, wrists crossed and reins loosely held as though embarking on perilous journeys was something he did every other day. His sightless eyes rolled upward, but something about his tranquil confidence suggested he did not miss much of what was going on around him. Keris half expected him to have an aristocratic name but he introduced himself simply as Meldor and he wore no domain symbols. His voice was a mellifluous bass that sent shivers up Keris's spine.

Next to him was a man of about thirty who gave his name as Graval Hurg, merchant. He did not seem to have much control over the dapple-grey mare he rode. She skittered this way and that, bumping into other mounts, generally upsetting everyone. The blind man's horse, however, did not budge an inch, and eventually its rider reached out and grabbed the dapple's bridle. He pulled her over until her face was next to his horse's own and the mare, surprisingly, calmed. Hurg apologised abjectly, and Keris stared, wondering just how a blind man had been able to reach out so unerringly for something he could not see.

The other two men in the party were young. Both were from Drumlin and they had arrived together, but Keris doubted that they were friends or even that they were long acquainted. Prime Beef and Scrag Ends, she had thought irreverently on meeting them. Prime Beef was well dressed, well mounted and had two pack mules. He was solidly built, with a neck as wide as his head and a torso of hard curves that could have been carved from stone. He wore his shirt unbuttoned to the waist but the muscles he flaunted seemed ugly to Keris, somehow artificial. After a while she decided it must be because they were the result of weightlifting and exercise, rather than the natural outcome of hard work. When she glimpsed a gold domain symbol around his neck a few minutes later she knew her surmise was probably correct. The man was a Trician, a trained fighter. She spent a moment wondering why he was not riding with a Trician fellowship, until the obvious answer occurred to her: none would have been headed for the Eighth Stability. The question was rather: what was a Trician doing wanting to ride on the Long Pilgrimage?

Scrag Ends, who gave his name as Quirk Quinling, could have done with more muscle, not less. He was a reedy, hollow-chested and narrow-shouldered youth with a number of irritating nervous mannerisms. He chewed his lower lip, pulled at his sideburns, picked at the skin at the edge of his fingernails, fidgeted unbearably before he said anything. He gave the appearance of being habitually uncomfortable in the presence of others. Yet, just when Keris was ready to dismiss him as an uninteresting nonentity, he said something about his own meagre luggage fitting into a Trician's manicure box with room to spare, a remark that masqueraded as self-deprecating but was more truly aimed at Prime Beef's extraordinary amount of baggage. It was enough to tell Keris that there was more to Scrag Ends than first met the eye.

His mount was an underfed palfrey and he had no pack animal at all. Davron Storre took pity on the palfrey and told him to transfer the packs it had been carrying to one of the mules belonging to Baraine of Valmair, Prime Beef. Baraine was outraged and only the threat of being left behind to wait for another guide to the Eighth – who would not leave for at least three weeks – had secured his grudging acquiescence.

Confound the Unmaker, Keris thought, what an unpromising lot of travelling companions this is. A guide who doesn't know how to crack a smile, an old woman who looks and smells like a greasy kitchen stove, a muscle-bound spoilt brat of a Trician, a young man who's already scared out of his wits, an old man who can't see where he's going, a rule-chantor who talks too much, and a fellow who can't ride as well as a sack of yams. A moment later she added: and a thief who stole from her brother and walked out on her dying mother. She sighed inwardly. This promised to be an awkward crossing.

She listened as Davron gave last-minute instructions, noting how those deep rough tones of his carried. 'My assistant,' he was saying, 'will be joining us once we leave the Stability. His name is Scow, and he is one of the Unbound, but I will not tolerate that you treat him any differently because of that. In fact, you will obey him as you would obey me,' he added, and singled out Baraine of Valmair for a hard stare. 'This trip is always dangerous; in addition, for some reason, crossings this year are especially hazardous. Ley lines change with a rapidity we have never seen before; the Wild are especially vicious and the Minions seem more numerous. You can perform devotions for the Maker all you want, but He doesn't see too many kineses out there. Lord Carasma rules in the Unstable and it is unwise to forget it. Given these dangers, it is essential that orders are obeyed, instantly and without question. If you stop to argue, you may well end up dead. As a guide it is my duty to get you to your destination untainted and alive – but in a dangerous situation neither Scow nor I will stop to help anyone who disobeys an order. Remember that.

'Remember too that, although much of the vegetation is edible for both you and your mounts, all animals, birds and so on are Wildish, and it's definitely not advisable to provoke them unnecessarily. No matter how harmless they look, they are all tainted and you will have enough trouble with them without deliberately setting out to hunt them down. In other words, until we reach the first halt, the only meat you will eat will be what you have brought with you.'

His eyes swept around the group, missing nothing of their reactions to what he was saying. 'I ride in front,' he said. 'Scow normally rides last.' He looked at Quirk, who fidgeted nervously under his gaze.

'Today's ride is not an arduous one, nor is it particularly dangerous because we will still be close to the Stability. However, it is wise to be alert at all times, and prepared for the unexpected.' With that remark, he turned his horse and rode out towards the Unstable. The blind man followed, giving his horse its head. Graval's mare danced this way and that before finally trotting off after them.

'Charming fellow.' Baraine of Valmair had waited until Davron was out of earshot before muttering the words and then adding, more loudly, 'You take care of the mule, Quinling, or I'll snap you across my knee.'

The woman, Corrian, cocked her head at Baraine. 'And you're another charmer,' she told him, grinning to display her mouth of blackened, cracked teeth. 'Tell me, young fella, do the muscles in your arse match those of your mouth?' Baraine jabbed his heels into his horse, but Corrian rode after him, pressing him with embarrassing questions in a penetrating voice.

Quirk Quinling gave a nervous laugh. 'Baraine really — um — is a bit much,' he said to Keris and Portron. 'I met him last night for the first time, you know, and he spent several hours complaining about how his servant had broken his ankle and had to be sent back to Drumlin instead of making the crossing, dancing attendance on Baraine. One would have thought the poor man had done it on purpose.'

'Maybe he did at that,' Keris said grimly. She had already decided she did not like Baraine of Valmair.

* * *

They crossed the kinesis chain about ten minutes later. Even if Keris had not seen the Chantry House beside the track, and glimpsed another, tangled in the mist, off in the distance, she would have known the moment they crossed from stability to the Unstable: something seemed to hit her hard in the middle of the chest. For a moment she felt that the air had been sucked from her lungs, and then she was through into another world.

Beside her Chantor Portron chuckled. 'Felt it, did you, lass? Don't let anyone be telling you there's no power in kinesis!' He waved a hand at the Chantry House. 'Think on it: there's been someone performing kinesis devotions there, and in each of the Houses that circle each of the stabs, every minute of every hour of every day of every year for nigh on a thousand years. Eight circles of unbroken kinesis . . .' He sounded smug, so she refused to comment on the marvel of it — but she was impressed. She hadn't expected to *feel* the barrier. Or was it perhaps the Unstable she had felt?

For the first mile the land seemed very much like that around Kibbleberry village. If she looked back, she could see where the Impassables snagged the clouds, while ahead the forests and grasslands of the Unstable showed as patches of dark and light green through cat's-cradle wisps of early-morning mist. Yet she was aware of a difference without at first being able to identify its nature. Then it came to her that it wasn't one thing but several: the land smelt different. Not bad, or foul; just different. And the sounds had changed, too. The background chirping of meadow birds and crickets, the sough of wind through grass and trees, all that had subtly altered the moment the kinesis chain was crossed. The birds had slightly different calls; the insects sawed different songs; the grasses rustled with a different timbre. The changes were slight but somehow sinister.

Keris shivered slightly and then chided herself for over-sensitivity. She'd always wanted to travel the Unstable, hadn't she? *Well, here you are, you fool — be happy!* She straightened in the saddle and looked ahead. The track gradually became fainter and fainter and finally disappeared entirely. They would not see another, she knew, until they reached the outskirts of another stability; the Unstable did not allow those who passed to mark its surface. Here Nature was under the sway of the Unmaker's hatred for Creation. It was a world being unmade . . .

'Yet the lack of tracks doesn't seem such a bad thing,' she remarked to Chantor Portron as they rode. 'A road scars the landscape, after all. In fact, when you think about it, much of what we do harms the world irretrievably. Why, think of the stone quarries in the First. They are only used when it's absolutely necessary – my father used to say it was no good asking for new stone until you could powder your face with the remains of the old, Chantry's so strict about it – but the quarries are still a scar that will last for generations –'

'Ah, my dear, you're not understanding the true nature of what you're seeing here,' he murmured sadly. 'Or, rather, you're not understanding its un-nature. The Unmaker promotes Chaos. And anything that is going against what is natural promotes the chaotic. It's not natural that a blade of grass, crushed under the hoof of your horse, should straighten its wee self up again after you have passed. It's a negation of the true cycle of life and death. And it is therefore evil.'

'Something is not being destroyed, but rather remade – it seems a good thing.'

'The battle between good and evil is much more complex than merely creation versus destruction, Maid Kereven. Think of it as a battle between Order and Chaos, where the Unmaker may do good on his way to evil and the Maker can be forced – perhaps not to evil, but to a certain hardness of heart in order to achieve a wider good. Am I sounding boringly pedantic, lass?'

'No. You sound more sensible than the devotions-chantor back in Kibbleberry. You should have heard the things he worried about: who was sleeping with who, or how much money the congregation was dropping into the collection.

And whether people wore regulation clothes.'

'Most people are appreciating such guidance, lass,' he chided, knowing this last was directed at him. 'We must do our best to keep the Rule — otherwise Lord Carasma will destroy all we have.'

She looked sceptical. She had heard it all before, but no one had ever proved it to her satisfaction.

He caught the look. 'Keris, the Maker made this world according to certain universal laws. Within a Stability, if I am falling off my horse — Maker forbid — I will always be falling down. Not up. Within a Stability, life ends in death. Water freezes when it's cold enough, becomes steam when it's hot enough — all these things are constant. They are the rules by which things exist — or did, until the Unmaker came. As we ride out into the Unstable, you will see that those sorts of laws are no longer always applying.'

She was impatient. 'Yes, yes, I know all that. But what proof is there that it is the *Rule* that keeps instability — the unmaking of the world — at bay?'

He waggled a jewelled hand at her. 'Ah, proof, proof. Why is it the young are always wanting proof? It's faith that you should be having, child! No one can offer you proof of the kind you mean, as well you know, but perhaps you should consider this: Minions sell themselves to the Unmaker in exchange for immortality, which is an unnatural state. Yet, if a Minion enters too far into a Stability, he dies. He cannot survive where there is Order, because Order will not tolerate what is unnatural, and therefore chaotic. That too is why the tainted die if they live in a Stab. Some people think it is the Maker that destroys them, but it is not so. It is simply that their innate unnaturalness cannot exist in an ordered world that operates according to the laws of Nature and Creation. To unbind a man, to taint him, to make him untouchable, is to introduce an element of Chaos. Death is an integral part of being alive; to put an end to Death is also to introduce that element of Chaos into the world. True Chaos can only exist in the Unstable. In a Stab, we emphasise the opposite of Chaos: sameness, day after day, year after year. This is Order. It discourages unnaturalness, it kills Minions or the tainted. And it is the Rule that maintains it.'

'Why the kinesis chain, then?' she asked, persistent. 'It shouldn't be necessary. Order should be enough.'

'No one I know is willing to take that risk,' he said drily. 'Kinesis reinforces Order – I can't be offering you proof, but it's what I believe.' He dug into his saddle bag and drew out his feather fly switch with the jewelled handle and used it to brush away the insect-like fliers that were beginning to bother them. 'Here in the Unstable the Unmaker has shattered the natural order and that is the beginning of the ultimate disintegration of the world, perhaps even of the universe. Look around you as we ride, Keris – you will see the beginnings of the end . . . And the Unmaker rejoices with every blade of crushed grass that springs back to life. All such "miracles" are manifestations of Chaos. And there, ahead of us, is another such if I am not mistaken.' He pointed with his switch. 'That must be Scow, Davron's Unbound assistant, I suppose. And, by the look of it, he rides a tainted beast as well. Most of them do. Untainted horses don't like the touch of the tainted any more than we ley-lit do. Probably that beast was his horse once.'

It was hard to believe. The animal the tainted man was riding was huge; its body had the shape and the size and solidity of one of the old stone tombs of Drumlin Chantry House, and its legs were as thick around as shrine pillars. Its face was more aquiline than equine – it was definitely beaked – but its head had two wide-curved horns with ends that pointed forward. Its dimpled hide was a deep, rich brown.

'Sweet Creation,' Quirk muttered from behind Keris. He pulled nervously at the hair in front of his ear. 'Do we have to ride with *that*?' He sounded more frightened than contemptuous.

She hardly blamed him. Not only was the beast frightening, but the rider's appearance was not reassuring, either. As with all tainted humans, he still had a basic human form. However, in his case the proportions had changed: his head was built on a grand scale, perhaps twice normal size, and his outsized face was circled by an animal's mane. The hair — fur? — of it cascaded down on to his shoulders, hiding his neck. His hands and feet were huge; the rest of him was normal, if large.

'Poor fellow,' Portron said softly. 'A great evil has been done to him.'

Davron Storre was the first to come to the waiting figure. He reached out and brushed the back of his hand against the back of the man's — a strange form of greeting Keris had never seen before, but the Unbound man seemed to expect no more.

'This is Scow,' Davron said as they rode up, and then introduced them, adding a few succinct words of information he apparently thought his assistant should know. 'Corrian,' he said. 'Never been in the Unstable. Says she can gut a man with a knife, no trouble, and doesn't think the odd Wild is much different. Graval Hurg, merchant. Has been on a short one-way pilgrimage ten years ago. Not a good rider and not ley-lit. Not armed. Young muscles here is Baraine. Tells me he knows how to use those arms he carries. The girl is Keris. Says she can down a flying pigeon with an arrow. She seems to be able to manage that crossings-horse of hers.' (Patronising sod, Keris thought.) 'The other youngster is Quirk. Unarmed. Ley-unlit. He has been in the Unstable as a child. The plump gentleman is a rule-chantor, Portron Bittle; experienced and ley-lit — and armed only with kinesis, of course. That's it for this trip, Scow.'

The large mouth parted in what could have been a grin, and Keris was horrified to see that the tongue inside was catlike: pink, rough and long. 'Guess we'll manage,' he said. The words were guttural, as if the enlarged mouth and throat had problems with human speech. It was the first time Keris had ever come face to face with one of the Unbound, and she was a little ashamed of her interest, and her revulsion. She tried to focus her curiosity elsewhere, to wonder why – for example – Davron had not introduced Scow to Meldor, the blind man.

The morning was relatively uneventful. They traversed a wide meadow, then rode through a patch of woodland. They saw nothing that was frightening, although much of the plant life seemed alien. The only obstacle they came across was a swift-flowing stream that would have presented few problems if Graval's horse had not slipped and crashed into Meldor's mount, unseating the latter. Fortunately he managed to control his fall and suffered no more than wet feet.

When they stopped for a break on the other side of the stream, Keris was amused to see Davron consulting a map – her own; Thirl, she was glad to note, had indeed sold him one of the few maps she'd had time to colour. She felt a moment's smug pleasure, but said nothing.

While Davron was deciding what route to take through the forest ahead and Scow was bringing water to the boil over a small fire, Graval Hurg sat disconsolately beside Meldor and apologised at length for his ineptitude on horse-back. 'Clumsy me,' he moaned. 'Wherever I go, things go wrong. I bring bad luck. Calamity.'

'I doubt it,' Meldor said, emptying water out of his boots. 'And I hardly think being tipped off my horse into a stream on a pleasantly warm day is a calamity.' His voice, Keris decided, was one of the most amazing she had ever heard. It was deep, yet sonorous. He never raised it, yet it seemed to carry. She thought: It soaks into one's bones . . . When Meldor spoke, everyone else was silent, just to listen.

'You know,' Quirk said into her ear, 'if the Maker came to walk among us like a human, I think He would look just like Meldor. Tall, imposing, regal, calm, possessing a sort of mature self-restraint –'

'Blind?' she added.

'Maybe. I'd like to think He's blind, then –' he looked

down at himself with a self-deprecatory grin '– then He wouldn't be influenced by outward appearances. Otherwise Baraine might be headed for Heaven's Ordering, while I'm damned to the Disorder of Hell.' She smiled, liking him.

'Your drink,' Scow said and handed Meldor a mug of hot char. Meldor, Keris noted, took the mug without hesitation or fumbling.

'How do you do that?' she blurted out.

His mouth smiled at her, although his eyes could not. 'Smell, the feel of air movement against my skin, tiny sounds – the rustle of clothes, a stone underfoot – nothing you would even notice.'

He moved away and Portron muttered under his breath so that only Keris could hear: 'I keep on thinking I've seen him somewhere before. I just wish I could remember where.'

Scow had brewed enough char for them all, and Keris was glad of it. She had no idea what it was made of, but it seemed to make her feel less tired. Graval somehow managed to spill much of the contents of his mug all over Corrian; fortunately she was wearing too many layers of clothing to be scalded, but her invective was rich anyway. Most of it Keris simply did not understand, but Graval certainly did. He went several shades darker.

'The man's a menace,' Baraine growled at Keris's side. 'He tripped over me a moment ago. Got me right in the instep with his boot. I'll feel it for days.'

We are a happy little group, she thought.

Later, when they stopped for lunch, the fellowship broke up into small gatherings. Portron and Keris sat together and shared their food; Meldor the blind joined Scow and Davron Storre; Quirk Quinling, Corrian, Graval Hurg and Baraine of Valmair initially sat down together, but it wasn't long before Baraine went off alone and Quirk wandered over diffidently to join Portron and Keris with his piece of cheese and dried fruit.

'Ah – do you mind – er – if I sit with you?' he asked. 'That awful woman keeps on making – um, begging your pardon — indecent suggestions to me.' He gave Portron a horrified look. 'How can she do that? She must be sixty if she's a day, and she said she could teach me more in an hour than, er — ah, perhaps I'd better not say the rest. It's disgusting. *She's* disgusting.'

'I hope,' Portron said mildly, 'that you are not thinking what she says is disgusting simply on account of her age. Youth is not after having a monopoly on the joys obtainable between the sheets, you know. However, I grant you that Mistress Corrian is somewhat forward with her suggestions, and I would be guessing that she gives scant thought to the Rule when it comes to putting them in to practice. Nonetheless, just remember before you are too rude to her that you have a long way to ride with her at your side.'

Keris blinked and tried to hide her surprise: Portron often did not talk the way she thought a rule-chantor would — or indeed, should. He was looking across at Quirk, his face a picture of fatherly benevolence. 'Why did you choose to take such a long pilgrimage, lad?' he asked.

Quinling's shoulders slumped and he laid his plate aside. Without even being aware of what he did, he began to pick at a hangnail. 'I guess because I'm stupid,' he said at last. 'I wanted to prove something to my father.' He looked up at them both miserably. 'He's a courier. You may have heard of him.'

Keris stared. 'Quinling — *Camper* Quinling is your father?'

He nodded.

She went blank with surprise. Camper was one of the best couriers in the Unstable. He was fast, reliable and renowned for making one of the most astonishing crossings of all time. Chased by a horde of the Wild, injured by a Minion arrow in his back and a ley cut across his thigh, he had ridden into one of the worst ley storms in history, only to emerge, several days later, almost skinned alive — and still carrying the letters entrusted to him.

'He has a reputation,' Portron said.

'Exactly,' Quirk agreed. 'And I was expected to follow in his footsteps. When I was ten, he took me into the Unstable, just to make sure I was ley-lit. Well, I wasn't, so that was the end of any idea of my being a courier — and you know what? I was *glad*. I hated the Unstable. It scared me silly. We were attacked by some half-wolves and we met this awful tainted fellow who was quite, quite mad . . . I was terrified. My father was disgusted with me. He said I was a coward, and he's been saying it ever since.'

'That's awful,' Keris said.

'Well, it stopped mattering after a while. It is true, after all. I *am* frightened. I always have been, of just about anything you like to name: the dark, loud noises, girls who smile at me. Awful old women like that witch over there, Tricians like Baraine — they all scare me, and they're nothing compared to what's out there.' He waved a hand at their surroundings. 'I was weaned on stories of my father's adventures, and I know the sorts of things that can happen to you. I'm petrified that — that I shall be tainted . . .' His voice had trailed away to a whisper. He looked down at his finger: he had made his hangnail bleed and he put his hand behind him in embarrassment.

'So why in the name of all Creation did you choose to go all the way to the Eighth Stability?' Keris asked.

'To prove something, I suppose. Stupid, eh?' He gave a smile that contained considerable charm and whimsy. 'I just had to show my father for once in my life that I could do something brave.'

She struggled to understand. She, who had so little fear of the Unstable, who had wanted to make the journey with her father ever since she was old enough to understand where it was he went, found it hard to comprehend the depth of Quirk's fear.

'He came to see me off, you know,' he said. 'He introduced me to Master Storre, just to make sure that I really was going to join a fellowship bound for the Eighth Stability. That I wouldn't change my mind at the last moment. He was right, of course: if he hadn't come, I'd probably be heading for the Second right now . . .'

'You're a remarkably brave man,' Portron said. 'And a remarkably foolish one, too. It's your life, lad, and you must learn to have the ordering of it.'

As long as you obey the Rule, Keris thought sarcastically.

Quirk hardly seemed to hear the chantor. 'I just hope I'm not tainted by the lines,' he said and wandered away to wash his plate in the stream.

'And I'm wondering about the kind of man the lad's father must be,' Portron said softly, 'that he can't even buy his son a packhorse and a decent mount. A courier could afford better than that poor old palfrey, surely.'

'He could,' Keris agreed, 'but Camper Quinling's as mean as a starving tomcat that's found a steak. His miserliness is legendary.' She banged down her plate in disgust. 'Chantor,' she asked, 'why? Why do we all have to make this stupid, idiotic, dangerous journey? Why does Chantry insist on it? Why does Quirk have to take this absurd ride when he doesn't want to? Why can't we all stay in the Stability we were born in, if that's what we want?'

'You know what the holy writings say –'

'Oh yes, I've heard them often enough. And, if I believed what they said, then I wouldn't believe in the Maker! How could I? How could I think that the Being who created the wonders of this world is also so stupid as to insist that we make this journey to save our souls from eternal damnation, just to prove our faith? He is surely not so petty, nor so stupid.'

Portron drew in a deep breath. 'No, I don't think he is. And it's my belief there's a simple answer. Without the pilgrimage, few would come to the Unstable. A handful of couriers, traders, adventurers – that's all. The Unstable would become wholly the Unmaker's realm. Lord Carasma would grow in strength, ultimately strong enough to destroy all stability. The presence of pilgrims – ordinary people worshipping the Maker – curbs the Unmaker's power. Each of us brings a little piece of Order and the Maker with us when we come. We are stronger than we know and we weaken him. That is why the Maker bade us undertake the Pilgrimage. It is the only explanation that makes any sense.'

And it did make sense, of a sort. She lapsed into silence to consider it. Portron chatted on, somehow changing the subject to an involved reminiscence of how he had fallen off the roof of the Drumlin Chantry House in a thunderstorm.

Keris heard none of it.

Chapter Eight

*And I say unto you, beware the Ley, for ley is a force of the
universe that can unmake the created, remould the flesh and
lie in the hand of Lord Carasma as a thread to be a noose for
humankind. Yet remember too that the Maker is loving and
so within the heart of that which wreaks devastation can be
found the hope of salvation for the wise.*

Generations II: 3: 3 & 4

Davron Storre led them to the top of a small ridge that
evening, and it was there he called a halt for the night. Keris
looked around the place with an odd sense of familiarity. She
recognised it, for all that she had never been there before,
because Piers had always used it as a triangulation point
when mapping the area. Baraine of Valmair, predictably,
protested about its exposed position and the meagreness of
the amount of water that trickled out of the spring on its
slopes. Nor would he accept Davron's tersely given reason
for the choice: 'It's safe.'

When he began to question Davron's ability to lead a
fellowship, and the guide turned a gaze on him that was as
black as pitch, Keris stepped in without really thinking. 'It's a
fixed feature,' she said. 'That's a place which is almost
impervious to ley change. It's as safe a haven as can be found
anywhere in the Unstable.'

Baraine stared scornfully at her. 'How in Creation could
you know that?'

She deliberately misunderstood him. 'Because we're

leaving footprints.' The others looked down. It was true: there were footmarks and hoofprints everywhere.

Quirk looked up in quick interest. 'I've heard of them! There are other places like this in different parts of the Unstable. Most halts are built on fixed features. The funny thing about them is that they are almost always a similar size, and, although the Unstable eats away at the edges, they are almost always straight-sided. Queer, huh?' Then, when he saw that everyone had transferred their attention to him, he started to blush and subsided, pulling uncomfortably at the neck of his shirt. Hurriedly he turned away to fetch his tent and the others drifted away to unload their pack animals.

As Keris began to unbuckle her own packs, she found Davron regarding her steadily over Tousson's back. She had the sense that for the first time he was actually seeing her, as a person, a personality. A woman, not a child. A thinking human being, not a faceless entity he was guiding. 'Kaylen's mapshop,' he said. 'You were serving in Kaylen's mapshop.'

He had finally recognised her. She nodded.

He continued to regard her. His expression was strange, as if he was having to rummage around for the right words to say. Finally one side of his mouth quirked up in a lopsided expression that wasn't quite a smile. 'Ah,' he said, 'I won't tell if you don't.'

She stared. 'Pardon?'

'I won't tell anyone you took Piers Kaylen's horses if you don't tell anyone that cats don't like me.'

She was speechless for a moment. *How did he know?* Then she thought: He can't; he's guessing. Perhaps he had no idea she was Piers's daughter; perhaps he thought she *was* a shop assistant who had taken the opportunity provided by Piers's death to steal the horses. She blushed furiously.

'Bull's-eye,' he murmured.

'Why don't cats like you?' she blurted.

'I tie sticks to their tails when no one's looking.'

She stared, trying to fathom through the nonsense what he really wanted. It should have all been a joke, but she knew it wasn't. Her cat had been terrified — and he really didn't want anyone to know. Once again she felt his shame. It was agony for him to have this conversation, and she had no idea why. 'You'll have to try to curb the desire next time,' she said, hardly aware if she was making sense. The conversation was absurd, but somehow the undercurrents ran deep and dark.

He strove for lightness. 'Oh, I will, I will.'

'Your secret's safe with me, then,' she said, but her flippancy was forced.

He sketched a kinesis of thanks and turned away, but not before she had seen the beginnings of a flush creep up his neck. Oh Creation, she thought, what was all that about?

As she erected her tent, she covertly watched not Davron, but Meldor. The blind man fascinated her. It was hard to accept that there was nothing more to his skills than sharpened hearing, smell and touch. As Scow aided him by pitching his tent and preparing food, Meldor helped and reached for things with unerring accuracy. During the day's ride he had not seemed to need instruction either. His abilities seemed uncanny, a match for the magic of his personality. Davron may have been the guide, but sometimes Keris felt that it was Meldor who was the leader. He exuded a calm confidence, a sense of contentment that was almost contagious. He had an old-world courtesy that was supposed to be the hallmark of Tricians and it seemed to serve him well. He could be friendly with a man like Quirk and not seem condescending, yet he could command respect from Baraine. If he made a suggestion to someone, they followed it as if it had been an order.

During the course of the day it had become clear to her that Meldor was not just a member of the fellowship, but he was part of the trio who had travelled together for some time: Davron, Scow and Meldor. The implications of that were intriguing, but Keris could not seem to make any sense of the combination — and that worried her.

Once the camp was fully erected (not without incident: Graval Hurg managed to tear a hole in Quirk's tent with a clumsy swing of a peg mallet) and the animals tethered for the evening, Scow called for two volunteers to descend the ridge once more with him to collect some fodder for the horses, explaining that the last time he and Davron had passed this way there had been some plants, the roots of which made excellent animal food, growing a little way ahead.

Graval and Portron declined, saying they were too tired; Corrian (with a disgusted look at Graval) remarked that it was a job for the young 'uns; Baraine did not even deign to reply, so it was left to Quirk and Keris to volunteer.

They took Tousson, Keris's packhorse, to carry the fodder back, but they themselves went on foot. It was a short scramble down the ridge to sheltering trees, and at first Scow seemed confident that he knew the way. Ten minutes into the forest, however, they abruptly came upon a steep-sided gully cutting across the route they were taking.

Scow grimaced. 'This wasn't here last time we came this way. It must have moved.' He hesitated, glancing up and down the gully.

The short, twisted trees clutched at the eroded slopes with a tangle of roots. They writhed into the soil like living worms, yet without ever managing to drag themselves entirely beneath the ground. Above, branches drooped, heavy with blood-red blossom and clumps of glossy brown wrigglers that crawled in and out of the flowers. The air was fetid, gravid with expectation, almost as if awaiting an explosion of violence.

'Ley,' Keris whispered, and was sure of it. The gully was drenched with the unnatural.

Quirk cleared his throat. 'I don't think I like this place very much,' he said, his voice suddenly high-pitched. 'Keris, are those tree roots *moving*?'

'Yes,' she said tersely. What was it Portron had said? 'You feel it corroding the very earth beneath your feet.' That was it exactly.

Still Scow hesitated, assessing the need for fodder against the dangers of crossing the gully. 'I think we had better go back,' he said. He turned on his heel and then staggered, almost falling. He had stepped into some kind of hole.

Keris blinked, puzzled. She had seen no hole there a moment before. Scow moaned and clutched at his leg. The earth seemed to have closed in around it; his calf was half buried.

'What is it?' Keris asked, still not aware that anything was terribly wrong.

His face greyed with shock and pain. 'Something's got hold of me –' He sat down heavily, still grasping his leg.

She and Quirk knelt beside him. 'Midden and Maker,' Quirk gasped out. 'It looks like something is trying to swallow him!'

A white ring of bone or shell encircled Scow's leg. Keris touched it tentatively with a finger; it was rock-hard and unyielding. Not even a knife blade could have fitted between it and Scow's flesh. 'What is it?' she asked again. If this was the mouth of something, then the rest of the animal was buried in the soil. She scrabbled with her fingers around his leg, brushing away the dirt. Just beneath the surface there was something hard and impenetrable and ivory-white. It radiated – flat – in all directions. She and Quirk were kneeling on top of it. They exchanged glances and edged away from Scow a little.

'Can we pull you out?' she asked.

His lips tilted up in an ironical twist that told her the thing had him gripped far too tight for tugging to make any difference.

'I know what it is,' Quirk said, his face suddenly sick with shock. 'It's a bilee. My father told me about them . . .' He looked up at Scow and his words trailed away.

Keris stood up and kicked at the creature; nothing happened. She tried bouncing up and down on it. It never budged. She knelt again and began scraping more earth away, wanting to find out the size of the thing, or if it had some vulnerable place.

111

'That won't do any good,' Scow said from between gritted teeth. 'I've heard of bilees too. They are huge. Larger than that tainted horse of mine. Shelled, with just the one mouth opening . . . They lie in wait, buried in the soil. They are of the Wild . . .' He shuddered. 'You can't kill them. You can't break them open. You can't force them open. You can't do a damn thing to them that makes a breath of difference.'

Quirk cast an anxious glance behind into the gully and then looked back at Scow. 'Bile juices,' he stuttered. 'Acidic. They digest prey, bit by bit. The mouth sucks more in as they finish with what they've got –'

Keris was appalled. 'Unmaker take you, Quirk – shut up!'

'Go for Davron and Meldor,' Scow said, 'and make it quick. Tell them to bring the axe.'

'I'll go,' Quirk said hurriedly. 'I'll take Tousson.'

'Is it – hurting?' Keris asked when he had gone. She knew it was a stupid question the moment she asked it, but her thoughts seemed to have become mired in horror.

His cavernous mouth gave a lopsided smile. 'I can bear it. It's got to eat through my boot first.'

With some embarrassment she realised *he* was trying to comfort *her.*

He shrugged, resigned. 'There's only one way to free yourself from a bilee alive.' He glanced down at his leg.

Tell them to bring an axe. She felt the blood leave her head and was glad she was not standing. 'My father lost a leg to one of the Wild,' she said finally, unable to halt the words she heard herself saying. 'It never stopped him from doing anything –'

His long tongue lolled out and she thought, incredulous, that he was able to be amused by her graceless attempts to find something to say that might be of use. 'Ah, lass, let's talk of something else, eh?' He was sweating now, and his large hands were gripping his leg so tightly the skin below was whitening. 'And let's hope that that young man finds his way back to the ridge – and can then guide Davron back here.'

He glanced upward. Beyond the canopy of leaves overhead, the sky was darkening.

She looked at the nearest of the dwarf trees along the gully edge, remembering the masses of wrigglers squirming in and out of the flowers. She could no longer see them, but their stench permeated the air; or perhaps it was the reek of the trumpet-shaped blossoms themselves. The place was corrupt, unclean. It was more than just the stink of putrefaction: it was the odour of . . . wrongness. She felt nauseated. 'It wasn't far back to camp,' she said. 'Quirk could hardly get lost.'

'He could put his leg into another one of these,' he replied, nodding towards the bilee.

'No. Don't even think it. Anyway, he was riding Tousson.'

'He reminds me of myself,' he said. His face was ashen now. 'Before I was tainted. Full of fears. I was a farm boy, you know. Just a simple lad, anxious to get the pilgrimage over and done with so I could go home and never leave again.' The words were flowing out, streaming away from him as he tried not to succumb to the pain that ate into his foot. 'I never wanted to go on a pilgrimage. I was scared. So frightened. My lass was there with me — Tilly, her name. A lot like you, I suppose. Nothing much to look at, but as good a kid as ever breathed. Kind, gentle, loving. Loved animals. Had freckles across her nose and a laugh like a new-born donkey. I'd known her all my life, pulled her pigtails and pushed her into the village pond when she was a kid. And suddenly there she was, smiling at me and I couldn't pull my eyes away . . . I could hardly believe that she wanted me. *Me*, Sammy Scowbridge.

'It was the first ley line that got me. The guide tried to rescue me, but the Unmaker is not so easily thwarted. Ley-life, the pain, Keris — the pain.' She didn't know whether he meant what he was feeling now, or what he had felt then. Perhaps he referred to both. She reached out to put her hand on his bare arm even though it was an inadequate gesture. His skin burnt under her fingers and she jerked

113

away. Untouchable. He was untouchable. He did not seem to notice her reaction. 'When I crawled to my feet, on the other side of the ley line, I looked for Tilly. To see if she was all right. And she was looking at me. Such a look. Pain, grief, tearing grief, such horror and worst of all – the revulsion. The overwhelming revulsion she couldn't hide.' He shuddered, and tears slipped down his huge cheeks.

'How long ago was that?'

'Five years. Just five years. Hard to believe, eh? I'm only twenty-five. Sometimes I feel a hundred.'

'Was Davron Storre the guide?'

He shook his head. 'Oh, no. Davron wasn't a guide then. Although I did meet him shortly after I was tainted . . .'

'Not a guide then? I would have thought he had been a guide longer than five years!' Davron Storre: he seemed so competent. He reminded her of Piers sometimes, the way he moved with an easy grace but never relaxed for a moment, as if he saw and heard and sensed things that others missed. The *tautness* of him . . .

'He's only twenty-nine.'

She sat back on her heels, staring. She had thought Davron closer to forty. 'Only *twenty-nine?*' What could have etched an extra ten years of pain and living into his face? What awful catastrophe had turned a young man into someone with eyes like that?

Scow gave no explanation and she knew he never would. It was Davron's story, not his. 'It's a hard place, the Unstable,' was all he said.

'You don't seem at all like an overly nervous farm boy now,' she said, and then blushed. 'Oh, Chaos, that didn't come out quite the way I meant it.'

She saw the tilt of his lips even in the dimness. 'I know you weren't making snide remarks about my present – er – imposing physiognomy. Keris, when you lose everything you ever had, what is there left to fear? As for the – what shall I call it? Assurance? A man can't move in the company of men like Davron and Meldor, and not have a little polish rub off on him. I have changed more in five years than most people change in a lifetime.' He released his leg for a moment to touch her, as if he wanted to reassure himself of something. She resisted the impulse to snatch her hand away from the fire of his fingers. 'You're ley-lit, aren't you?' he asked, removing his hand.

'I don't know. Maybe — how can you tell?'

'You feel this place, in a way I can't. I can see what it is, but you — your skin crawls just to be here because tainted ley is strong here: it's what is known as a ley-mire. A place where the unbreaking of the world is at its most active. A place inhabited by the very worst of the Wild, and the very oldest of the Minions. It bears the touch of the Unmaker — and you feel it into the deep of your bones. And the touch of my hand burns you, because of the tainted ley in me.'

She nodded.

'That's the tragedy of the Unbound,' he said. 'Davron and I have been together five years. He saved my sanity, my life. And I believe I helped him. We love one another as deeply as friends can — yet he cannot endure my touch for more than a moment or two. He has to steel himself just to place a hand on my shoulder. We are as brothers, but he must sit on the other side of the campfire. He is my closest friend, but I cannot hug him. Pity the tainted, Keris. The ley-unlit turn from us in revulsion because they cannot understand. The ley-lit feel our tragedy for they can see our humanity beneath the cloaking evil — but they must reject us because their sensitivity cannot endure the presence of Chaos, of unbinding, that lives within us. Davron and I travel together, but we walk apart.'

She understood now the strange gesture with which the two men had greeted one another. A touch to the back of the hand was all Davron could tolerate. 'Have you — have you heard of a place called Havenstar?' she asked.

He gave a short bark of laughter. 'Where wizards cure the Unbound with magic? Don't believe the tales, Keris. There is no cure for my . . . condition. If ever the Unmaker was destroyed and Order restored to the Unstable, we tainted would die. Order would kill us within a month or two. We are already unnatural and there is no way back – none. I shall live and die in this flesh. I am a man, with all a man's desires and feelings, but I wear the guise of a monster and must toughen myself to bear the look in other men's eyes. In a woman's eyes. We tainted have only one another in the end.' He looked straight at her and she knew he was telling her he had seen the way she'd felt when she had first met him. Revulsion, pity, compassion, fascination – he had seen it all, and despised it for what it was even as he had understood it. Then he smiled again, as if to tell her that he knew she now saw him differently.

'But the tainted live in halts,' she said slowly, following her own line of thought. 'Fixed features, like the one on the ridge. And there is stability in such places. It must be of a slightly different kind to the ordered stability of stabs . . . If we could find out how such places were made . . . If we could duplicate the same forces that created such areas . . .'

He grunted. 'If ever you find out, tell me.'

'It was done once,' she pointed out, but he had retreated behind a barrier of pain.

It was a relief when she heard the coming horses.

Meldor, Portron and Baraine had come with Davron and Quirk, and they had brought lanterns with them. The light was needed now; it was almost dark under the trees. Quirk sent Keris a speaking look. 'That damn horse of yours *bit* me,' he hissed at her as he dismounted. He rubbed his backside meaningfully.

Davron slid off his horse and came straight over to Keris and Scow. For a moment he let his eyes rove around, taking in the scene, then he ignored Keris and flashed a smile at Scow. It was the first time she had seen him give a genuine smile to anyone and the effect was startling. He suddenly changed from a block of granite to a handsome man. The years dropped away and she could see that, yes, perhaps he was only twenty-nine. The obsidian shone, the face softened, the lines smoothed away . . .

'Thought you had more sense, Sammy,' he said. Sammy. Not Scow. His voice could never be anything but gravel on the move, but the tone was affectionate.

'Didn't look where I was going,' Scow replied with a shrug. 'You bring the axe?'

'Yes, but that's a last resort, my friend —'

'Don't waste your time, Davron. Let's get it over and done with.'

'There are other ways.'

Scow glanced blankly from Davron to Meldor and then seemed to understand what the guide meant. His face hardened. '*No.* You have no idea what might happen. And what about . . .?' He gave a sidelong look at Portron.

Davron shrugged.

Scow continued quietly, calmly, 'Come on, Dav, let's be practical here. This is me, Scow, remember? I can take it.'

'Maybe you can, but who says *I* can?' The words were simple enough, but there were levels of meaning beneath them: they all heard it.

'I'll do it,' Baraine said without emotion. 'I'm reckoned a pretty fine axeman back on my domain.' They all knew he was probably not boasting: the rich young bloods of the First ran log-chopping competitions among themselves, just for fun — and probably to irritate Chantry, who frowned on almost any tree-felling as unacceptable change, but who were often powerless to intervene when the great Trician families were involved.

Keris saw the look Davron shot Baraine and thought it enough to frizzle his eyelashes; Baraine did not even notice. She could not bear the thought of that elegant hunk of prime beef chopping off Scow's leg and then going home to boast about it to his upper-crust friends as though it was some sort of adventure. Even Portron, who had knelt beside Scow to perform the kinesis of supplication, could not hide the expression of distaste that crossed his face at Baraine's words.

Only Meldor seemed unmoved. He dismounted and walked

unaided to Scow's side. 'Sammy, why have we done what we have done, if not for moments such as this? If we lose sight of smaller needs in our search for the greater good, then we lose our humanity.'

Scow just looked at Portron and Baraine.

'We'll send them away,' Davron said.

'I'm not going anywhere,' Baraine drawled and moved closer.

Portron looked indignant. 'I'm certainly not budging either. Kinesis may be of help —'

'Chantor, this is the Unmaker's realm,' Davron pointed out impatiently.

'It matters not a whisker,' Meldor said, and he was speaking to Scow. 'Let them see.' He too knelt, but not for devotions. He laid an unerring hand on the bilee where Keris had uncovered it and beckoned Davron to join him.

Something about his determination made Keris step back nervously. Davron laid both hands on the bilee.

'What are they doing?' Quirk murmured in Keris's ear, his uneasiness making his voice squeaky. Even Baraine, who had not bothered to dismount, and Portron, who was continuing his devotions, watched with wary eyes.

'I don't know,' Keris said.

Nothing happened for a long while. Then slowly the air around the bilee seemed to glow faintly. A thin red wisp of mist, moving like vapoured breath on a cold morning, gathered around the hands of Meldor and Davron — was drawn perhaps from their hands — then lightly skimmed the bilee . . .

The skin across Keris's forehead tightened and her hands tingled but she did not move. She knew only that she did not like the feel of what was happening.

Portron scrambled up abruptly, his face a mask of rigid shock. For a moment Keris thought he was going to intervene, but he controlled the impulse and remained standing, straight as a rhumb line on a map, radiating revulsion.

'What — what's happening?' Quirk whispered, and Keris

118

realised he could not see the glow, or the faint ribbon of mist.

'I don't know,' she repeated.

The tension in the air increased, the glow deepened. The temperature around them seemed to drop; Keris found she was shivering. Baraine dismounted and, his gaze intent on the bilee, edged closer.

And then the ground around Scow erupted.

Green liquid from the bilee squirted into the air in a stinging fountain. The glow around Davron and Meldor shattered into a thousand tiny comets of molten colour that shot through the air in every direction, trailing fiery feathering. One of them hit Keris on the cheek. It burnt coldly, winter's ice on her face; she flinched and scrubbed the hurt away.

Scow fell backward, ejected from the bilee like unwanted garbage. His foot – minus his boot – was covered in green slime and all three men were spattered with the same foul bile. Where the bilee had been there was now a depression in the ground.

Ley-life, Keris thought in blankest astonishment. Somehow they *exploded* it!

'Water!' Davron snapped.

Both Baraine and Quirk ran to the horses to fetch waterskins. They washed away the slime from Scow the best they could and then loaded him on to his tainted mount. No one spoke. Keris glanced across at Portron: he was still rigidly angry and deliberately refused to catch her eye. At her side, Quirk was pale with fear and Scow was equally colourless as he fought his pain. His leg was intact, but the skin was raw, stippled with pinpoints of blood and oozing fluid.

Meldor wiped away the bile and remounted his horse wordlessly. Neither he nor Davron seemed affected. Baraine was suddenly displaying an unaccustomed animation, as if he had just been watching a show put on for his benefit. He turned to Davron, wanting to ask something, but one look from the guide's black eyes halted the question before he could form the words.

They rode back to the ridge in silence.

It was Meldor who doctored Scow back in the camp. How, when he was sightless, Keris did not know, because he and Scow and Davron all disappeared into Scow's tent. The rest of them, subdued, fended off the questions from Corrian and Graval, tended the animals, ate their supper and turned in for the night.

Keris could not sleep. She was tense with reaction, still thinking over what had happened and unable to make sense of it. Finally she could stand it no longer and left her tent to go to Portron. 'Chantor,' she whispered at his tent flap. 'Are you still awake?'

'Oh, aye,' he said. 'Sleep and I have parted company this night, I think.' He sighed. 'Come in, lass, and take a seat on my bedroll there. Surely, circumstances are unusual enough for us not to be bothered with conventions tonight. In fact, I have been half expecting you. You saw, didn't you?'

'The glow, you mean?' she nodded uneasily. 'What was it? What did they do? *How* did they do it?'

He sighed again. 'I don't think there is the slightest doubt but that you are ley-lit, lass. That was ley you were seeing. They were working the ley.'

'*Working* the ley? You mean, *using* it? But — that's impossible, isn't it?'

' 'Tis surely an abomination! The way of the Unmaker and his Minions.' The anger in his voice was clear, but there was something else too: fear. 'Now I know why Davron made such a fuss when Baraine and I insisted on accompanying him and Quirk back to Scow and you. He didn't want us seeing what he was going to do. I said I had to go — that Scow may need a man of colours at such a moment. And Baraine was just curious. But Davron ordered us to stay.'

'And you disobeyed?'

He looked uncomfortable. 'Well, not exactly. I protested, I felt I had to. There are times when a chantor has to make a stand. Anyway, in the end Meldor said we could go. He told Davron it didn't matter. I suppose he thought that, as you

120

and Quirk were going to see, it made no difference if Baraine and I were there as well.'

'They are — Minions of Chaos? Meldor and Davron?'

'And Scow their tainted servant . . . I don't know, Keris. There was a time when the ley-lit could *feel* the presence of a Minion, but of late it seems the Unmaker's servants have learnt to conceal themselves better.' He slumped a little and his voice in the darkness seemed to be that of a tired old man. 'Maker help us all if that's what they are, for none of us will reach safety again.'

'I have seen Davron in the First Stability, twice, at Kibbleberry. The last time wasn't long ago. He couldn't have been a Minion then.'

'You are offering me hope, child — but, if they aren't dedicated to the Unmaker, then it's still a dangerous game they play. An abomination in the eyes of Chantry. Ley will subvert them, corrupt them, perhaps even kill them . . . That way there lies only evil. I should confront them, but I fear, lass, I fear. If they are truly the Unmaker's servants 'tis certain death to be challenging them. I wish I could remember just where I've seen Meldor before. It might be important . . .' His voice trailed away. 'I'm just an old rule-chantor from the Order of Kt Ladma. I'm not even a good chantor.'

That was too much for Keris. If someone like Portron could not cope with what faced them, how could she? She said goodnight and scuttled back to her tent.

But she could not sleep. Fear chilled both her body and her emotions. Disorder be damned, she thought, you wanted to come to the Unstable, Keris my girl. You've wanted it all your life!

But it seemed a lifetime ago that she had thought of herself as a butterfly touching the first freedoms of its new life, and rejoicing in the joy of it.

Now she thought of Sheyli, and of Piers, and cried a little.

Keris woke to find someone shaking her foot through the covers of the bedroll. She sat up, immediately wide awake. It was dark, but she had no trouble recognising Davron's outline against the cloudless sky. He was kneeling down and had pushed the tent flap aside to reach in to her feet.

Fear flooded through her, unbidden, unwanted.

'Your turn on guard duty,' he said. 'You and Portron, till dawn. Two hours.'

She nodded, trying to contain the fear. 'How's Scow?'

'Fine. Meldor gave him something to help him sleep, and he dozes still.'

'And is what happened yesterday evening another secret you don't want told?'

She felt rather than saw his smile. 'Bit late for that now, I think. Tell whoever you want — Portron certainly will.'

'Is this what you are so ashamed of — using ley?'

The smile became a chuckle, but there was more pain than mirth in it. 'Ah, no, Keris. *That* I am proud of.' He dropped the tent flap and moved away. She dressed and pulled on her boots, wondering why her mouth had suddenly gone dry.

Oh Maker, she thought. Why, by all that's dark in Chaos, didn't I stay in Kibbleberry?

Chapter Nine

And Kt Gredal held fast to his faith as the Wild sprang upon
him and tore him asunder. His blood poured forth, but still
he called not upon the Unmaker to leash his unmade beast.
Instead, when he turned to the Lord of Chaos, he said, 'The
people hereafter shall bind themselves with devotions, and
you shall be defeated. Chaos shall be no more.'

Knights II: 3: 3–6 (Kt Gredal the Anchorite)

The second day on their way was worse than the first; the
third worse than the second.

The land grew more and more alien, more and more
grotesque. When Scow lit a fire to make tea on the fourth
morning, the flames burnt cold and greenish and the water
refused to boil. Then, as a seeming reflection of the twisted
landscape, things began to go wrong with the progress of
the fellowship as well. Throughout the day, Graval's mare
caused a hundred different problems by spooking the other
mounts. A pack loosened unnoticed on one of Baraine's
mules and chose to fall just as they were wending their way
across a chisel-sharp col, and was irretrievably lost into the
canyons below. Corrian's mount somehow cut its foot and
had to be rested; Corrian rode her pack animal while its
packs were distributed among the other animals – all of
which slowed the progress of the fellowship.

Keris had grown up with tales of the Unstable, yet nothing
had prepared her for its reality, for its sheer unpredictability.
They rode down a gully sweltering in fetid heat, rounded a

123

corner – and were faced with a howling gale of freezing wind and lashing rain. They brushed up against bushes, only to see them crumble to dust. They pushed their way through a sea of waving grass tall enough to dwarf a mounted man, only to find that on the other side there was bare earth honeycombed with bottomless holes. Keris had drawn these things on maps, she had heard Piers and others speak of them, she had imagined them – that morning, she had even heard Davron tell them what to expect, and she had glanced at her own map as well – but still everything came as a shock, usually unpleasant. The gullies were bleaker, the heat and cold more extreme, the grasses more savagely serrated, the holes deeper, the rain more viciously determined than she had dreamt possible. They were her words on the map, it was her lettering that said, 'jagged gullies – hard going . . . sea of grass (beware cutting edges) . . . holed ground – dangerous.' Yet when she saw those places it was as if she had never anticipated them. All her confidence, her youthful arrogance, ebbed away.

And to think I dreamt of being a mapmaker, she thought. I wouldn't even last five minutes out here alone . . .

She thought of Piers then; six months in every year he had spent here, sometimes alone, mapping and surveying the dangers. The route they followed was his. Piers himself must have investigated a dozen others looking for the safest way, the least arduous, the least treacherous. She gained new insights into her father's tenacity and courage, just by experiencing a little of what he too must have endured.

Still, it was hard to convince herself that they had it any easier than a mapmaker searching out a route, especially when it rained most of the afternoon. The clouds that brought the rain roiled just above them in ugly brown colours; the water stained everything the same dun tint. It even tasted sour on the tongue. Once or twice she thought she saw dark shapes slinking through the rain, shadowing them. Once or twice she caught the stale stench of rotten-ness that went along with any creature of the Wild, and she dreaded the night ahead. 'Slashers, or some such,' Davron said within her hearing. He glanced across at her. 'Probably their ancestors were just cute domestic cats before the Unstable tainted them.'

Their mounts slipped and skidded and even fell. She was glad of Ygraine's grumpy stolidity, her sure tread – but both Quirk and Corrian ended up in the mud once. Fortunately neither was hurt, nor did the animals bolt. Corrian swore as she rode on, brushing mud and gravel out of her clothing. Keris had never heard those particular oaths before either; of many she could not even guess the meaning, although it was obvious most were sexual in origin. By now, Keris had divined just what sort of profession Corrian must have followed back in Drumlin city.

Sometimes they were forced to lead the horses, and Graval spent the time skidding and sliding, complaining about his boots, and somehow managing to stumble into the others or get in their way. 'I'm sorry,' he'd say. 'Terribly sorry. Didn't mean it. It's these boots – smooth soles, you know. Should have got hobnailed, but I didn't know – Oh, sorry –'

'If the blighter says that one more time, I'll clobber'm with 'is own muckin' boot,' Corrian muttered. 'Clutch-footed muckle-top. Thought there wasn't a man in the world I wouldn't take to bed if I was desperate enough for a poke, but, believe me, I'd draw the line with that one. Gives me the creeps, he does. Like a miserable gutter-cur that sneaks around the midden and has nivver learnt to look a man in the eye. Apologise, apologise – why the shit doesn't he just learn to do something right for a change, instead of muckin' things up and saying sorry after?'

It was a sentiment that they all had considerable sympathy for, even Portron, who did his best to be charitable on principle, and Meldor, who seemed to be able to remain equable in the worst of situations. Davron, Keris noticed with some surprise, was sucking in his cheeks as if he was having a hard job not to laugh. She had not thought him to be

125

a man who would find humour in the graphic earthiness of Corrian's plain speaking, but, then, she was beginning to wonder if she understood anything at all about him.

They camped that night on a hill slope, sheltered by an outcrop of rocks. Fortunately by then it had stopped raining and the fire burnt normally, but the cloud was still low, cutting off the view and darkening the landscape, and there was little wood to be had for burning. They built only one fire between them, and everyone contributed something to a single stew. Baraine complained (as he produced his contribution of sweet yams, a thick cut of dried meat and a handful of grain kernels) that he was contributing the best food and he expected to get it back again. Corrian bared her gums at him and asked if he would like to carve his initials on each grain kernel first, just so he could be sure he received the frigging right ones back.

Baraine stalked off and Keris looked around to find that Corrian and she had been left alone to attend to the stew. 'Just because we're women, they think we can do the cooking,' she grumbled. She minded the assumption, rather than the task.

'Aagh, that's the way of the world,' Corrian said, puffing a cloud of black smoke over the yams she was peeling. 'If it irks you, lass, skim off the sweet meat for y'self first and then piss in the pot.'

Keris looked at her carefully to see if she was joking, and decided she was not. The old woman grinned at her. 'It's called the battle of the sexes, love, and I've been at it for nigh on fifty years. Maybe longer. My ma always said I started on the job in me cradle. Who cares if *they* don't know they've been done in. *We* know, and that's what counts. Stick together, I say, and do the dirty on 'em.'

Keris scraped some more root vegetables, supplied by Meldor, and added them to the pot. 'Why did you come on this pilgrimage, Mistress Corrian?' she asked. 'Why this one – and why now?'

The woman clamped her teeth down on her pipe and

laughed a rather nasty cackle. 'No one calls old Corrie the Pipe "Mistress", lass. No need to be proper with me, I'm just a one-time whore turned madame, born and bred in Drumlin's Cess, and I don't need no fancy words to call me what I'm not. But you want to know: why a pilgrimage now? Well, first because I've nivver been on a pilgrimage. And second – I reckon after a lifetime of whoring and thieving, I'd better look proper repentant in the eyes of the Maker. No short pilgrimage would take care of my sins, lass.'

'Repentant?' Keris asked, remembering a number of lewd suggestions Corrian had made to the males of the party – from Scow to Chantor Portron – about what they could do if they came to her tent or, for that matter, if they just took a few minutes out behind those bushes over there . . .

Corrian leered. 'Hard to ask a pussy not to stiffen its tail when the toms come sniffing around.'

'Looked more like the pussy sniffing out the toms to me,' Keris said, poking at the fire to help it along. She was beginning to learn how to talk to the old woman without blushing.

Corrian's bright little eyes peered at her in interest. 'Ah – I like you, lass. Straight out of a chanterie class, but you've got spunk. And a good head on you. Tell me, which one of the toms are you wriggling yer backside for?'

'I missed out on a chanterie education, and I don't think I'm – er – wriggling at all yet.'

'Slow, love, slow,' the woman chided. 'This is going to be a dull journey – you gotta have an interest on the way.' She put the last of the yams in the stew and considered. 'Forget Quirk. I know his type – born to lose. Hopeless case and probably couldn't get it up anyways. As for Baraine – well, he's a meaty hunk, but that type doesn't go for plain faces. All for show, he is, and you're not the showy type. If he did pick you up it'd only be because there was nothing else, and he'd drop you at the first sign of summat better – and, for him, better may well be a pretty lad rather than a lass. Portron? Nah. Chantors are bad luck. Too much conscience in types like him even though he's got an eye for a bit of tail. Back in the Cess, half our customers were encoloured bastards. Unable to live the straight and narrow Chantry says they must, yet unable to admit it in public – sneaking around us whores in the dead of night instead for a quick fumble. They make sorry lovers, I can tell you.' She grunted her contempt and passed on to Scow instead. 'The tainted one? He's out, with those looks of his, unless you've got a hankering for the grotesque and I bet you haven't. And I've heard that if you're ley-lit it ain't possible anyways – too painful. They're not called Untouchable for nothing. Graval – now there's a possibility, if you don't mind creeps down your spine. Ah, maybe I exaggerate and he's just a fool. Who knows? I've been wrong often enough. Meldor has class – you could do well for y'self there, love, and he can't see either.'

'Thanks,' Keris said drily, and then, when Corrian did not continue, she added, 'You've missed out Master Storre.'

'Ah – so it's him that interests, is it?'

Keris gaped at her. '*Storre?* Me and *Davron Storre?*'

'Ah. Well, maybe not. Anyways, that man you don't mess with, love. He carries his storm with him wherever he goes – any woman worth her juices can see that. He's trouble and heartbreak and more besides. He hates himself, that one, and that type's always bad for a woman to be around. You get beat up, or dragged down, one or t'other, with a man like him. I like a man who can laugh, myself.' Corrian sighed sadly. 'Not that Davron wouldn't be a good poke, mind.'

Keris busied herself lifting the pot lid to stir the stew. 'It's no wonder you feel in need of the longest pilgrimage,' she said.

Corrian leered some more, still puffing, and not in the least fazed. Keris had not expected her to be.

Over dinner Davron asked everyone to gather around and then told them what to expect the next day. None of it was good. 'Tomorrow,' he said, 'we meet our first ley line. It's a small one, or it was back when it was mapped a month or two ago. But it's new — it never used to exist here, and new lines are more unpredictable than old ones. Worse, it's an offshoot directly from the Snarled Fist, and such lines can be powerful.'

'What's it called?' The question came from Quirk. They all knew he was not in the least interested in the line's name; he just needed to say something to cover his fear. The first ley line, small or not, was always the most dangerous for someone who was not ley-lit.

'The mapmaker has given it the name of the Dancer.'

'Can't we ride around it?'

Scow answered hastily before Davron, in exasperation, had time to give a sharp reply. He shook his maned head and said, 'If we could, we would.'

Davron continued, 'Once we reach the ley line, I will escort you, one at a time, across. There is just one thing to remember: obey all orders, no matter how silly they seem. If I tell you to stand on your head and gesture a Chantry praise — then do it.' He emptied the dregs from his mug on to the ground. 'That's all.'

Quirk sighed and muttered to Keris, 'As an after-dinner speech, that one seemed designed to wreck the digestion.'

Portron overheard and said, 'Perform your kineses, lad, perform the rituals, and you'll feel fine.'

'Yeah,' said Quirk, 'trouble is, out here, how's the Maker going to see them?' But he waited until the chantor was out of earshot before he said it.

Later that night, as Keris was passing through the camp on her way back from relieving herself away from the tents, a handful of words drifted out from Scow's tent into the silence of the night: 'But Margraf, would she know, do you think?' Keris stopped dead and turned her head towards the tent. Shadows cast on the canvas wall told her that Scow, Meldor and Davron were all inside. One of them had spoken, but the words had been said so softly it was impossible to say whose voice had given them life.

129

The conversation murmured on, indistinct and desultory.

Keris turned away, irrationally sure the speaker had been referring to her, but it was not that which she found disturbing. It was the word Margraf.

Once there had been a single monarch of all Malinawar. A Margrave or a Margravine, he or she had been addressed by the honorific 'Sire'. The monarch had vanished with the Rending and the coming of the Unstable; instead each stability had a Margrave and each of the eight was addressed as Margraf. They commanded the Defenders and controlled the domain lords of their respective stabilities, but everyone knew that true power resided with Chantry's Sanhedrin. What could a Margrave do, when every aspect of life was subject to the Rule, which he himself — as Commander of the Defenders — was bound to enforce? Two Hedrin from each stability combined to form the sixteen-person Sanhedrin, and it was they, interpreting the Holy Books, who said what was the Rule and what was not; it was they who in truth ruled what had once been Malinawar. The Margraves were the law enforcers, not the lawmakers.

None of it interested Keris much. All that concerned her now was that there were eight Margraves, and certainly none of them was sitting inside Scow's tent. Who, then, had been addressed as Margraf? And *why*?

Later, just as she was dropping off to sleep, she had a disquieting thought: what if the Minions of Chaos had some sort of pecking order in their ranks? What if the most important of them was addressed as 'Margraf'?

Davron? Or Meldor?

Could Davron be a Minion? Her cat had been terrified of him . . . And she had noticed that Scow always groomed and saddled his horse for him. But the animal didn't seem skittish when he rode it — and he had been well inside the stability when he had come to Kibbleberry. No Minion could do that. It was *just* possible that a Minion could enter a border town for a few hours at a time — Piers had told her that he had heard of one or two such cases — but that was all.

Her thoughts went on, troubled and confused. What about Meldor? A Minion would never be blind — would he?

She and Portron were on guard duty together again that night. This time it was Meldor who came to wake her. Much to her surprise she realised that he had mounted guard alone. Sensing her astonishment he gave one of his enigmatic smiles and said, 'In the dark, I do better than you do, you know. Be especially vigilant tonight, Keris; we are close to the ley line and the Wild are difficult when influenced by ley.'

Difficult. She could have thought of a better word.

She took her bow and arrows and her throwing knife with her and set off on a round of the camp, passing Portron on the way. He did not look happy.

Twice she saw shapes move out in the darkness and smelt the stench of the Wild; once both she and Portron caught a glimpse of lights like half a dozen huge fireflies twinkling among nearby rocks. (Fireflies — hadn't Piers mentioned magical fireflies once?) But Portron dismissed the notion of fireflies altogether. 'That's ley of some kind,' he said, and his voice was edged with hate. 'Minions using ley to light their way. They dance it out of their fingertips.'

'Should we tell Davron Storre they are here?'

He shook his head. 'They are no danger when they light their way, Keris. It's when they attack with stealth that they are dangerous — keep an eye on the lights, by all means, but watch the darkness more, for it's there that an attack would be coming from.' He proceeded on his way, varying his speed, sometimes doubling back, sometimes stopping, sometimes hurrying, as he tried to make his progress around the camp unpredictable. She copied his style, realising how much more effective it was than a sentry's steady tramp, and as she walked she tried to comfort herself with the thought that her father had rarely mounted guard at all. Travelling alone as he sometimes did it would not have been possible; but then it was also easier to hide the camp of one or two men than the camp of a whole fellowship. And this camp, Keris thought, is certainly not hidden from Minion eyes . . . She felt the quiet menace drift in towards her, and shuddered.

Half an hour before the first of dawnlight, Graval emerged from his tent. He complained of stomach problems and made a dive for the camp perimeter. Keris barely had time to warn him not to go too far. 'Don't worry,' he hissed back out of the darkness. 'I'm not going any distance – and first sign of trouble I'll scream so loud I'll wake the camp.'

She worried, though, especially as the sky was beginning to lighten before he returned. 'What did you put in that damn stew?' he grumbled as he passed her on the way back.

Rarely had Keris been so glad to see the dawn. Circling the camp in the dark – jumping at every movement, seeing things where there was nothing to see, dreading what she *did* see, imagining every sound was an approaching creature of the Wild or a Minion – she had spent the several hours of guard duty in a state of constant tension.

Davron was the first person up. He nodded in her direction and went to Scow's tent – to check on his assistant's foot, she supposed. Portron made signs to her from the other side of the camp, indicating that he wanted to put an end to his guard duties in order to perform his morning kineses, those of the Obeisance devotions. She nodded her acknowledgement, and continued on her rounds.

There wasn't much to see yet. A ground mist hugged the land, blocking off any sight there might have been of the ley line. But she knew it was out there, somewhere. It came to her as a far-off pulsing that was neither sound nor vibration, but rather a thickness felt as an emotion. It did not remind her of the place where Scow had nearly lost his foot; she could not sense wrongness, but rather . . . excitement. She thrilled at its touch, and that shocked her.

She turned away and circled the camp once more. By the time she had returned to the same spot facing the ley line, the mist had retreated a little to uncover a group of ochre rocks some fifty paces away. They were – as was much of the landscape of the Unstable — an unnatural shade, too bright to be normal. They crouched along the slope like animals about to spring on prey, bright brassy animals with block-like heads and solid haunches. She turned away, aware she was being fanciful, imagining things . . .

And could not resist turning back, to take another look.

One of them had moved. It *was* flesh and blood, not stone. It had crept up the slope in the few seconds that her back had been turned. It had no eyes, no face, just a blank yellow mass for a head — yet she felt appallingly threatened. She unslung her bow from her back, fitted an arrow with fingers that trembled, grateful that her bow was strung and that she now wore the leather bracer on her arm as a matter of course.

'Master Storre,' she said, her voice penetrating and harsh, vibrant with an appeal for help.

The animal leapt towards her. There was unexpected power there in those block-like hindquarters. As the creature opened up in the first bound, she saw what there was to fear: the mass of its head was nothing more than rows of jagged teeth that meshed and unmeshed with crushing power in two lines across its face. No mouth: its whole face was toothed.

She released the arrow on its way. It thunked down into the earth, penetrating the soil just in front of where she expected the animal to land, some thirty paces away. A second and a third arrow followed in quick succession. The beast skidded to a halt, its huge paws furrowing in the dirt, its face ending up only inches away from the embedded arrows.

It crouched looking at her — if indeed it could look. There were no visible eyes, no nostrils, no ears: just those teeth interlocking like the jaws of a giant nutcracker. She became aware of Davron standing on one side of her with a throwing knife held by the blade, raised to throw, and Scow on the other, bandaged foot and all, battle axe in hand, ready to let fly. The three of them stood like that, waiting.

And the creature backed down. Its companions slunk

away still looking like blocks of stone, hunkering off on plate-sized paws with their stomachs scraping the ground; the leader stood facing the camp for a moment longer, then joined them.

There was a collective sigh of relief. When Keris turned it was to see everyone else standing behind her in various states of undress. Her call had evidently been even more penetrating than she had known.

Baraine lowered his own bow and glanced contemptuously at her arrows sticking out of the soil. 'Trust a woman to miss,' he said in disgust.

'She didn't miss,' Davron said in a level voice. 'Have you forgotten what I said about it being unwise to kill the Wild? A death in the pack only makes the others vindictive. Far better to frighten them off.' He looked around the group. 'Well, what are you all staring at? Excitement's over. Go and have your breakfast and break camp. Keris, you go and get the arrows — we don't want to waste any.'

They all turned away, leaving Keris feeling somehow crestfallen. Fighting off Wild might have been second nature to Davron and Scow, but it was still new to her. She had not expected thanks, exactly — but, well, *something*. She sighed and began to unscrew the tension on her bow. Then, as if he had heard her thoughts, Davron turned around and came back. He stood looking at her for a moment and she felt an absurd desire to have him take her in his arms and pat her on the back and say, There, there, there's no need to cry.

Instead she continued to attend to her bow, dry-eyed.

'You did well,' he said at last. He sounded diffident, embarrassed, as if he had forgotten how to praise and the words no longer came easily. 'Who taught you to use a bow?'

'Piers Kaylen.'

'Are you any good with that throwing knife?'

She shook her head. 'Not really. If I can have two or three practice shots first, at the same target from the same place, then I have no problems — but that's not much good in an emergency, is it?'

134

He gave a grunt of assent. 'It's not your distance judgement that's at fault,' he said, 'not if your archery is always so good; it's just knowing how many turns of the knife to the distance. I could probably teach you, given the time.' He looked down at the knife he was still holding by the blade. 'A thumb's width to the left of your left-hand arrow,' he said. 'Four and a half turns with this knife.' He let fly casually, with only the briefest of glances at his target. It buried itself in the soil — a thumb's width to the left of her arrows.

They walked forward to retrieve them.

'You're Piers Kaylen's daughter,' he said, a flat statement of fact. 'Piers wouldn't have taught any shop assistant how to use a bow like that.' He gestured at the arrows. They were buried several inches into the hard-packed ground, each several inches apart, evidence of the strength and accuracy of her draw. 'Why did you say your name was Kereven?' He bent to retrieve her arrows.

She said, 'My father died. My mother was dying. My brother wanted to marry me off to one of his beer-swilling friends. He was going to turn the shop into a tavern. I didn't want to be married and I didn't want to be a tavern wench, fending off drunken hands up my skirt. And so I ran away. I didn't want my brother finding me, so I lied about my name.' She took back her arrows and he pulled his knife out of the soil and brushed it clean.

'Why Kereven?' he asked, standing up and looking straight at her.

She blinked. For a moment she could not think why — then she knew. *The name of the trompleri mapmaker.* Kereven Deverli. *Stupid.* Why in all Creation had she chosen that name? 'It was the first name that popped into my head,' she said truthfully.

His black eyes branded her with his disbelief and her heart turned over in fear. She made as if to go, but he caught her arm in an iron hand. 'What do you know of me? Of us?' he asked, pulling her across to him, so that she was close enough to have been in an embrace. Blinding terror swept through her, although he uttered no threat. The same feeling she had known in that gully with its bilee trap, the same feeling the Wild had given her as it leapt — she knew it again. And she knew beyond any possibility of doubt that Davron Storre, guide, was somehow tainted with the touch of the Unmaker. Not tainted physically, like poor Scow, but tainted nonetheless, in some more subtle, more terrible and much more dangerous way.

He released her arm and then repeated, 'What do you know of *me*, Keris Kaylen?' There was no menace in his voice, just a sense of urgency, of strain, of shame.

It was because of the name. Kereven. Something to do with the map — it had to be.

She found her voice at last, was able to breathe again. 'Nothing. I know nothing. What — what is there to know?' *He's just a man. There's nothing there to fear. He is just a man, an ordinary man. Corrian was right. He despises himself. Because he has done something awful, and he can't forget it.* And then she remembered the cat. The churning fear of the animal . . . *He isn't ordinary, damn it!*

She turned to walk away from him up the slope towards the camp. Her heart was beating fast enough to have given a heart attack to a horse, and her emotions were as teased out as hackled flax. Perhaps the worst thing of all was her memory of something she'd seen in those black eyes. Desire. The desire of a man for a woman . . . For the first time in her life she had seen something in a man that spoke of a need for her — a need beyond just passing lust — and she had seen it in the eyes of a man whose very presence could stultify her with fear.

'Hey, Kaylen,' he called suddenly from behind her. 'Are you ley-lit?'

She turned, still walking, astonished at the joyousness of his tone — and then stopped dead. He was standing where she had left him, waving a hand to indicate the plain below. The mist had retreated fully, and the ley line was revealed.

She choked, overwhelmed.

She had heard so much about ley lines, how terrible they were, how dangerous. Why had no one told her they were so gloriously beautiful? Not even the trompleri map had prepared her for such magnificence.

'Why, yes,' she said. 'It seems I am.'

Chapter Ten

*Fear not Lord Carasma when you walk the paths of stability,
for he is less than the Maker and your devotions will be as a
wall around you. Fear Lord Carasma only when you walk the
land that he has made his, for the earth trembles beneath his
feet and the Maker cannot hear you.*

Knights IV: 8: 9–10 (Kte Fessa)

Davron ducked into Scow's tent. The tainted man lay propped
up on his bedroll with Meldor unwrapping his bandages and
giving him a lecture at the same time. 'Of course it's going
to hurt if you will rush around the place waving pikes at
slashers –'

Scow corrected him politely. 'It was a battle axe, actually.
And stone myrcats. And, thanks to Keris Kereven, I didn't
have to do much rushing.'

'Well, I can't get everything right; I *am* blind, you know.
Davron, how does this look to you?'

Davron eyed the healing leg with distaste. 'Disgusting?'

Meldor appeared to take this to mean it was healing
nicely, because he looked satisfied and began spreading oint-
ment over the scabbing skin.

Davron watched, face expressionless. He said, 'You were
right. She is Piers Kaylen's daughter.'

'Of course,' Meldor said complacently. 'You had only to
look at her to know she wasn't some shop assistant who'd
stolen a couple of crossings-horses when her master died.'

Davron grunted. 'Chaosdamn, Meldor, I'd like to know

just how you see so much when you can't see at all.'

Meldor straightened up and regarded him. His eyes may have been sightless, but the look was somehow penetrating. 'Perhaps it is not I who see so much, but you who see very little. Davron, you have been so caught up in your own misery that you no longer know *how* to look. There are other people out there with their own troubles, their own miseries. Judge people by what they *are*, not by first encompassing them with your own experiences. Not every woman is Alyss of Tower-and-Fleury; not every mapmaker is Kereven Deverli; not every Chantor carries the same Holy Book.'

'You would have me trust everybody, Keris Kaylen included?'

'I would have you think more with your brains and less with your bile. But enough of this; I don't wish to argue with you, my friend. We have enough problems without adding to them. Tell me about Keris.'

'She admitted her identity. The problem is — why is she here? Why is she bound for Pickle's Halt?'

'Her father *did* die there,' Scow pointed out.

'So she risks life and limb to take a look at his grave? Which won't exist any more anyhow. She's got more sense. No, she has a reason — but what? And that's *not* bile talking, Meldor.'

'You think she knows about the trompleri map,' Meldor said. It was a statement, not a question.

'It seems likely.'

'We don't *know* Piers Kaylen had it,' Scow said.

'Now that's stretching coincidence too far,' Davron replied. 'Of course he had it. Who has it now? That's the problem.'

'She doesn't surely. Ouch — that hurts!'

'Sorry,' said Meldor. 'No, she can't have it — that's why she's bound for the halt. She knows about it and wants to get her hands on it. But what do we make of the name she chose as her own: Kereven?'

'There's a lot more to that young woman than is first

visible,' Davron agreed. 'Something tells me she knows more than she should. About us, I mean. She – well, she could be a danger.'

'She mentioned Havenstar to me,' Scow said.

Davron looked interested. 'Did she now?'

'Oh, come on,' Meldor protested. 'She's a mapmaker's daughter – of course she's heard of Havenstar. That doesn't mean she knows anything about it that approximates to the truth.' He rewrapped the last of the bandage and tied it with deft fingers. 'However, keep an eye on her, Davron. We don't want any more complications.' He stood up and faced the guide. His eyes remained unfocused and unseeing, yet he still gave the impression of perception. 'Use her if need be; if she knows more than we do about the map, we must have that information.'

Davron nodded. 'Of course.' He looked down at Scow. 'Are you all right now? We have to get started.'

Scow nodded and stood. Davron went to the tent flap to go out, but turned back in the opening. 'She's ley-lit, by the way.'

'Naturally,' Meldor said placidly. 'I never thought otherwise.'

When Davron had gone, Meldor said in soft tones, 'There's a brew stirred up there, Scow; the girl's a catalyst. It won't go unnoticed by Lord Carasma. Keep a watch on things.'

He did not specify what things he referred to, but Scow seemed to know what was meant. 'You were hard on him,' he said.

'Not as hard as he is on himself. There never was a chance for exoneration, Scow – he has always known that, so he seeks to atone, to expiate. But expiation will not help unless he learns first to forgive himself. And, for the overly proud man Davron once was, that is the hardest thing of all.'

Keris, Portron and Baraine stood together on the hill slope, watching the ley line.

Keris had ached to be ley-lit – but she was no longer so

sanguine about its advantages, not now as she stood there on the slope of the hill near the camp and watched the ley line move below her.

When she finally dragged her eyes away to glance behind, it was to see Graval and Corrian and Quirk striking camp, utterly unaware of that glorious corridor of colour and light and movement below. 'They can't be ley-lit,' Portron said sadly. He had also seen a ley line before, but the sight had obviously not lost its power to impress him. He had been standing next to Keris, bemusedly muttering at intervals, 'And to think such beauty is the work of the forces of evil, lass,' and, 'Hard to believe the Maker didn't have a hand in the making of it, to be sure!'

Keris looked away from Quirk and the other two, back to the line. 'Why can't they see?' she asked. The question was a rhetorical one; no one knew why some people were ley-lit and others were not, except to say that the tendency ran in families.

'It's the Maker's will,' Portron replied.

Beyond him, Baraine stood transfixed, arms hanging loosely by his sides in the way the Kibbleberry village simpleton stood when his mind was blank. His only comment had been an amazed, 'The power . . . holy creation – the *power* of it!'

A moment later Quirk came to stand beside Keris. His colour was bad; she was reminded, absurdly, of uncooked chicken skin. 'Ah – I guess it's the ley line you're looking at, isn't it?' he asked. She nodded. 'I – I can't see anything,' he said. 'Just a line of whitish mist, as if there is cool damp air lingering along the banks of a river down there.' He ran through a string of nervous gestures: a tug at the hair in front of his ear was followed by a clearing of his throat, then he chewed his lip and tugged his hair again, all before he could bring himself to ask miserably, 'Keris – er – could you tell me what you see? If it's not too much trouble?'

It was a more difficult question to answer than he realised. She found it hard to find words to describe something that was so alien, hard to find the right similes. 'It's a little like a ribbon,' she said at last, 'lying across the land. In some places it is twisted; in others crumpled; in others smooth. It is about two hundred paces across, I would guess, and it extends as far as I can see in both directions. There's no way around it.'

'Yes, but what is it *like*?' he persisted. 'That is, if you don't mind telling me . . .'

She wondered what to say. The ribbon itself did not move – or rather it did not appear to do so. She assumed that, if it travelled sideways, then the movement was imperceptible. However, inside, in the fabric of the ribbon, it moved all the time. Blues and purples and reds shimmered and changed and flowed. In some places the hues rose above the ribbon in solid waves, only to splash down in a backwash of foam or disappear into whirlpools of colour; other areas seemed calmer.

Above the ribbon the air was coloured too, tinted. A tunnel of translucent mist, pinks, mauves, copper . . . The hues swirled and twisted and skeined; they plunged down, fountained upward – it was as if a capricious wind played along the tunnel to move mist veils through the air. Balls of light shot past and vanished full speed into nothing; showers of coloured sparks tumbled and then winked out.

No words could do it justice. Finally all she could say was, 'It's a band of moving colours. Beautiful. And rather . . . strange. Alien.'

She paused, acknowledging to herself the truth of what she saw. *None of it was real*. There was no wind, no waves, no ribbon of colour. She would have known that much, even if she'd known nothing about ley lines. What they were looking at were forces, not realities. Wild energies, fields of magic power. Those sparks would not burn, those balls of lightning would not blast anyone to pieces – but they were dangerous nonetheless because they represented the forces of ley, and those forces could indeed kill. They could kill ley-lit and ley-unlit, without distinction, in ways that were unpredictable.

She said, 'I see Magic, Quirk, and it frightens me even as it seduces with its beauty.'

'It frightens *me*,' he said unhappily, 'and I can't see a darn thing. Sometime this morning I'm going to have to ride into that, and I keep thinking that I'm not going to ride out of the other side looking the way I did when I went in . . .' He turned away and plodded back towards his dismantled tent.

Baraine watched him go and then turned to Keris, saying just loud enough for Quirk to hear, 'What a whey-faced scaremonger! What was he thinking of, joining this fellowship? Does he even know we're heading all the way down to the Eighth, or is he so witless he mistook our destination?'

Meldor, who had approached them on silent feet, also heard and turned on Baraine with unexpected ferocity. 'The bravest men are those who feel fear yet still perform the deed. Remember this: that man elected to join this pilgrimage, knowing he was ley unlit. Knowing he had tens of ley lines to cross and any one of them could taint him. Is that not bravery? I wonder if such a man is not worthier of your birth than you are, Baraine of Valmair.' He strode off, with all the assurance of a sighted person, leaving both Baraine and Keris gaping after him. It was the first time Meldor had shown the least sign of anger towards anyone, and the words were spoken with the cutting edge of a well-honed axe.

Baraine ruffled up, but said nothing. He turned his back on the line and headed back into the camp to strike his tent. Keris looked at Scow, who had just limped up. 'Would I be wrong,' she said thoughtfully, 'if I suggested that Meldor gets a little peevish to see one of the highborn act without honour, because Meldor is himself a Trician?'

Scow grinned at her, but would not confirm her suspicions. 'I haven't told you how much I admired what you did this morning,' he said, 'with that creature of the Wild. You acted with courage and good sense. Davron tells me you are Piers Kaylen's daughter, so I suppose we shouldn't be surprised. Your father was one of the best in the Unstable, and undoubtedly the greatest of all mapmakers, with the possible exception of Deverli. He'll be sorely missed.'

'Thank you. And you can tell Master Storre that he talks too much. I don't want the whole world knowing who I am.'

'Why not? Piers was a fine man.'

'Maybe because I want to be me, not just Piers the Mapmaker's daughter.' Perhaps because I don't want the whole world to know I'm the daughter who left Sheyli when she was dying . . .

He nodded. 'I think I can understand that, a little. Back home I was always young Sammy, Tomal Scowbridge's son. My father was larger than life, you know, and I was just a kid who could never match up. No one remembered me when my dad was around. That's one thing getting tainted put an end to, I guess,' he added with a wry grin. 'Everyone remembers me now. But I don't suppose Davron will spread your identity around. As you may have noticed, he's hardly a gossip. More the taciturn type.' His eyes continued to twinkle at her, overly large but full of good humour.

I like him, she thought, and wondered what in the world he saw in Davron Storre.

As they rode out towards the Dancer, Keris considered the oddities of this fellowship she had joined. All those years as a child hanging around the mapshop, with her ears flapping as she listened to adult talk, had taught her much about human foibles and how to judge people, but this group had her baffled.

Why was Meldor or Davron — or Scow? — addressed by one of the other two as Margraf? What had Davron meant when he had asked, 'What do you know about us?' How had they used ley to free Scow from the bilee? If one of them was a Trician, why was he travelling like this, without servants, in the company of commoners? How was Meldor able to 'see' so much when he had no eyesight? His abilities were too uncanny to be explained away by any glib reference to the senses of smell and hearing and touch. And why did Davron and Meldor and Scow spend so much of their time together in serious discussion? It did not take a particularly perceptive person to see that something was worrying them, and worrying them badly.

Baraine Keris thought she understood: he was the sort of fool who had decided he would enjoy playing at being an ordinary fellow with common folk and was finding it not nearly as enjoyable as he had expected. He would stick it out, though, and then go home and make fun of them all. In any story he ended up telling, he would be the hero and the rest of them would be figures of fun.

Portron, Quirk and Corrian were all probably exactly what they said they were, but how did Graval fit in? A trader who thought he was bad luck? He seemed so ineffectual; ludicrous even, riding a horse he couldn't control, bumping into people, dropping things, tripping up — it should have been clownish, but it was somehow not funny. Whenever he came near her, Keris tensed as if he was somehow going to spill something all over her or step on her toes. She was not the only one who felt that way, either: all of them were making an effort to dodge Graval, even Portron, although she could see that the chantor felt guilty about it. Keris herself felt sorry for Graval, but she wanted to feel compassion from a distance.

As they rode parallel to the Dancer, searching for a suitable place to cross, she looked over to where Davron rode, mounted on that magnificent crossings-horse of his, all hidden emotion and guilt. What was the matter with him, that his presence alerted her senses to the Unmaker? What was it that had made a man like that — obviously competent, physically personable, who had the assurance of a Trician — into a man who despised himself? He was the biggest mystery of all, but she wasn't sure she wanted it solved. Sometimes solutions brought their own problems.

Portron noticed her watching the guide and said with a twinkle, 'Ah, lass, why don't you ride with him a-ways? I'm sure he can be telling you more interesting tales than I.'

Her instinct was to reject the idea immediately, but Davron

had turned his mount towards the ley line, and her interest overrode her distaste for being in his company. She urged Ygraine up beside him as he approached the ley. 'I'd like to learn about ley lines,' she said without preamble. 'Would you teach me what the different hues and the movements signify?'

She thought for a moment that he was going to refuse; knowing his reluctance to explain anything, she would not have been surprised. Instead he stared for a moment, shrugged and said, 'Why not?' He waved a hand at the line. 'The colour is toning down now, but it's still not suitable for a crossing. We'll ride on a bit further and I'll tell you what you are looking at.'

The lesson was not an easy one. To someone with experience each subtle variation of colour meant something, and the flow of forces through the air could be read like a handbill – but it was hard to be literate when there were thousands of variations to be learnt. 'You see that spiralling swirl there?' he asked. 'When the spiral is tightening like that, all energy is being trapped. The areas around are then safe, but the problem with such spirals is you never know when they will become too tight. Then they uncoil with horrendous force. As they lash free, the ground heaves and anybody nearby is likely to be killed.'

'Have you seen it happen?'

'Once, when I was much, much younger. I was in an escort party. The guide misjudged and we were caught too close when a spiral unravelled. Luckily, no one was hurt.' He gave a reminiscent smile. 'I was closest and was caught in the backlash – it stripped the clothes off me. I suddenly found myself without a stitch of clothing, in full view of a party of giggling young women. I was seventeen years old – and totally humiliated. I had to scrabble around – bare-arsed – trying to retrieve my trousers and shirt while the ley whisked them around in a whirlwind. Some of my fellow guides still bring up that incident when they want to take me down a peg or two, the sods.' The smile broke out into a grin and she was amazed at the difference it made to him. He was not only suddenly much younger – he was *human*.

He waved a hand at another patch in the ley. 'See that deep purple colour there? It signifies a basic instability where anything can happen. It's to be avoided at all cost – unless there are force lines in a figure of eight above it. A figure of eight is highly restricting to ley energy . . .'

Having made the decision to teach her, he was relentless. When she complained she could not tell the difference between subtle gradations of colour, he remarked that it took years of study to be competent at ley-line crossings. 'You won't learn one hundredth of what there is to know today. And even someone with your father's experience could be wrong from time to time: the ley is Lord Carasma's realm, not ours.'

She shivered slightly.

'Scared, Kaylen?'

'Yes,' she admitted. 'Aren't you?'

She looked across at him as she spoke. The flare of pain in his eyes caught her unawares – aching, rending pain, as if his very soul had been torn. His answer when it came seemed prosaic by comparison, even as the words shocked her. 'For myself? No, not in the least. Ley is . . . seductive. I look forward to being in contact with it.' He glanced across at her. 'Is that too honest for you, Keris?'

She didn't answer. All her fear of him came flooding back.

'Well,' he continued, 'if it makes you any happier, I do fear ley for those I escort. My job is to get everyone where they want to go, untainted, unhurt, and as quickly as possible. One trip in every four, I fail. Either someone gets tainted, I lose someone to the Wild or a Minion or a whirlstorm or the unpredictability of ley, or even just a stupid accident like a fall from a horse. One trip in every four, Keris, I lose someone in my care. Yes, I fear ley lines.'

She felt compelled to offer him some comfort. 'Could anyone else do better?' she asked.

'I can answer that,' said Meldor, who had ridden up

behind them, unnoticed. 'The reply is an unequivocal no.'

'And quite pointless to the dead or tainted who were in my care,' Davron said evenly.

They rode on, in silence this time. She glanced nervously at the ley line, and wished they could get the crossing over and done with. Yet she felt no evil from it. Danger, yes, but no wrongness; not like the area around the bilee. The ley line bubbled with strength rather than evil, she was sure of it. But didn't Chantry say that the lines were cracks in Creation, through which the Unmaker's wickedness entered the world?

Davron said suddenly, 'Kereven is the first name of a talented mapmaker; did you know that when you took on the name?'

She jumped and answered too quickly. 'I've never heard of him.'

'Kereven Deverli. He's dead now,' he said. 'He mapped the southern Unstable. He was even better than your father, I think.' He reined in his horse to study the ley line, and dropped the subject, much to her relief. 'I think this might be it,' he said. 'See – the tint all along here is a soft blue. The ground colours appear flat, their movement is smooth. The patterns are definitely unaggressive. The flow of energy in the air is sluggish . . . yes, I don't think we'll get a better place than this to cross.' He turned to Meldor, who halted his horse beside him without prompting. 'What do you think?' Davron asked him.

Meldor sat very still, sightless eyes staring upward, sensing the line in other ways. His lips parted slightly, his head cocked to listen; every now and then he would take a deep breath. 'It's a bad line,' he said to Davron in his rich, aristocratic voice. 'A lot of localised turbulence and pent-up angers, as if Carasma has been around lately. I don't like it. But it seems quiet enough here and this part may well be the best of a bad choice . . . There's a lot of suppression, though, Davron. Stay alert.'

'Let's check it out. The rest of you, stay here.' He

and Meldor swung their mounts into the line without the slightest hesitation, leaving their pack animals behind.

'What's happening?' Quirk asked a moment later. 'Can you see Davron and Meldor?'

'Can't you?' Keris asked.

He shook his head. 'The mist is too thick.'

'They are riding slowly. Picking their way. Davron's leading; he keeps looking down, up, around — at the colours of the line, I suppose.'

Quirk stared hard, and fidgeted. The others had joined them but nobody spoke much. Tension ached in the air around them: they all knew that one or more of them could die in the next hour or so. It was useless to remind themselves that most fellowships came safely through crossings. Useless to remember that only a few pilgrims were ever tainted, fewer still were ever killed. They were standing there, facing the ley, feeling its magic, knowing the Maker probably could not answer their prayers, and fear saturated them to the bone.

I'm ley-lit, Keris thought. I can't be tainted, yet I'm frightened. How much worse it must be for the ley-unlit.

'Let us perform kineses,' Portron said, and dismounted to kneel on the ground. 'Reverence, I think,' he added, referring to the second of the four daily devotions.

'What's the point? The Holy Books say the Maker can't see us when we're in the Unstable,' Barainc grumbled, but, as the others dismounted one by one and went down on left knee, right hand to the heart, he joined them. Even Scow participated in the rituals (hand from heart to forehead, signifying the sincerity of one's thoughts; both hands to right knee, showing piety; forehead to knee, indicating reverence; fingers curling in submission . . .), although Keris noticed that his eyes never left the line for a moment. It was worse for him, she realised: he couldn't see what was happening any more than Quirk, Corrian or Graval could, and Davron was his friend. Meldor too, perhaps.

'So far, so good,' she whispered to him. (Right forefinger

to earlobe, signifying willingness to listen to the word of the Maker . . .) 'They've reached the other side and nothing changed that I could see.'

He smiled gratefully.

A few minutes later Davron was back, without Meldor. 'All right,' he said, 'let's get moving. Corrian, you first. Lead your animals — you can't ride through a ley line unless you've got a mount that's trained to it.'

Corrian dismounted, groaning. 'Middendamn,' she said, 'in the past when I've felt this stiff, at least I'd been riding the right sort of animal.' She leered at Davron. 'Lead on, laddie.'

They set off, Corrian stumbling on the unevenness of the line, yet doing her best to hurry. Her pipe was clamped tight in her mouth, but the pipeweed had gone out — an indication of how flustered she was.

The minutes dragged on as Portron continued his devotions and the rest dropped out one by one to watch the ley line. Quirk started biting his hangnails; Baraine looked contemptuously in his direction. When Corrian was safe, Davron returned and took Graval. Still there appeared to be nothing unusual happening within the line, and, if Davron was tense, he allowed none of it to show on his face. Portron followed Graval, then it was Scow's turn.

Baraine looked relaxed; Quirk was almost turning himself inside out with worry. Davron should have taken him first, Keris thought. He can't realise just how scared the man is.

'Quirk reminds me of what I once was,' Scow had said. Scow the farm boy, so unsure of his worth that he had been unable to believe that the woman he loved could possibly love him back. And Quirk was an ineffectual man with no innate sense of his own value. Piers had once remarked that such men easily fell prey to the Unmaker's tainting. There was nothing inside them to give them the strength to resist ley when it attacked. Keris was pierced by a feeling of tragic inevitability. Quirk was going to be tainted and there was nothing any of them could do to stop it.

Baraine grinned as Davron chose Quirk next. 'Careful you don't foul yourself, boy,' he said.

She doubted Quirk heard him. As he walked into the line, pulling his mount and one of Baraine's mules, his face was a picture of utter misery. Keris found herself making a kinesis against bad luck.

But Davron was right: the Maker did not respond to too many of the kineses performed in the Unstable. He certainly did not answer that one.

When Davron and Quirk were halfway across the line, the ground erupted beneath their feet. '*Back!*' Davron shouted. '*Leave the animals!*' He himself was still mounted, and he swung his horse through a spray of earth and rock, reaching out to grab Quirk with the intention of hauling him up on to the front of his saddle. Quirk dodged him and ignored his shouts. He had dropped the reins of his own mount but he was still struggling to calm the pack mule: Baraine's animal.

'Leave it!' Davron roared.

Still Quirk would not leave the beast.

Damn you, Baraine, Keris thought, dry-mouthed. This is your doing.

Something was being pushed up out of the soil in front of the two men: rocks. Boulders, like huge mushrooms. Earth cascaded off them, knocking Quirk to the ground and unseating Davron. The crossings-horse took off towards Baraine and Keris; Davron fell badly. A wave of colour swirled through the air. Purple, a deep rich purple, billowed through the indigo. It engulfed Quirk momentarily, then dissipated like steam from a boiling pot.

Davron lay unmoving.

Without thinking, Keris grabbed Baraine by the arm, 'Come on,' she shouted, 'we're closer than the others. We have to help.'

Baraine resisted her. 'You're mad!' he said. 'I'm not risking my neck for someone so stupid he'd die for a pack animal! That — that tainted brain!'

She released him to pluck her bow from her back and tighten

the string. 'Who's the coward now?' she asked savagely as she dived into the ley line. She felt the evil then. It engulfed her, soaked into her pores. Stench and power and danger were inseparable. The ground was still heaving; the fingers of rock thrust further upward. They were as yellow as the myrcat that had attacked them. She was staggering as she ran, vaguely aware that Baraine – goaded by her accusation of cowardice – had indeed followed her.

She reached Quirk first, half stooped towards him, and halted in horror. He wasn't Quirk. He was already changed. Tainted. She had an impression of flickering colour, of a skin that was no longer skin, of a smooth greenness, of patterns like painted eyes, of an almost saurian face on a still human head. He was half covered with earth and his body was twisted, knotted – like rope. He was changing before her eyes, and the transformation was hideous. And he screamed, endlessly, with pain.

She staggered on to Davron. He was half up, pushing himself away from the ground. A shower of earth caught them both, and she dipped her head to shield her eyes.

'You damned fool,' he said, the words wrenched out of him, full of pain. She wasn't sure whether he was referring to her or to Quirk.

She turned back to ask Baraine to help her support Davron, expecting to find him right behind her. Instead he was some way back and he was standing still, pooled in yellowish light. Bands of ochre played around him, twining across his body, between his legs. Yet he did not seem afraid; there was a cynical half-smile on his face as if he was listening to something he knew was only partially true but which amused him nonetheless. It was a look that froze Keris to the bone.

She turned back to Davron to find he was staring past her to Baraine. 'Oh midden,' he whispered. 'The Unmaker.' He stood up, leaning against her. 'Kaylen, in the next few minutes you arc going to pay for being foolish enough to follow us into the line.' He took her by the shoulders, facing her now, fingers digging in hard. She felt an unpleasant

152

tingling through the cloth of her shirt where he touched her but had no time to think about it. The eyes that looked into hers were not angry, as she had expected them to be. They were filled with fear; no, something more than fear: something more stark. And his concern was for *her*, not himself. He had to take a deep breath before he could even speak again. 'Get out of here if you can. If you can't, then prove yourself worthy of your father. Now *move*.' He pushed her away, back towards her horses and safety, while he turned back towards Baraine. 'Valmair,' he shouted. 'He has no hold over you unless you grant it to him!'

Keris tried to run, but tripped on moving ground and fell flat. Baraine turned, smiling towards them both. 'I know,' he said. 'He has just explained that.'

'The price is your soul.'

Keris struggled to rise as Davron answered, but the ground would not stay still.

'I know that too. But what use is a soul if one has eternal life? He offers me nothing that I have not already yearned for, Storre – nothing.'

'Minions can still die, Baraine. The immortality is just from disease and old age, not from wounds or accidents.'

Keris thought that she had never seen anything more chilling than the smile Baraine gave the guide: it was completely without humanity. Davron reached out to Keris, hauling her to her feet by the yoke of her jerkin, without taking his eyes off the Trician. 'Keris, please try,' he whispered, begging her to move, pushing her away from him, still without looking at her.

She tried to move, but never finished the first step. Something came ploughing towards them both, churning its way down the length of the ley line. It was huge, insect-like – vaguely – and heart-stoppingly awful. It rushed at them so fast there was no time for Keris to grab for her knife. She dropped her staff and bow and dived through the air to the right; Davron broke to the left.

He moved faster than anyone she had ever seen, even her

father. He had a throwing knife in each hand long before she had even managed to get to her feet; one hit the creature in the eye, the second thudded home deep into its throat.

Then a sweeping antenna whipped across to hit him full in the chest. It was studded with thorns the size of a man's hand and it ripped the shirt from him, to score scratches deep into his flesh. She was dimly aware that he was wearing an amulet that had been hidden under his shirt: she glimpsed the symbol on it and felt the shock of recognition, but there was no time to think about its implications.

By this time she had managed to get a hand to her own knife. She didn't have any trouble with the distance this time: the animal was looming over her like a cliffside. She whipped the blade one and a half turns into the other side of its throat.

It collapsed then, although it was probably Davron's knives that had done the trick: hers was just an extra. Davron grabbed at her as she tried to make up her mind which way to run to avoid the toppling body.

'Typical bloody woman,' he said, yanking her to safety. 'Can't ever make up her mind.'

'Typical bloody man,' she snapped back, 'always so damn sure he knows what's best for a woman.' She was grateful, though, and if he had been anyone else she probably would have fallen into his arms in tears. Instead she just glared and tried not to think about the amulet he wore. It had grown into his flesh, was part of him, melded into his skin. It had a cross on it, like a multiplication sign. The cross of wrongness, within a diamond. A parody of the plus sign of Chantry symbolism.

The cross of wrongness – the symbol of the Unmaker and his Minions.

She looked around for Baraine, but he seemed to have disappeared.

'Oh midden,' Davron said again, dabbing ineffectually at the blood welling up from the scratch marks on his chest. 'I think the beast has fallen on poor Quirk. Let's have a look.'

They skirted the body trying not to think of what they

154

might find on the other side. 'A cross-country tramp just to get around the thing,' he muttered. Keris resisted an impulse to touch him, to tend his bleeding, to seek support for herself just by touching another human being. *Remember the sigil, you fool!*

Quirk had not been flattened after all. He appeared untouched. If it was Quirk. Keris had a hard time trying to convince herself that this . . . person was indeed the nervy youth from Drumlin. He was only semiconscious, which was probably just as well. He would need time to get acquainted with himself again and she doubted that he was in any fit state to start. He was naked, lying on his side. What had been done to him had been carefully thought out. Whatever was responsible for his tainting had known of his diffidence and had taken the indefinite nature of his personality and made it his bodily reality. He was still human, yet he was a chameleon, fated to be always attuned to the background behind him, always fading away into his surroundings, of indefinite colour, blurred edges and partial invisibility.

Keris turned away and was spectacularly sick.

'Stop that,' Davron said, without a trace of sympathy. 'We've got to get him out of here –'

'Better he died –'

'That's not for you to decide.'

She opened her mouth to say she did not know what, and closed it again. Suddenly, out of nowhere, a stranger stood before them, with his arm around Baraine's shoulders, and the sight of him took her breath away.

A man – no, not a man: a god. Tall, naked, spectacular. *Large*. Large in body, large in personality. Large elsewhere too – 'well hung' was the phrase Keris had heard her brother and his friends bandy about. He exuded musk and sexual tension; sweat glistened across his skin. He was gorgeous. And totally evil.

She wanted to close her eyes, to refuse to see, because she knew who he was.

He was Carasma the Unmaker.

Chapter Eleven

Lord Carasma exists only in true Chaos at the heart of ley, for only there is power to be found. To extend his realm must he subvert Humankind to his bidding. Blessed are the ley-lit who resist his blandishments; damned are they who obey his behest.

The Rending XII: 23: 7—9

It never occurred to Keris that it was ever possible to actually see the Unmaker. He was a figure of horror tales, a nebulous, fabulous being akin to — although less than — the Maker, and one didn't expect to meet *Him*. Carasma the Unmaker was portrayed in the holy writings as taking on human dimensions when he tried to pervert the holy knights of the past — but appearing to living people in present times? To *her*? She knew he often subverted the ley-lit into being his Minions, but she had imagined this was achieved by some cosmic struggle within the mind of those who were tempted. She had not expected a personal appearance.

And yet she never doubted that it was him, not for a moment; no human man could have exuded such power, could have shimmered with something so manifestly bad, could have glowed with such a seductive light, could have pierced her with such a look to see her weaknesses . . . No ordinary man could have reduced her to a mass of sexual urges and revulsion just by looking at her.

Davron stood beside her, unmoving, with a surprising passivity. He seemed neither worried nor pleased — just accepting, as if he acknowledged that there was no way any ordinary mortal could run from the Unmaker.

When he spoke, though, she knew him well enough now to hear the thread of urgency underlying his words, even as his tone was measured and calm. She knew him well enough to recognise that he chose every word with care and she would do well to listen with equal care. 'Remember, Keris,' he said, 'the Unmaker is governed by the Law of the Universe. He cannot kill us directly, he can only subvert us, or unmake us.' Obliterate them, he meant, as if they had never existed. Erase them from being, so that their souls died as well, and the memory of them disappeared from all who had ever known them.

She shuddered.

'You have the Maker within you,' Davron went on, 'and therefore cannot be unmade unless you agree to it. Nor can you be enslaved unless you go to him of your own free will.'

He did not need to warn her that the Unmaker had a hundred different ways to make a person succumb to his suggestions of servitude. Nor did he have to warn her that Carasma could send the Wild after her, or his Minions, or use the power of the ley line – and all of them could kill without waiting for the victim's permission. Torture, bribes, seduction, threats, tricks, traps – Carasma the Unmaker used them all directly or indirectly on occasion, and probably sometimes all at once.

'Yeah,' she said. Her tone was dry but her voice wobbled. 'I guess Baraine didn't listen to your warning.'

The Unmaker smiled. 'Baraine is mine now. We have struck our bargain, and it is sealed.' He looked down at the man beside him, and bestowed on him an obscene smile of proud possession. 'Baraine liked the idea of eternal youth. He has such a splendid body and he could not bear to think of it rotting into old age.'

Carasma fingered the silver pendant he was wearing around his neck: the pendant was the 'X' cross inside the diamond; it was the one adornment to his nakedness. He

157

touched it with his hands and took from it a replica, pulling it out of the original with just the touch of his fingers. This he dropped over Baraine's head. It dangled for a moment, then melded to the Trician's chest, fused to his skin. Keris gave an involuntary glance to Davron's amulet. The sigil was identical. She bit back her nausea. *She was standing in front of the Unmaker, in the presence of two of his Minions.*

Baraine looked at Davron and her with a mixture of arrogance and defiance. Davron ignored him and she tried to do the same.

'So,' the Unmaker said, switching his attention wholly to the guide, 'we meet again, Master Storre.'

'Yes.' Davron remained apparently imperturbable. Keris thought: As well he might – he is dedicated to the service of Carasma, of Chaos . . . 'It was inevitable, as we both know.'

Carasma inclined his head. 'As you say. But it is not you I deal with today. Your time for service has not yet come, Master Guide. I await the moment that will bring the greatest grief to all . . . No, today I deal with the woman at your side.'

Davron raised an eyebrow just a fraction. 'Her?' he asked, and the word contained a slur of contempt. 'She is worthy of your attention?' He turned to look at Keris, as if seeing her for the first time. Then he gave the faintest of shrugs, as if to say he couldn't understand, but, well, if that's the way you feel, go ahead . . .

The Unmaker seemed amused. And then Keris lost sight of Davron and of Baraine. And of Quirk, still lying at their feet, and of the animal they had killed. They all slipped away and it was just the Unmaker and her, facing one another across a kaleidoscope of sliding colours.

'You were made to serve me,' he said.

'I doubt it.' Her mouth had dried out. Her tongue was glued to the insides of her cheeks.

'Master Storre serves me,' he said. 'Do not look for help there. What are your greatest desires, Keris Kaylen of Kibbleberry? I can make them come true, in return for your pledge of service. I can give you eternal life and youth as well. Just name what it is you want . . .'

'There is nothing for which I would surrender my immortal soul. Nothing.'

'Not this?' he asked, and gestured with his hand.

She was looking at a shop. There was a sign swinging over the door and on it she read: KAYLEN'S MAPS AND CHARTS. She walked towards it, opened the door and went in. It was exactly as she had pictured it in daydreams, even after she had known it was an impossibility: the shop she would one day own. The shop where she would sell her maps. There were the master charts, there the drawing boards, there the rows of paint and ink pots, the leads and brushes and pens. The walls were covered with charts. Her charts. She reached out and took up one of the master skins, rolled it out on to the counter top. It was good, and it was signed with her name. She released it and it curled back up, hiding its secrets.

Through an open door she glimpsed another room, filled with surveying and camping equipment. She turned her head and saw through into the parlour. A man was standing, with his back to her, warming his hands beside a fire. She felt a wash of love and knew that this unknown man was her husband. At his feet a child played, wobbling on baby legs. Her son; she knew that too. She wanted to walk into that room, to speak, to make that man turn so she could see his face. Instead, her feet took her the other way, out through the back door of the shop into the yard. It was clean, neat and spacious. There were stables, carts and fine crossings-horses. All hers. A stableboy was brushing down a riding hack. Hers.

She turned and tried to re-enter the shop.

And it was gone. There was only Carasma and herself once more.

'You can have it all,' he purred. 'That's my promise, and I cannot lie to strike a bargain or the bargain is invalid. All your dreams can come true, Keris. All. For six months in every year you can live in a stability and serve only yourself and your dreams; for six months you can roam the Unstable to make your maps and serve me. Everything you ever dreamt of, and for such a little price. As Baraine has said so aptly, of what use is an immortal soul if you can be bodily immortal? Imagine, Keris, all you ever wanted . . .'

She forced herself to speak. 'Not all, I think. It is not plain maps I wish to make, Lord Carasma. Not any more. I want the secret of trompleri mapmaking – and that is the one thing I think you cannot dare to give, because a trompleri map would help humankind to thwart the Unstable. Fellowships and traders could find the weakest parts of ley to cross; they could see the presence of your Minions and the Wild and avoid them. There would be few deaths in the Unstable then, and more people would come to weaken you. There would be fewer of the ley-unlit tainted, fewer of the ley-lit made into Minions. People would see where the ley is strong; they would know where not to go; they would see it there, on their maps –' She was babbling, too frightened even to know if she was making sense; too frightened to know if she was saying things that would be wiser unsaid.

He stared at her, and the triumph in him died as he somehow reached out with his mind to test the truth of what she said. The look he gave her then was pure rage. For a moment she expected to die, sure he would strike her, universal laws or not – but he reined in the passion, bridled it with a colder hate.

'Will you turn down this?' he hissed, and made another gesture with his hand. She was back in the shop. This time there was someone behind the counter: Sheyli. Her mother as Keris had known her before she was ill, smiling, full of strength and vigour. Sheyli, somehow well and whole.

'My mother is dead,' she said coldly. 'Even you cannot bring back the dead.'

'You left her for dead,' he corrected. 'But that was only a few days ago. She lied when she told you she was so close to death. She lives still, weaker, but she does live. My word on it.'

She drew in breath sharply. 'How do you know?'

'The same way I know your name. Ley gives me the power. I may not be able to create havoc in a stability, but I can see into it. And I could do good there — I could give your mother back her health.'

'If . . .?'

'If you will but serve me.'

'No.'

'Think on it.'

And she did. *Sheyli could live.* Be healthy again. And she, Keris, could hold herself straight again, free of the guilt she had felt ever since she had ridden away from Kibbleberry. It would all be so easy. She could have it all. And it wouldn't be such a terrible sin, would it? She would be doing it for Sheyli — *No.* Sheyli would not want life at such a price.

'No,' she said to Carasma. 'No. Not even for that. Not even for trompleri skills. Not even if you could bring back my father again. Never — at any price.' But inside she wept. *Forgive me, Mother.*

She still expected to die. Carasma had two Minions right there somewhere at his disposal. He had the forces of the ley line he could turn on her. He could whistle up some of the Wild . . .

She waited for death. Instead he stripped her naked. One moment she was clothed, the next, the clothes had gone. He knew she had never revealed herself to any man; he knew how vulnerable she would be, bared to him like that. She willed herself not to move her hands, not to try to cover her nakedness. She tried to stand proud, but felt shamed nonetheless as he let his eyes wander over her body and his member swelled to taunt her.

'No, no, not me, little Keris,' he mocked as she shrank away. 'Let me give you what you *really* want.'

And he was gone.

She was standing beside Davron once more. Of Baraine and Quirk there was no sign. Davron was as naked as she was. He was staring at her, and his expression was appalled, then yearning, then sickened. His skin glistened, and he moaned. She was in no better state. She felt she had been stimulated beyond endurance, although she had no memory of such happening – and the lack of memory was worse than remembering would have been. She was wet between the legs, desperately wanting something more and not quite sure what it was but longing to find out. She was taut all over, turgid – even her nipples stood up like pinnacles. She was on the brink of something miraculous, but unable to plunge over the rim and find out what it was.

She yearned to reach out and pull Davron to her. She wanted to feel his hands on her body. She wanted him to kiss her, to do things to her that she could not detail because she lacked the experience of them, but knew would feel good. She was just an inch away from something wonderful –

'No,' he said flatly. 'Keris, no.' He was willing her not to touch him and there was horror on his face. And something else too: the wolfish craving of a man who had been denied too long and had just been offered a feast.

Her hand froze as it reached out to him. She deliberately dropped her eyes to his amulet, searching for a way to kill her desire. She moved her lips, spat out a word at him, packing it full of loathing and contempt: *'Minion!'* It was as much to save her own integrity as to scorn him, because in her heart she knew the truth: the Unmaker may have stirred her passions by some abnormal means, but he had not directed them. She had done that all by herself. Just as she had peopled the dream-shop with a husband who would have worn Davron's face had he turned . . .

She stumbled away, revolted, back towards where she had left Ygraine and Tousson. She was weak with reaction, still shuddering with self-loathing and unfilled longing – and still filled with fear. She expected to die. She expected the ley line to erupt under her, she expected Davron's knife in her back – and part of her had even given up caring.

She was sobbing when she reached the edge of the ley line safely. She stepped out and went to where Tousson stood patiently waiting. With tired and shaking fingers she untied one of the bundles and took out another set of clothing. She dressed and was just putting on her spare pair of boots when Davron arrived.

She shrank back against the flank of her packhorse, but he barely looked at her. 'Here,' he said and threw her knife on to the ground at her feet. He had also brought back her bow and quiver, as well as his own knives. 'Sorry, couldn't find our clothes,' he added. It didn't seem to worry him that he was still naked. His lack of clothing enabled her to note that he was no longer obviously aroused and she felt a momentary relief.

He went to get more clothing for himself, but when he reached his packhorse he simply leant, face down, arms spread, against the pack on the horse's back. His shoulders heaved, shuddering, but with what emotion she couldn't tell. She had to quell the absurd desire she had to mother him. *Mother a Minion of Carasma, for Chaos's sake! Am I tainted mad?*

She slid down the side of her horse until she was seated on the ground, then rested her head on her arms. She *was* mad. She should have got on her horse and fled. But she didn't have the energy to go anywhere. Her legs were weak, her hands shook. A while later she became aware that Davron was rummaging in his pack for his clothing and for something to dress the cuts on his chest. They looked nasty: skin slashed open on a background of raised welts.

'What happens now?' she asked finally, not knowing whether she cared.

He gave her a weary look. He was pale, she noted. In fact he looked sick, with none of a Minion's triumphant arrogance as she had seen in Baraine. 'You're in no danger now,' he said. 'What the Unmaker wanted to do he has already done. Tomorrow he may have other ideas, but today you are safe.'

'He wanted me dead,' she said. 'For a moment there I'm sure he wanted me dead. You could have killed me for him. Yet you didn't — why not?'

163

'Because he never got around to asking me to.' A stark answer, with the ring of truth to it. Its corollary was chilling: had the Unmaker desired it, Davron would have killed her, without question.

'He did want us to – to –' She couldn't put it into words. 'You didn't do that either.'

He gave the slightest of cold smiles. 'If he'd ordered it, it would have been done. He assumed it would happen, that's all, and his assumption underestimated us both. Fortunately. You would have found it a painful experience.'

She stood there helplessly, and wondered what she should do. He was clumsily bandaging himself, too proud to ask her to help, and she made no move to offer it. He was a Minion of Chaos, a servant of the Unmaker, one of the evil ones who killed and tortured and raped at Lord Carasma's whim. And she was alone with him.

No, not quite alone. It was only then that she noticed Quirk was still with them. Someone (Baraine perhaps?) had laid him, still unconscious, on the ground behind Baraine's horse and mule. Davron saw him at the same time and bit off an exclamation. 'I was looking for him everywhere! I thought he was still in the line.' He went to kneel by the tainted man, and then glanced around, taking stock. His own packhorse was still there. His mount had wandered back, and seemed quite unruffled by its experience: crossings-horses were used to the vagaries of ley. They had lost Baraine's second pack animal and Quirk's packs with it, and Quirk's mount was nowhere to be seen either. 'We'll use Baraine's tent for Quirk,' Davron said. 'I'm not going to take him across the line again just now. Come on, Kaylen, snap out of it. You're wandering around like a two-year-old who's lost her mother. Help me – we need to get Quirk comfortable and warm. He's in shock.'

She forced herself to move, to act. Together they erected the tent, settled Quirk in it the best they could, and then fixed their own tents. She worked automatically, not speaking, not wanting to speak, avoiding even looking at the guide.

164

He built a fire and put on some water to boil. She set about cooking a meal, using Baraine's supplies because they were the best they had and Quirk would doubtless need nourishing food. By the time she had finished, Quirk was stirring. Between them, they managed to coax him into eating and drinking, then he drifted off to sleep. He did not seem to be fully aware of what had happened to him.

As she left the tent, Davron jerked his head towards the fire. 'Sit down,' he said, 'and have this.' He pushed a mug of char into her hand, careful not to let his fingers brush hers. 'You and I have to have a talk.'

She sat down obediently where he indicated, and sipped the drink. Scow's char, except it did not seem to taste as good as when Scow brewed it. She needed it. 'Why talk?' she asked, forcing the words out. 'We both know you have to kill me. If I tell anyone you are a Minion of Chaos, your little masquerade is over, and doubtless you don't want that.' With reason. Anyone known to be a Minion could be killed on sight; in fact it was considered the duty of citizens of any stability to try to rid the Unstable of Minions.

He sat down opposite her, warming his hands on his own drink. 'I am not a Minion of Chaos,' he said. 'A bonded servant of Carasma, yes, but I'm not a Minion.'

'What's the difference?' she asked dully.

'Barring accidental death or murder, a Minion has eternal life, for a start. A Minion has surrendered his soul. A Minion has renounced the Maker. A Minion has sworn to serve the Unmaker without question for the rest of his days. I have done none of those things.'

'What *have* you done? And why should I believe you anyway? You wear his sigil,' she said, pointing to his arm, now covered with his shirtsleeve.

'On my arm, not around my neck. I have to perform one task for the Unmaker, just one. And only within the Unstable. That is all he can ask of me. And then I shall be free of him. That is perhaps why he did not *order* me to hurt you – he wants me for some more important task.'

'Oh, great. Thanks. My welfare is rather important to me, you know.'

He ignored that. 'And you know I'm not a Minion because you know I can go deep into the stabilities. You've seen me in Kibbleberry. If I were truly a Minion, that would be impossible.'

She refrained from pointing out that it would have been possible for him to have sold his soul after she had seen him in Kibbleberry. 'This task you have to do?'

'I do not know what it is.'

She stared at him. 'How can you live, knowing that one day you will have to do something that will be . . . vile and cruel and utterly beyond forgiveness? That you won't be able to stop yourself performing this . . . deed?'

He did not answer but that flush of his was travelling up the back of his neck and into his face once again. She watched it, mesmerised, intrigued by the idea that someone who had sold his labour to the Unmaker could actually still blush. 'Why don't you stay in a stab, away from *him*?'

'Do you think I haven't tried? He won't let me. After a week or two, he . . . drags me back. Somehow. No matter how far I go, I have to return whether I want to or not.'

She took up her knife and went to hand it to him, handle first. 'Kill yourself,' she said.

He ignored the knife. 'Would *you*?'

'Kill you?'

'Kill yourself if you stood in my shoes.'

She sheathed the knife and considered. 'I don't think I *could* live, knowing that something so terrible was in my future. And I don't think I would have made such a bargain in the beginning.'

'Ah, yes. You turned down whatever it was he tempted you with and therefore are in a position to scorn those who act with less virtue. You can despise those who forget their honour, who betray what you feel they should stand for.'

She wanted to shout at him: *I denied my mother a second chance at life — that gives me the right to feel self-righteous!* But

166

the words would not come. She could not speak of Sheyli to him.

'Perhaps the Unmaker just didn't offer you anything that you cared enough about,' he said, and there was more than a trace of bitterness in him.

'Oh, I cared all right.' She had killed her mother a second time . . . She drove away her guilt with anger. 'You and the Unmaker struck a bargain, like a couple of traders haggling over a sale: one task in return for — what? What did he offer you, Master Storre, that was worth a life lived knowing that you are a walking future catastrophe to humankind? Knowing that one day you will explode into action at Lord Carasma's bidding, even if what is required of you turns your stomach? You may be asked to kill and maim and murder and rape and mutilate until your task is complete. And, because you are a strong, talented, intelligent man, you will do an excellent job. What in heaven's name was it he offered you in return for *that*?' When he did not answer, she added, 'Yes, I would rather die than live knowing that something so dreadful lurked somewhere in my future.'

The pain in him surfaced, stark and immediate. 'I can't,' he whispered. 'I can't. Maker knows, I *have* tried . . . But I'm . . . I'm too much of a coward? Too selfish? *I just can't take my own life.* Is that a crime, Keris? *Is* it?'

'Don't ask me for exoneration. You don't have that right.'

He was silent for a moment. 'No, I don't. I'm sorry.' He fiddled with his mug and then tipped the dregs into the fire. 'I don't want to have you blabbing to everyone you meet that I am a Minion, or indeed that I am a bond-servant of Lord Carasma, so that I end up dead by another's hand. We both know there's an open hunting season on the Unmaker's servants. I would beg you to keep your own counsel on this.' He gave a lopsided smile. 'Another secret for you to keep. At least you know why cats don't like me.'

'Do Meldor and Scow know you wear Lord Carasma's sigil?'

'Yes.'

She did not want to think about the implications of that. 'Are you threatening me?'

'No. You are in no danger from me, unless Carasma demands it. If that were to happen I could make no promises. Remember, though, that you are out in the middle of the Unstable and I'm your guide. You need me – and do you think it would help the safety of this group if you told them I'm the Unmaker's bondsman? Keep your mouth shut, Kaylen. Besides, if Carasma thinks you are a danger to me, he could make life very uncomfortable for you. I am important to him, that I do know. I think he would perform any vileness to ensure my safety, and my anonymity. Do you understand me?'

The dryness was back in her mouth. 'Why hasn't he had me killed already?'

'He can't order your death. Not so long as you are the Maker's. To do so would be to risk his own viability here, perhaps his own existence, even. If the Minions happened to kill you on their own initiative, I doubt that he would quibble – but he can't *order* it.'

'Couldn't he have contrived it so that the ley killed me? An upheaval in the ley line?'

'Without breaking the Law of the Universe? Difficult. Ley lines do kill, but purely accidentally, simply because they are focuses of unstable power. Carasma needs to conserve the power of the ley. Every time he uses the power, for whatever purpose, the ley line is weakened. Look at it.'

She turned reluctantly. The line was calm and almost colourless. Directly opposite them it seemed narrower than it had been.

'That's because it took power to materialise the Unmaker, power to taint Quirk, power to call in that Wild to divert me while Carasma corrupted Baraine. If the Unmaker taints too many people, if he corrupts too many, the ley lines would start to dry up.'

'I thought the whole purpose of a ley line was to kill or taint people.'

His lips smiled, a little, but his eyes remained troubled. 'No.

Ley has other purposes, more important to the Unmaker. Ley comes from the destruction of the world, and is then used to destroy more of the world.' His gaze fixed on her, firelight dancing in the blackness of his pupils. 'The need to conserve ley is the reason why Minions do not often use ley power to kill; why they prefer knives and other conventional methods — or the strength of one of their Pets. But don't feel too safe, Kaylen; Carasma may well let it be known that he has no love for you, which could be enough to give Minions the hint. From now on you had better watch your back — and hope that Carasma expects me to take care of your . . . disposal, to protect myself.'

'Why don't you?'

'Do you really think I —' He stared at her. 'By the Maker, Keris, I don't deserve that from you.'

She didn't answer.

'We'll stay here the rest of today and tonight,' he said finally. 'Tomorrow we'll join the others. I hope Quirk will have recovered enough by then to make another attempt to cross the ley line.'

She ignored the sickness in her stomach and asked, 'The others?'

'They will wait for us.'

He reached out to take the empty mug from her. For a moment their eyes met again and he read in hers something that she herself had hardly known was there, a nebulous, terrible thought that he forced to the surface with his next words. 'You are wondering if you should kill me,' he said. 'To stop me doing Carasma's bidding.' The harshness in his voice was softened by acceptance; the gravel whispered. He plucked his knife from his belt and thrust it into her hand, hilt first, just as she had tried to do to him. 'Then do it. Do it now. I'd rather die now, like this, than lie awake all night wondering just when I'm going to be killed. And perhaps this way would be the best — perhaps you are right, and I have been wrong all along, to try to live.'

She read his willingness to die in his eyes; he may not have killed himself but from her he would accept it. Worse, she saw his uncertainty: *he did not know if she would do it or not*, and it unmanned her. The thought that he could even think of allowing it, could think of standing there while she plunged the knife into his throat or heart, stripped her of any desire to do so.

The knife dropped from her fingers and she saw his gaze change: his uncertainty and pain flickered away into the lingering remains of his yearning for her. For one brief, impossible moment she responded by a quickening of her pulse, a rush of blood through her body. Then, sickened, she turned away.

He was a bonded servant of evil, everything she had been taught to despise. How could she possibly want him?

Chapter Twelve

— *He who hammers evil at his last should be counted evil,*
even though the shoes he makes fit.
— *If poison is cast on the waters yet the dead fish be sweet,*
why should the customer complain?

Sayings of the old Margravate

Keris had to wake Quirk to give him his supper that evening.
He sat up groggily when she laid a hand on his shoulder, then
his focus sharpened as he caught sight of himself by the light
of the lantern she had brought into his tent. His thin arms
lay across the brown of his blanket and the skin was the
same colour as the wool. Where the material was roughly
mottled, or speckled through with lighter streaks, so were
his arms.

With tentative fingers he explored one arm with the
fingers of the other, seeking reassurance. Its texture was that
of skin; the rest was illusion, a trick of light and colour. He
flung back all his covers and sat up. Shocked, he stared at the
rest of his body. He was naked — they had put him to bed as
they had found him — but in his panic he did not care that
Keris was there.

His body had not changed in shape: he was still too thin,
he still lacked muscle; his ribs still showed across his torso.
But he had changed in colour. His lower body blended in
with the blanket he lay on; his upper body merged into the
green colour of the tent at his back. When he placed his hand
on the ground next to his bedroll, the fingers fused visually

with the soil he touched. Keris had to look several times just to make sure he actually still had a hand.

'I'm *tainted*,' he said, stupefied with horror. 'I'm tainted, aren't I? It really happened.'

Keris nodded.

He touched the skin of his chest and stomach. 'It still *feels* like me.' Suddenly aware of his nakedness, he pulled a single blanket up over himself. And saw, in appalled fascination, that, where cloth touched his skin, it too blended into the background, as if it had been contaminated by his body. For a moment he was blank-faced, then his expression changed as the realisation hit him that any clothes he wore would behave as his skin did. He shuddered and looked up at Keris. 'What — what does my face look like?'

'We'll talk about it in the morning,' she said and bent to give him his plate. 'Right now I've brought you your supper —'

'Don't patronise me, Keris.'

Her head jerked up in surprise. It was the first time she had ever heard Quirk be assertive.

She reddened, knowing she was in the wrong. 'Sorry. You look — er — Oh Creation, Quirk, he changed your — your eyes. I'll get my mirror.'

A few moments later she handed her glass to him, trying not to show her dread of his reaction. His face was still human, except for his eyes. These were now mounted at the top of mobile mounds ringed with wrinkles of skin: they were a chameleon's eyes, completely saurian, able even to tilt up and down and sideways without any movement of the head. The pupil was a black slit in a yellow background.

He stared for a long time at his reflection, then handed back the glass. 'I guess I knew,' he said at last. 'The way I blink is different. The way I see things is different. I knew there was something. I'm a sort of lizard, aren't I? A . . . chameleon, that changes colour according to the background. And more than that — I'm a reptile that changes the colour of anything that touches its skin.'

Fury swelled inside her. 'You're a human being, Quirk! A *man*, not a damned – damned – gecko.'

He sighed. 'A camouflaged human being who has to spend the rest of his life living in a place that scares the teeth out of his sockets. *Keris, I can't ever go back to a stab.* From this moment on, I am one of the excluded! Ley-lit, what am I going to *do*?'

'You'll go on living,' Davron said, from the entrance to the tent. He came in and crouched by Quirk, giving him a quick visual once over. 'You'll adapt to life here. The worst has already happened, Quinling.'

Keris, thinking him insensitive, glared at him, but Davron was unrepentant. 'How do you feel?'

'As well as can be expected?' Quirk suggested tentatively after some thought, a strand of his old self-deprecating humour surfacing. And then, 'Why, I think it cleared up my sinus problem. Now, that has possibilities, doesn't it? Quirk Quinling's guaranteed remedy: half a gold to all who want a drastic cure for sinusitis . . .' When they did not laugh, his mood changed. 'The Unmaker did this, didn't he? It wasn't just a random change by the ley – this was carefully thought out. The bastard has a cruel sense of irony.'

Davron looked puzzled. 'Pardon?'

'I saw him, when I was rolling around feeling as if I was being turned inside out like a leech on a stick – Chaos, the pain! I saw him and knew who it was. He was laughing. He knew I was a nothing, a nonentity, so he's made me even more so. Now I have no physical identity free of the background around me. I am always to be – blurred. A shade intangible.' He paused, then swore. 'Well, damn him! I'm more than that! You're right, Keris, I'm a human being, not a blasted colourless iguana, and I'm going to fight that bastard and all he stands for even if it kills me.' A moment later he gave a crooked grin, sheepishly amused by his own vehemence. 'Which it probably will, I suppose. Kill me, I mean.'

He's right, Keris thought. It was a deliberate cruelty. A

173

diabolical alteration tailored to mock an individual. It was all she could do not to send Davron a look of pure hate. How could he even *think* of serving a creature who delighted in devising such torments?

On the other side of the ley line, Chantor Portron Bittle lay back on his bedroll, and tried not to remember what he had seen that day. That animal erupting up out of billows of ley, a confused movement of figures trapped in ribbons of misty colour. Scow, clamping a huge hand on his arm, anchoring him to safety, telling him that Meldor had said the Unmaker was there. 'There is nothing we can do,' the Unbound had said. 'Not when Carasma is involved.' And then, more kindly, 'Davron will look after her as best he can.'

But he did not trust Davron. How could he trust a man who played with the evil of ley?

And that final glimpse of Keris, naked, in the swirl of colour – a glimpse that had hit him like a butted head in the belly. *Maker save and protect her* –

He remembered Maylie. Keris was so like Maylie – like Maylie had been, when he had known her. A strange mix of innocence and innate wisdom, of shrewdness and trust. Boyish figure, yet possessing surprising muscular strength. A nondescript face, hair of an indeterminate shade – nothing about Keris was memorable, yet somehow she could never be forgotten, just as he had never truly forgotten Maylie, though he had tried. Tried hard, for twenty years, and sometimes he had indeed put away all thought of her, until something came to remind him – a woman with the same turn of the head, or the same habit of biting her lower lip when puzzled, or the same way of sounding cross. And now there was Keris, who reminded him all the time of what he had once possessed, for such a short time, so long ago.

Nine months, twenty years in the past; that's all they'd had . . .

And now he was once again travelling towards a woman and a child, just as he had twenty years ago. He had no hopes of recapturing what was past and precious; it had gone, swept away by the Rule. Whoever it was he was going towards, she was not Maylie. And the child would not be Maylie's daughter.

Nine months, and a child they had never seen, to last them a lifetime. It had not been enough. It would never be enough. *Ah, Keris, please be all right. Please be all right. Maker grant that you have the courage to withstand.*

To cross the ley line the next morning took all the courage Keris had, and what she did have was not enough to stop the dryness rising in her throat and nausea permeating her gut once more. She had declined Davron's offer to take Quirk first and come back for her. 'We can all go together. If anything goes wrong I'll look after myself,' she told him, 'while you attend to Quirk.'

Quirk took the crossing in his stride, calmly following the guide as if he was off for an evening stroll. 'Sure, I'm afraid,' he said to Keris as they started out, 'but I'm done with being scared witless. Master Storre is right: the worst thing that could possibly happen has happened already; what more do I have to lose?'

Keris was not so indifferent. By the time she arrived safely on the other side of the ley line, she was sweating like a steamed-up window in a crowded tavern and her knees were so weak she had to cling to the saddle when she dismounted. Scow greeted her with a grin and an amused, 'Arthritic joints at your age, Keris?' He held out a water skin.

'Shut up,' she growled, straightening up and attempting to look nonchalant. She took the skin and drank, glad to wet the dryness of her throat.

She looked across to where Davron was confronting Meldor – and it *was* a confrontation, she felt sure, although Davron's words were mild enough. 'I could have done with some help,' he said as he dismounted. 'You must have known Carasma was there.'

Meldor nodded. 'Yes, I knew. I just didn't think that it

was the right time to draw attention to myself.'

'And what of us? One tainted, Meldor, and one subverted to be a Minion. That's a high price. We could have lost Keris as well as Baraine, if she hadn't been strong enough to resist — and you weren't to know what else he wanted.'

'I knew it wasn't you,' Meldor said calmly. 'This is neither the time nor the place. It was just a warning. A way of weakening you, if you let it.'

Davron gave him a dark look. 'By the Maker, Meldor — I hope that, when I really need you, you don't decide that it's "not the right time" and turn your back.' He walked away, leading his horses, and his shoulders were knotted with tension.

'Hey,' Scow said to Keris, who was still trembling, 'it's all right. You did just fine. If the Unmaker appeared to you and you withstood, you should feel proud.'

'Yeah. Proud and petrified, that's me. The Unmaker didn't take my refusal kindly. The day of reckoning has just been postponed, that's all.' She grimaced at him. 'How's your leg?'

'Much better, thanks.'

'Keris, lass.' Portron, his face a picture of fatherly concern, came hurrying over from where he had been comforting Quirk. 'Are you all right? Meldor said the Unmaker appeared —'

She cut him off short. 'We'll talk about it later.'

'Let's go,' Davron called. 'We don't want to hang around a ley line any longer than necessary.'

As she hauled herself back into the saddle, she happened to catch sight of Graval's face. He was looking across to where Quirk, attempting to mount Baraine's horse, was making a mess of the procedure. The animal had not yet quite come to terms with his new rider's peculiarities and was shying away in panic; when Quirk accidentally touched the horse's hide with his bare hand, the touch stung, which did not help matters.

Graval was amused by the unequal struggle between the

slightly built man and the determined animal, especially as Quirk — and his clothes — faded in and out from one set of colours to another as his background changed. 'Chaosdamn, Quirk,' Graval crowed, 'you're like a child's kaleidoscope. Turn the handle, and goodness me! You're a new man!'

You bastard, Keris thought uncharitably and went to help Quirk.

During the next few days Keris gradually began to accept the bizarre as normal. The rocks that twisted into impossible shapes, the sudden shifts of wind and weather, the weird coloration of the landscape, the beast that attacked them and was killed with a single knife throw from Davron (it had three heads), the streaming ribbons of cloud that would appear suddenly out of nowhere and drift among them long enough to spook the horses and assail them with strange smells.

They crossed three more narrow ley lines which were exactly where Piers's maps said they would be, and a fourth that was not. It had shifted sideways, leaving the grey swath of a burn mark behind that took them half a day to cross.

They passed a number of wooded gullies that were heavy with ley yet did not contain ley lines. Called ley mires, as Scow had told Keris, they were always dark places, deep in muck and smells and strange creatures, overhung with twisted growths, and saturated with coloured miasmas that hurt if inhaled. The ley-lit had no problem seeing and avoiding such foul holes, but Keris was struck by how different they seemed from the ley lines. The lines were dangerous, thick with power; mires were just downright evil. The word that came to mind was corrupt.

'I don't see much difference,' Portron said when she asked if he felt any distinction between the two types of ley. 'Both sorts of places are anathema to anyone who serves the Maker.'

Davron, though, disagreed. 'Of course there is a dif- ference. Mires are places that Minions and their Pets have

177

made their own. Such holes are thick with misused ley, and are often the den of very old Minions – people whose humanity has been well and truly lost across centuries in the Unmaker's service.'

'And the ley of ley lines?' Keris asked.

He shrugged. 'It's just different.' She had an idea that there was much more he could have said, but did not.

Sometimes they saw other people; they passed a courier going in the opposite direction, and he stopped for a cup of Scow's char while Davron questioned him in detail about the way ahead. Once they passed a trader and a train of mules carrying goods from the Fifth Stability to the First; he had three of the Unbound in his employ as well, each mounted on a tainted beast with a hide like armour and horns like sabres. Another time they found a whole encampment of the Unbound, perhaps four or five families of about thirty people, including children born in the Unstable to tainted parents.

This group operated a ferry across the Flow and charged for their services. Davron paid them partially in Baraine's dried meat – meat was one thing that was not available in the Unstable, and those who lived there were always desperate for it. Portron was shocked by Davron's casual appropriation of Baraine's things; but, when the chantor protested, Davron gave him one of his branding-iron looks and Portron did not pursue the matter.

As she helped to load the horses on to the ferry, Keris eyed the children playing at the water's edge, aimlessly throwing sods of earth into the water, and then at the ferry itself when it began to pull away from the bank. 'I didn't know the tainted could have children,' she blurted out to Scow. She was fighting her revulsion; the children seemed more twisted than their parents. One girl had a hump of loose flesh on her back and some deformity of the spine that doubled her over to such an extent she scrabbled about on all fours. The other children, seeing the ferry was now out of range, threw earthen clods at her instead. Keris winced as one particularly large lump caught her on the ear and she gave an animal yelp.

Scow turned saddened eyes towards the youngsters. 'Yes,' he said, 'it's possible for us to bear children. But they always seem to lack the intelligence of their parents. They . . . degenerate, generation to generation, until the family finally dies out because the fourth or fifth generation don't have the intelligence to look after their young properly. The Unstable is a hostile world to children; without care they quickly fall victim to ley, or to predators. Did you know the Minions hunt humans for food? The younger the better.' He turned his regard from the children to her. 'I would father no children in this place.'

She nodded dumbly, unable to speak in the face of his tragedy.

Davron Storre used the Kaylen maps well; he was an expert at finding the best route through a trackless environment; and his foresight meant that many problems were avoided rather than confronted. Like Piers, Keris thought. I wonder if they knew one another? She had not asked him that.

What Davron was not always good at was dealing with people. He had little patience at the best of times, and none at all with stupidity. He treated Quirk no differently now that he had been tainted, which might have been wise, but he was rarely polite to Graval any more, evidently finding the man's constant carelessness and effusive apologies too irritating to bear. He ignored Portron to the point of insult, and, although he sometimes seemed amused by Corrian, he was less tolerant when she deliberately needled Graval or Portron. Most of the time, however, he just seemed self-contained and remote. If there was pity for Quirk within him, he never showed it. If there was real concern for his friends, it was impossible to read it in his face or words. If there was any anger at Baraine's acceptance of evil, he never let it be seen. If he still desired Keris, he never showed it. He performed a job, and did it well, but he gave the impression that, if he had lost the lot of them in some cataclysmic upheaval, he would have just shrugged and ridden on.

Keris knew by now that it was all a façade. Davron cared. He cared deeply. He cared enough to take meticulous care of their safety even at the risk of his own; he cared enough to take the trouble to make them as comfortable as possible in arduous circumstances. He had done his best to save Quirk from tainting and to divert Baraine from the Unmaker. She remembered too well his heaving shoulders after they had emerged from the ley of the Dancer when he had known he had failed in both those endeavours. And she knew he was deeply shamed by the bargain he had made with Carasma – she had seen that in his face, in his eyes, in his blush. He wasn't indifferent to them all, then, just somehow holding himself apart. Was it shame that kept him so self-contained and remote from most of the rest of the fellowship? She thought it may have been and didn't know whether to despise him – or pity him.

To her surprise he did spend more time talking to her than he had done in the past. She was not sure why, because he made no special effort to encourage her to like him, or even to trust him. In fact, sometimes she thought the reverse was true and he actually wanted her to see him in as bad a light as possible. 'Don't turn your back on me, Kaylen,' he'd say when they were alone. 'Never forget that one day I will serve the Unmaker.' Or, after he had explained something about the Unstable to her, 'Arm yourself with knowledge, Keris. You never know when it may be necessary. I'll teach you all I can, and who knows – one day you may be able to use it against me.' And he would give his lopsided ironic smile.

At least he now *saw* her, acknowledged her as a person in her own right, and was prepared to listen to what she had to say. She had in some way proved herself, but the thought brought her no satisfaction. She herself was uneasy in his company, worried by her knowledge of his bondage to the Unmaker, unsettled by the nature of her own attraction to him.

She made no attempt to talk to Scow or Meldor about Davron's bonding to the Unmaker. They knew about it, they had done nothing, and Meldor had used ley to release Scow from the bilee – it all pointed to the two of them being in some way committed either to Lord Carasma, or at least to the dangerous use of ley. She wanted nothing to do with any of them. It even upset her to see that Scow was spending much of his time with Quirk, teaching him the survival skills of the Unstable, explaining to him the various ways it was possible to make a living outside of the stabilities, helping him to come to terms with his tainted nature.

Day by day Quirk seemed to grow in confidence; perhaps it was Scow's doing. He began to delight in his camouflage abilities, and practised stalking through the camp, challenging them all to see him. He had decided to add to his name – as many of the Unbound did – and had chosen to be known as the Chameleon. Keris was glad to see his renewed joy in living; she was just afraid that, along with the aid, Scow would somehow involve Quirk in Davron Storre's affairs.

Just thinking about it made Keris irritable. The trouble was she *liked* Scow, and respected Meldor. And she found Davron physically attractive – while all the time her instincts were screaming at her to have nothing to do with any of them.

In the end she morosely tried to avoid them all, which meant that she had a choice of Portron's loquacity, Corrian's vulgarity or Graval Hurg's ingratiating flattery and disastrous clumsiness.

Portron questioned her on every aspect of her encounter with Lord Carasma, only to be thwarted by her noncommittal answers; she did not want to talk about it. She had not come to terms with her guilt yet, and there was hardly an hour went by that she did not wonder if Sheyli had died. (*Perhaps she is taking her last breath right now and I'm not with her. Perhaps she died last night, alone. Thirl wouldn't stay home just because she's dying . . .*)

Fortunately it was easy to sidetrack Portron on to some other topic, so that he was the one who ended up talking.

One night Davron told her to mount guard duty with Meldor, which surprised her. Up until then she had always been paired with Portron, and Meldor, as far as she knew, had done his stint alone.

They kept the middle watch, and when it was over she went to wake Corrian and Graval, who had the dawn stretch. She poked her head into Corrian's tent, to find her sprawled out on her bedroll with her mouth open. Her pipe had fallen out of her mouth and was lying on her blankets with all the pipeweed spilt out of it in a black dottle. There were several old burn marks on the covers and Keris made a mental note not to pitch her tent so close to Corrian's another time. Once the woman was awake, she went on to Graval's tent, only to find he was already up, roused by Meldor.

'I want to talk to you,' Meldor said quietly and led her off to his tent, with his usual unerring sense of direction, deftly stepping over tent pegs he could not see on the way.

It was the first time she had been inside his tent. She was not surprised to find it more luxurious than her own. It was tall enough for Meldor to stand up inside and the central pole was made of sturdy but lightweight whipwood. His blankets were woven of fenet wool, the finest and warmest yarn in all the stabilities, and the undersheet of his bedroll was well padded. There were several other signs of wealth: a warmth-stove that burnt chips of compressed mata leaf, a cake of fine-grained soap lying in a tortoiseshell dish, a soft towel of bedraggle cotton from the Fifth.

'I'm afraid I don't use a lamp,' he said. 'Do you mind sitting in the dark?'

She refrained from telling him that the stove gave off sufficient glow for her to see by, and even took comfort from the thought that he did not know everything about his environs after all. 'Not if all you have in mind is talk,' she said bluntly.

He laughed softly. 'You have no need to worry, Keris. Sit here on the bedroll. I wish to discuss Davron's situation with you. Tomorrow we reach Pickle's Halt, and it disturbs us that you may be considering passing on what you know to other people.'

'Can you give me one reason why I should not?' she asked as she seated herself. Even as she spoke she wondered if he would say, Because we'll kill you if you do.

He was more circumspect. 'Davron is not an evil man, merely a tormented one. Scow and I are with him all the time he is in the Unstable, every trip. When the time comes, we hope to sabotage the Unmaker's plans for him. If we can't, then Davron will die. Scow and I are pledged to kill him.'

'He *knows* this?'

'He suggested it.'

'You're all mad. Snatching at dreams, hoping Davron will be able to escape the final reckoning. Do you think the Unmaker will let any of you ruin his plans? You can't watch Davron all the time – one day you'll wake up and find him gone, and the horror will have begun before you've even worked out that he's left your guardianship.' She paused, then added, 'If you are still alive.'

'The Unmaker is not all-powerful. He can be thwarted.'

'I thwarted him,' she said, 'but, believe me, I did not have the impression that he would let me get away with it for very long.'

'You intend to betray Davron.'

'Betray is an emotive word, Master Meldor. Let's just say I haven't made up my mind what to do.'

'You leave me no choice, Keris. I did not want to do this, but you have forced it upon me –'

Her hand flew to the knife at her side and she began to move, to flee. She never even reached an upright stance.

Light – a tendril of colour – seeped out of Meldor and spiralled itself around her arm. It stung like nettle rash. She released the knife she held: she no longer had the strength to hold it. She was forced to release a hold on her will also, and felt it drain away like water pouring from a jug.

'You will neither speak of nor write of Davron's bondage to anyone but the three of us: Scow, Davron and myself,' Meldor said. His deep voice was beautiful; it caressed her as it bound her to his will. It seduced, even as it wove its bonds. 'Within the hearing of others, you will keep your counsel on this matter. You will not mention to anyone who does not already know it that Davron and I use ley. You will not talk of our affairs to others.'

The light faded away and she rubbed her arm. 'You *bastard*,' she said in outrage. It was the first time she had ever used such a word aloud, and under the circumstances it felt good on her tongue. She knew he had somehow taken away her freedom of choice; she would not be able to betray Davron's secret. She felt violated. And furious.

She picked up her knife and stood up, almost shaking with rage. 'Keep your filthy ley practices to yourself; I want no part of them.'

'I'm sorry,' he repeated. 'Too much rides on what we do to allow you to blunt our blade with your interference.'

It was only when she was outside the tent that her anger subsided enough to allow her to feel real fear. Who were these people? Who was this Meldor that he could sap the will away from someone and make them into a reluctant accomplice? She wanted to throw back her head and shout to the world, *Davron is bond-servant to the Unmaker!* But the words would not come. Nothing would come. When she tried even to think about betraying Davron her mind seemed woolly – vague – as if she could not quite remember . . .

Damn the lot of you, she thought in a fury.

Chapter Thirteen

And the Minions of Chaos serve the Lord in all things, with their Wild Ones tied to them by chains we cannot see, Pet and Master both glorifying in the Lord's dread service. Beware, Pilgrim, for I say unto you, there is naught you can do against such servants if Carasma has sent them after you. Fall instead to your knee, hand on heart, and make your peace with Creation, that you may one day be at one with That Which Was Created.

Pilgrims V: 22: 6

'You're *Piers*'s daughter? By all that's dark in Chaos, what are you doing *here*, girlie?'

The large green troll blinked at Keris from across the other side of the table in the halt common room, while she resisted the temptation to respond to the 'girlie' by calling him froggie. Instead she asked mildly, trying not to feel five years old, 'Why not, Master Pickle?'

'Your father wouldn't have liked it for a start. This is not a pilgrim trail for ordinary people, lass, at least not from the direction of the First.'

'I'm not particularly ordinary. I'm ley-lit, and I'm a master mapmaker's daughter. *Piers*'s daughter — that counts for something. I came because I want to know how he died. And why.' She fingered the end of the staff propped up against the table. It was Piers's blackwood staff that he had taken everywhere with him and she had brought it down from her room on an impulse, thinking that perhaps she would give it to Pickle. The wood was warm and smooth under her hand. Comforting.

'Krissy, Krissy, what does it matter how he died? He died, and a fine man he was. Remember him for that. I'll get you included in a party of Chantry dignitaries or some other suitable escort heading north for the First —'

You wouldn't say that if I was Thirl, she thought, but said, 'Thank you. I'd appreciate that. But I'll be going to the Second, not the First. And I'm not going anywhere until I have a few answers, Master Pickle.' She clutched the staff a little tighter, seeking reassurance.

Pickle spent a moment gazing at her, then looked into his drink, considering. She took the opportunity to look around the common room.

Davron, Scow and Meldor were together as usual, talking to another Unstabler. They were all drinking some of the local brew that was the end result of a distilling plant in Pickle's cellar, its basic ingredient known only to Pickle, which was probably just as well. Corrian had already disappeared upstairs with a toothless trader known as Gasp the Smell; Graval and the Chameleon were nowhere to be seen and Portron, who had borne in mind what Davron had once said about kineses in his presence, had retreated to the stair hall to hold a small devotions session. The only other occupants of the common room were a group of Defenders morosely regarding their glasses and eyeing — even more morosely — the tainted waitresses.

'Why should I give you any answers?' Pickle asked finally. 'You wouldn't like 'em if you heard 'em.'

'Because Piers was your friend and I'm his daughter.'

He stared at her again, still considering. She stared back, refusing to be intimidated. He leant his bulk across the table towards her, and the slab top groaned. 'Stubborn,' he growled.

She nodded, and did not lean away from him, even though his breath did smell of tebblewitz yams and garlic.

'Your dad said you had twice the gumption of your brother Whatsisname — Tirl.'

'Thirl.'

'He stayed at home, I suppose.' She nodded again. 'All right, lassie, I'll give you the full story, but you won't like it.' Blandishments had not worked so now he was aiming to punish her recalcitrance. At least she knew she was going to get the truth, with no glossing over the unpleasantness of a messy death.

He settled back in his especially reinforced chair. 'Your dad had dinner with me the day he arrived, everything as normal, although he'd had an unusually rough trip. After dinner, he went on up to his room to avoid a kinesis session. Several of the ley-lit followed him up to buy maps.

'Some time that evening, two . . . creatures climbed the stockade wall into the yard. A Minion and her pet Wild. My stableboy was killed. His head was bitten off and his heart eaten out of his body. The guard at the gate went to investigate, and he too was killed. He was ripped open and all his guts spilt into the hay — all without either of them having a chance to rouse the house. The intruder and the Pet then climbed up to the second storey and entered the building through a shuttered window, by ripping the shutters off their hinges. Nobody seems to have noticed the noise — the room was empty at the time and most of the halt guests were still downstairs.

'They then sniffed along the passage until they came to a room occupied by an unbound man called the Mantis. He was a stranger around here, and we don't know much about him. He opened the door to 'em, poor fellow. What exactly happened after that, we don't know. Certainly he was tortured. His throat was crushed at some point, perhaps to stop him screaming. Later — we don't know how much later — he was killed. His room was thoroughly ransacked.

'Then the bastards went to Piers's room. Piers put up a bit of a struggle. Nothing much, you understand, but by this time people had heard things and were beginning to come out of their rooms asking what was going on. I was called from down in the common room. I came upstairs, and saw that there was blood seeping out under the door of the Mantis's room. I opened the door and found him. By then the Wild must have killed Piers as well; I'm not quite sure how. You can take your pick: when I saw him, his neck was broken, his ribs were stove in, and something had taken a great bite out of his neck — maybe after he was dead — and drunk his blood.'

Keris looked down at her hands. She had been moving a pile of crumbs left on the table from one place to another. He died, she told herself. How doesn't matter. How doesn't matter —

But it did. Terribly.

Her hand strayed to caress the top of Piers's staff again. 'Go on,' she said, and the huskiness of her voice, the unbearable lump in her throat, wanted to spill over into helpless tears. 'Girlie' be blasted, she thought. I won't act the way he expects me to —

He went on, 'I came out of the Mantis's room and started looking around for Piers. Damn good man to have in a fight with those knives of his, Piers was, and I was pretty sure whatever had done that to the Mantis was still around. But Piers wasn't there. And that wasn't like him — we were all out there in the passage making enough noise to wake a hibernating puckleworm.' He sighed. 'Then that thing came bursting out of Piers's room. The Wild — with its maws all covered in blood. Piers's blood, dripping down from its mouth and matting its curls of wool . . . Horrible thing. Sort of like a pear-shaped dog with talons and too many teeth for its mouth — they were stuck out all over the place, I remember. Couldn't close his jaws over them . . .'

This time it was Pickle's voice that was husky. He took a drink from his mug. 'The Minion came next — a bitch with reddish hair, the colour of moggie fur. Name of Cissi Woodrug.'

'You *knew* her?'

'Yep. Friend of mine once, back in the days before she was corrupted. Ley-lit daughter of a courier who took her with him on his trips after her mother died. Hard as nails was Cissi, but cute. Very cute in a brittle kind of way. Knew the Unstable like most people know their own hearths.'

He paused but Keris didn't say anything.

'She looked me straight in the eye and said, "'Lo there, Pick. Long time no see." Piers's blood was all over her. If there was any justice in the world she would have been struck dead, right there and then, just with the look I gave her. "You going to kill me too, Ciss?" I asked.

' "Nah," she said. "Next time maybe. I reckon you'll suffer a bit over what happened to your friend the mapmaker – so why cut short a man's suffering? That's not the way of a Minion." She was alive with ley; it crackled all over her. Not that I could see it, mind, but that's what the ley-lit said afterwards: she sparkled with ley like cracklewood in a fireplace. I reckon that's what gave her protection against the stability of the halt. She and that Pet of hers had somehow absorbed enough ley to shield themselves.

' "What did the Unmaker have against Piers?" I asked, but she didn't answer. "Gather everyone in the building in the common room," she ordered, imperious-like. Well, we did. We didn't have all that much choice. That Pet of hers winkled everyone out of the rooms, right down to the cookboy, poor lad. Several of the Defenders who were here then tried to rush her and the animal. The bitch's dog was too fast for most of them, and the man that almost got to her with his pike, well she sort of swept him aside with the weapon in her hand and he let go of the pike with a yell you could have heard halfway to the Fist. His hands were burnt to the bone.'

He gave an involuntary glance at a spot in the middle of the room. 'Men bleed a lot when they've been torn apart,' he said softly, 'and she was right. Sometimes you suffer more when you live to remember –' Then he shrugged. 'What more is there to say? She lined us up and asked us one by one if any of us knew anything about some map or maps that the Mantis had, or that Piers had. Special maps, she called them.

Well, no one did – and I reckon that was the truth. When a slobbering beast with his teeth still dripping blood looked up from what he was eating and licked his chops, and that bitch looked down into the depths of your soul with her red eyes, I figure no one could have lied to save their old granny, let alone a map.'

He took another drink, draining his mug this time. 'And that's it, lass. Cissi left us. Walked out with that beast, calm as you please, although I think the stability was getting to them both a bit by that time. She was fidgeting. That Pet of hers took the cookboy with him as a late-night snack. He was the eighth. Oh yes, and there was the baby too. Chaosdamn, how could I have forgotten? It died as well, just because it looked tasty, I reckon. It was swallowed whole, gulped down just like that, still crying its heart out.'

They were silent for a long time after that. Pickle ordered himself another drink and sipped it, but Keris just sat, hands cupped around the end of the staff.

'Tell you one funny thing,' Pickle said after a while. 'We found the ownership papers for Piers's horse in the Mantis's room, and for the Mantis's horse in Piers's room. Never did figure that one out. Anyway, I put the scrip for Ygraine in with Piers's things when I packed 'em up to send them to you. Piers's things had been ransacked too, of course, and the room itself torn to bits. Chaosblast of a mess.'

'Did you ever find out anything about the Mantis? Who he was, where he'd come from?'

'Well, of course I asked everyone who passed through for the next few weeks. I wanted to know if he had any family or anything; anyone who should be told. An Unbound from down south said he'd known him. The Mantis was a loner, he said, but he had been in service from time to time with a mapmaker from the south. A man called Deverli. And that was all I ever found out about the poor fellow. Not much of an epitaph, is it? Maker knows what his real name was.

'Tell you another odd thing, though, Keris me girl. That little group over there –' he nodded towards Meldor, Scow and Davron '— they were through here a day or two before either the Mantis or Piers arrived, and they were looking for the Mantis. And they asked after Piers too. I told 'em I reckoned Piers would have been heading back to Kibbleberry by then. It was late in the season, after all. They left; the Mantis and Piers arrived a day or two later. But I guess they've already told you what all that was about.'

The muscles in Keris's face tightened. 'No,' she said. 'I can't say they've mentioned it.'

'They were back a couple of weeks later as well. Asked me about what happened. Wanted to go through the Mantis's things. I let 'em   didn't seem much point not to. There wasn't anything of value. Wanted to see Piers's gear as well, but I'd long since sent that off with Blue Ketter. They also spoke to the Kitten — she's the chambermaid here. The one with the whiskers. It was her that packed up Piers's baggage — I just didn't have the heart. He was a good friend, Piers.'

Keris looked up from the pile of crumbs. 'I think I'll go to bed now, Master Pickle.'

He nodded. 'I told you that you wouldn't like it.'

'I didn't expect to like it. But I still wanted to know.'

'We buried him outside the stockade wall. But . . . you know how it is.'

'Yes, I know.' The Unstable would have wiped away every scrap of evidence that there ever had been a grave. And, according to Chantry, Piers would never be at one with That Which Was Created. Instead of being returned to Creation, his body was now part of Chaos, and his soul — well, whether it would ever find its way through to the Maker was a question to which nobody knew the answer.

Chantry said everyone must make their pilgrimage. Chantry excluded the unwanted to the Unstable. Chantry refused to allow the Unbound back into the stabilities, even for the short time they could bear to be there. Yet Chantry also told you it was a terrible thing to die in the Unstable. *Damn Chantry, damn them all*.

She stood up abruptly and picked up the staff. Suddenly

she knew she would never be able to part with it. 'Good-night, Master Pickle.'

He nodded sadly and began to play with the crumbs she had left behind.

To leave the room Keris had to go past Davron's table, but he reached out to touch her sleeve as she passed. 'Keris, there's someone here I'd like you to meet.' He indicated the stranger at the table. He was a small, bright-eyed man wearing the rough leathers so preferred by Unstablers. 'This is Rossel,' Davron said. 'He's a pedlar –'

'– of pins and needles, string, thread, hobnails, charms, scissors, whetstones and knives,' the man said. 'If you have any needs, lass . . .'

She smiled at him. 'Not at the moment. I'm Keris.'

'Kaylen,' Davron added, ignoring her instinctive gesture of annoyance at his giving her full name. 'Piers's daughter. I wanted you to hear what he has to say, Keris. There is something odd happening to the south, and I wondered what you, as a mapmaker's daughter, might make of it.'

Rossel nodded – and dropped his pedlar's demeanour as swiftly as his spiel. He may be a pedlar now, Keris decided, but once he was much more than that. He spoke like an educated man; the cheery bonhomie of a pedlar had suddenly become the inquisitive intelligence of a man more used to research than selling. She wasn't surprised: most of the excluded had held jobs vastly different from the ones that earned them a living in the Unstable. 'It's good news, we hope,' he said, bright eyes fixed on hers. 'There have been a number of patches of stability – fixed features – popping up out of nowhere. Seven, to be exact, that we know of. Down near the Eighth Stability.'

'How big are they?' Keris asked and sat down on the chair Davron proffered. She hadn't intended to stay, but all her emotional fatigue vanished at the idea that new stabilities were appearing. Hope, she thought. Hope, at last.

'Oh, not that large. Larger than the old fixed features, though. All more or less the same size. I haven't seen them myself, but from what I hear they are all about a mile long and not quite as wide. And all with edges ruled as straight as a sober man heading for his bed on his wedding night. From what I have been able to find out, they all appeared around about the same time. But why, and how, we don't know.'

'Did anyone see them appear?'

'Not so far as we can find out. There was a camp near one of them and the people there said they heard a funny noise during the night. There was a slight earth tremor accompanied by a flash of light bright enough to illuminate the inside of their tents. Then, when they woke in the morning, there it was on their doorstep, so to speak: a fixed feature.'

'If only we could find out how it was done. And by whom. Or by what,' Scow said softly.

'If only we could replicate it,' Rossel said. 'There's one not-so-good thing about them, though. It seems that the tainted don't like them. They say they start feeling sick if they enter one for long.'

'In that case, they may be more like an ordinary stability, rather than a fixed feature,' Davron said, frowning.

'I don't know what to suggest could have made them,' said Keris. 'I've often wondered about what caused fixed features. Some people used to say that they were just remnants of the old Margravate, just as the eight stabilities are. But, then, why do they always have straight edges? My father took me once to the huge Chantry library in Drumlin to see the map they keep there, under glass. It supposedly dates back to the days shortly after the Rending. There are no fixed features marked on it at all – not one. Which seems to indicate that they were something that developed later.'

'And unfortunately, as we all know,' added Meldor, 'that post-Rending period in our history was one of terrible turmoil, mass starvation and so on. Records were lost, momentous events weren't even recorded . . . I doubt whether we'll find the answer by looking back.'

She shrugged. 'I'm sorry, I can't be much help. The best I could suggest would be that all the new areas are marked on a map — accurately, mind — to see if there is any clue provided by their relative positions or their orientation. If it turns out that they are randomly scattered, I don't know what else to suggest.' She stopped speaking, suddenly aware that she was giving useful information to people who may not have the best interests of the Unstable at heart. 'If you'll excuse me, I am tired. I think I'll turn in. Glad to have met you, Master Rossel.' Before any of them could protest or detain her, she was gone.

Davron sighed. 'Suspicious as a kitten faced with a pack of dogs,' he said.

'Do you blame her?' Scow asked.

Davron laughed and shook his head. 'No — Creation, what a fellowship trip she's had for her pilgrimage! Just two weeks into the Unstable, and we've had enough excitement for half a dozen trips. It's a wonder she hasn't been demanding her money back.'

Rossel raised an eyebrow. 'That bad, eh?'

'Worse,' said Meldor. 'Believe me, this news of new fixed features is the only good thing we've heard in weeks. Thanks for bringing it to us, Ross.'

'Good luck that I found you. Where do you want me next?'

'I think — I think the time has come for us all to go . . . home.'

'Home, eh? I've no quarrel with that. Tomorrow you can tell me why you look so glum about it, but right now, if you fellows will excuse me, I'm for bed as well — I'm whacked. I've had a horse under me so long today I can't get my knees together.' He deposited some coins on the table and headed for the stairs.

Scow signalled the waitress for another drink and glanced across to where the haltkeeper still sat. 'What do you think Pickle told Keris?' he asked Meldor.

'The details of what happened to Piers, I suppose.'

Scow nodded thoughtfully. 'Maybe that's all she ever

came here for. Maybe she doesn't know about the maps. Maybe they've all gone, if ever the Mantis brought them here to start with.'

Davron's face hardened. 'Of course he did. Cissi Wood-rug believed they were here. She questioned the Mantis, who put her on to Piers because he'd already sold them to the mapmaker. It's logical, isn't it? The Mantis knew we were hard on his heels. Maybe he even knew the Unmaker had got a whiff of the maps' existence and wanted to destroy them. He meets a mapmaker and he knows a mapmaker would pay the earth for a trompleri map —'

'But neither he nor the mapmaker have them when Cissi the Minion looks,' said Meldor.

Davron gave a low laugh. 'Maker, she must have been furious when she realised she'd been a shade too hasty in killing the only two men who might know where they were.'

'If only we'd waited longer,' Scow said, 'instead of assuming that the Mantis was still ahead of us —'

'None of that,' Meldor said. 'We did what we thought was best at the time. We weren't to know we'd missed him. The point is that the maps were probably passed to Piers, and Piers hid them somewhere, somewhere here.'

'And left some sort of message among his things that told his daughter about them,' Scow suggested, 'else why is she here, and how did she know the name Kereven?'

'It's possible,' Meldor agreed. 'I think the time has come for us to talk to Keris Kaylen.'

'Talk?' Davron asked, with a grim laugh. 'She won't tell you a thing! Use ley, Meldor. Force her.'

'Davron, Davron, there are better ways. She's a —'

'She's a foolish child trying to ride a horse that's too big for her — out of greed, I imagine. Probably thinks she can make a fortune out of the map. Doesn't she realise her father died because of it? Or maybe she doesn't care.' He drained his mug and stood up. 'I'll be in my room if you want me.'

Meldor gave the faintest of smiles as Davron disappeared

upstairs. 'Do you think, Sammy, that just possibly our friend has found Kaylen a shade more attractive than he wanted to?'

'And *that's* why he's acting like a mule with a headache lately?' Scow was astonished. 'She's not much to look at. Ley-life, Meldor, why would he hanker after a mouse when he married a woman like Allys of Tower? Allys is as beautiful as a summer's day is long!'

'A mouse? Is that how you see Keris Kaylen, Sammy?'

Scow swilled the last of his brew around in the bottom of his mug. 'Well, not quite. Her teeth are too sharp for a mouse, perhaps.'

'Go on.'

They both knew that they did not speak of Keris's looks. 'She *is* young, but hardly a child. A woman who hasn't yet been touched, let's say. Wants very much to be strong and has many elements of a rebel, yet lacks the real strength of a true dissident — yet. At the moment she's . . . a mixture, I think. Very capable in many ways, but unsure of herself. Scared of the Unstable, but refusing to show it. Swings between being confident and feeling insecure, between being excited by adventure and being terrified of it, between knowing what she wants — and not knowing at all.' He grinned and his tongue lolled out. 'Pretty much as we were at that age, I suppose, and nothing that that age won't cure, one way or another.'

'I think perhaps you do her an injustice. Most of us weren't like that, not at her age. She's lived all her life under the Rule, but it has chafed, and she's angry. She's already been questioning — *we* didn't question until we'd lived without the Rule, until we'd seen other ways, heard other ideas. She's special, Sammy.'

Scow nodded thoughtfully. 'You think she's already questioning Chantry? She still spends most of her time with the chantor.'

'And who else is she going to spend it with? Corrian? Graval? I don't think she's too enamoured of Chantry. If

196

Portron was the usual sort of rule-chantor I don't think she would have spent five minutes in his company. Portron just had the good sense to see that preaching to her wouldn't gain him anything. He may be a true believer, but he hates contention, religious or otherwise. At the first sign of disagreement or unpleasantness he backs away.'

Scow smiled. 'Yes, I've noticed.'

'I think I shall have a word with our host over there. If my senses tell me correctly, he's still there — and half awash, I'd say.'

Scow looked across to Pickle. 'Definitely half sunk. Potent stuff, this brew of his.'

Pickle looked up as Meldor came across to his table and his green face sagged a little deeper into depression. 'Damn it all, Margraf,' he said, 'have you any idea of how hard it's becoming to get staff around here? Anyone with any ambition or nous finds out about Havenstar, and the next thing I know they're off. And it's all your fault!'

Up in her room, Keris was going through her things, sorting out clothes to be washed or repaired, and generally looking through her gear to see what needed attention. It was late but she was too frightened to think of going to bed yet. Her head was bursting with the one thought: Piers had been killed for the map which she now had in her baggage. He — one of the most competent of all Unstablers — had been killed right in this very building, surrounded by Defenders and canny Untouchables like Pickle. Killed by a Minion and her Pet. *For a map.*

Now she did not know what to do. Hide the map somewhere? Destroy it? Keep it and assume that the Unmaker's Minions had no way of finding out she had it? It's very presence terrified her. She even wondered if the Unmaker had tried to subvert her for some reason connected with it — or whether she had been just a random choice.

She had no answer — and no one to ask.

She emptied out her quiver on to the bed so that she could

check over her arrows, and a pile of sand came with them. 'Darn,' she muttered. Where in the name of Creation had that come from? She must have laid the quiver down on the ground at one stage, and accidentally scooped up some sand into it. She took up a pinch and put it in the palm of her hand. She fingered it, thinking that it looked very much like a powdered form of the soluble iron salts she used as a basis for her inks. She was running short of it, so instead of throwing it away she poured it into one of her empty paint pots instead.

She was stowing the pot away with her mapping things when someone knocked at her door. *He opened the door to 'em: the Mantis, her father —*

'Who is it?' she asked, her voice several tones higher than normal.

'Meldor. I'd very much like to talk to you.'

'Do I have any choice?'

He chuckled. 'Only about the time. It can wait until tomorrow if you are tired.'

She opened the door. 'And then spend all night worrying about what it is you're going to order me to do this time?' she asked. 'No thanks.' She did not know whether she was relieved or dismayed to see that he had brought both Davron and Scow with him.

'A drink?' Scow asked and showed her a wine skin and several of Pickle's pewter mugs. 'This is good Eighth Stab red, not Pickle's gut-wrenching brew.'

Keris had never drunk alcohol in her life, but it suddenly seemed a good time to start. 'Thank you.' She waved a hand towards her bed. 'The accommodation is somewhat cramped, but take a seat.'

Scow poured a mug and handed it over. She sipped tentatively, uncertain whether she actually liked it.

'We want to know why you chose to come here, to Pickle's Halt,' Meldor said, sitting down. Davron settled next to him; Scow joined Keris on the floor, back to the wall.

'I would have thought that was perfectly obvious,' Keris said.

'Don't be ridiculous,' Davron said. 'You didn't come here just because your father died here –'

Meldor frowned at him and interrupted. 'Keris, we believe your father was given some items that belonged to us just before he died. We want them back.'

'You were looking for my father before he even arrived here,' she accused.

'Not exactly. We were looking for the Unbound who also died here that night: the Mantis. Look, let me begin at the beginning.' He accepted a mug of wine from Scow, and said, 'We had a friend. A man named Kereven Deverli, a young mapmaker. He was a very talented young man, brilliant. Better, perhaps, than your father even. He did not make standard maps for pilgrims though; he was more interested in – well, in trompleri maps.

'I assume you know what they are?'

She gave a curt nod.

'He believed that the best way to make the Unstable safe for pilgrims was to rediscover trompleri techniques. Davron and I know more about ley than any man alive, and he came to us because he thought we might be able to help him. Well, we did help him: we found him a place to stay, we paid him – and he promised to let us know if he uncovered the secret of the technique. And he did, apparently. He made a number of trompleri maps. He sent word to us, but unfortunately, before we arrived to see what he had done, the Unmaker discovered what he was doing and sent a tainted traitor to kill him and destroy all the maps.

'It seems, though, that some maps survived. How many we don't know. It could have been just one. Anyway, it – or they – were spirited away by Deverli's assistant, the Mantis.'

Keris listened without comment, sipping her drink. She tried to sense whether he spoke the truth, but could make no judgement. How much eyes normally betray a speaker, she thought. But with a blind man there is no expression there to tell the listener anything.

'If the Mantis had then brought the maps to us, he might still be alive,' Meldor continued. 'Unhappily, he tried to sell them. We heard about that, and Minions got to hear of it as well. They reported back to Carasma, who sent Cissi Woodrug after him. He fled as far and as fast as he could. We came after him as well, but somehow missed him. We thought he might be heading for Piers, believing that a mapmaker would buy such maps, so we headed for the First after leaving here. Davron went to Kibbleberry, as you know, but Piers was not there. By then, in fact, he was dead. When we found out that, we all came back here, but could find nothing. We were prepared to think that the maps had been irretrievably lost – and decided to return home. Then, when we were gathering together a fellowship in Hopen Grat, you turned up.

'And we began to wonder just what was bringing you to Pickle's Halt.'

'And came to the conclusion it was the maps,' Davron added.

Keris looked from one to the other and shook her head in wonderment. 'Let us for a moment suppose that were true,' she said, 'and I certainly don't admit that it is, what in Creation's ordering makes you think that I would voluntarily tell you about where the map – maps – could be found, or what happened to them, or indeed hand them over to someone who is bonded to the Unmaker? You're all out of your tainted little minds!'

'We had nothing to do with your father's death,' Meldor said. 'In fact, that was the last thing we wanted. With Deverli dead, we need another skilled mapmaker to try again to find the secret of trompleri maps. We had hoped to have the maps to show Piers, and then to ask him to discover their secret.'

Scow leant over and refilled Keris's mug. She said, 'And if he had, do you think he would have told you, just like that?

My father was a very moral man. He would never have helped anyone who had dealings with the Unmaker.'

'Oh, damn it all,' Davron snapped at her, 'we want the secret so that we can defeat the Unmaker, not help him!'

'*Defeat* the Unmaker? Defeat *Carasma*?' Keris stared at him. 'Who do you think you are? The Maker?'

Scow stifled a laugh. Davron threw up his hands in frustration.

And someone screamed, loudly.

They all turned their heads to listen. The screaming – several voices now – grew louder and more frantic. Keris's heart lurched painfully.

'Downstairs, in the common room,' Meldor said as they jumped up. There was a moment of confused congestion as they all tried to leave the room at once, then Davron shot out, closely followed by the others. Keris – having paused to snatch up her knife – was last.

The screaming may have come mostly from the common room, but the cause of the panic was in the entrance hallway, where Portron had been holding his kinesis meeting, and they came upon it the moment they turned the corner on the stairs. They halted as one.

Portron was lying on the floor, propping himself up groggily on one elbow. His bald patch was streaming with blood. Pickle was in the doorway to the common room, blocking it with his bulk. Graval was at the front door of the Halt, trying to lift the beam that was the bar to the door. He could not budge it: it would have taken Pickle to raise it, or perhaps several ordinary men.

There was something very strange about Graval. He seemed to be in great pain. His face was contorted. He kept on releasing the bar to grab at himself, to slap at his clothing and his skin as if he wanted to put out sparks of fire that had showered him. Yet there was nothing visible there.

Pickle took a step towards him, but Graval gestured with a hand and a band of colour distorted the air between the two men. The haltkeeper staggered back as if he had been punched.

It was not entirely Graval's problems that had caused the screaming. The hysteria of several of the halt's staff and guests was prompted by fear of whatever it was that was throwing itself against the door trying to break it down from the outside.

It had to be huge. The thick slab door was juddering, *bending* under the blows. The hinges — massive chunks of iron — showed signs of stress. The bar itself seemed to be holding, but the brackets that kept it in place had already cracked. In between blows, the sound of splintering wood was audible to them all; it seemed that the creature was not only trying to break the door down, but was also clawing the wood, *shredding* it from the outside.

Scow stared. *'Chaosblast.'*

Graval shook an agitated finger at Portron. 'You did this!' he screeched. 'You with your endless kinesis! Oh, Lord help me! I cannot stand it —' He turned back to the door, throwing his whole weight under the bar in one last desperate attempt to raise it. 'Pet, Pet, come Pet . . . help me . . .'

The creature outside the door redoubled its onslaught.

Pickle turned to Davron in outrage. 'You! You brought that creature here. Into *my* halt! Another Minion, here, in my house —'

But none of them needed Pickle's anguished accusation to the guide to know what Graval was, and what he was doing. He was calling his Pet to break down the door.

Keris was ice cold. She had stopped several steps higher up the stairs than Davron and Meldor. She made her decision and acted all in one fluid second that seemed to stretch for ever, and knew even as she threw her knife that she was going to kill a man.

Chapter Fourteen

And the Minions of Carasma gladly do his bidding in the world he cannot reach, for he is tied to the ley whence he draws his power. And therein, poor pilgrim, lie both your despair and your hope. Remember with hope that the power of the Unmaker is finite; remember with despair that the Minion and his Pet are the monsters of Chaos that will dog your footsteps on their master's bidding.

Pilgrims XX: 32: 6

Graval remained standing for a moment, almost as if he had been transfixed against the massive slabs of the door by the knives that protruded from his throat.

Keris stared, uncomprehending. Knives. Two of them. Side by side. Only one of them was hers.

Graval was not pinned to the door — it was an illusion; he slowly slid down to his knees and then toppled, already dead. There was an initial fountain of blood as the knives dislodged, then the flow thickened on his clothes, on the floor: hot raspberry jam clotting in the pot, blood gelling on the flagstones.

The hammering at the door was frenzied.

Keris felt her own knees going. She lowered her eyes to Davron, to find that he had turned to look up at her. His face was expressionless. 'Not bad for someone who said they can't be accurate with a knife throw,' he said. The words seemed neutral, bland. Ridiculous. They had just killed someone . . .

He did not wait for a reply but grabbed her by the arm and hauled her up the stairs. 'Get your bow,' he said urgently. 'That Pet might not give up just because its master's dead.' At the head of the stairs he peeled off in the direction of his room; she ran for her own, propelled half by his parting push, half by her own fear. Her hands were shaking as she gathered up quiver and bowstave, as she fumbled to string the bow. They came down the stairs together, already fitting arrows to the string, suddenly comrades, linked by death, by the knowledge that they could soon be fighting for their lives.

It had taken a great bite out of his neck and drunk his blood –

There was now a semicircle of Defenders gathered around the door, pikes at the ready. Some of them had been maudlin with liquor a few minutes earlier, others asleep, but they all looked alert enough now, white-faced perhaps, but tersely vigilant. The pounding on the door shattered more of one of the brackets holding the bar, and the upper hinge broke with a grinding snap of metal.

Keris and Davron stayed up on the stair so that they could get a clear shot over the heads of the Defenders the moment the door burst in.

'Your knives,' Scow said solemnly and handed them back as if he was taking part in some kind of ceremonial. Keris was glad to see that they had been wiped clean and that Graval's body had been removed. Portron had also disappeared and Pickle was now armed with several wicked-looking choppers from the kitchen.

Still in a state of shock, she heard the officer in charge of the Defenders instruct his men to hold back to give the archers a chance once the door broke, and realised he was talking about her and Davron. The officer was a large blond man with a precise way of speaking and an accent that was so aristocratic it was almost a parody, but he exuded an air of competent calm. He, at least, was immune from panic.

Keris shivered. There wouldn't be much time for those arrows.

Davron glanced at Meldor. 'Ley?' he asked quietly.

More of the bracket for the bar splintered. Pickle was trying to reinforce it with a plank of wood torn from a bench. Meldor stood tall and calm. 'Not here, last resort only.'

'More *light*,' Pickle was roaring to his staff, 'we need more *light*!' There were wall candles in the hallway, but no lamps.

And then there was a final crack, sharp and explosive. The door was hurled inward, knocking several of the Defenders to the floor. There was a howl of wind — a blast of air — and then there was no light at all except what came from the common room. Both Keris and Davron let loose an arrow, but in the sudden dimness neither risked a second shot for fear of hitting the Defenders.

There was a stifled silence — a silence of suppressed breathing, of halted movement, of burgeoning fear. Keris had an impression of a vast shape outside the door, something lumpish and dark.

Someone moaned, a soft sound of undiluted terror. Darkness filled the doorway, blocking out the night. A smell of musk, wet fur and stale urine stung Keris's throat with acid potency.

Then the darkness lurched and vanished.

'It's *gone*!' someone said, incredulous.

A servant brought a lamp, the doorway was illuminated — and there was nothing there. The Defenders cautiously edged their way out into the yard and Davron and Scow went with them. Pickle began dispensing orders in a bellowing roar, calling for hammer and nails, that lumber down in the cellar and be quick about it, and how about some action from you lazy lot of tainted layabouts?

Servants scurried this way and that while Keris sank down on to the stair and leant her head against the rough wood banister. Her eyes were on the gouge marks across the front of the door: the slabs were furrowed from side to side to a finger-width depth and the edges of the scoring were charred. A smell of burnt wood lingered on, together with the more unpleasant stench of the Pet.

Someone sat down beside her and she looked to see the Chameleon. 'Bit of an anticlimax, eh?' he said.

'Where were you? I didn't see you,' she said.

'Oh, I sort of faded out into the woodwork,' he replied cheerfully. 'I'm getting very good at that sort of thing. I don't suppose it would have helped me one whit against whatever that thing was, but I felt loads safer.'

She gave a reluctant smile. 'Ley-life, Quirk – what *happened*? Graval –'

'He sort of went mad, I think. He'd been out in the yard all evening, and then Master Pickle told him he'd have to come in because it was time to bar the door, so he did. Chantor Portron was still performing kineses. Graval went into the common room and had a drink. He sat all huddled up like it was cold. He was rubbing his arms and wiggling around in his seat, then he – well, he sort of went berserk. Dashed out and struck Portron down, cursing him. Next he laid about with a chair, scattering all those who had been performing kinesis. Then that thing came to the door, and Graval was trying to get out to it – or to let it in, or something . . .' He hesitated, powerless to stop his shiver at the memory. 'You know the rest.'

Meldor, who was still standing on the stair in an attitude of relaxed interest, said, 'There was too much stability here for him. Portron's kineses must have been the last straw.'

'You knew he was a Minion?' Keris asked and did not try to hide the note of accusation that crept into her voice.

'Indeed no. Although I should have wondered. All that clumsiness. It was to make us wary of him, so no one wanted to come near. If any of us ley-lit had touched him, we'd have known. We'd have felt his corruption, his perverted ley. And that lack of control over his horse – the poor beast must have sensed his true nature, and been in a panic the whole time.'

'But why did he join a fellowship in the first place?'

'To spy: why else? Keris, how else does the Unmaker know what is going on in the Unstable if his Minions don't tell him?'

'I thought — I thought he was sort of like the Maker. All-seeing —'

He smiled a little. 'Blasphemy, Keris. Better not let Portron hear you speak of any such resemblance!'

'But — but he knew things — about me. How could he have known such things? He knew how I felt, what I wanted most . . .'

'Yes. Face to face in the ley, he can read any of us like a book.'

'He knew my mother was alive still.'

'No — but he might have known she was not yet dead.'

'There's a distinction?'

'Chantry believes that all souls must pass the way of the Unmaker first, before being made at one with That Which Is Created. Carasma weeds out those on which he has a claim. He would know that your mother had not yet passed his way. But, other than that, his powers outside ley lines are limited. He controls indirectly, through his Minions and their Pets and his paid servants. They are his eyes and ears. This is the first time, though, that I have heard of him placing a Minion in a fellowship — an indication of how important at least one of us is to him. It is not easy to find a Minion who can withstand a stab — even a sinkhole like Hopen Grat — for long enough to deceive a guide and join a fellowship. Graval was a very special man. I could admire him, if he had not chosen the wrong path for his talents.'

Keris clamped her lips into a thin line, trying not to remember the sound of a blade thudding into throat tissue.

Davron re-entered the hallway. He was holding a dead hen in his hand, one of Pickle's layers. Its neck had been cut open, but not quite severed.

'Any sign of — of whatever it was?' Keris asked him, but her eyes were on the blood-drenched bird.

'It left a trail of ichor. I think both our arrows are still in it. We followed the trail to the stockade fence, but no further. None of us had the stomach for going any further, not tonight. I don't think it will trouble us again.'

'Nor at all, I imagine,' Meldor said calmly. 'Not wounded and with its master dead. Why the – er – chicken, Davron?'

The Chameleon and Keris exchanged glances. Useless to wonder just how Meldor knew the guide was carrying anything at all.

'Touch it,' Davron suggested, and held it out.

Meldor reached out and rested his fingers on the feathers of the bird's back for a moment. 'Ah. A worship sacrifice. It has been dead for several hours, I think.'

'A what?' the Chameleon asked.

Keris tried to look at Quirk. His voice seemed to come out of nowhere; in the dim light of the hall, he kept fading away into the background, indistinguishable from the treads of the stairs and the hand-hewn walls of the halt where the bark still clung to the planks in leprous patches.

Meldor wiped his hands on his kerchief. 'The only way for a Minion to contact his lord while not in a ley line is for him to perform a rather nasty ritual of worship that must involve a slow death by bleeding. I'm surprised Graval was content with a hen; bigger prey offer a stronger contact. We are lucky he didn't decide to use one of our horses – or even a man.'

'Reasons of stealth, I imagine,' Davron said. 'He wasn't intending to go mad and be killed. He wanted to continue his spying on us.' Pickle appeared in the doorway and Davron handed the chicken to him. 'You may as well cook it.'

'One of my best layers,' Pickle said morosely. 'Do you know how hard it is to keep a chicken untainted in this place?'

'From now on, Pick,' Davron said, carefully avoiding looking Keris's way as he spoke, 'I want you to tell every single guide that comes through here that they had better check their fellowships for the presence of Minions from now on, *before* they leave the stabs. Suggest they ask their fellowship to strip to the waist – all Minions carry the chain and sigils of Carasma.'

'Oh, the women in the fellowships will love that,' said Quirk. 'Are you going to ask *Corrian* to take off her clothes tomorrow, Master Davron?'

Davron winced at the thought and Pickle laughed. 'Somehow I think enough people have checked Corrian out without Davron having to resort to that,' he said.

'Let's go to bed,' said Meldor. He suddenly seemed saddened, and the touch of distress aged him.

They climbed the stairs together, in silence, Meldor and the Chameleon ahead, Davron and Keris behind. There were a few scattered goodnights at the top and they went off into their respective rooms. Or so Keris thought, until she stepped into her room and realised that Davron was right behind her. She could not help flinching away.

If he saw her reaction, he ignored it. 'We left our wine,' he said by way of explanation. He picked up the wine skin, and her mug. He topped it up from the skin and handed it to her. 'Drink this,' he said. 'You have need of it.'

She took the mug with fingers that felt weak.

He filled his own mug. 'Keris,' he said gently, 'don't lose any sleep over it. You did the right thing at the right time, and there are a number of people who can be grateful to you – to us – tonight.'

She blinked, wondering at his understanding, staggered that – of all of them – he was the only one to know how she felt. To know how scarified she had been by the sight of her knife in a man's throat, the blood gushing, the light snuffed out, the life gone . . .

'I remember,' he said, and he had quelled the harshness in his voice, 'what it was like the very first time.' He spoke almost absently as if he had forgotten she was there, and she knew he was looking beyond her, into some place in the past which was outside her knowledge, yet now within her understanding. 'I was out on one of my first patrols with the Defenders. I was just a kid, but then – so was he. He was an Unbred who had somehow escaped the rulechantors. He'd had fourteen years or so of life in the

209

stability, life that he should never have had at all — but that didn't make his death any easier for me.'

'He was deformed?' she asked.

He nodded. 'A crippled arm and leg at birth. Hidden by his parents on their farm — until the Rule Office found out about him. He was a bit too old for them to smother by then, but still an affront to their ordered souls. They were surprisingly magnanimous — they commanded us to take the lad and abandon him out in the Unstable. He didn't want to go, naturally enough. We talked, and I felt sorry for him. Then he jumped me on guard duty one night. I didn't mean to kill him — but that's what ended up happening. Considering his disability, he was surprisingly strong.' He paused, sipping his wine absent-mindedly and Keris allowed the silence to continue. 'I assume that he wanted to die rather than face exclusion,' he said at last. He looked at Keris then, and she saw to her surprise that he had tears in his eyes. 'It was a long time ago . . . but I can't forget. He may have wanted to die, but I lost something that night: I never felt young again. The first time . . . is difficult. And perhaps, even worse than that, is the fact that it gets easier . . . It shouldn't. Killing someone should *never* be easy.'

She nodded, unable to trust herself to speak.

'Keris, Graval, at least, had forfeited his right to life. Don't let it touch you too much. *He* wasn't worth it.' He waved his wine skin at her still untouched glass. 'I'm — I'm sorry you've had such a bad journey on your first trip into the Unstable. It happens that way sometimes. Anyway, drink your wine and go to bed.'

She nodded. 'Thank you,' she whispered, '. . . Davron.' No title, just his name.

He went to the door and stood there, looking at her, sharing his pain, understanding her own. And then he was gone.

She closed the door and picked up Piers's staff. She hugged it to her, missing her father, wanting her mother. Wanting Davron. By all Creation's ordering, what sort of man was this Davron the guide? What kind of a man was it who could ride the Unstable with all the stolidity of a donkey pulling a millstone around in an endless circle, knowing what was in his future? What kind of man could hold on to his sanity knowing that one day he would do the Unmaker's bidding – yet who could be sensitive enough to know how she had felt at Graval's death?

Keris drank the wine as if it was water and wished she had more.

She dreamt of Davron that night. It was a dream disturbing enough to wake her, and it left her filled with uncomfortable feelings she could not pin down and with the odd sensation that her skin was too small for her body. Her insides seemed compressed, spiralled too tight, in need of release. Even her nipples swelled against her nightdress.

She rolled over, flat on to her back. She knew what it was she felt – she had Sheyli's frankness to thank for that – but she did not welcome the sensations, not when they came accompanied by dreams of Davron Storre. Sheyli might have been explicitly frank when she spoke of the physical manifestations of desire, but no one had ever explained to her how it was possible to want a man who had done something as despicable as give his promise of servitude to the Unmaker. A man who may one day have to kill her, if that was what he was ordered to do. She shivered and waited for the dawn.

Keris was late into the common room for breakfast. She had not slept well and both her body and mind felt leaden. She was glad of the strong brew of char that the waitress served up, but was less attracted by the griddle cakes and honey that came with it. And still less happy when she overheard snatches of conversation from the group at a nearby table. There were several tainted men sitting there: one who had a mouse-like head; one with fangs and slit-eyes, and a third with a face so flat that the nostrils were only holes without a nose. 'I tell you,' the mouse was saying, 'there are dragons. Or something similar. Flying creatures that eat chantists and let the tainted pass.'

'No, Havenstar can't be like that,' the fanged man protested. 'My friend has been there. He wouldn't say much, but he did say –'

Keris missed the next bit, and heard only the flat-faced man laugh and observe that he rather preferred the idea of dragons that ate chantists.

The next few words that she heard clearly came from the mouse: '– not making it up. It was possible to fly in their embrace. Imagine that – fly!'

She lost the rest of the conversation, because Meldor made his way unerringly across the room towards her and slipped into the empty chair at her table.

'Greetings,' he said. 'I'm glad to find you: we never did get to finish our conversation about maps yesterday.'

'I have nothing to add to what was said,' she replied, raising her voice a little to be heard over a volley of hammering that came from outside. Pickle's employees had evidently been set to reinforcing the halt's defences. 'Meldor, are you a Trician too?'

There was a momentary pause before he asked, 'Too?'

'Davron told me last night that he was once a Defender, and that means Trician to me.'

'Ah. Yes, *he* was, once. He forfeited that right when he became an Unstabler, of course. Before that, he belonged to a minor domain house of the Fourth Stab. He was Davron of Storre then. Nobody of any particular importance in the Trician hierarchy.'

'And you?' she persisted.

He shook his head. 'What makes you think I'm Trician?'

She shrugged. 'A certain . . . assurance. A quality of leadership. An unconscious assumption you seem to make that you will be obeyed. And your accent.'

'No. Those things – if I have them – didn't come from a Trician background. I was born, as far as I know, the son of a wheelwright somewhere or other. I never knew either of my parents, and was never even told which Stab they were from. I was a third son and as a consequence I was given

212

over to Chantry immediately after birth. As you doubtless know, too big a family is considered inimical to Order.'

She nodded. Everyone tried to limit family size, using one method or another, but accidents happened often enough and Rule-chantors were ruthless in ferreting out additions to families that had already reached optimum numbers. She made a gesture of distress, remembering Aurin.

'A wheelwright has need of only one son to maintain the business,' he continued, 'whereas Chantry can never have too many chantors. Especially since so many lose their lives serving fellowships during crossings.' His voice was toneless; she could not tell what his feelings were. 'I was wet-nursed by a chantora breeder in Dene. That's in the Seventh. Later I was sent for Chantry training in Salient.'

She almost dropped her cup. 'You were a *chantor*?'

'Is that so hard to believe?'

'Yes. Somehow it is.' She had thought him too much an individual, too independent, to have ever submitted to the regimen of a religious life.

'I was not given any choice in the matter at the time. Now of course I have no ties to Chantry. They cast me off when I lost my sight, you see. Blindness is also inimical to Order.' He sounded amused rather than bitter. 'I was excluded from all stabilities, thrust out into the Unstable after fifty years of service to Chantry. Strange — they never do that to the deaf; only to the blind. I sometimes wonder if that's because a lot more of the elderly, Hedrin-chantors included, go deaf rather than go blind. But perhaps I'm just a cynic. However, there's nothing like being on the receiving end of injustice for awakening one to the reality of the Rule's innate iniquities. I became an unbeliever overnight.' The thread of amusement was still there, as if he was laughing at the man he had once been.

'You no longer worship the Maker?' she asked, and wondered if he had turned to the Unmaker instead.

'On the contrary, I worship him every day of my life. It is Chantry I no longer believe in. Chantry and the Rule.

Not to mention the idiocy of kinesis. But this is not what I came to talk to you about –'

'Still trying to pry information out of her, I see.' Davron, appearing at Keris's elbow, laid an arrow on the table in front of her plate and Scow drew up two chairs for them to sit down. Both men were dressed in riding clothes.

Keris picked up the arrow and turned it over in her hands. 'This is mine.'

'That's right,' Davron said. 'You left it lying around in the chest of a rather nasty animal last night.'

'You *went after* that thing?'

'Scow and I, yes. This morning. Found it dead a mile or so into the Roughs. He was already being disintegrated by the Unstable, but we did manage to salvage the arrows. Mine finally did the trick, I fancy. I got him in the eye; more luck than skill, I'm afraid. Yours was lodged in his chestplate, which helped to weaken him. Dangerous shot to make, that, though, Keris; Pets are often reinforced there – with fur, scales, thickened skin or whatever. Better to go for the throat, or the underarm or the groin.' He gave a sudden grin. 'As I was *trying* to do.'

A waitress came by and dumped some mugs of char and a plateful of food in front of them. Davron helped himself and passed the plate to Scow. 'And now, Keris, it's reckoning time. About the maps –'

'I didn't come to Pickle's Halt to find a trompleri map,' she said carefully. 'If you'll think back, you'll know I wasn't intending to come here at all at first. I was booked to travel to the Second.'

Meldor gave Davron an enquiring glance and the guide nodded, remembering. 'What made you change your mind?' he asked.

'My brother. He came to Hopen Grat looking for me. You were leaving that morning; the guide to the Second wasn't going for a day or two.'

'You were running away from your brother? Why?' Meldor asked.

'Because I didn't want to be branded as a thief.'

'Ah,' he said in sudden comprehension. 'The crossings-horses. Of course.'

'And a few other things. My dowry money. Mapping equipment, camping equipment. It is all legally my brother's. He wasn't going to use them; he didn't want to be a mapmaker. I did. He was going to bribe the local Rule Office so that he could become a tavernkeeper. He wanted me to marry a friend of his. So I ran away from home — I knew I could never be a mapmaker of course, but I wanted to go to my uncle in Salient in the Second. When Thirl, my brother, came after me, I decided to go with you instead. I wanted to speak to Pickle about my father's death anyway, but most of all I needed a quick passage out of Hopen Grat. I intend going to the Second Stab now.'

Davron settled back in his chair with a sigh. 'So much for all our hopes. The trompleri maps really are gone, lost . . .'

'And so is our only hope to find a mapmaker who might have been able to duplicate Deverli's work,' Meldor added. 'There's no one in any of the Stabs who has Piers's imagination —'

'Imagination?' Keris asked without thinking. 'My father was a practical man, not an imaginative one.'

'Not imaginative?' Davron raised a disbelieving eyebrow. 'Of course he was! Why, you have only to look at his maps.'

Suddenly Keris was tired of hiding her talents, and she could not even be bothered to think through the implications of her confession. She said acidly, 'My father was a rank traditionalist when it comes to mapmaking. Mind you, he was probably one of the best surveyors who ever lived and the accuracy of his maps is phenomenal — but he would never have altered the format one brushstroke from his father's and his grandfather's day if it had been left up to him.'

They all stared at her. It was Davron who broke the silence. He gave a low chuckle of appreciation. 'It was *you*,' he said. 'You've been drawing all Piers's maps for the past five years! All the coloured ones were yours. All the revolutionary changes in style and presentation – they were yours.'

Keris nodded and stood up. 'Thank you for returning my arrow, Master Davron. I'm sorry I'm not able to help you with regard to the map. Now, if you'll excuse me, I have things to do.'

Scow and Meldor exchanged bemused looks as she made her way to the hall stairs. 'I'll be damned,' said Meldor. 'Can that be true?'

'Oh, yes,' said Davron. 'I knew Piers and now I know her – oh, yes.' An amused smile played around the corner of his lips. 'The maid's a devil, Margraf.'

Meldor looked annoyed, but the annoyance was with himself. 'I underestimated her – and I was the one who said she was special. Careless, careless.'

'Now what?' Scow asked.

'That's obvious,' Meldor said. 'We persuade her to come with us. We need an innovative mapmaker of talent, and, if she made those Kaylen maps, she's the person.'

'And just how are you going to do that?' Davron asked mildly. 'She trusts me about as much as a minnow trusts a pike, and you not much more. What bait can you possibly use that will persuade her to travel in the company of a man who could well turn around and kill her any time? Or are you going to coerce her with ley? It would be a big mistake.'

'You were the one who advised it before.'

'Only so that we got to hear the truth. But for mapmaking we would need her cooperation. Coercion would not achieve that.'

'No,' Meldor agreed, 'and I would never consider it. There are other ways.'

'Just don't tell her the truth about Havenstar,' Davron warned. 'That won't persuade her to do anything except run for the nearest Rule-chantor. She wasn't happy with our using ley to free Sam from the bilee. She'd be appalled if she knew what we were really doing with it.'

'I think I know exactly what to use for bait,' Meldor said slowly. 'And I'll be very surprised if she doesn't find it tasty.'

Chapter Fifteen

If a dog barks at a mountain, does the mountain suffer?

saying of the old Margravate of Malinawar

Chantor Portron regarded Keris anxiously. 'So Master Pickle has arranged for you to go to the Second? But no fellowships go that way from here, surely?' The chantor had found Keris out in the stables grooming her horses, and now he dodged around after her keeping up a flow of conversation as she attended to Ygraine.

'No, but traders apparently do. They come from the Third, stop by the halt to make deliveries, then pass on to the Second. Master Grossbik and his wife make that particular crossing all the time. I'll be safe with them. And they are willing to take a couple of maps as payment. Don't worry about me, Chantor. I'll be fine. How's your head, by the way?'

'Ah, a wee bit of a headache, that's all. I hit the wall when Graval pushed me, but it's fine now. Master Davron's fellowship is off tomorrow too, I'm thinking.' He hesitated, as if he had reservations about that, but then added, 'I'll not be sorry to be leaving this place. I'm anxious to be reaching the Eighth as soon as possible, and all in one piece, too.'

She smiled. 'After a journey like this one has been, you'll be needing that retreat once you get there.'

'Well, to be honest, it's not really a religious retreat I'm on, lass. I'm after fathering a babe for Chantry. Looking forward to it, I am at that. My second. Bit worrying though, for a man of my age: it's a long time since I had experience with — er — well . . . But I shouldn't be saying that to a maid! Me and my tongue.'

She straightened up, forgetting the grooming. 'You're after doing *what*?'

He blushed slightly and went on the defensive. 'All on Chantry's business, lass. When numbers are down, 'tis the duty of selected chantoras to bring another babe to Chantry and I've been chosen to father one such. The mother-to-be is a rule-chantora of my order. 'Tis an honour much appreciated among us chantors.'

Shock jerked a sharp reply from her. 'I'll bet it is!' He looked hurt by her blunt cynicism, but she went on relentlessly. 'So that's what Meldor meant when he referred to a breeding chantora! This is not a holy practice that is much discussed with the uncoloured public, is it? I've never heard of such — although I've heard much made of the chastity and celibacy of Chantry men and women. Tell me, on what grounds were you chosen? Do you know the chantora concerned?'

He looked horrified. 'Of course not! This is not a matter of — of personalities, Keris. Or desire. Or choice. 'Tis our duty, and the selection of the pair is a matter for Hedrin-chantors to decide.'

'It is to be hoped your chantora also thinks it an honour,' she said drily.

'Well, of course she does! She is to be allowed to bear a child, a privilege that all women must be coveting, surely.'

She stared, both fascinated and repulsed. 'And the — er — logistics of this liaison?'

He looked increasingly uncomfortable, aware that he had somehow lost control of the conversation. 'Logistics? Ah well. I stay in the chanterie until such time as — er — the chantora has evidence that she is . . . increasing.'

'And then?'

'Why, then, I will be returning to my Rule Office, and she to her duties. The child, when it is born, will be taken to another chanterie, to be raised there by others under a name not known to us, of course. The chantora may well become a wet nurse for some years, to other chantora infants, or to those taken from their overproductive mothers and given to Chantry.'

'Not given,' she said involuntarily. 'Not given. Taken. Wrenched from their homes and true families —'

'Keris, Keris,' he said reproachfully. 'It's the Rule. Why, think what would happen if the population of the stabs was allowed to grow freely — how could people be fed? Housed? We *have* to exercise control, for the greater good of everyone.'

'Control?' she asked bitterly. 'It seems your idea of control is to breed yourselves, at the same time as preventing others from doing so — or taking away the offspring they do have! Is that just?'

'It's just a question of regulation,' he protested. 'Of keeping numbers right. Chantry has to be obtaining its chantors from somewhere, and the younger they come to the service of the Maker the better. At the same time, Order must be observed, and large unruly families are threatening Order, you know that. There is no place in the father's trade for surplus sons, for example, and no marriage opportunities for the surplus girls — it just wouldn't do, you know.'

'No,' she said. 'No, it wouldn't, would it?' She took a deep breath, aware that she was losing her composure. 'Tell me,' she said more calmly, 'why don't you allow a breeding chantora to feed her own child? Why give her someone else's instead of her own?'

'A chantora's job is not that of a mother, Keris. Nothing must come between her and her duty to Chantry. It is felt that caring for her own child would be too much of a distraction. Similarly, children brought up by strangers must surely be more dedicated to Chantry rather than to their families. Some of the greatest chantors in Chantry history have been men and women who did not know their own parents, who started life as chantry children raised within the confines of Chantry walls.'

219

Oh Maker — poor Aurin! Sheyli would have loved you so much . . . She thought of Sheyli's anguished 'There's not a day but I don't think of him —'; she thought of Meldor's 'I never knew my parents. I never even knew what stab they were from —'; she thought of Davron, ordered to abandon a crippled boy in the Unstable, one of the so-called Unbred who were ordinarily suffocated at birth because of birth defects; she thought of the young chantora waiting for a man, a paunched, balding, white-haired man she did not know, waiting for him to arrive and impregnate her.

Tyranny, she thought. The worst kind of tyranny of all — the tyranny of guilt. And of love. *If we love Creation, we must serve the Rule and bow to the tyranny of Chantry. If we don't, we commit a sin against all humankind . . .* Aloud she repeated bitterly, 'It wouldn't do at all.' She bent to Ygraine's foreleg again.

Portron, made uneasy by her tone, looked around for an excuse to leave. 'I must ask the stableboy to groom my palfrey,' he muttered, and disappeared.

Keris attacked her task with unnecessary force, ignoring Ygraine's rather startled snort.

'Keris?'

She straightened again to eye dubiously the new silhouette in the doorway. This time it was Meldor who blocked the light. 'I'm here,' she said. 'Although how in all Creation *you* know that beats me.' She sounded sour, and did not care.

He did not appear to notice her tone. 'We're leaving for the south tomorrow,' he said. 'I have a proposition for you.'

'No,' she said.

'You haven't heard it.'

'I don't need to. The answer's still no.'

'You want to be a mapmaker. I can make that dream come true. Come with us tomorrow, and you can have your own shop, your own equipment. Staff to help, if you want. Tainted assistants to take you into the Unstable. All paid for.'

She eyed him carefully. 'I seem to have heard a rather similar offer once before. The only thing was, there was a rather large and unattractive snag concealed in the deal. Something about serving the Unmaker, I seem to recall.'

'I do not serve Carasma.'

'No? Then perhaps the sediment dirtying the bottom of the glass is of other origins. Let us see: you are offering to make me a mapmaker?'

'Yes.'

'In return for . . .?'

'Your promise that you will search for a way to make trompleri maps, and that, once you have found the secret, you will share it with us.'

'And if I didn't find it?'

'I'll take the chance.'

'Why do you want trompleri so badly?'

'To defeat Carasma, why else?'

She paused in her task to look at him. Was he lying? She thought so; at least he was not telling the whole truth. She started on the stiff hairs of Ygraine's mane. 'The answer's still no.'

'You ran away rather than be forced into a marriage you didn't want. Won't the same thing happen to you at your uncle's? You will be expected to marry. The Rule demands it of you. Keris, I offer you everything you ever wanted, I know it.'

'Do I have to remind you what happened to your last mapmaker and his assistant?'

'We will protect you —'

'Ha! Can you tell me how? Once the Unmaker decides on an Unstabler's death, he's doomed, for all that Carasma can't do the deed personally. Sooner or later. Perhaps crossing a ley line. Perhaps in an attack by the Wild. Or by Minions. Yet I can't be a mapmaker by staying in a stability. If there's a secret to be found about trompleri, it'll be found right here, in the Unstable.' She threw the rug back over Ygraine and turned to Tousson, who nipped at her bad-temperedly and then deliberately stepped on her foot.

She pulled the animal's ear and it reluctantly lifted its

hoof. 'You miserable sod,' she said. 'I know you did that on purpose. The answer's still no, Meldor.' She started brushing the horse's coat. 'And – quite apart from the danger – I have a very good reason. Several good reasons. You travel with a man who's a bonded servant to the Unmaker. And you mess with ley. That's enough to make up my mind.'

'You are aware I could . . . coerce you.'

'I suppose so, but I doubt whether I'd ever find the answer to trompleri techniques if you made a slave of me.' She had no idea how closely she was echoing Scow's words earlier that day and did not comprehend the flicker of appreciation in his eyes. He stood for a while longer, listening to the sounds of her brushing, the satisfied snuffling of the horse, then he turned and walked away. She watched him go: straight-backed, undefeated by her rejection.

She leant her head against Tousson's back and stifled a desire to weep. She knew he was right: there was no way out for her. She was a woman, born to fit the mould made for her by her sex and her father's profession, born to obey the Rule because to disobey was to risk the destruction of what was left of the world. The tyranny of guilt.

You fool, Keris, she thought. You ought to go with him. The destiny he offers is better, surely, than that which awaits you in Salient. You *know* what awaits you in Salient. Boredom. Subjection to the Rule for the rest of your life. Is that what you want? The more rational side of her replied: In Davron's company, you may not make it further than the next camp down the trail.

She sighed and sat down on the feed bin in the stall. What in the name of all Creation should she do?

Keris was packing away the horse comb and brush when Davron came. She shot him a flat look and flung the horse blanket back over Tousson. 'What do you want?' she asked ungraciously.

'Meldor seems to think I might be able to persuade you to come with us.'

'He's mad. It's *because* of you I won't go. Are you insane, the pair of you? The moment I found a way of making trompleri maps – if I ever did – you would be making a worship sacrifice to tell your Lord to send his Minions down on my head.' She did not really believe what she said, but she derived a childish satisfaction from saying it nonetheless.

'I'm no spy for Carasma, let alone one of his worshippers,' he said mildly. 'Be rational, Keris. I am sure that you can see that my one hope is to destroy Carasma's power. Then he can't command me to perform this task for him. And one way to break his hold is to have trompleri maps. With people able to travel through the Unstable with a minimum of risk, there will be more and more Order here, less Chaos –'

'And, while all this is going on, Lord Carasma just calmly watches? The first thing he'd do would be to order his servants to hunt down the mapmaker – just as he did with Deverli. And, even if he didn't, you need more than trompleri maps to bring Lord Carasma to his knees. Sweet Creation, we're talking about the Unmaker! He has ruled the Unstable for a thousand years. He destroyed old Malinawar – all except a few islands of stability in this hellish sea. Perhaps he destroyed the whole of the rest of the world. I know he wiped away a whole mountain of the Impassables – who's to say he could not also wipe away everything beyond the borders of what was once the Malinawar Margravate?'

She untied Tousson and led her to the feed bin, retying her there as she added softly, 'I've read the histories: my father bought us a copy of Torgath's *Annals* when I was a child. Once there were oceans of water, and lands across them where our ships sailed; once there were whole countries to the west and south that we traded with – and what have we left of all that? What happened to all those other places? They haven't come to our rescue. Doubtless they suffer from Carasma's depredations just as we do. Perhaps they never discovered how to prevent the encroachment of Chaos; perhaps they are all dead. And yet you want me to believe

223

you have a way to bring Carasma to his knees — with a few maps? Don't make me laugh!'

She ducked under Tousson's neck and came to face him, hands on her hips. 'And that's not the only hole in this offer of yours. There are other gaps large enough for a whole ley line to flow through. Meldor says he'll set me up as a mapmaker — as if any Rule Office would tolerate a woman mapmaker in their jurisdiction. Not even a bribe of treasury proportions would buy such an aberration.' She gave him a contemptuous look. 'You must both think I'm awfully stupid.'

He was silent for a long moment. Then he shrugged. 'I'm sorry. Yes, I suppose it must seem that way. I think it was more that we expected you to take a lot on trust. We did not intend to set you up in a shop in a stab, you know. You are right: Chantry would not countenance it. We had other ideas.'

'Do you really expect me to follow you *without* a full explanation of what you are up to?'

There was another long silence. 'All I can say is that — as unlikely as it may sound — if trompleri techniques can be rediscovered, I believe there is a possibility we may free ourselves of the Unmaker. At the very least, a great many people will be saved from . . . what happened to Quirk, and what happened to Baraine.' He had half turned away, avoiding meeting her eyes. 'Yes, I'll admit it: I want this too, more than you could possibly guess, for myself. For my own wellbeing. You are . . . probably my only chance. But I would not ask you for myself, because you are right: join us and you could die. Die horribly, and die soon. I am not worth that kind of sacrifice from anyone. I neither ask it nor expect it nor desire it for myself. But I have dedicated my life — what dregs I have of a life — to bringing down Carasma. And a trompleri map could help do it.'

She stared at him. 'You want revenge!'

'Chaos above, what sort of a man do you think I am? That I would go after the Unmaker for *revenge*?'

'Then what do you want?'

'For the Unstable, for Unstablers — I want security. For myself . . .' He paused and when he finally spoke again she barely caught the words. 'I want peace.'

His expression was as bleak as a midwinter's day in Drumlin's Cess; her irritation vanished.

He went on, 'My advice to you as a friend would be to leave us. To get as far away as you can go. It would be safer — but it wouldn't be *right*, Keris. This is everyone's fight. Our stabilities are prisons and the walls are closing in on us . . . We have to fight back or one day there will be nowhere for us to live, no place for our children.'

She could not speak. She rubbed her arms for warmth and wondered why his words made her feel so cold.

He said, 'Join us, Keris. There is no reason that Carasma should suspect you to be a master mapmaker. A woman? It's unheard of! There is nothing that will make him fear you —'

She gave a dry laugh, trying to dispel the coldness of her fear. 'Creation, Davron, you underestimate him! In the ley line, he turned me inside out. What do you think he first offered me? And what do you think I replied? This will make you laugh. I told him a career as a mapmaker was not enough: nothing less than granting me the ability to make trompleri maps would be enough to make me give up my soul to him. And I didn't really mean it. We both knew that was the one thing he could never allow.'

His shock rendered him speechless.

'I think there are more of his spies about than you know,' she said. 'Graval had you fooled — you didn't even suspect that he was ley-lit, as he must have been, let alone suspect what his loyalties were. How many more of Carasma's Minions are there, travelling in disguise in fellowships, lurking here in the halt even, somehow shielding themselves from the touch of Order?'

'We will put an end to that. All Minions wear a sigil; we can check. We are sending out warnings.'

She went on relentlessly. 'Anyway, Carasma didn't need

225

spies to find out all about me. He knew who I was the moment he drowned me in the ley of the line he occupied. He knew my innermost desires and my guilt. He knew I was haunted by my mother's death. Spies, and an ability to touch the minds of those he confronts in the line: a lethal combination. Don't talk to me about my safety, Master Guide, because I don't believe in it.'

He stared at her, still silent, then made another frustrated gesture with his hand. 'You are right. Go home, Keris. Or go to your uncle. At least you will be safe.' There was no bitterness in his voice; what she heard was worse than that. It was a hopelessness so corrosively pungent it seemed to poison the air between them. For a moment they continued to look at one another, and in that moment she saw once again the echo of his desire for her, that inexplicable stirring of a man of experience and position, for her. Then the echo faded into despair and he turned to go.

He has made the decision to kill himself, as you once suggested to him. The thought came unbidden and stayed to poison her choice. *No,* her more rational self protested. *He wouldn't do that.* And then: *Oh, he wouldn't fall on his knife, perhaps. But there are other ways of dying . . .*

She had a sudden vision of Sheyli. Of her mother sending her away to have a chance at life. And she, Keris, accepting the chance that had meant a betrayal of the woman who had given her life.

'Wait,' she said, panicking.

Davron turned back, pausing merely as a courtesy, without hope or expectation.

'You — you have decided to die,' she said.

Emotion twitched at one corner of his mouth. 'That was once your advice. It has begun to look more attractive. But no, I have not decided to take my own life.' She noted the careful wording and her heart lurched, stricken, as if it was all her fault. 'Would you perhaps go with Meldor, if I was not there?' he asked, carefully neutral.

Her heart hammered. *As if — as if I cared,* she thought,

surprised. And I don't even like the man.

He said, 'I can't jeopardise Meldor's plans by my presence any more. And perhaps, if I am not there, you will ride with him. He needs you, Keris. Help him. Help him bring down the Unmaker. That is his aim. I was just along for the ride, after all . . . Ah don't look so upset – I'm not going to cut my own throat.'

'There's more than one way to kick a dog.'

He did not try to understand. 'I promise I won't actively seek death, either.'

He's lying, she thought. He'll challenge every Minion he sees. He'll be a one-man rampage across the Unstable until something gets to him before he gets to it. Shut up, Keris! You are swamping yourself with guilt!

'Wait,' she said to Davron again, as he turned to go once more. 'Perhaps I'll go with you and Meldor and Scow, if –'

He continued to wait, without expression.

She took a deep breath. '– if you tell me why you made this bargain with the Unmaker. If you tell me what you gained from it.'

The blackness of his eyes flashed with a brilliant anger. 'What difference does that make?'

She struggled for the right words. 'If I can understand what makes a man strike such a bargain, then perhaps I won't . . . fear you so much. Despise you so much.' I might understand why my instincts tell me to trust you, she thought.

A chuckle of reluctant amusement broke through his anger. 'Ley-life, but you have an honest streak, Kaylen!' He regarded her, smile fading into calculation, apparently debating her tentative offer.

With sudden premonition, she thought: I'm not going to like this.

He leant carelessly against the door post of the stall, in control again. He was suddenly the Master Guide once more, the man who had waited for customers back in Hopen Grat and had stared more at her horses than at her. 'What could the Unmaker offer me?' he mused in bitterness. 'I had everything I ever wanted . . . I'll tell you, Keris, what he offered — and you can see if you dare to judge me.'

And she listened while his words went through her like a cold shafting of ley. 'He offered me the life and sanity of my wife. Of my daughter. And of my unborn son. I took up his offer. *And I'd do it all over again*. There, does that answer your question?'

Chapter Sixteen

*It is written that, before the Rending, many were the wild
creatures that lived in the Realm of the Maker. The fish of the
sea were wondrous to behold; the birds of the sky were a joy
unto the eyes of Humankind; and the animals that walked
the Margravate were too numerous to count. Some were
fearful in aspect; others were venomous. Many were
dangerous. But this I say unto you: none were as dangerous
as the Wild, for the Wild were created by the Unmaking.
They are a perversion and, should they cross your path,
beware.*

The Rending 9: 10: 2

A day's ride and the Roughs, the plains that surrounded
Pickle's Halt, were behind them. The horses, fresh after
their rest and well fed on the halt's fodder, did not like the
pockmarked surface of the plains, and the echo of their
hooves resounding from the hollowness of the land beneath
them made them capricious and skittish.

'It's getting worse,' Keris heard Scow mutter to Davron.
'The spaces below are widening.'

The guide nodded, seemingly imperturbable, although
Keris wondered. 'I'm afraid you are right,' he said.

Just at sunset they reached the long line of the cliff barrier
that bordered the southern edge of the plains – a blue band of
rock stitched on to the flat land like coloured braid around the
hem of a chantor's robe. It was called the Sponge. They camped
there, a bare hundred paces from the cliff, for the night.

Keris eyed the Sponge uneasily as they erected their tents in the twilight. She had heard her father speak of it often enough: '. . . full of the Wild,' he had said. 'Even the Minions hate it. And no way around.'

It stretched as far as she could see in both directions and it rose into the air four times the height of a tall tree. There was no way over the top either, not with horses; the only route was through.

Before the light was completely gone from the sky Keris walked over to take a closer look. It was just as Piers had described it to her: rubbery in texture, blue in colour, consisting of interlocking bridges and pillars and columns, passages and holes and arches. There wasn't a straight line or a flat path or a large cavern anywhere in it – just twisting warrens and niches, holes and wells and walls.

There *was* light. It filtered in through holes from above, through entrances along the sides, then through the network of spans and cavities, funnels and warrens until it was a dim and diffused blue. There were many entrances and exits; the problem was that, once inside, it was very easy to become lost. Nor was there any point in marking a path for the next fellowship to follow either, because the passages kept on changing. Spans fell, others grew; holes filled in, burrows opened up; exits disappeared and new entrances split open. A guide had to find his own way through each time he passed that way. Piers had used Ygraine as his guide; the canny old crossings-horse had never seemed to have trouble finding a short route from one side to the other. Other Unstablers used dogs or ferrets. One or two boasted that they did not need animals to sniff out a route: they could do it themselves.

Keris was still contemplating the structure when the Chameleon, Portron and Corrian joined her. None of them seemed any more comfortable with the sight than she did. 'A cheese with holes,' the Chameleon remarked, wrinkling his nose in distaste. 'How far through, Keris? Do you know?'

'A day's journey if Master Davron knows what he is doing

and we're lucky. But the width varies, and it's all too easy to get lost inside.'

'Cheeses never have that many holes. At least not where I come from,' Portron said. 'It's more like a honeycomb.'

'Blue cheeses, maybe, but blue honeycombs?' Corrian asked, somehow managing to light her pipe and talk at the same time. ''Sides, honeycombs are regular. This is a maze gone bonkers. Reminds me of the slums of Drumlin Cess, and it stinks just as bad, too.'

'What *is* that smell?' the Chameleon asked.

'The Wild,' Keris said, the curt words cutting through the air.

'Once I saw someone sliced up in a street fight,' Corrian mused, puffing. 'Made a right proper job of him, they did. His lungs were a bit like that: all spongy and holey. Maybe that's why they give it that name. The Sponge.'

'My father said he heard that it was named after something that came from the sea. When there were seas.'

The Chameleon poked at the blue chunk of wall in front of him. It gave slightly under his fingers like a living thing. He drew back hurriedly. 'An animal?'

'I don't know. A kind of plant perhaps.'

He rubbed his cheek, his nervousness obvious. 'Well, let's hope this is not alive. I don't like the thought of walking inside something that's still – er – capable of digestion.'

'Let's be getting back,' Portron said. 'It's getting dark.' But when Quirk and Corrian began to walk back towards the camp he ambled behind, forcing Keris to slow her pace to his. 'You haven't told me just why you decided to come with us,' he said. 'This is a dangerous route, lass –'

She cut him short. 'I've decided to become an Unstabler, Chantor. I am now in Meldor's employ.'

He gaped, then shut his mouth with an audible snap. 'Doing what?' he asked finally.

'I'm a mapmaker.'

'Impossible! It's a man's profession –'

'No one cares for such proprieties in the Unstable.'

'But who would be after buying your maps?'

'Do you know, I've been thinking about that and I've come to the conclusion that Unstablers wouldn't care a flea's purse for anything but the accuracy of the map, and the ease with which it could be read. Ordinary people might jib at buying a woman's map, but not those who know the Unstable – and who know maps.'

'You will be breaking the Rule. Opposing Chantry, and all that Chantry stands for.' He waved his fly switch at her in agitation.

'Oh, I'll probably have a shop in some bordertown like Hopen Grat where Order doesn't operate and no one takes much notice of the Rule and rule-chantors.'

'Maker help you, Keris! That doesn't make it *right*. Besides, you *know* Meldor and Storre are messing with ley. You *saw* what they did. How can you *think* of working with a man who has deliberately sought to make the power of the Unmaker's realm his?'

She sighed, in her heart agreeing with him. 'Chantor, why didn't you tell people at the halt about it? Why didn't you tell the Defenders that Meldor and Davron dabble in the forbidden?'

'Believe me, I was wanting to. But somehow . . .' He shivered and stopped, holding her back. 'He told me not to, and I *couldn't*. Keris, there is evil abroad in that man.'

'In who?'

'Meldor. I wish I could remember where it was I've seen him before.'

'If you felt he was evil, then why are you here?'

'Because *you* are, disorder be damned! I might still be back in Pickle's Halt, waiting for the next fellowship to pass, if you hadn't announced you were riding out with Davron. I was thinking of dropping out of the Fellowship until I knew you weren't.'

She was taken aback. 'Oh. Oh, Creation. I never meant –'

He sighed. ''Tis too late now. You're a headstrong lass, Keris Kaylen, and I'll be hoping that you have a change of heart. 'Tis never too late to return to the Rule and the protection of Chantry.'

'You won't – you won't deliberately make trouble for me, will you? With Chantry, I mean.'

He looked uncomfortable. 'I – er – Yes, well. I'm not looking to stir the burnt crust at the bottom of the pot. I'm too old for crusades.' He had a sudden thought. 'What is Master Meldor wanting a mapmaker for?'

She hedged. 'An investment, I imagine. Doubtless he thinks there is money in maps.'

He looked over to where Meldor was warming his hands on the single campfire. 'I've been scouring my brains to think where I've seen him before.'

'Probably in a chanterie somewhere. He was a chantor, once.'

'Meldor?' He continued to stare at the blind man. 'But I've never seen him bend a knee in kinesis, nor read the Holy Books.'

'I said he was, not is. He's blind, Chantor Portron, and, quite apart from the fact that he'd find it hard to read anything, doubtless you know what the Rule says about the blind.'

'Oh. Yes. Sometimes it's hard to remember he can't see. Anyway, just because he's not allowed to stay in a stab doesn't mean a chantor should be giving up his calling. He can serve the faithful here as well as –' He paled and almost fell. 'Holy ley-life!' he breathed.

She reached out to take hold of him, but he pulled away from her and stumbled over to his tent, as if he was in a state of shock. Well, she wondered, what was all that about?

A moment later her thought was echoed in words. 'What was all that about?' Davron asked, coming over to her.

'I don't know,' she said. 'Are we having only one fire tonight?'

'Fuel is scarce. From here on, there's hardly any trees. But don't suppose I have to tell you that.'

'No.' She knew what lay on the other side of the Sponge:

the Wide and then the Flow — ley line and river, running parallel. Somewhere the Snarled Fist, where four lines met and mingled. And then beyond, a land that would be increasingly hostile and unmade.

'I haven't thanked you,' he said. 'For being here. For agreeing. For giving me hope.'

'I didn't do it for you,' she said, incurably honest. 'At least, not in that sense. I was afraid of what you would do if I didn't — I didn't want another burden of guilt loaded on to my shoulders.'

'Another?'

'I ran away from my dying mother. I left her when she needed me most because . . . because it suited my — my convenience. It is hard to live with.'

'Ah.' He rubbed the back of his neck and the look he gave her was tinged with embarrassment. 'You — you shouldn't have felt that you could be responsible for what I might have done. My decisions have always been my own.'

'Yes. And my mother's decision to ask me to leave was hers, yet it makes no difference. The guilt is there. It always will be,' she added simply. 'It is something I am learning to live with and I had no wish to add to it.'

He nodded and she had the impression that not only did he understand but was reluctantly amused by it, as if what she said struck too personal a chord within him. She guessed that he too knew what it was like to suffer from those insidious tendrils of guilt entwining themselves into one's conscience. She sighed. 'Davron, I don't have the faintest clue of how to set about making a trompleri map. I don't have ideas. I don't know where to begin.' This time she was very much aware that she had dropped the honorific 'Master'. She was determined he was going treat her as an equal, but found herself blushing anyway.

He said, 'We will introduce you to people who knew Deverli. And others who might have ideas. We'll tell you the same things that we told him. He found the secret — so car you.'

234

'Well, I hope you take better care of me than you did of him.'

His lips twisted, but it was hardly a smile. 'I'll try. And . . . I'm sorry about your mother. I remember her. I met her several times. The very first time I came to Kibbleberry, years ago, I remember that I noticed she had edged her petticoat with lacework. I saw it, peeping out from underneath her skirt. It impressed me that someone would go to all that trouble just to please themselves – and taunt Chantry in a way that only she knew about. I liked that. I thought her a woman of . . . dignity and integrity.'

Ornamentation was only for chantors, for the glory of Chantry, but Sheyli, for all her piety, had possessed a stubborn streak and she'd had a love of beautiful things. Davron was right: she had indeed been a woman of integrity, refusing ever to surrender that core of herself to the Rule. Keris looked up at the guide in wonderment; he could hardly have known Sheyli well, yet he had sensed so much.

'Hey, Keris – do you have some food for the fire?' Scow called out. 'We don't have much fuel to keep this going.'

'I'm coming.' She left Davron and headed for her tent, wishing all the while that it did not matter to her that he was married. With children. But it did matter, and it was becoming increasingly hard for her to convince herself that he meant nothing to her.

Infatuation, she thought, disgusted with herself. That's all.

But then she would remember the shame in his eyes and the way he drew on some inner resource to damp it down. She would recall the way he had grieved at Baraine's defection and Quirk's maiming. She would remember the turn of his head, the fluidity of the way he moved. She would remember the way he had sensed her turmoil at Graval's death, the way he had tried – not to comfort her; he was not a man to offer platitudes – but to make her strong. There was even something intriguing about his hardness, something enticing in that obsidian blackness; there was something attractive, too, about the weakness within that he strove to conceal, something fascinating about a man who blushed so easily and yet whose weapons of choice included a whip. He intrigued. He repelled. And something stirred inside her in response.

And there was no way he could ever be for her.

Oh, Creation, why is nothing simple any more?

It was not easy to find a way through the Sponge. A chosen route could suddenly end in a blank wall or a dead-end passage; or it would simply narrow down so much that a horse couldn't pass. In the soft blue light it was sometimes difficult to see the holes that suddenly opened up in the floor, or to make out the unevenness that snagged their feet. There were sills and nodules and humps and loops, and they could have been designed to catch unwary boots. And somewhere within were the Wild that made their nests and webs and dens and burrows there.

They walked the animals and plodded on. Tousson tossed her head and banged her neck against Keris's arm. 'She doesn't like it,' Scow remarked. He was bringing up the rear, behind them.

'No. I don't blame her.'

'Yes. Watch out here, it's slippery. It's wet for some reason.'

She glanced ahead. In front Corrian was swearing because she had bumped her head; Portron was talking to his palfrey trying to keep the nervous animal calm; and the Chameleon – now a pale blue to match his surroundings – was padding along with his animals, quiet and unobtrusive.

Funny, she thought, how Quirk moves differently now that he's the Chameleon. He walked softly, with a confidence that seemed innate, like an animal in its home territory. In company he might still agonise over what to say and he was certainly a dithering mess of nervous mannerisms, but at other times his camouflage seemed to cloak him with assurance as well as hiding him. It seemed his maiming had changed him in an unexpected way.

She looked past him but could not see Davron and Meldor — they were hidden by the numerous twists and turns — but she knew which one of the two men led them. 'Scow,' she asked, 'how does Meldor know his way?'

The tainted man shrugged his massive shoulders. 'He senses the route somehow. Don't worry — I've never known him to get lost in here.'

'I'm not worried.' And she wasn't. The blind man had that certain quality of leadership that made people feel secure in his company. Even Portron, with all his reservations, seemed to feel it. Charisma, Keris thought. Such men can be dangerous to humankind — and to Chantry.

For most of the morning they had to walk in single file through the narrow confines of passages and linked chambers, and conversation was not always possible. It was not until they stopped for lunch, when the configurations of the Sponge forced the party to break up into twos and threes, that Keris was able to talk to Scow again. She ended up sitting next to the unbound man in a hollowed-out chamber that was barely large enough for the two of them. Their mounts were crowded together in a wider passageway; the others were scattered in other chambers. It was then that she asked the question that had been nagging at her, that shamed her to ask, but that she was unable to resist. 'What is Davron's wife like, Scow?'

She thought he might dodge the question; instead his eyes softened. 'Who told you he was married?' he asked.

'He did.'

'Ah.' He seemed surprised. 'Alyss. Alyss of Tower-and-Fleury. She was — is — the most beautiful woman I've ever laid eyes on. No, perhaps beautiful is not the correct word. Lovely, that's it. She is lovely. Moonlight and quicksilver. At least that's what she was like when I first met her, before — before Davron's trouble. Full of life, a woman who made you feel more vital just by coming within your range. Gentle, loving . . . Red hair, green eyes, fair skin and fine bones. A soft heart that hates to see pain or suffering. She was there when Davron's party found me, after my tainting. I'll never forget looking up and seeing her bending over me like some sort of heavenly vision.'

'Where is she now?'

'Back in the Fifth, I suppose. Davron does not speak of her any more, although he – he goes to the Fifth whenever he can.'

And they were going to the Fifth now. Doubtless Davron would go and see her. Moonlight and quicksilver. Keris felt sick. No one would ever describe Keris Kaylen that way; more like pebbles and porridge, or something else equally commonplace and unattractive.

Even the name sounded special: Alyss of Tower-and-Fleury. Damn her.

Then Davron was there, towering over them both where they sat. 'Scow, go and talk to Meldor, will you?' he asked quietly. 'He's worried about the weather.' He waited until the unbound man had gone, then added, 'My wife is none of your business, Keris.'

He had heard. He wasn't angry; it was hurt she saw in his eyes, pain of memories that were almost too bad to endure, and that made it worse. She reddened and looked away. 'Forgive me. Are we going on now?' She gathered up the remains of her lunch and began to pack it away so as to avoid looking at him.

He nodded. 'Meldor thinks it's going to rain.'

'It has been growing darker.'

'Clouds,' Meldor said, joining them with Scow in tow. 'I've been smelling rain coming for some time. That could make things a lot worse.'

Keris looked upward. The domed roof immediately above her head was holed; she could see more vaults and bridges layered higher still above like some child's haphazard effort to build something fabulous. It had an exotic beauty: a deep rich blue in the shadows, a paler translucent colour elsewhere, and none of it symmetrical or smooth. 'Would rain come in?' she asked.

'The light does,' Scow pointed out.

'The Wild are also closing in on us,' Meldor added calmly. 'I think we are going to have a rough afternoon.'

Nobody said anything. There was little point.

They heard the rain some time before they had other evidence of it, but eventually it filtered down in rivulets, wetting the floor and walls and making things twice as treacherous. The dulling of the light did not help, either.

'Sometimes I think this trip is jinxed,' Scow muttered to Davron as he picked himself up after a nasty fall. 'I can't remember another that has gone as badly as this one.'

'Nonsense,' Davron snapped. 'Graval was the only jinx we had.'

Keris reflected on that, and realised its truth. The pack that was lost, the torn tent, the lamed horse, the trouble they'd had from the Wild, the numerous other little pinpricks that had occurred to make life unpleasant – it could all have been the maliciousness of a Minion; he could even have called in the Wild to attack.

She shivered, and did not know if it was the cold or fear that prompted it. There was a smell in the air that seemed to be drawing her on, something more than the stink of the Wild. Sometimes she caught a hint of colour in the air, a pinkish glow that faded when she concentrated on it, but which she seemed to catch sight of through the corner of her eye from time to time.

The trickle became a torrent as the day wore on and more of the rain found its way into the Sponge. Sometimes they were wading knee deep, worried about stepping into a hole; just as often they were drenched by water that gushed down chutes from above. They were cold and wet and tired, and Keris fretted that her second pair of boots – now her only pair – would not hold up under the constant soaking. She walked with the aid of Piers's staff, prodding at the floor in front of her when the water was deep, and took comfort from the thought that her father had probably used it for just that purpose on occasion.

Gradually all thought of the Wild faded into the general misery. They trudged on, cursing.

When the attack did come, it came with a vicious ferocity that caught them unawares. One minute they were just tired and irritable – the next they were besieged on all sides by a scurry of black beasts. Keris had an appalled glimpse of hairy arms and legs and thin bodies, of swinging animals and snapping teeth, then she was knocked aside by the horses. Ygraine and Tousson panicked, tore the reins free and were gone. Keris landed hard, cracking her head on a ridge of the floor, bruising her back on her quiver. There was no time to clear her ringing head – one of the black creatures leapt on her prone body from above. It was the size of a thin five-year-old child, and was vaguely human-shaped. The thick stench of a Wild overwhelmed her. A wrinkled face that had a mouth of pointed teeth was inches from her own; clawed hands pulled at her shirt. She tried to struggle up, gasping in horror but unable to scream. The ink-black face moved away from her own to hover over her chest. With an oddly human grip, the hands tore her shirt open and she knew without the slightest doubt that it was after her heart.

She groped for her knife but could not reach it. With her other hand she managed to poke at the bright red eye that glared into her own, and won herself a moment's respite. Then while still seeking her knife she found the knob of Piers's staff instead. She jerked the other end of it into the animal's midriff with a force that she didn't know she could muster, prone as she was. The Wild collapsed, retching, and she rolled out from underneath. One wild swing of the staff thudded into the black head and the creature collapsed at her feet, suddenly seeming small and insignificant. She dragged in breath, wondering how she had done it.

There was no time for congratulations. She was leaning back against the wall and water was cascading over her face and shoulders, blinding her, but she could see that she was surrounded. A circle of five or six of the same black creatures were closing in on her, snarling. Several of them were

240

climbing down from above, taking their time, knowing that she could not kill all with a mere staff, or even a knife. Her bow — unstrung because of the damp — was strapped to her pack on Tousson and the crossings-horses were long gone.

And then Davron was crouched in the doorway. His clothing was ripped and a ragged gash scored an arm. He had his whip, yet the beasts ignored him. When he kicked one of them, snapping its back with the power behind his boot, when he lashed at another, opening up a deep cut on its neck, the others simply moved away and closed in on Keris instead. She thought: They know him by the sigil he wears; and she felt her old anger at him well up. He plunged in among the Wild, lashing out at them, but they dodged away to make forays at Keris instead, to slash at her with claws and teeth even as she tried to ward them off with her staff.

Davron seemed to be without his knives and he had problems using the whip in such a confined space. She caught glimpses of his face as he whirled among the creatures, and recognised the desperation there.

Then those above dropped towards her, snarling.

She screamed then, thinking herself only the rip of a claw away from death. And the room erupted with sparks and colour and power. Ley, she thought, and was slammed back into the wall. Power. It was like the force of the wind, but the air was still; the breath was driven from her body, yet nothing touched her. Around her the Wild folded up into pathetic heaps of skinny limbs and skull-like heads. They were shrunken, as if life itself had had dimension and it had been sucked from them, leaving only a husk behind.

Keris gasped in air and pushed herself away from the wall. Davron was lying prone in the middle of the chamber, face down, whip still in his hand. And all the Wild were dead.

She had no idea what had happened.

She picked up her knife and glanced around, but there was no sign of anyone else, no movement of any other Wild. She could have been the only living thing left inside the Sponge. The silence was appalling and served only to emphasise her memory of what had gone before — sounds that had barely registered at the time: Corrian screaming obscenities, Meldor yelling at someone to run, the scream of horses, the snarl of beasts, the grunts and thumps and thuds . . . Now there was only the sound of running water.

She knelt at Davron's side, fearing the worst, not wanting to know if whatever had killed the Wild had also killed him. Knowing it would be better for everyone if he was dead. Wanting it so — and knowing that, if it was, it would be more than she could bear.

She went to roll him over on to his back and then paused. There was a vibration coming to her through the floor of the Sponge. A thundering of hooves. A snorting sound. She whirled to her feet to meet this new attack, and saw the last thing she had expected. It was Stockwood, Scow's enormous tainted mount. The beast was out of control, gasping and dribbling, swinging its vast head and knife-edged horns, pounding through the tunnels of the Sponge in an agony of mindless fear. Several of the black creatures were clinging to its back, biting into its hide.

And it was heading straight for her.

There was nothing she could do for Davron. There was no time for anything, no space to fling herself where she would be safe from those swinging horns . . .

She ran.

And Stockwood thundered after her. His huge feet trampled Davron, but that did not slow him. The horns were a bare few inches from her back and she ran as she had never run before. There was no time to duck into a side passage — she never even saw one until they were past — she just ran and ran. Behind her the crazed animal pounded on her heels. When passages opened up in front of her, when both she and the animal were presented with a choice, it followed her. One of the Wild fell off and was crushed beneath the hooves; the other was brushed off against the wall in a narrow archway, but still Stockwood ran.

Keris was terrified of slipping, of falling beneath those

huge hooves with their immense iron shoes. A gap opened up in the floor in front of her; she took it at a flying leap. Stockwood followed, heaving his bulk after her. The edge crumbled under him, but he recovered and was soon on her heels once more. Her breath laboured. She felt the tip of one of the horns against her buttock and sped up, knowing she could not last much longer. *What a stupid way to die.*

And then an arm came out of nowhere and snatched her sideways, pulling her through a narrow hole in the wall and into the safety beyond. Stockwood blundered straight on and the sound of his charge faded into the distance.

Keris, paralysed with fear, felt the thud of her heart in her chest and thought she might die of terror. She looked down at the arm that still held her. It blended in with the background . . .

'*Quirk!*'

She collapsed against him, and he clutched at her to prevent her fall even as he tried not to touch her skin, knowing that would hurt her. 'It's all right,' he said. 'It's all over now.'

'Oh Maker – *Quirk*! I've never been so glad to see anyone before in my whole life.'

His face turned an even darker blue. 'Er – well, thanks. Um, Keris – your . . .' He made an embarrassed gesture at her shirt even as his eyes were fixed on a point above her head and she realised her breasts were bare. Blushing, she pulled the edges of the cloth together and tied them. 'Are you hurt?' he asked, pulling at an ear and avoiding meeting her gaze.

'No. I mean, except for a few cuts and bruises. Are you?'

He shook his head. 'I stood still, right at the beginning, and those beasts just didn't see me. Then, when nothing was looking my way, I took off. I know that wasn't very brave, but I've never said I was brave,' he said. He sounded lost and lonely. 'I don't know the first thing about fighting. Once my father saw I had no ley, he could never be bothered to teach me.'

She took a deep breath. 'You saved my life just then.'

'Er – well, at no risk to my own. What happened to the others? Meldor was in the lead ahead of me but I didn't see what happened to him.'

'Davron's hurt. How badly I don't know. I never saw any of the others at all. Corrian was in front of me, but when we were attacked she had just turned a corner and was out of sight. Davron and Scow were behind me at the time.'

She stepped back into the passage she had fled down and looked back the way she had come. 'There were so many passages – I have no idea how to go back.'

'Nor do I. Come to think of it, I don't have the first idea of how to go on, either. Keris, we have no food, nothing. Can you get us out of here?'

She paused and took another deep breath. She smelt the ley ahead of them, felt the seductive pull of it. 'Yes, I think so.' She took another reluctant look behind. If she tried to retrace her steps . . . But it was hopeless. She would never find Davron again. If the water rises, he could drown, she thought. If he isn't dead already. I can't leave him like that. 'I've got to go back for Davron,' she said. I can't go on abandoning people just because it suits my convenience.

He accepted the implications of her statement. 'Do you know how to get to him?'

She shook her head. From where she stood she could see five branches in the passage and she had no idea which one she had come down. Water had already washed away any tracks Stockwood may have made.

'There are the Wild back there somewhere,' the Chameleon said.

They may have eaten him by now, she thought. No, they wouldn't do that. They think he serves the Unmaker. 'You don't have to come with me,' she said.

He gave her a look laden with meaning. 'If you think I'm letting you out of my sight, your brains are tainted. I think we ought to get out of here and leave Davron to look after himself – he's the guide, after all – but, if you're going back then so am I. I'm far too scared to stay here alone, or to go on alone.'

They tried. She put her back to the pull of the ley and searched the way she had come. They never found the gap she had leapt, nor the bodies of the two Wild Stockwood had killed, nor any of the others.

Finally it was Quirk who called a halt. 'It's getting dark, Keris,' he said. 'I think we should try to get out of here. We have no light, nothing.' He stared at her, his slitted eyes frightened. 'The Wild . . . at night . . .'

She nodded miserably, turned and followed the thread that pulled her onward. Ley. It was calling, and she answered the call, even as she feared.

They broke free of the Sponge at sunset. They emerged from an entrance at the base of the barrier on the southern side, and found themselves overlooking the Valley of the Flow.

Vaguely Keris took in the camp a few hundred paces away – not theirs but someone else's. Vaguely she saw the Flow, the colours of the Wide as it snaked across the valley floor . . . But it was the eruption of ley that drew all her senses. The place where four ley lines converged, snarled, combined in a tangle and poured upward into a perpetual mushroom cloud of colour and power and movement. She looked and feared and felt its tug pulling her, enticing her to approach, asking her to immolate herself on its pyre.

'What's the matter?' the Chameleon asked, worried. Keris, what is it?'

'Ah, sweet Creation, Quirk – can't you see it?'

He stared in the direction she gazed and saw nothing, felt nothing.

He shook his head. 'Mist. That's all.'

She whispered, 'It's the Fist. The Snarled Fist. Ley-life, Quirk, it's *huge.*'

Chapter Seventeen

Men who would escape their fate are as eggs in the hands of a blind juggler.

> *saying of the old Margravate of Malinawar*

The camp belonged to a trader called Tom the Cheap and his half-dozen tainted staff. He had come up from the south and intended to cross the Sponge the next day. Keris knew him, but he did not recognise Piers's daughter and she did not enlighten him. To her annoyance, he seemed smugly pleased that they had been attacked by the Wild, and he made no attempt to conceal the sentiment. 'They're less likely to want to get her filthy teeth into us, if they've ate a couple of you lot,' he explained. There was no malice in the remark, but he evidently had no particular love for other people and took their tragedies in his stride.

Keris, relieved, saw that Scow and Corrian and Portror were already there, sharing the trader's camp. The chantor came bustling over, full of concern. 'Ah, lass, you're a sight for anxious eyes to behold! And right sincerely it is that I've been performing kinesis dedicated to your safety. Are you hurt?'

She shook her head. 'What of you?'

'Scow got us out of the Sponge,' he said, nodding toward the tainted man, who grinned at Keris with his usual animal smile. 'With the Maker's grace, of course. And our horse turned up on their own. I think your Ygraine led them out. That monster of Scow's found his own way out later.'

'The others?' she asked. 'Davron? Meldor?'

'No sign of them yet. And Corrian's pack mule is missing too.'

Corrian glowered at them. 'I broke my best pipe. And the replacements are all in my packs. Now what the midden am I supposed to do without my pipes and baccy weed?'

Everyone refrained from remarking that she seemed to be doing quite well: she had her teeth clamped hard on the stem of a new pipe bought from Tom, and she had stuffed it with his best pipeweed. Apparently her money had been on her person, not in her packs.

Keris turned to Scow. 'Did you see what happened to Meldor?'

'He yelled at me to get Corrian and Quirk and the chantor out of there. I couldn't see Quirk, but I found Corrian and Portron. Meldor went back down the passage to find you and Davron. We grabbed Meldor's crossings horse — it led us out.'

'You just left Meldor?'

He gave Keris a stolid look. 'When I get a direct order, I obey it. Meldor and Davron can look after themselves a lot better than I can. And now you had better get your tent erected. Do you mind sharing with Corrian tonight? If her mule doesn't turn up she has nowhere to sleep.'

'Only if she promises not to smoke that damned pipe inside the tent,' Keris said ungraciously.

'Upstart,' Corrian muttered. 'Dunno what the young are comin' to these days. No respect for their elders.'

Keris erected her tent and then gratefully accepted a plate of stew from Portron. 'The trader says he'll have his Unbound guard the camp tonight,' the chantor said cheerfully, 'which means we can get a good night's rest.'

Keris stared at him, wondering at his tone, and finally realised that Portron was hoping Davron and Meldor would never appear. She said nothing, but she knew she would not sleep until she saw that Davron was safe. But he's not safe, she thought. How can he be safe? He was unconscious, lying there on the floor, and the water was coming in. Maybe he was already dead. Stockwood was huge, and he was trampled.

She ate her food stoically, even cleaning the last of the gravy from the plate with a piece of damper bread that Corrian had baked in the ashes of the fire. But she tasted none of it.

Corrian did not share Keris's tent after all. It seemed that Tom the Cheap was happy to share his bed with a leathery old woman – once she had convinced him that she was not tainted. He had questioned that anyone so unattractive could possibly be that way naturally. This insult Corrian took in her stride, remarking loudly as she made her way to his tent that all pussies looked alike in the dark. Portron drew in an indignant breath and stalked off to bed; predictably, Quirk blushed. A few minutes later he too went off to his tent, leaving Scow and Keris by the dying embers of the fire.

'I saw what happened to Davron,' she said without preamble, and described what she had seen. 'Even if he was just temporarily unconscious, Stockwood galloped right over him –' She stopped, unable to go on.

'Meldor will find him.'

'Meldor's blind. The Wild might tear him to pieces.'

'He is not defenceless.'

'Oh stop it, Scow,' she said irritably. 'You're just as worried as I am.'

He grimaced, tongue lolling out. 'Yeah, I guess so. But I can't go back for them; I'd never find the way. And Meldor is stronger than you realise.'

She poked a stick idly at the ashes around the edges of the fire. 'He uses ley,' she said. 'That's it, isn't it? Somehow he uses ley to see. To replace the sense he lost, or at the very least to enhance those he still has.'

Scow said nothing.

She went on. 'And that's why he thinks he can fight the Unmaker – because he knows how to use ley. He ignores the strictures of Chantry. He thinks he can bend the ley to his bidding without himself being corrupted.' She paused. 'He's mad. As mad as Davron. No one can fight the Unmaker except by creating Order.'

'Ah, yes. The rigidity of Order and the Rule. The inflexibility that allows no variations, nothing unusual. That expels the blind and crippled, that sends us out into the Unstable to be tainted in the first place. Is that the kind of life you believe in, Keris?'

'What else is there?' she whispered. 'You want the truth? I *hate* it. I always have. All my life I've wanted to break free. I wanted to be a mapmaker. I wanted to wear trousers. I wanted to ride into the Unstable with my father. I wanted not to go to Chantry on rest days. I wanted to argue with the mentor in Chantry school. I wanted to read books that never mentioned the damned Rule − ley-life, I wanted a hundred different things! I loathed Chantry − I despised their laws and their spying. I detested their pettiness and their sanctimonious ways. But I never fought them. Not really. Oh, I might have been a little cheeky, but that was all.

'You see, in my heart I believed − no, I *believe* − that, without Order, Chaos comes. That's a *truth*, Scow. We all have to make sacrifices. For some, it's harder than others, I know. But that's not the fault of Chantry, or the Rule. It's the Unmaker who has done this to us . . .' She continued to poke around in the ashes. 'I've come with you all, but deep inside me I feel that I have committed a terrible sin. I've come with you for half a dozen reasons − and most of them are selfish. Basically, I think I'm a very selfish person.' She unearthed some of the wood from the fire and pushed it back into the flames. 'What sort of wood *is* this?'

'Not wood at all,' he said absently. 'Tom the Cheap hacked a few chunks off the Sponge.' He threw several more pieces on to the dying fire where they flamed blue, and then began to whittle at another piece with his knife. 'I don't think I will be able to sleep tonight.'

'Me neither.' They sat for a while in silence, until Keris

took note of the knife he was using. 'That's an unusual blade — why is it so shiny?'

'It's the kind of metal it is made of, I think. Meldor gave it to me. He thinks it probably comes from the times before the Rending, when people knew how to make such marvellous things.'

'That old? But that's a thousand years —' She thought of the metal caddy back in the mapmaker's shop in Kibbleberry. 'Is it possible for something to be so old?'

'Well, no one knows how to make metal like this now. Mind you, I don't think it could have been used continuously for a thousand years. It would have been worn away by the sharpening. And I think the handle has been replaced, maybe even several times.'

She mused, 'When I was little, I used to wish I lived back in the days of the Margravate of Malinawar, when ships used to cross the oceans. I would dream about the sea. Water stretching out as far as the eye could see — but it's hard to imagine. What colour do you think it would have been? Brown, like the Flow? Thick and green, like the Gebbish River back home? Or perhaps tea-coloured, like the Warbuss, where it flows through Taggart's Wood.'

'One day you'll be able to ride to the sea again, and see for yourself. In your lifetime.'

'Do you really believe that?'

'Yes, yes I do. You don't know Meldor as I do. I love Davron as a friend, a brother — but Meldor: I would follow Meldor to the other side of the Waste if he asked it of me. He will do what he says: free us all.'

'That's ridiculous. A dream, a foolish dream. Like mine, of seeing the ocean.'

'Keris, if we don't free ourselves, who will do it for us? Chantry? Their only answer is failing. The kinesis chain has retreated in half a dozen places over the past few years. You'll see that when you approach the Fifth. With each passing year, the areas of stability grow smaller. The Eighth is in danger of being cut in two. Keris — *Chantry and the Rule are not keeping Chaos at bay any more.* And they certainly have no idea of ever regaining what has been lost. No one has had that idea – not one has *considered* casting the Unmaker down and reclaiming what was ours – until Meldor. Meldor has a dream, and such a dream is worth fighting for.'

'If it was possible, wouldn't the Maker have done it before now?'

'Read the Holy Books, Keris. Chaos was brought to Malinawar because some of humankind supported Carasma the Unmaker. It is our belief that only humankind can defeat what they themselves brought about by their folly. All the clues are there, in the writings. We have ignored them too long, misinterpreted what was written, insisted that things were allegories when what was written was the literal truth. The Maker gave us the answers through His Prophets and His Scribes and His Knights – but we have chosen not to listen.'

She stared at him and was silent.

He looked up from his whittling to see why she had not replied. 'Do I surprise you?'

'You astound me.'

'They are Meldor's words, of course – but I have come to agree that he is right.'

'But you sound more like a chantor –'

'Oh no, never that. Chantry uses the Holy Books to justify stability and lack of change. Meldor tells us to study them with a view to finding out how the world can be altered, how the Unmaker can be defeated. Meldor is a deeply religious man, but his views are not those of Chantry.'

She was appalled by the hint in his words. 'There can only be one religion. One way. To even think anything else –' The ultimate heresy. The only crime – except being born Unbred – that was punishable by death.

'He will explain it to you better. Ask him.' He grinned at her, rather like a large friendly dog.

She looked away, out towards the Sponge, now a black outline against a starlit sky. 'If he's alive.'

'He will live. He has not yet fulfilled his destiny. And your trompleri maps will be part of the plan – you'll see.' He held up the piece of the Sponge that he had been carving. He had created a rough representation of Stockwood, horns and all. 'It would be a terrible irony, would it not, if my oversized hack has killed Davron?' His hand tightened on the carving for a moment, as if he wanted to crush it, then he tossed it into the fire and watched it burn.

She stood up, restless, and turned to look at the Snarled Fist. She had been aware of it ever since she had emerged from the Sponge, aware of it through the corner of her eye, on the edge of her consciousness, but after her initial gaze she had avoided looking at it directly. It was too overpowering. Too compelling. Too downright dangerous. Now she forced herself to look, forced herself to absorb its reality and face its power.

Below her the Wide flowed through the night like a broad river of churning light. Beyond it, somewhere out in the darkness, was the true river known as the Flow, while to her right, streaming through the Sponge one after the other, came the maelstrom of the fickle Wanderer, and the narrow ribbon of the Dancer. Their confluence with the Wide was a clash of force, a vortex that sent power and colour upward into a perpetual mushroom cloud of roiling purple and livid billows. It created its own light; it glowed and sparked and flared and flickered, sometimes like playful lightning, sometimes with the ferocity of brushfire, sometimes cold and eerie as fox fire.

The Snarled Fist, feared and avoided by all Unstablers – and there it was within an hour's ride of where she stood . . .

'It pulls me,' she murmured. 'I feel it all the time. Like a restlessness inside me.' *Like that moment in the ley line when I wanted Davron to love me.* 'I feel that I want to walk into it.' She shivered.

Scow watched her face, not the ley. 'I cannot see it. I cannot feel it. It does nothing to me.' He shrugged. 'Meldor exults in ley, you know, but Davron is more cautious.'

She turned away from the Fist and looked back at the Sponge. 'The ley I saw — the ley that killed the Wild that were attacking me — where did it come from?' He was silent. 'It was Davron, wasn't it?' When he continued to keep silent, she made a small sound of exasperation. 'Scow, I *know* it was him. I just want to know why he collapsed. Was he — did it kill him too?'

The tainted man shook his head. 'No, I shouldn't think so. But Davron is not like Meldor. He doesn't have the same sort of skills. I suspect he misjudged and drained himself, not only of ley, but of his own . . . energy. He probably fainted.'

She wanted to ask how he had obtained the ley. She wanted to ask half a dozen questions — but they all died unasked. 'There's someone there,' she whispered. 'There's someone coming.' And the hope that surged in her was painful and told her far too much. *I mustn't.*

Meldor and Davron appeared at the edge of the fire's glow, one leaning into the other. Davron was partly supporting himself on Piers's staff, which Keris had thought she had lost for ever.

Scow jumped to his feet, grinning. 'Maker be thanked!' He went forward to help Meldor, but Keris saw that it was Davron who suffered, not the blind man. Meldor was tired, but he held himself erect and the blood on his clothes was Davron's, not his. It was Davron who was in pain. The cut on his arm had been roughly bandaged, but the bandage was blood-soaked. Freed of Meldor's support, he limped hesitantly to where Keris stood, and halted a step away. The look he gave her was concentrated, as if he had blocked out the rest of the world.

Keris remained where she was, unable to move, afraid she would give herself away. Afraid of what she was feeling. She took no joy in her relief that he was safe; every particle of desire and love she felt was suffused with an equal horror. *He is bonded to the Unmaker. He is married, he is Trician, his wife is beautiful. He plays with the evil of ley. One day he will answer the Unmaker's summons . . .*

She said, 'I thought you must have died —' *Don't let me love you*.

He spoke at the same time. 'I thought the Wild must have taken you —'

They stopped, then Keris started again. 'Stockwood trampled you —'

Meldor laughed, and the spell was broken; the world came back with a rush. Keris stepped back, flushing, wondering how obvious she had been. Davron turned away, smiling at Meldor, then looking back at her to share the joke. 'I said to Meldor that I felt I had been trampled by a herd of horses. I guess Stockwood is about equal to a herd of normal beasts. Ley-life, Scow, I swear he must have broken every rib I have. I need to be strapped up — and, whatever you do, don't make me laugh.'

Scow put a hand on his shoulder by way of apology and the three of them made their way to where the Unbound man had erected Davron's tent, and disappeared inside.

Keris, left alone by the fire, felt the prick of helpless tears and was not sure which of her numerous miseries was responsible. I shall have to learn to swear out loud, she thought. Maybe then I wouldn't need to cry all the time.

'You shouldn't have said that to her,' Meldor said some time later, after listening to all Scow had had to say. 'It was too early.'

Scow gave a shake of his reddish mane. He was seated on the floor of Davron's tent, next to the guide's bedroll. Meldor, although he must have been tired, remained standing. The only concession he made to fatigue was to lean against the centre pole of the tent. 'Sorry,' Scow said. 'I was not thinking — I was worried, wondering if you might both be hurt, or dead, and I didn't know whether I should go back for you, or not.'

'There, you did the right thing. If you had gone back, we'd probably have had to turn around and go and look for you. But make no mistake about it: Maid Kaylen's still not to be trusted. She's still tethered to Chantry, and just because she's had a few frustrations doesn't mean she's ready to change her allegiance. There's a streak of righteousness there and she doesn't have the trauma of being tainted to help her change, not like Quirk.'

'As long as she doesn't go to Portron,' Davron said. Now that he was clean, fed and rebandaged, he was feeling much better, especially as Meldor had applied ley to help the healing process. Nonetheless, he was not entirely comfortable, as his constant shifting of position showed.

'Keris run to Portron? She won't,' Scow said with certainty. 'Even if she wasn't ley-coerced. She has a well-developed sense of fair play, and, anyway, anyone with half a mind can see that she's halfway to loving you, Davron.'

Davron winced and said nothing.

'Anyway,' Meldor said, 'you're not to trust her yet. Either of you. Certainly no mention of Havenstar. Although if she loves you, Davron, maybe we can use that.'

The blackness in Davron's eyes flashed dangerously. 'One of these days I might just run a blade into your guts, Meldor.'

Meldor did not seem disturbed by the threat. He looked down at the guide with a shrug. 'I don't have your scruples, Maker be thanked. If I did, nothing would ever be done. Now, what about your ley, my friend? Can it wait until tomorrow night?'

Davron shook his head. 'I'm afraid not. I need it, Meldor. The lack of it is an ache right through my bones to my soul.' He hesitated. 'I didn't know — I never guessed. I didn't really know until this moment. Meldor, if ever we win, totally win and banish ley from this land, we who have taken the ley will die of its lack, just as surely as the Unbound will die of too much stability.'

Meldor nodded calmly. 'I've always known that.'

Davron took a deep breath. 'You never warned us. Was that . . . just? Ley-life — how can you ask men to fight for a victory that will bring only certain death to them?'

'Won't it be worth it?'

'I may think so, but others may not. If they knew they were doomed, would they follow?'

'I did,' said Scow softly. 'Others of my kind may believe what the Margraf tells them of a better world where we will all be whole again, with the Unmaker vanquished – but I am not so sanguine, and I know Meldor well enough to know when he equivocates. If there's a total victory, we're all doomed, Davron. That's our tragedy. But we will go on, nonetheless – for the Tillys of this world, and the Allyses. For children like your Mirrin and Staven. So that one day they will not have to make a crossing.'

Meldor pushed himself away from the tent pole. 'Perhaps you should both put your faith in Havenstar,' he admonished them. 'Haven't I told you it will be our salvation?' He went to the tent flap, saying, 'Try to sleep for an hour or two, Davron. I will come for you when the camp is quiet, and we will go into the ley together.'

Keris could not sleep. Too much had happened that day; she had been too close to death too many times; her emotions had been scored and scarified and shredded. She was exhausted, but sleep would not come. When someone scratched at the canvas of her tent she was almost relieved. 'Who is it?' she asked.

'Quirk.'

She unlaced the tent opening and poked her head out. She strained to see him against the darkness of the ground beyond, and thought she glimpsed his small eyes, perched as they were in moving mounds of ringed flesh. 'Is something the matter?'

'Something woke me. I looked out to see Meldor and Davron. I followed them. Keris – I think they went into the ley.'

'One moment.' She withdrew into her tent and hurriedly dressed, ignoring the momentary pain of her scratches and aching muscles.

When she emerged from the tent, Quirk clutched at her

arm worriedly. 'I don't know if it's any of our business, but I followed them. They were stopped by the trader's sentry but he let them pass. None of them saw me, of course. Meldor and Davron just went straight down towards the mist, where you say the Wide is. What should we do?'

'I'll take a look.'

He guided her through the camp, then distracted the sentry with noise while she slipped past. A moment later he rejoined her. He pointed. 'They entered over there somewhere.'

'Yes, I can see them.'

'What are they doing? Keris, they didn't go to . . . to meet Carasma, did they? Could they be . . . Minions?'

Towards the centre of the line she could see a swirl of ley hues. As the clot of colour teased out more thinly she caught glimpses of Davron and Meldor standing together, close enough to have been in an embrace. A twirl of ley, pinkish in colour, wrapped them around in a spiral, tied them one to the other. And then she saw: there was no end to the top of the spiral. At the bottom it eased out of the ribbon of ley; at the top it disappeared into them both. Was absorbed through their skin, into their faces.

She turned away, troubled.

'What did you see?' Quirk asked, watching her anxiously. 'Is *he* there?'

She shook her head. 'No, they are alone. They are . . . absorbing the ley. For its powers.'

'Ah.' He thought about that and nodded. 'That's what they used to dispose of the bilee, I suppose.'

She nodded in turn.

'That's illegal,' he remarked. 'And it's what Minions do.'

She was silent.

'Keris,' he said, 'I don't know what to do. They want me to come with them. They want to fight the Unmaker. You know I have become friendly with Scow?'

She nodded.

'He's a fine chap. The best.' He pulled at his earlobe. 'He

says there's a place where the Unbound can live and be safe.'

'Havenstar? I've heard of it. But Scow told me it didn't exist. At least, that's what I thought he meant.'

'Well, I don't think it's like rumours say – with sorcerers and all that, to make us human again. I don't even know if it's called Havenstar. Scow didn't use that word. But he says there is a place. Keris, I'm scared of the Unstable. I've always been scared. I hate it. I hate the thought that, out here, there are Minions and the Wild just waiting for an opportunity to rip us apart – I want to be *safe* again.'

'They make use of ley. And they will lead you into confrontation with the Unmaker. You will be far from safe in their company. In our company,' she corrected. *For am I not one of them too?* 'You will be hunted by both Lord Carasma *and* Chantry, if you are not careful.'

'Oh, but I'll be there, in that place – safe. They won't want *me* to fight; they know what a coward I am.'

She sighed. 'Quirk, Quirk, can't you see? They want you for what you are. The Chameleon.'

In the light she saw his blank uncertainty.

'A spy, Quirk. You are the perfect spy. Not even the Minions can see you if you stay still, move slowly. Although the Wild may smell you, I suppose.'

'Oh.' He stood very still and his outline, even in the light from the ley, blurred away into the background. 'I'm stupid, I suppose.'

She did not know what to say, but stood there quietly while he thought things through. He roused himself after a while with an odd smile. 'Ironic, isn't it? When Carasma changed me, and other Unbound, with his wretched ley, he brought into being instruments that might bring about his downfall. Scow with his great strength, other men who have the strength or claws or senses of animals . . . A man who wears the perfect camouflage. In the end we are the ones who will bring him down. Not Chantry.' He turned his sad eyes towards her without moving his head. 'What else is left to me, Keris? I cannot enter a stab. I have to take what

Meldor offers; it's all I'll ever have.'

Sweet Creation, she thought. Is there no end to his tragedy? She gave one last glance back at Davron and Meldor, where they stood oblivious to her gaze as they drank in forbidden power, and then she and the Chameleon turned to walk back towards the camp.

Chapter Eighteen

Watch for the Knight who sees the night but not the stars, for he shall show thee another way that shall make the sighted of Chantry stumble in the dark, even as his gait is smooth.

Predictions II: 5: 17

They stayed two days in the camp beside the Wide. The trader, having sold another mule to Corrian, moved on, but Davron needed rest so the fellowship stayed. Keris spent half the time trying not to think about Davron, and the other half trying not to think about the Snarled Fist — and succeeded in neither endeavour.

Once, seeing her eyes follow Davron as he limped about the camp, Corrian jabbed her in the ribs. 'Come on, love, why don't you bed the hunk 'stead of lapping 'im up with your eyes? You're not so innocent that you don't know how you would enjoy it!'

'He'd only take me because his wife's not around,' she said and then blushed because she sounded like a sulky child.

Corrian laughed. 'So? So? What does it matter? Enjoy!' Then, seeing the grief in Keris, she lowered her voice. 'Listen, love, don't you hold with all this crap that Chantry doles out 'bout the pleasures of the body being a sin and all. Sex is an urge, like wanting a drink of water when you're thirsty, or wanting a bite to eat when you're hungry. 'Tis Creator-given, just like the thirst and the hunger. You slake one and assuage t'other — then Chantry tells us not to scratch the third itch we've got, because that one's a sin for the unwed. Makes no sense now, does it?'

Keris could not help smiling. 'Corrian, I thought you were supposed to be on this pilgrimage as atonement for your sins. You'll not earn many points if you sleep with anyone who'll have you along the way – and try to urge others to do so as well.'

Corrian grinned at her wickedly. 'Ah, lass, 'tis not bedding men that was my sin. It was the thieving. And a few other sundry – er – blunders over the years. Chantry can rave all it likes about fornication, but I'll not believe that anything so sweet, that gives pleasure to both sides of the bed, can be a sin!' She puffed at her pipe, her face suddenly pensive. 'Mayhap there's summat not so good about living off the earnings of the girls, though, I'll grant you that. If I live through this damn trek, I'll not do that again. At least, I'll *try* not to do that again – but, believe me, I'll still be humping between the sheets on my own account till the day I die. Listen, lass, if it brings pleasure to you and him –' she jerked a head at Davron '– there can't be aught wrong with it.'

'He's married –'

'So? She's not *here,* is she? If she wanted 'im to be faithful, then she ought to be at his side when he needs her. Anyways, she'll never know. He's not so daft he'd tell her.'

Keris sighed. Perhaps Corrian was right. Perhaps it was better to have a moment's pleasure and a sweet memory, than to have nothing at all. But I'll be damned if I'll seduce him, she thought. If he asks, I'll . . . think about it.

Her spirits felt no lighter once she had made the decision, partly because in her heart she recognised an empty jug when she saw one. She wanted more than just pleasure. She sighed again: what was the point anyhow? She did not believe he would ask. Why should he? He was married to a beautiful, lovely woman and in another few days he would be seeing her. She had borne him children. He had loved her so much that he had bonded himself to the Unmaker in order to save her . . .

What wouldn't I give to be loved like that . . .?

But she was freckled and skinny and rather plain, and few men gave her more than a passing glance. If he wanted her at all, and perhaps he did a little, it was just because she was there and there was no one else.

The days they spent in camp went slowly. Meldor took Scow back into the Sponge to retrieve Corrian's packs; he and Davron had come across them on the way out. Her mule had been killed and eaten, but the Wild hadn't been interested in the packs.

On the second night, Keris found that her tent pegs were being obliterated by the Unstable, and her tent was almost blown away as a consequence. The others hastily loosened and moved their pegs to prevent the same thing happening to them, while Scow whittled some new ones out of the Sponge for Keris. 'I hope that darn blue thing is not alive,' she muttered, 'or it may just decide to roll over in revenge one dark night and flatten us all to paste.' Scow found that idea hugely amusing, but then there was little that Scow could not find worthy of laughter or a smile.

Portron came over to help her repitch her tent. 'Just in time, I think,' he said as he hammered in the last of the new pegs. 'It's going to rain. Keris, could I talk to you for a moment?'

She hid a sigh. 'All right,' she said, waving him inside the canvas just as the first raindrops fell. 'But I should warn you that I think I know everything you're about to tell me. If you want me to change my mind, then you'll have to come up with something new.'

'New?' he asked in despair. 'What else can I tell you? There is nothing more important than your immortal soul, and you endanger that just by being here, in the company of –'

She cut him short. 'Chantor, what is it you know about Meldor that I don't know? You recognised him, didn't you?'

He looked at her in an agony of feeling. It was now raining in earnest and the sound of the water on the canvas of the tent almost drowned out his stifled reply. 'Yes. Finally. I remembered where I had seen him before – it was in the Chanterie of Kt Ladma. He was there for a few nights, oh, about twenty years ago. He led the kinesis devotions and preached the sermon at Prostration one night, I recall.'

'And . . .?' she prompted.

'He wasn't called Meldor then,' he said bitterly. 'He was Knight Edion of Galman. Of the Knighten Ordering – the holiest and wisest of them all.' Tears welled up in his eyes. 'How could he be deserting Chantry, Keris? We revered him. Above all others, we revered him. When he spoke, our hearts were swelling up like puff-pigeons just to be hearing him. He was preaching such ideas – brotherhood, understanding . . . People strewed flower petals under his feet when he walked in the town, in recognition of his learning and piety. And then one day he disappeared . . .'

Her mind reeled. A man so saintly it was said that even the Sanhedrin knelt when he entered a room. A man who had led a life of wandering austerity, owning nothing, relying eternally on charity to feed and shelter him – a Chantry Knight who had chosen a life of teaching, Edion had embarked on journeys to all stabilities, dispensing the word of the Holy Books, expounding, explaining and enlightening. Even Keris had heard of him. He had brought a message of hope, rather than obedience, and the people had loved him, loved him more perhaps than his fellow chantors had.

'He didn't desert Chantry; Chantry deserted him. They excluded him,' she said, 'because of his blindness. Or maybe because he spoke too much truth. They threw him out, removed him from the Knighten Ordering and excluded him. After the kind of life he had led, the kind of man he had been. It was unjust.'

'Such a knightly man should have been able to accept the burden,' he said. 'He could have preached in the Unstable. Maker knows, there's enough work to be done here among the tainted and the Unstablers – instead he turned to the forbidden. To ley.'

'You'd like to denounce him, wouldn't you?'

He ducked his head to avoid her gaze. 'What's the point? He'll stop me if I try. Let him go his own evil way – but without you. I don't care what *he* does.'

She stared at him in surprise. 'You should care.'

He caught her look of surprise and reddened. 'I – er – right now I'm just a traveller. Like anybody else.'

Why, she thought, all he cares about is getting himself to the Eighth so he can bed his chantora. Portron did not want to involve himself in Chantry controversy along the way. She felt a sharp disappointment, which was irrational, seeing that she really did not want Meldor to face Chantry wrath.

Portron shook his head sadly. 'He wasn't really a Trician, you know. The "of Galman" was honorific, bestowed on him by Chantry because of his saintly character. I can't believe it of him – that he would come to this.' He was still shaking his head in disbelief as he left her.

The ley crossing of the Wide – long dreaded by Keris – passed without incident. The colours of the line remained pale and dormant around their feet; there was no hint of Lord Carasma or his Minions.

The fording of the Flow, which Keris had not feared at all, was much worse than crossing the Wide. A thick yellowish cloud of vapour like teased wool hung over the river that morning; after they had entered it, the particles it contained stung the throat and eyes and sang in the ears. Worse, it was impossible to see further than a horse's length ahead. Worried by its unpleasantness, Keris failed to keep a watch on the person in front – Corrian – and, the next time she looked, there was no one there. No Corrian, no horses or mules, no fellowship.

She called out, but the sound of her voice was muffled and thin, suffocated in the mist-smoke. Nervously she urged Ygraine on. Beneath its feet, the water of the river was sluggish and shallow, no part so deep that a horse couldn't walk it. The horror was in being closed off from the rest of the world, in being out of touch with the others — and in hearing that keening sound in her ears.

Keris tried to convince herself that a fog could not sing, but the dirge went on, whispering its melody intimately into her head with each tendril of vapour. There were no words, just a tuneless song — more a lament — that faded in and out as the vapour thickened and thinned.

Once or twice she thought she caught glimpses of shapes wading through the water, shapes that were too small to be mounted riders, but then the fog would close in and whatever it was would vanish. She kept swinging around, trying to find the others, but there was no sign of them. She was no longer sure she was heading the right way, and was forced to halt Ygraine. She looked down at the water, trying to decide the direction of its flow so that she could orientate herself, but the river seemed stagnant, lifeless.

Is this also part of the disintegration of our world? she wondered. A river that does not flow. That has no sea to flow to any more . . .

She gave Ygraine her head and gripped Tousson's lead-rein tighter. Over to her left there was a violent splashing, but she could see nothing. The water reached Ygraine's belly and the horses were slowed; not even her urging could move them any faster.

Then, out of the yellowish fug ahead, something dark loomed: rocks. A low huddle of rocks barely breaking the river surface, and someone crouched on them. A naked youth. She halted, uncertain. Through the smudge of the mist, the boy grinned at her, a mischievous grin of glee. Even partially obscured, he seemed beautiful, golden, lithe — all slim muscle and youthful strength. Water glistened across his skin, slid down the midline of his chest to be lost in golden curls. Keris looked for the Unmaker's sigil, but there was none. He stood and turned his back. For a brief second he looked over his shoulder and smiled, then he dived into the water — and vanished. She drew a sharp breath at what she had seen as he had unfolded himself from his crouch and turned his back: the triple set of swollen nipples on his chest, the grotesquely elongated penis below (an animal's appendage rather than a human's, surely), the viciously taloned feet and spurred calves, the furred and ridged back ending in a tail . . .

She dug in her heels and slapped Ygraine across the rump, not knowing why fear clawed at her insides, urging her to run. *Wasn't he just an Unbound man, to be pitied?*

But something told her otherwise. The face and arms and thighs had seemed human, but the rest had been more than just a distortion of a human form. The rest had been pure animal, corrupted animal. A half-forgotten tale heard in the mapmaker's shop slid into her mind: *they say Minions breed with their Wild sometimes and the offspring are . . .*

Are what? Vile? She had forgotten. She was not sure she wanted to remember.

The water shallowed; Ygraine heaved her way out of the river on to the sand of the bank – and propped, startled as more figures loomed in the fog. It was the animal-youth again, and this time he was not alone. A man stood with his arm draped casually across the naked golden shoulders. He was immaculately dressed in a Trician's costume, yet with additional gold chains and brooches and other ornaments forbidden to the unencoloured. His shirt was unhooked to the waist to show the sigil fused to his skin, as if the owner was proud of his allegiance.

Keris recognised him, and went cold all over.

Baraine of Valmair. Prime Beef. Ley-life, how could she ever have mocked him by privately calling him that? He was not funny now . . .

She sat very still and debated what to do. Plunge back into the river? Try to get a knife into him – them – before Baraine used ley on her?

Impossible . . .

'Maid Kaylen.' He sketched the kinesis of formal greeting. She merely declined her head. 'Baraine.'

'So we all meet again. What happened to Graval?'

She withstood the temptation to lick dry lips. 'He died — of a sore throat, I believe. Came on quite suddenly. Alive one minute, then —' She clicked her fingers. 'Dead, just like that.'

He stared, doubtful, as if he could not decide how much she knew.

'It seems the immortality of Minions is not so . . . long-lasting after all. You *did* find out he was a Minion, I suppose?' She pretended to examine her nails. 'Better watch it, you scummy bit of boglife, or you may find yourself absorbed into the Unstable with no soul to live on afterwards, either.'

The creature at his side sensed Baraine's anger. It bared its teeth in an animal gesture of rage, and lashed its tail.

She pretended to ignore it. 'Why, Baraine?' she asked. 'Why did you give yourself over to Carasma? You had everything a man could want, surely. Looks, wealth, position — in the Maker's name, *why*?'

He stroked the arm of the creature next to him, allowing his hand to trail lower and lower, until it was buried in the creature's genital hair. He smiled. 'That is why, girl. This is why.'

She still did not understand and he saw her bafflement.

His eyes narrowed. 'Can you be so innocent, so stupid? Try to imagine — if you can — what it is to lust, yes, and to love, but never to be allowed to fulfil that lust, that love. Because Chantry says it is a grave sin. Because Chantry says it is a perversion. Because Chantry says one man cannot lust after another. Imagine, if you can, what it is to live afraid even to let your eyes roam in the wrong direction, always to have to hide your love.' He snorted. 'By Chantry's Rule I was already condemned to the Hell of Disorder anyway. What did I have to lose? Here I can love whom I please, for ever. Here I will never grow old. Here men can lust after me for all eternity.'

A tumult of emotion stirred in her: fear, understanding, compassion, revulsion — she could feel it all. The Rule, she thought. Causes always seem to be rendered down to the same thing: the damned Rule. He's right. He shouldn't have had to hide his desire, or his love, any more than I should have had to quash my desire to be a mapmaker. Or Thirl his need to be something other than a mapmaker.

Reading part of what she felt on her face, he said harshly, 'I don't need your compassion, girl.' He smiled, and it was not a nice smile. All Keris's fear came flooding back in. 'That's better,' he said softly. 'That's better. I wonder if I should let Carve here loose in your direction. He's not very . . . fastidious in his tastes.'

She kept her eyes on Baraine. 'No. I can see that.'

There was no mistaking Baraine's anger this time. He raised a shaking finger in her direction.

She shuddered, the rest of her courage vanishing. *You fool! You're going to die because you couldn't keep your damn mouth shut —*

And then there was a snorting heaving horse between her and Baraine, the sound of a cracking whip and a wild cry of rage.

Davron's cry. Baraine's answering pain.

A gaping line of red was opened up across Baraine's face and chest. Blood dripped from Davron's whip as he whirled it back for another strike.

And then the scene froze as if time had stopped. The Wild was crouched, poised to leap, spurs extended; Baraine's hand was raised, about to make some gesture towards Davron — his fingers crackled with ley; Davron's arm remained stilled, whip motionless. Then with a deliberate gesture of contempt, the guide lowered his arm and rolled up his sleeve to display the sigil on his amulet. 'Dare,' he said, and his voice was thick with contempt. 'Just dare, and see what happens to you.'

One Trician to another, Keris thought. Ley-life, how he hates Valmair! With sudden clarity she knew why: in Baraine Davron saw himself — the Trician who had betrayed the code of his class by bargaining with the Unmaker. It was not Baraine that Davron despised, it was himself.

'We'll meet again,' Baraine said softly. 'You'll rue the day you struck me, Davron of Storre.' He turned away, beckoning to his Wild to follow.

Pure Chantry theatre, Keris thought, but somehow she could not laugh at Baraine. Even as he turned away, the cut on his face was closing up, healing.

Davron swung his horse to face her. The rage in him was intense and dark. For a moment she thought he was going to seize her, shake her unmercifully.

The moment passed.

'Damn it, Kaylen,' he said, 'what have you got for brains? Sitting there like Lord Carasma himself, trading insults with a Minion —'

'You heard,' she said weakly.

'Enough. Were you out of your tiny little mind?'

'It was either that or blubber. Thanks, anyway. For making a habit of timely rescues.'

He took a deep breath. 'Oh *shit,* Keris —' He was looking at her helplessly, his expression a mixture of pain and horror. It seemed a long time before he had gathered himself together enough to say, 'Please don't do that again. I don't think I could stand it.' He turned his horse away from the river and called back over his shoulder. 'Come on — the others are waiting for us.'

Chapter Nineteen

Beware the fence that devours the crop.

old saying of the Margravate of Malinawar

They were never free of Minions and their Pets after the crossing of the Flow, except for the one night they spent in a halt, when at least they felt reasonably safe. Otherwise, sleek black shadows haunted them by day, slinking away if anyone approached too closely; shapes hunkered down around their camp at night, growling softly. Sometimes Keris would catch a glimpse of Baraine, mounted on a horned beast, with his tailed Pet mounted behind him. At other times there were different Minions, men and women she did not know. They kept out of accurate bow range; they were careful and furtive.

They waited and followed.

Keris thought of the trompleri map and tried to contain her fear.

She was not the only one who worried: Portron spent more time than ever in kinesis devotions; Quirk often preferred to walk rather than ride ('I'm less conspicuous that way,' he explained). Corrian defiantly spat in the direction of their unholy escort, but her occasional muttered 'Bloody unnerving bastards – what in all the muck in the midden are they waiting *for*?' showed that her defiance was more for show than as a result of indifference.

Davron and Meldor ignored the followers with superb aplomb – perhaps because they knew that Scow, more pragmatically, rarely took his eyes off them.

'What are they up to?' Keris asked Scow when her nerves could stand it no longer.

'I don't know,' he admitted with a laugh, then added more soberly, 'I suppose the Unmaker lost his spy when Graval Hurg died, so now he's had to resort to this.'

'Were you spied on before Hurg turned up?'

'I don't think so. At least, no more than most fellowships are. I think we may have drawn attention to ourselves over this business of the trompleri map, unfortunately. Until then, I don't think Carasma took too much notice of Meldor – he was just a no-account blind man who rode with Davron, and Davron was just a guide who would one day have to do the Lord's bidding.' He shook his maned head unhappily. 'I think perhaps it's beginning to occur to Carasma that there's more to us than that.'

'Then why not wipe us out one dark night in a Minion attack? It would be so easy.'

He smiled ruefully. 'Possibly. Probably. Do you think we don't know it? But, Keris, apart from the difficulties the Unmaker has with regard to directly conniving at the death of those who follow the Maker, he *wants* us alive. That way he will learn more – about who supports us, for a start. And let me tell you another thing about the Unmaker and his Minions that may cheer you: they don't have much of an understanding of time.'

She did not understand and told him so.

He explained: 'If one has eternal life, urgency has little meaning. Ordinary humans are driven to act now, to act quickly, to try to fit a lifetime of living into a short time span. The Unmaker and his ilk have no such sense of urgency, especially those Minions who have been around for a few hundred years – most of them spend a great deal of their time sleeping. Even the Unmaker finds it difficult to prod them to action. His best servants are those who have been recently corrupted and have not yet forgotten what it is like to be human. But even Lord Carasma is slower to act than he should be. It is his weakness and has often been our salvation. Meldor believes that the world could have been long since disintegrated, if the Unmaker had worked at his unmaking with human dedication.'

And so they rode on, taking more care with their guard duties at night, being more watchful by day.

About them, the land changed. There were no trees at all now. Nothing that could be thought of as normal vegetation. The horses nibbled on rounded bulbs that pushed their way up out of the soil like giant grey pearls, and fortunately seemed to come to no harm as a result. The ground itself was twisted: red earthen waves, frozen in time, remained poised as if to break on the heads of the riders as they passed; sculptured rocks seemed poised in the midst of cataclysmic upheaval, their towers and cliffs and boulders abruptly halted in the middle of their heaving and twirling and undulating. Everything seemed momentarily caught in some hiatus of movement, giving the impression that if they were to turn their backs then everything would begin to move again. The rock tower would spiral upward, those boulders would fling themselves off that cliff, that wave of earth would break into thundering surf.

And indeed sometimes things did move. They would wake in the morning to find that their surroundings were not quite as they had been when they had gone to bed; they would occasionally see the land shift before them, as if a giant were turning over in his sleep under the soil somewhere, disturbing his covering. It was a world in the process of disintegration, of being unmade. Meldor's right, Keris thought. Things are growing worse. Father never told me that it was like this.

Portron apparently agreed. 'I keep on expecting to wake one morning to find there's a hole in the world, a place where there's . . . a nothingness,' he confided to Keris one day. 'A place where the ultimate unmaking has already been achieved and nothing is left except . . . space. A void. An –

an absence of anything.' He rubbed his bald patch anxiously. 'It wasn't like this when I passed through here twenty years ago.'

Keris shivered. She did not want to hear.

The changes made their journey difficult; Davron was always consulting his charts – not Kaylen maps now, but the work of Way Letering of Dormuss Crossways, a town in the Fifth. 'Ley-life,' Davron would complain, 'I wish this fellow could draw maps like yours, Keris! Come, tell me what you make of this.'

She would bend her head over the skins, only too aware that he was being careful not to brush against her as they stood together. 'It's changed since I was here last,' was his constant comment. 'The land is becoming more and more unstable.'

And she would shiver at the implications, even as she worked to interpret the maps and make sense of their own position in a changing land. Letering's maps had never been as good as hers and Piers's; now they were often next to useless. Still, she thought, he does have an interesting way of showing the relative height of hills and mountains. I'd like to talk to him about that. In the meantime she did what she could with his maps and her compass and theodolite, the latter now minus its telescope. By studying present configurations and comparing them with the past landscape as drawn in Letering's charts, it was often possible to work out the best routes around recent changes.

And so it was, after several false turns down dead-end valleys and several days lost in backtracking, that they came within sight of the Fifth Stability. Davron signalled a pause and rode with Meldor and Scow to the top of the small rise overlooking the kinesis chain to check on their position, while the rest of the party waited patiently below. Overhead, the stingray mantas circled with lazy undulations of their wings, viewing the humans below with their piggy eyes set on the underside of their triangular heads.

'More spies?' Scow asked, noticing them. But neither of

the others answered. There was no way of telling.

'We're right where Keris said we'd be,' Davron said. 'I can see the border town of Edgeloss.'

'And the Minions?' Meldor asked.

'They have dropped back.'

'Doubtless they feel the kinesis chain. Davron, we have to throw them off.' He turned to Scow. 'I'm sorry, Sammy, but you and I and Quirk might have to enter the stab. At least for a while.'

Scow was stoical. 'A few days won't hurt us.'

'Skirt inside the kinesis line and try not to let Chantry catch you,' Davron said. 'The rest of us'll go in to stock up on supplies, and we'll meet you south of Middlemass, in the Unstable. You know that canyon with the waterhole?'

'Withering Hole?'

'That's it. We'll meet there in eight days.' He turned back to Meldor. 'This is all coming to a head. We can't go on like this much longer. I can't go on travelling with you if the Unmaker has realised what you are doing – or the task he will ask me to perform will be either your murder, or the destruction of Havenstar.'

Meldor gave the faintest of sad smiles. 'Davron, I have never at any time thought it would be anything else. Surely it is obvious that there is a certain . . . inevitability about it. Destiny, if you like.'

Davron dragged in a heavy breath. 'A case of the fence stealing the crop, eh? And, believing that, you have travelled with me all this time?'

'Companion to a guide has been a good cover, as you know. You have suited my purposes – and where better than to have your enemy than under your nose?'

'You think of me as your enemy?' The unbearable desolation in Davron's voice touched both of his listeners; it was the cry of a lonely man knowing his own abandonment.

'Davron, you are my closest friend and my greatest danger. You will destroy me – or I will kill you. Or . . . just perhaps, together we will destroy Carasma first. As I have said before, I believe I will have warning of the Unmaker's call to you. If that happens, you will die before I will let you destroy our dreams. You have my promise on that.' He then added briskly, 'Come, we waste time. You must ride on to Edgeloss.'

Idly Keris watched the manta rays circling, pointed tails ruddering through the air to keep them on track. Pets? she wondered. Or just Wild, descendants of some of Malinawar's vanished birds, perhaps, for all that they were featherless. She felt a moment's sadness. With the Rending, so much had gone or been irretrievably changed. Even if it was possible to restabilise the world, to banish ley, there was so much that could never return. *Extinction is for ever.* A tautology she had read somewhere that now plucked a strand of helpless sorrow within her. Damn him, she thought. Damn the Unmaker.

She pushed the thought away and looked over to Portron. 'Chantor, will you still be riding with this fellowship after the Fifth?'

'Oh, aye. I'm thinking so. As long as you do.'

'You don't have to. I don't need a guardian.'

'That's a matter of opinion.' He glanced towards Corrian and Quirk to make sure they could not hear. 'Keris, I'm not good for much, I know. I'm not much of a rule-chantor, never have been. I hate confrontations. I should never have been placed in a Rule Office. I might have made a better devotions-chantor, or a mentor — I don't know. But the Sanhedrin said rule-chantor and once a decision is made it can't be unmade. But even I can see I have a duty towards an unprotected lass riding in a fellowship like this one. I'll be seeing you as far as the Eighth.'

She did not ask what he thought he could do to protect her. She knew it was a question he would not be able to answer.

Edgeloss was very much like Hopen Grat, yet, in spite of its lawlessness, Keris was surprised at the surge of confidence she felt. For the first time in weeks she felt safe. Here there were no Minions, no Wild. Here the land was not going to erupt beneath her feet, swallow her up or do anything else impossible: tomorrow it would look exactly as it had done yesterday. Here she might be raped or knifed or robbed, but no one was going to use ley on her, rip her to pieces, or steal her soul. As they rode down the potholed dust of the main street she drew in a deep breath of contentment. Not even the unsettling memory of the deserted line of kinesis chain towers they had just passed – a good five hundred paces outside the present barrier – could disturb her sense of wellbeing.

She glanced across at Davron where he rode beside her, to see that he too had relaxed. The tight look around his eyes had faded. For a while at least he did not have to worry about being ordered to embark on some murderous task that would turn his stomach. Within the stability he was safe from the Unmaker.

'Where are we going?' Portron asked him, looking around with some distaste. 'This place is as bad as Hopen Grat.'

'There's a chanterie with a travellers' lodge in the next town: Dormuss Crossways. There's a shrine there to Kt Beogor, I believe – or is it Kte Sylgie? Anyway, doubtless you will be glad to be among your own kind again, Chantor.'

'Indeed I will. And it's Kt Belmatian, I believe.'

Corrian removed her pipe and spat. 'And what about me and my kind, Master Storre?'

He gave her a teasing grin. 'Stay here if you will, Mistress.'

She grinned back, impervious to the slur. 'Ach, nay. I'll stick with you. Two nights, you said?'

'Yes. Then we'll cross to the south of the stab, buying supplies as we go, and leave from the south. You will have time to visit the obligatory shrines in the stability along the way.'

She sighed. 'More time on bent knee — or worse. I do hate these shrines that demand you approach flat on your belly, wriggling along like maggots trying to get out of the light. And as for Abasement kinesis: down on your knees, up on your feet, down on your belly, up on your elbows, down on your forehead . . . My old joints don't like this kinesis business at the best of times, but Abasement is the buffalo's arse.'

Portron frowned, wondering if he should make some remark to exhort Corrian to behave herself, but thought better of it. It was Davron who replied. 'I don't know why not,' he said, his tone deceptively mild. 'Those same joints of yours don't seem to mind other sorts of exercise.'

Corrian cackled and pulled her mule around to skirt what appeared to be a dead body on the road.

'Should we do something about him?' Keris asked doubtfully.

Davron glanced down. 'No. He's beyond help. Did you know Dormuss Crossways is where Letering the Mapmaker has his shop?'

'Is it? Will I have time to see him?'

'Of course! Unless you want to linger around the shrine all day.'

'Not me,' she said, low enough so that Portron could not hear. 'If I was going to stay anywhere all day, it would be in a steaming hot herb bath, with lots of that lovely scented soap the chanteries make.' She sighed. 'It seems months since I had a good bath.'

The chanterie did not have any guest baths at all, but there was a public bath house just next door, so Keris had her bath — for a price, scented soap included. When she slipped between two clean sheets on a real bed that night, after a hot meal that had not been cooked with beef jerky and old vegetables, she felt she never wanted to leave again. Yet, when she woke in the morning to the sound of bells tinkling as the chantors hurried past her room to attend to morning

Obeisance, and when she smelt the whiff of the perfume used in the ceremony (always rosemusk for Obeisance), she felt uncomfortable. The Rule was suddenly once again too close, too oppressive. With an inward sigh she dug around in her packs to find a skirt: trousers might be all right to wear when riding in from the Unstable, but no chantor would tolerate her wearing anything but a skirt in the chanterie of the town.

Breakfast, hot milk and fresh bread still warm from the oven, was lying on the refectory table when she entered, although most of the chantors had eaten already. Davron sat at a long trestle table, alone.

She made the morning kinesis as she sat opposite him and poured herself some milk from the jug. 'Where's Portron?'

He returned the salute cheerfully. 'Obeisance. Where's Corrian?'

'Dead to the world. She had a tremendous argument with the dormitory chantor last night; did you hear? She wouldn't put out her pipe.'

She sipped her milk, surreptitiously watching him. In the Unstable he always seemed tensely alert, yet calm. Now it was the opposite. He was relaxed, yet somehow his calm had vanished. He was fidgeting and seemed to have shredded most of his bread rather than eaten it.

'I'll show you the way to the mapmaker's when you've finished,' he said. 'I have to walk that way myself.'

A chantor, who had been cleaning the other tables, stopped beside him. 'Master Guide,' he said politely, 'we don't waste bread here.'

Davron looked down at what he had done, seeming to notice the pile of crumbs for the first time. 'Oh, I'm sorry.' He picked out the biggest piece of bread and popped it into his mouth.

'It's the Rule,' the man said.

Davron raised a puzzled eyebrow. 'It's the Rule not to make a mess of one's bread?'

'Not to waste bread. We grow all the grain we can, but

we've lost a lot of land to Chaos since my grandfather's day.' He shook his head sorrowfully. 'I heard they are thinking they'll have to shift the kinesis chain yet again and abandon a village on the south side of the Fifth — and that's good farming land out that way. I keep on wondering when we'll be able to move the chain the other way — taking land away from Chaos — but it never happens.' He sighed and moved on to the next table.

Guiltily, Davron upended a cup over his crumbs and grinned at Keris. 'Let's go,' he said, 'before I have to do kinesis penance for the wanton destruction of a slice of bread.'

Dormuss Crossways was shabbier than any First Stability town. The houses seemed more ancient and the slate roofs were often so broken that they resembled rubble rather than tiles. The people seemed shabbier also. The Rule in the Fifth was more oppressive and stated that all encoloured citizens must wear grey, with black collars and cuffs. Boots had to be black and have a regulation number of hooks for the laces. Snoods and wimples had to be dark and even unmarried women had to have their hair done in braids tied with black laces. Men were obliged to wear narrow brimmed hats. Dressed in her fawn blouse and brown skirt, Keris felt positively colourful.

Just outside the travellers' lodge a few town workmen had dug up the street and then abandoned the workings. As Keris and Davron stepped out of their lodgings, they had to push their way through a crowd now gathered about the pile of unearthed cobbles, arguing heatedly. 'I wonder what that's all about,' Keris said.

'The chantors were talking about it this morning at breakfast. It seems the Rule won't allow anyone to quarry for more stone to make new cobbles, so someone decided they should just turn over the old ones — put the underside uppermost. Unfortunately they have just discovered that someone else had the same idea several hundred years ago —

and now they're arguing about which side of the cobbles is the most worn.'

They looked at one another and simultaneously burst into laughter, sharing an appreciation of the tale and all it said about the absurdity of stability life and the Rule.

They were still laughing when they were stopped a moment later by a rule-chantor. He was resplendent in crimson and gold, with the green braid of his rank and the purple of this Ordering adding still more colour. Both wrists were heavy with jewelled bracelets, and he had fringed his stole with lace as well as bells. His tricorn hat was ruched and spangled. Chantors in the First were always colourful, but Keris had never seen quite as much splendour as on this man. He held up an authoritative hand. 'Stop, please. Tell me why you are dressed this way.'

'Master Guide,' Davron said laconically, tapping his chest. 'And a pilgrim from the First.' He fumbled in his purse and produced the leather tag of a guide, duly stamped with the seal of the Sanhedrin.

The rule-chantor looked at it and carefully handed it back, before glaring at Keris. 'Your pilgrim's pass, please.'

She showed him the pass she had bought in Hopen Grat. He stared at the date, did a few calculations and then handed it back with a curt nod. 'You Firsters,' he grumbled, 'you don't know how to dress. If I had my way, you'd have to put on the clothing of the Fifth while you are here. You disturb the regularity of the Rule with your different garb, and it encourages disorder. In fact, the Sanhedrin should enforce uniformity throughout all the stabilities.'

'I agree entirely,' Davron said blandly. 'Everyone should wear *exactly* the same thing.' Keris just managed to keep a straight face until the chantor had disappeared around a nearby corner.

They continued on their way, swapping tales of Chantry absurdities. When she related stories of her verbal battles with Nebuthnar in winter school, Keris was amazed to find that she had the power to turn Davron's casual interest into chuckles and finally into helpless laughter. (Davron Storre, *laughing*?) When he finally pointed out the mapmaker's and then continued on his way alone, she felt a disproportionate regret. They had so little opportunity to feel carefree . . .

And Letering was not there. 'I'm sorry,' his wife said, 'but he's gone to buy more skins from the tanner's. I expect he'll be back in half an hour or so. I'm sure he'd be glad to meet you, if you're a mapmaker.' She sounded doubtful, dubious of the truth of Keris's statement about her trade, rather than her husband's willingness to meet a colleague. 'You can wait, or go for a walk. There's a nice stretch of river further along the road. Real picture it is now, with all the wildflowers and the view across to the domain.'

'Which domain is that?' Keris asked, suddenly alert.

'Tower-and-Fleury. Not a big place, mind.' The woman laughed. 'Even the Tricians aren't rich around here.'

'Oh. Would that — would that be the family of Alyss who married Davron of Storre?'

'That's the one.'

'She's there now?'

'Oh, I shouldn't think so. She's married, after all — but, then, how should I know? Tricians don't tell the likes of us what they're up to, do they?'

'No. Not very often,' Keris agreed.

She left the shop and went to look for the domain, driven by an overwhelming curiosity, by a bizarre desire to hurt herself. *Lovely Alyss, moonshine and quicksilver* . . . She did not doubt for a moment that that was where Davron had gone.

The river was barely more than a stream and the domain house in the distance — long and low with a slate roof — was set on the opposite side, surrounded by farm fields. The near side of the stream was a tangle of trees, bushes and under- growth into which a narrow path disappeared. It was not the kind of woodland scenery Keris was used to: the Fifth was much drier than the First and the vegetation was more stunted and tangled as a consequence. Still, it was suddenly good to see proper trees again, and feel the grass beneath her feet, grass that crushed beneath her shoes. She set off down the path, catching glimpses of the domain house through the growth as she approached closer.

What she did not expect was to see Davron.

He should have been in the house, surely – instead he was standing hidden among the trees, watching the buildings on the other side of the river, so intent that he did not see or hear her. She came to a halt, stood motionless, appalled. She was intruding and her intrusion was unpardonable – yet she could not bring herself to move.

From where she stood she could see what he was watching: two children playing in front of the house. One was a girl of about eight; the other a boy some two or three years younger. They were Trician children; she could see that much by the fineness of their black and grey clothes.

A plump middle-aged woman came out of the house and called to them. The girl promptly caught hold of the boy's hand and began to walk towards the door; he protested and pulled away. There was a scuffle, a child's shouted protest and several giggling chases before both of them ran off into the house and all was silent again.

It had been a short glimpse of ordinary daily life, without any particular meaning, yet it left Keris with a feeling of profound sadness. She glanced back at Davron and began to back away.

He turned and saw her, and stopped dead.

She had thought he would be angry. Instead he stood like a man on the edge of a chasm, knowing any minute that the edge would crumble beneath him. There was no room for anger in his despair. She stepped towards him, unable to do anything else. 'Why?' she whispered. 'Why can't you go and see them?'

The woods around them seemed hushed, quiet, waiting for his answer. He was silent for so long she thought he was not going to reply at all, then he said quietly, without emotion, 'Because if I try to see them, speak to them, she will tell Chantry that I wear this.' He touched his sleeve at the place where the Unmaker's sigil was fused to his biceps. 'I have not seen Mirrin — my daughter — since the day this was placed on my arm. I have never held my son in my arms, or heard him call me father.' He looked back at the building on the other side of the stream. 'Every time I come to Dormuss I stand here and watch the house, and hope that I will at least see Mirrin. Just catch a glimpse. Often I stand all day, and I never see her at all.'

She will tell Chantry? Alyss, his wife? Keris was stupefied. If Chantry knew about his sigil, Davron would die, condemned as an apostate. Immediately after the most summary of trials, with no time for any excuses. The woman threatened him with death, *yet he had done it all for her,* for Alyss, his wife.

Davron leant against the tree and Keris watched in growing horror as he began to cry, shoulders shaking helplessly as the grief of five years spilt over into the present.

Chapter Twenty

Nothing is colder than the grey ashes of an old love, nothing warmer than the bright coals of the new.

> old saying of the Margravate of Malinawar

Domain lords were allowed to have large families. The reason was obvious and undisputed: so many of their sons were destined to die in service to the people of their stability, to die – or to be tainted and excluded.

Thus, when Davron of Storre was born to the wife of a domain lord of the Fourth Stability, he already had four elder brothers and two sisters.

His father, Camone of Storre, was a large untidy man with untidy habits who had married a woman of fey charm and no self-discipline; the result was a family that enjoyed life in a state of eternal disarray and constant laughter. The children ran wild for much of the time, scattering their mischief through the house and the estate, leaving the consequences for the servants. Had they been less likable they might have been despised for their irresponsibility – but, like their parents, they were pleasant-natured and kind. They may have been fickle but none of the Storre brood were ever malicious. The more perspicacious of servants were in fact aware that the wildness and the self-centredness of the Storre children were products of their future rather than their present: the Storres knew that the sweetness of life, possibly the length of life itself, would for them be short-lived and they were determined to live it to the full.

Their existence was not completely without discipline. There were lessons and these could never be shirked. Arms training started for the boys when they were five and part of every day was dedicated to it thereafter; combat drills and exercises became an integral part of life. A variety of weapons was presented to them over the years, each needing to be mastered before the ultimate choice of a personal weapon was made.

There were other lessons too: those in reading and numbering and the Rule taken in the local Chantry school; others their father taught when he was home: pathfinding, map-reading, equestrian skills and similar attainments that would help them one day in the Unstable. The sons of Storre knew how to magnetise and read a compass, how to plot a course by the stars, how to live off the land. They could mount and dismount from a galloping horse by the time they were ten, or they could diagnose and treat common equine problems such as a sprained forelock or a bout of colic.

By the time he was twelve, Davron had passed all the written and oral tests needed to qualify him as a Defender, and he had chosen his preferred weapons: the throwing knife and the whip. For two more years he honed his skills within the walls of his father's domain, but by then the carefree years were already over: the first inevitable tragedy had come and left its scars. The eldest Storre brother was dead in the Unstable, killed by a Minion while riding guard on a large fellowship.

When he was fourteen, Davron started riding in the local Defender troop that policed the area against those who broke the Rule. A year later, his father died as a consequence of a combination of old injuries received in the Unstable, and another brother, retired from the Defenders after being mauled by a Wild, took over the domain. That same year, Davron – aged fifteen – killed his first human, an Unbred boy whose only crime was to have been born deformed. A few months later, sixteen-year-old Geralt Storre – the best loved of his brothers and the closest to Davron in age – disappeared after being tainted.

When Davron himself was sixteen, he rode his first tour of duty in the Unstable, crossed his first ley line, and discovered – against all odds – that he was ley-lit.

Davron Storre at that age was a pleasant boy, well liked by his male peers and the object of sidelong glances from Trician girls who saw something in him beyond the ordinary: a romanticism, a sense of honour, a thoughtfulness that was beginning to overtake the superficiality his early erratic upbringing had encouraged. At twelve Davron had been both shallow and spoilt. By sixteen, he was much more caring and introspective; he accepted responsibility and fought with courage. If he had a fault, it was pride – he was proud of his honour, of his integrity.

As a younger son, with no possibility of ever inheriting the Storre domain and thus being one of the landed gentry, he was destined to be a Defender, alternating guard duty on crossings with policing duties at home. There was no other profession open to him, although the domain of Storre would always be obliged to provide him with a home in one of the domain cottages.

Davron embarked down the expected road knowing there were no other options and it worried him not one whit. The first time he had ridden out into the Unstable as part of a guard contingent he had found himself enjoying it. He liked the comradeship of his fellow Trician Defenders; he enjoyed the exhilaration of the unknown, the danger of ley crossings, the sheer unbridled adventure of the ever-changing Unstable.

He began to read the ley lines, and, because he was ley-lit as well as being talented, promotions came quickly. He volunteered for more crossings than were required of him and gradually acquired the skills that would stand him in good stead later, as a guide. Both his mind and his body were being challenged, and as a consequence his personality developed more depth – but he never lost the strong streak of romanticism and honour.

At eighteen he fell in love.

Alyss of Tower-and-Fleury was on her pilgrimage when he met her. She was two years older than he was, but less wise and with much less experience of the world.

Taken with the black-eyed youth, who was all whip-cord and muscle, yet seemed gentle, she gave him every encouragement. By the time her pilgrimage was over, they had declared their love.

He courted her with letters and frequent visits; they were married immediately after his own pilgrimage at the age of twenty. Alyss moved to the Storre domain as custom dictated. At her insistence, and when he was given a choice, Davron opted for local law-enforcement duties rather than crossings assignments. As a married man, soon with a child on the way, he had no wish to be parted from his wife — and yet there were times when he regretted that he could not spend more time in the Unstable. If he had allowed himself to consider the matter, he would have realised that at heart he was an Unstabler. Stability with all its regulations stifled him. When he had to deal with Chantry, he had to subdue his hostility. The Rule irritated him. Only in the Unstable could he feel truly free.

Yet, when his daughter Mirrin was born, there could have been no happier man than Davron of Storre. He adored his daughter and resented the duties that took him away from her. As for Alyss . . . Had he known how Scow was to describe his wife to Keris, he would have agreed with the description. Alyss was indeed like moonlight: ethereal, beautiful quicksilver. She was a tease and a flirt and so much fun. She was kind and gentle and generous: she could never pass a hurt creature or a beggar child without stopping. He loved her as much as it was humanly possible to love, and, had the Unmaker not stepped into his life, he would probably have gone on loving her that way — and been happy in that love. He did not see that she was still untried, as yet untouched by adversity, callow. Even her charity was something that never caused her pain: it was the footman who passed her coppers on to the beggar; the maid who cared for the wounded bird she found; her physician who cared for the newly tainted boy they discovered in the Unstable. There was little below the surface of Alyss of Tower-and-Fleury, but Davron felt no lack and did not know the illusory nature of the dream he lived.

When Mirrin was three, Alyss found she was expecting another child, but this pregnancy did not seem to progress well. Alyss was tired and fretful and often ill. She was irritated by Mirrin's noise, discontented by the smallness of their house on the Storre domain, unhappy with Davron's absences on patrol. She harped on things that had not worried her before: her parents had never seen Mirrin, it was so long since she had seen her mother, she missed her home in the Fifth. She wanted her mother for this new birth. She was frightened. Please – could they go to the Fifth Stability? She could have the baby there . . .

Davron, while sympathetic, was more concerned about the danger. Crossings were becoming more treacherous. He knew better than most the sort of tricks a ley line could produce; he dreaded gambling the life of his wife and child on the unpredictability of ley. But he loved Alyss, and she pleaded so desperately.

He planned it carefully. It was to be a strong group with a large contingent of Defenders, too large surely for any of the Wild or the Minions to risk attacking. He was aware of the paradox: the larger the group, the more they drew the attention of the Unmaker, but he still felt at that time that it was worth the risk to have the security in numbers. He hired the best of guides; he himself would lead the armed escort; the men were his hand-picked elite. Every comfort was to be provided for Alyss and Mirrin: a physician and a chantor were in attendance. Alyss laughed at her husband for all his precautions, but he was determined that they should not come to harm.

Not far into the Unstable, they found and rescued a young farm boy called Sammy Scowbridge. Abandoned by his fellowship after having been tainted, he was almost dead of starvation and half out of his mind because of what had happened to him. They took him in and Alyss insisted that her physician give him the best of care. It was, however, Davron – hardly much older than the traumatised farm boy himself – who managed to restore Sammy Scowbridge's peace of mind. He saw something in the youth, in his tragedy, that tugged at him; inevitably he was reminded of Geralt's disappearance. His brother had been abandoned just as Sammy had, alone and on foot – and had never been seen again.

And so he spent time talking to Scow, brushing aside the differences between Trician and farm boy. He delved inside himself to find the wisdom to help Scow confront what had happened: the tainting, the betrayal of his love. Along the way he made the closest friend he would ever have. When Scow finally was able to look down at his reddish mane and say with mournful humour, 'But Tilly always said she *liked* men with hair on their chests,' Davron knew he was over the worst.

A day later they arrived at the Wanderer.

All seemed quiet. The guide was well pleased with the ley patterns, and Davron concurred. But the patterns lied – or perhaps the two men missed some subtle clue that would have told them all was not well, or perhaps it was a fact that when the Unmaker was present he could, if he wished, subdue the patterns as he sat in wait . . .

The main party was already across when Davron rode into the line as escort for Alyss, with Mirrin sitting on his saddle bow. Both mounts were well-trained crossings-horses, so he had seen no need to dismount.

They were halfway through when a thick mist of sulphurous yellow surrounded them. The air was clear where they were, but the artificial way the vapour swirled around told Davron that it was designed to cut them off from escape. When he reached out to touch one of its eddies, he was burnt by its acidity; when he breathed one of its tendrils, he choked.

'What is it?' Alyss asked, impatient. 'Why are we stop-ping? It's just a mist.'

'Don't move. It is harmful.'

She looked around, expression dubious. 'How can a mist be harmful?'

He felt a moment's irritation and quelled the feeling as unworthy. 'This is a ley line, Alyss. We had better dis-mount.' His voice was quiet as he tried not to show her the fear he had for her safety — hers and Mirrin's. Neither of them was ley-lit. They could both be tainted.

He helped Alyss down from her horse and she clung to him, trembling as she sensed his fear. He held Mirrin in his arms and cursed himself for ever agreeing to this trip.

And the Unmaker appeared.

He was naked except for his pendant. His skin glistened with golden sweat and open sexuality. He was aroused and his arousal threatened them all. His swarthy penis thrust through the tight curls of his golden pubic hair, its lividity ugly and menacing.

He feasted his eyes on Mirrin and Alyss, and laughed.

'What do you want of us?' Davron asked, dry-throated.

'You,' Carasma replied. 'You, Davron of Storre. You, to become a Minion of Chaos, mine to command for all eternity.'

Alyss saw and heard — and buried her face in his shoulder, weeping; Mirrin began to cry too, and her sobs of terror tore into him. He could not help his shudder. '*Never* —' he whispered. 'You would unmake my soul.'

'Of what use is a soul to him who will not die?'

'My soul is not mine to give,' he said with a courage he did not feel. 'I worship the Maker; my soul is His.'

The golden face tensed, its classic features suddenly seem-ing to take on hard shadowed planes, like an anvil. 'Come to me, or I taint your wife and child.'

Alyss moaned, sagged in his clasp. Mirrin, not under-standing, began to scream.

Davron felt the world crushing in on him. There was no direction he could turn, no route for escape no matter what he did — and he did not know what to do. The alternatives were each so terrible there could be no choice. 'I cannot,' he whispered, almost not believing that this could be happening. 'I cannot give up my soul; I cannot serve evil. *I cannot.*'

Alyss turned on him, twisting in his arms. 'Davron, for mercy's sake, *stop* him —'

'I don't know how,' he stammered.

Her eyes dilated with a horror so extreme he thought she might cease to breathe. He had never felt so helpless, never felt such inadequacy. All he held dear he had in his arms, yet he was unable to protect them. The muscles in his throat tightened.

'Let me show you what I can do,' Carasma said, and drew an image with a gesture of his hands. The yellow mist cleared a little — just enough to show a semblance of Alyss and Mirrin before them . . . Monsters, dragging themselves along the ground — with human faces. Mirrin, innocent and apple-cheeked; Alyss, silver-smiled and gentle. The rest was obscenity.

Alyss, the real Alyss, screamed. She beat at him with her fists, begged him to save her, to do what the Lord asked. Why was he frightened of a little mist? Let them ride away out of there, flee, anything, anything . . . Mirrin saw her face in the monstrosity before her, heard her mother's hysteria, and her own screams redoubled. Davron buried her face in his shoulder and rocked her.

He stood speechless, spirit-broken, knowing now all the colours of evil. The choking horror in his throat clamped his muscles tight, tearing his voice from him. He did not know it then, but he would never be smooth-voiced again.

'*If you loved me you would do anything,*' Alyss shrieked, her hands clutching, digging in, shaking him. 'What of Mirrin? You say you love her!'

And in that moment he left all his youth behind.

'Look on them as they will be, if you refuse,' the Unmaker purred. 'Look well, and ask yourself if you will be able to live with what you have done.'

'I will kill us all,' Davron said, his voice hoarse and painful, as he strove to hold his frantic daughter.

Alyss screamed at him, but he could not bring himself to hear what she was saying.

'Not yet,' Carasma said. The words were viciously joyful. 'Not yet. First I will taint them. Look, Davron of Storre, and see what your stubbornness has wrought.'

But, as he lifted his hand to point it at Alyss, she drew herself away from her husband, shuddering. 'No,' she said with sudden cold calm. 'No. I will not be tainted. I would rather give up my s—'

Davron knew what she was going to say. To her, anything was better than being tainted — or was it Mirrin's fate that concerned her? Perhaps she was going to offer herself to Carasma so that her daughter could go free, but Davron was no longer sure if he knew her. There had been a coldness in her voice that he had never heard before, as if she was a stranger who despised him.

He drew back his fist even as she started to say the words that would sell her soul to the Unmaker. And he hit her, hard. Her head snapped back and she fell senseless.

Mirrin struggled out of his arms and ran to her mother. 'I hate you!' she screamed at him. 'You hit Mummy! You're not my daddy never again!' They were the last words she had ever spoken to him, and they were to echo and re-echo in his memory like shards of hell, the pain of them never diminishing. Mirrin, with her head buried into her mother's clothing, crying herself almost into a stupor, never looking at him again . . .

Davron stared at Carasma, helpless. 'I shall make a bargain with you,' he croaked, his voice harshly unrecognisable to his own ears. 'I will not be your Minion, not ever, no matter what it costs me — or mine. But let them go free, without harm now or ever, and I will perform one task for you. One task, of your choosing — and at a time of your choosing.' He was gambling, and he knew it. Gambling that Carasma would give him time, time to suffer, and that in that time he would find a way out of his dilemma. Or kill himself.

Carasma hesitated, suspicious. 'Anything?'

'As long as it is to be done within your realm. I will do nothing in any stability. One task — and I shall be free of any obligation and safe from you and your servants.' Bile welled up into his throat and mouth. *Traitor! Betrayer of his class, apostate of his Oath to the Defenders, traitor to Chantry.* The moment he opened his mouth to bargain with the Unmaker, he lost his honour . . .

Carasma considered. 'What pain is there in that for you? I am beginning not to like you, Davron of Storre — I prefer you to suffer.' He sneered down at Alyss. 'I wonder what sort of baby will be born to a tainted monster.'

Davron swallowed the bile. Deliberately, he allowed his desperation to drag at his voice. 'One task, at the time of your choosing. Is that not punishment enough for any man?'

'No, not good enough. You will disappear into a stability and I will never see you again. You must swear to spend three-quarters of every year here in the Unstable. And if you do not keep your word — if you kill yourself — then I shall taint your daughter, or any ley-unlit issue of yours, any descendant through all time, when they come to do their pilgrimage. My word on it. *Now* do you accept my side of the bargain?'

He paled, knowing he would be saying goodbye to the life he had led. He plunged on, unable to think of an alternative. 'Yes, if I have your assurance as the Unmaker that, after I have performed your task, I — and mine — will be safe from your harm for all time?'

He smiled. 'The only harm that will come to you — and yours — will be what you will do to yourselves, Master Davron.' He began to nod in a self-satisfied way. 'Yes, I think I begin to like this. It has possibilities . . . Do you accept, then?'

It was worse than Davron had hoped for, but he knew it was all he was going to get. 'I accept,' he said. And the shame he felt at his capitulation began.

Five years further on he finally cried for what he had lost that day; cried because another woman had asked him why he could not see his children.

Keris wanted to take him into her arms, she wanted to hold him, comfort him, love him. She wanted to banish his pain, his tears. Instead she stood helpless, aware that he shrank from being touched.

She waited.

Finally he calmed, walked to the stream, washed his face, wiped it dry with his hands. He lowered himself to the ground with his back to a tree, his head tilted back to lean on its trunk, his knees bent to support his forearms. And, briefly, he told her what had happened that day in the ley line, when he had lost his world. 'She will not permit me near my daughter,' he finished, his voice flat, 'and she has hidden my son from me.'

She went to kneel at his side, still not touching him. 'I don't understand.'

A long pause. And then: 'Alyss forbade me to see Mirrin ever again, forbade me ever to see the child she was bearing.'

She searched for reasons, to excuse the inexcusable. 'She feared for their safety —'

'She knows Carasma is always bound by the terms of his bargains. No, she was . . . ashamed. Ashamed that I knew she had been willing to sell her soul to save herself — so she had to blame me, punish me. And she despises me, too. Despises me because I could not protect her as it was my duty to do, could not protect our children — without selling myself to Carasma.'

'You judge her harshly.'

He said in sudden anguish, 'I would have forgiven her anything, understood anything . . . except what she did to Mirrin — and Staven. She could have turned me in to Chantry there and then and I would have understood. Applauded her courage, even. Loved her still more, knowing the depth of her sacrifice to save the world from what I might do to it. And I cannot blame her for blaming me — Maker, how could I condemn her for something I do myself, every day of my life? No, it was what she did to Mirrin and the boy that I can never forgive. Never.'

She waited, understanding at last that he hated his wife.

'Mirrin — she was only three. Think about it, Keris. What she had seen, and heard. She had seen her own face on the shoulders of a monster. She had been threatened by the Unmaker and seen her father powerless to save her. She had seen me strike her mother senseless. And then Alyss forbade me to see her, forbade me to speak to her, forbade me to even say goodbye. "Come near her again, and I shall tell the world you wear the Unmaker's sigil," she said. So I left — turned my back on my daughter and her trauma. I accepted that, I accepted that as the price I had to pay. As my punishment, if you like. She will have her mother, I thought. Alyss loves her as much as I do. Alyss will be her support and her comfort.'

He paused, still not looking at Keris, and she knew she still had not heard the thing that had turned his love for Alyss into a cold rage against her.

'I left them there, and rode off with Scow. He offered to come with me. A few days later I met Meldor for the first time, and we have been together ever since. I have a bargain with him, too. I help him and he kills me when the time comes.' He gave a dry laugh. 'Not much of a bargain, is it? But I can't kill myself without endangering the future of my children — and my children's children.'

He dropped a hand to the ground and began to sift soil aimlessly through his fingers. 'Alyss went on to Tower-and-Fleury. But, instead of staying with her parents, she left Mirrin and rode off to the chanterie in Middlemass. It's a closed kinesis order that sends chantoras to the chain, and she told them she wanted to sever her marriage to me and replace it with one to them, as a kinesis-chantora. They told her that was only possible if she sacrificed something of great value. So she gave them our baby. Our son. When he was born she offered him to Chantry. He was taken from her, given another name, and sent elsewhere. She never even put him to the breast. And now he is untraceable, destined never to know his origins, destined to be a chantor.'

She drew in a sharp breath, and turned involuntarily to look at the house on the other side of the river.

'The girl was Mirrin,' he said, 'but the boy was her cousin, not my son. I have never seen him and never will. I will never know where he is, or even know his given name. I – I call him Staven.' He raised his face to look at her, and his gravel voice broke. 'Mirrin lost her father in circumstances that were inexplicable to her. Just when she needed Alyss most, she was rejected by her as well, with breathtaking callousness. My son was given over to strangers who only care to raise chantors for their cause. Mirrin and Staven will never know one another. For that – for all that – I shall never forgive Alyss of Tower-and-Fleury.'

He looked at her with helpless eyes, and she dropped her gaze. In her heart she cried for him, and knew that had she stood in Alyss's shoes his children would have been the most precious beings alive. *How could she have done that to her own flesh and blood? To his children?*

'I don't know why,' he said, as if she had spoken aloud. 'I suppose she feels that offering her son to Chantry will help to expiate her sin. Perhaps she would also have offered Mirrin, if her parents had allowed it. I don't know why she did the things she did. I don't know what stops her from telling Chantry about me – possibly she's afraid I would then tell the world exactly what she was prepared to do.' He shrugged. 'If so, then she knows me little. I have told no one that. Not Meldor, not Scow, no one – until now. And I'm not sure why I'm telling you. Perhaps –' His voice caught as he looked at her. 'Keris, it has become very important to me that you say you understand why I did what I did, if you can.'

She did not hesitate. 'Yes.'

The immediacy of her reply took him by surprise and he

stared, then laughed. 'Oh, Keris, dear, is there anyone as — as wonderfully *forthright* as you are?'

She said in surprise, 'I didn't need to think. Most women would have *honoured* a man who did what you did for her and for your daughter.' *I would have.*

'Oh Keris —' She wasn't sure what she had done, but some of the burden was gone from his voice, and she was glad.

He stood, giving one last reluctant glance at the domain house. 'Let's go. Was Letering out when you called? Were you wanting to ask him about trompleri maps?'

She accepted his need to talk about something else, a neutral topic. 'Yes. And also he has a way of showing the land height with lines and numbers. It's ingenious. I think he must use some form of vertical triangulation, using a theodolite. I have long thought it possible . . .'

She chattered on, trying not to think how much she would have liked to kill Alyss of Tower-and-Fleury for what she had done to this man at her side. She knew now who had put the polish on the obsidian blackness of his eyes.

She went to him that night.

She did not know or care why he had been assigned a single room; she was just glad it was that way. She waited until the last service of the day, the Abasement, was finished and the last of the drifting perfume, moonflower-wine, had dissipated. When the chanterie was finally still and quiet, she crept along the stone-flagged corridors to his room.

He opened to her knock immediately, as if he had been wide awake and waiting. There was even a candle burning by his bed. He gestured for her to enter — but he remained remote, standing away from her. 'Is there something wrong?' he asked.

She shook her head dumbly.

He understood then. His face changed, darkening as he flushed. 'Oh no, Keris. No. I thought you understood. I thought you knew — it's not possible.'

She stammered in turn. 'I thought — I thought — I know

your wife was very beautiful, and I'm plain, and I have no experience –'

He groaned, and she stumbled into embarrassed silence. 'You don't understand,' he whispered. 'Sweet Creation, you don't understand. It's not possible.'

She rushed on. 'I'm not asking for anything permanent. I know you're a Trician, and I'm just a mapmaker's daughter, but I thought – You *did* want me, I know you did –'

'Keris, Keris – hush. Of *course* I wanted you. *Want* you. I've wanted a lot of women in the five years since I was bonded to the Unmaker. I've never taken one of them, and I never will. I am cut off from the tainted, and from the normal, and from the ley-lit – Carasma's little joke on me, you see, because I didn't specify it in our bargain. I can never lie with anyone as long as I wear this.' He touched the sigil on his arm. 'Except a Minion, I suppose. And that I will never do.'

She looked at him, uncomprehending, not wanting to understand.

Gently, so very gently, he took up her hand and – eyes never leaving her face – he allowed his lips to brush the back of her fingers. She felt the first jolt when he touched her hand, but that was just the beginning. His lips were burning incandescence. The pain screamed through her, searing, pulsing deep, molten metal being poured into her veins. It lasted only for the second that he held her, for the moment of his kiss to her fingers, but it had her sinking to the floor, dragging in deep breaths, praying for the memory of the agony to become bearable.

Gradually the wild beating of her heart calmed. She looked down at her hand: it was unmarked. She stumbled to her feet and stood before him and her eyes filled with tears. When he reached out again she refused to flinch, but all he did was stroke her hair. Tenderly he wound a strand around his finger, touching the only part of her that would not feel the fire of his fingers.

She turned away then, blindly groping for the door. She

barely heard his whispered words as the door closed behind her, but they echoed on in her head as she ran crying along the corridor until she did not know whether they had been her words, or his.

'I'm so sorry. Forgive me. Forgive me.'

Chapter Twenty-One

*She has magic in her colours, despair in her heart and gives
beauty she does not have. She will vanquish the Lord or die
in the ley because of him. In her hands are both salvation and
death.*

Predictions XII: 2: 23

Ley-life but I feel old, Keris thought. How long ago was it
that I left Kibbleberry? Four weeks? No, it must be more like
six. Yet I feel I've aged ten years . . . I was a child, and now
I've grown up.

She looked across at Davron, where he rode to the side
and slightly ahead of her. His clothing was, like hers, stained
with dust and sweat; his seat on his crossings-horse was
relaxed, yet there was something about the way he held his
head that told her he was alert and watchful. I am beginning
to read him so well, she thought. Is this what it is like to be in
love – to look at someone and know how they feel?

They were riding through a land that seemed utterly
without redemption. Dry, harsh red in colour, slashed
through with bottomless fissures and crazed with cracks – it
was easy to think of it as being already partially unmade.
What had Portron said? 'I keep on thinking I'll come
across a hole in the world . . . A place where there is
nothingness . . .' Well, there were holes enough in this
landscape to make him think his worst nightmare was
coming true.

The chantor was riding beside her, his shoulders slumping

a little with fatigue. He had lost weight in the weeks since they had left the First; his paunch had slimmed to a more flabby, less noticeable roundness. She wondered idly why it was that he was so protective of her. There did not seem to be any reason that she could see: she had never given him any encouragement to think that she might be amenable to Chantry interference in her life and she did not think that he was guilty of falling in love with someone thirty years younger than he was.

Her eyes strayed back to Davron. Solid, sorrow-laden, troubled Davron. I must have been mad, she thought. Whatever made me think that he felt anything for me? It was just the reaction of a virile man who hasn't had a woman for five years . . . It wasn't me he wanted, it was just relief. I wish that knowing that made a difference — but it doesn't. Before, I just wanted him; now I love him, and it hurts . . .

Ley-life, how I love him . . . Creation, his courage.

The only way he could find freedom would be to change the whole world, and that was what he was trying to do, knowing all the while that he would probably lose. And yet he refused to surrender.

Helpless to aid him, she considered the way he wrapped himself around with his protective shell, the way he kept himself under tight control all the time, waiting — endlessly waiting, knowing that his life could end in his madness as he attacked all he cared to maintain and protect — a dishonourable end to a man who placed great store by his honour. There was something heart-rending about the kind of courage he possessed just to go on living.

'Sheesh!' The Chameleon's disgusted remark came from behind her. She turned and, as always, found herself disorientated by her first impression: he blended into the landscape behind him so perfectly that it seemed at first glance that his horse was riderless. She was endlessly fascinated by his invisibility, by his harmony with the surroundings. 'Another of those damn fish-net bridges,' he was saying. 'Keris, will you hold my hand this time?'

'Are you mind-tainted? I'll be too busy holding on to the ropes.' That wasn't quite true: usually she had both hands fully occupied with dragging a reluctant, blindfolded horse across a rope-and-board bridge that was about as stable as a tattered pennant flapping in the breeze. Luckily there was always the Unbound to help, but even so it was an ordeal.

Ahead, Davron and Meldor were already dismounting to talk to the tainted who maintained the bridge, probably the same individuals who had originally built it. Bridges never lasted long: the landscape changed around them too much, and too often.

'There seem to be so many more people in the Unstable here than there were north of the Wide, don't there?' Quirk remarked as they drew up. 'We keep bumping into the tainted all over the place.'

'Others beside the Unbound, too,' Keris agreed, dismounting.

'Yeah. Those renegades yesterday, for example. None of you ley-lit ever did explain to my satisfaction just what happened to the clothing of that couple of spike-headed bastards who were leading them.' A group of excluded thieves, led by two stubble-tonsured thugs, had tried to rob the fellowship, only to think better of it when Meldor had released a bolt of colour from his fingertips that had set their leaders' clothes smouldering. Neither the Chameleon nor Corrian had seen the ley, but they had seen the effects of it.

Keris grinned. 'Meldor took a dislike to their fashion sense and performed a little sleight of hand, that's all.'

Quirk wanted to question her further but was interrupted by Portron, who was dismounting beside him. 'Davron's negotiating with this lot on a price for use of that cat's cradle, I suppose,' the chantor said, eyeing the bridge ahead with considerable misgivings. He wiped the sweat from his face with his sleeve. 'Creation, what I wouldn't give for a bath!'

To Keris the discussion between the guide and the tainted bridgemen did not look like a bargaining session over how much the toll was; as far as she could tell, the Unbound greeted Meldor and Davron as old friends. In fact, after a few minutes, the two men were invited into one of the tents in the camp erected some distance away.

Keris had noted before that Meldor appeared to be well acquainted with many of the tainted they had met since they had left the Fifth Stab behind. Some of them had even seemed to treat him as if he was still a knight. Women had run alongside his horse, just to touch his foot; men had reached for his hand or knelt at his feet. As for paying to cross any of the numerous bridges they had been forced to use, as far as she could tell no money had ever changed hands. On the contrary, once, she had even seen what appeared to be a bag of coins pass the other way, from the Unbound into Davron's hands. Although she supposed she could have been mistaken about its contents.

Still . . .

She glanced towards the tents, but there was no sign yet of Meldor and Davron emerging. Scow was talking to some of the others there, and after a while he took something from one of them and headed back to where she and the rest of the fellowship were waiting.

'Probably wining and dining him,' Portron said, referring to the Unbound and Meldor. He sounded sour. He was even less enamoured of the blind man since his further use of ley against the bandits.

'Very likely,' Keris agreed. *He's being entertained as if he is among his own people* . . . Her own thought startled her. His own people? These Unbound, once pilgrims, now wanderers forced to roam the Unstable, seeking a way of making a living, seeking a place where they could be safe for a while? These scattered groups of refugees they had encountered – the outcasts of the stabilities: the thieves, the deformed, the blind, all those excluded from stability by the Rule? Yes, perhaps they *were* his people. He too was an outcast, rejected by Chantry – not that you'd ever know it now. Meldor did not act like anyone who had been rejected. In fact, he seemed to have grown in stature since they had left the Fifth. He had become more regal, more confident, as if he was shrugging off a disguise he had been wearing and was now assuming a different mantle — that of leader. A respected leader.

'May as well dismount,' Scow said to the Chameleon, coming up with a handful of dried animal turds that the Unbound had given him for fuel. 'I'll make a fire and we'll have some char while we are waiting.'

Quirk slipped from his horse, stretched and rubbed a sore back. 'I won't complain about that. Anything to delay looking down through something that's more holes than wood and rope, and knowing that there's nothing under me for as far as the eye can see — and probably a whole lot further.'

'Where do they get the makings of a bridge from, anyway?' Corrian asked. She was already digging about in her packs for nosebags for her animals — and some pipeweed for herself. 'We haven't seen a tree since we left the Fifth. Never thought I'd miss a tree — but I'd give up a night with someone young and warm in my bed just to see a decent greenwood down the path aways.'

Scow grinned at the thought of Corrian relinquishing the chance of sex merely to see a forest. 'Wood for use in the Unstable usually comes from the Unstable. It works like this: travellers pay to use the bridge, bridgekeepers buy what they need from traders. The traders, who are usually excluded themselves, buy in the border towns or from other Unstable camps. Life's hard and unpredictable — but people survive.'

'How much trouble do people like this get from Minions?' Keris asked, looking over towards the tents.

'Oh, not that much. Why would Minions bother? The Wild are another matter, but then we tainted can be a bit formidable ourselves.' He nodded in satisfaction as the fire caught. 'Did you notice that huge fellow with the horns over there?'

Corrian gave an evil grin. 'Yep. Tell me, do his nether regions match the size of his topknot?'

He raised an amused eyebrow. 'And of what possible interest would that be to you?'

'None of the personal kind, I suppose,' Corrian said with a sigh.

'The worst problem the tainted have is the Unstable itself,' Scow continued. 'Its unpredictability. The lack of natural laws. You never know when it's going to rain, or in fact *what* it is going to rain. You never know what season it will be tomorrow. You have to continually move your tents, and yourself. Oh, and that reminds me of some more bad news. Meldor says the Minions have found us again.'

Portron moved uneasily where he squatted by the fire and gave a quick look around. 'How does he know?'

'Oh, he knows,' Scow said, deliberately vague. 'He says there's a pair up on that cliff up there.'

Keris sighed. 'I suppose it was inevitable. These canyons have to be crossed, and all they had to do was watch any of the bridges along the way.'

'But why would they bother?' Portron asked. 'What's so special about us?'

Keris could have kicked herself. Why in all Creation had she said that? 'Nothing that I know of,' she said cheerfully. 'I meant that, if the Unmaker wants to keep track of what happens in his domain, he doesn't have all that much difficulty in doing so.'

'I have some good news as well,' Scow said, stirring the char. 'This particular canyon is the second last one. The last one is tomorrow — and that one's not bottomless, just a couple of hundred paces down. The Deep flows through it.'

'That's *good* news?' Quirk asked.

'And why not? It means we won't have to walk through ley. Believe me, a bridge over it is better than a walk through it.'

'I'll drink to that,' Corrian agreed, ladling out some char for herself and Keris.

And now what? Keris thought. The Minions have found us, therefore so has the Unmaker . . .

'Drink up,' Scow said, glancing towards the camp of the Unbound bridgemen. 'It seems the meeting's over and we're on our way again.'

As Keris arrived at the near end of the bridge, Meldor was waiting for her. He sniffed the air as she came up, as if to identify her, and then said, 'I would like to talk to you tonight. Join me for supper in my tent.' No 'please', she noted, or any other indication that it was a request rather than an order, but somehow he sounded meticulously polite. He managed to convey the idea that, while he was doing her an honour by inviting her, she was important, special. How does he do that? she wondered. Ley-life, but he's a clever man.

'As you wish,' she said.

He nodded casually and patted Ygraine, murmuring into the horse's ear, calming the animal as it eyed the bridge with its ears back.

'It's all very well for you,' the Chameleon said sourly to Meldor as he pulled his reluctant mount forward. 'You can't see how far it is down there.'

'Being blind does have some advantages,' Meldor agreed.

As she edged over the bridge a few minutes later, leading Ygraine, Keris felt as though the world was being split through like a broken apple beneath her feet. No matter how she stared into the fissure below, she could see no end to it. It plunged down and down – and down – until there was no seeing any longer. 'And I'm hanging over this, like a spider in a web, supported by a few flimsy strands of hemp,' she muttered to herself. 'There's a Minion up there somewhere spying on us, I'm in love with a man I can never have, and in my packs I have something the Unmaker wants desperately to destroy. I must be insane – I could be safe with Uncle Fergrand in the Second now.' She shook her head sadly. 'Keris Kaylen, your brains are tainted.'

'Another drink?' Scow asked and showed Keris the wine skin. 'We stocked up again in the Fifth.'

'Thanks, but I haven't quite finished this one yet.' She settled back more comfortably on the floor of Meldor's tent, propped up against his saddle. Piers's blackwood staff was on the ground beside her: she had taken to carrying it when she was walking around the camp because she liked to think it gave her some of Piers's confidence. She was not, however, confident enough to tempt fate by refilling her mug of wine. 'I think one cup of that stuff is enough,' she said, 'if I'm also to absorb whatever it is you want to talk to me about.' She looked to where Meldor was lying back against the fenet wool of his bedroll. 'I enjoyed the meal, Master Meldor, and I thank you for the invitation. Now perhaps you should tell me what it is all about.'

Meldor nodded to Scow, who then hung up the wine-skin on the tent pole and slipped outside. Guard duty, she thought. To make sure no one hears what is said? They had a stranger in the camp that night, a courier named Gawen who had just arrived from the opposite direction and had asked if he could share their company for the night. Even couriers, it seemed, could feel the need for human companionship once in a while. Davron had made him strip to the waist first, but once they were sure that he wore no Unmaker's sigil he had been made welcome.

Scow's absence from the tent only served to make Keris more aware of Davron's presence. The master guide sat on the groundsheet, bent knees supporting his forearms in front of him. He was not looking at her, any more than she looked at him, but it did not do any good – he filled Keris's thoughts like too much festival pudding filling the stomach. Disgruntled and restless, she thought: The wretched man exudes enough sexuality, just by being, to make me aware of him even if I never glanced his way.

'We thought it might be a good idea if you knew a little more about ley lines. Or rather what we think about them,' Meldor said without preamble. 'It may help you to find a solution to the problem of creating a trompleri map.'

She nodded. 'I've heard it said that the unmaking of the

307

world causes cracks. Ley – the evil of disorder – then enters through the cracks from the Chaos of the unmade parts of the universe.'

'Yes, and I've heard them described as the Unmaker's claw marks,' Davron said drily. 'There are any number of theories.'

'And you're about to hear another,' Meldor added, 'which we happen to like better. Keris, understand this first: as a chantor, I spent more time studying the Holy Books than any man alive. I believe that the Maker told us in those writings what had happened to us, and how to correct it. Unfortunately, we did not always listen. His words, given to certain knights and prophets, were mixed up with those of much less holy men, many of them bigots or idiots – or both. The problem has been to try to sort out which are the true words of the Maker, which the words of power-hungry men from Chantry, and which the words of sincere men who didn't talk with the authority of the Maker.'

'And you think you've managed to do it.'

He smiled faintly at the dryness of her tone.

'Ley lines are not some sort of fault lines,' he continued. 'A true reading of the Holy Books tells us that they were lines of power, not evil. The beginnings of the unmaking of the world made cracks, true enough, but these cracks released power from the fabric of the world, not evil from Chaos beyond.'

'That's a convenient way of excusing your use of ley, I suppose,' she said.

Meldor was unruffled. 'Look at it this way, Keris. Think of a wood fire: where does the heat come from?'

She blinked. She'd never thought about it, but it was an interesting question. Where did it come from? 'From the wood, somehow. By the burning?' she suggested tentatively. Obvious answers which really did not explain anything.

He pointed to her blackwood staff. 'So there is heat trapped in here, which doesn't feel hot while it is trapped, and which is only released if the wood is burnt. Let's not call it heat, but power. A power that can cook food, warm our bodies — or be used for destructive purposes. Similarly, I believe there is power sealed up in the world, which is only released if the fabric of creation is torn, as the Unmaker has torn it here in the Unstable. And that power can be used for good purposes or for evil, just as the power in wood can.'

'Power?' she asked. 'Not evil?'

'That's right,' Meldor agreed. 'Power. Magic, if you like to use that word; I don't. It is too imprecise and implies things like spells and incantations, which I believe are so much nonsense. Magic is just a form of power, like the heat trapped in the wood. A fire is not evil although it can burn your house down. Similarly magic — or power — is neither good nor evil.'

'You really believe a ley line is not evil?' She was incredulous.

'It isn't. Not innately.'

'Tell that to Quirk,' she said, but she felt the stirrings of interest.

'Or me?' Davron asked softly. 'But I have come to think Meldor is right, Keris. Just as a careless child is burnt by fire, a ley line can taint the ley-unlit. In other words, where the Unmaker is not involved, tainting is more of an accident. The ley-unlit should not be asked to cross ley lines, any more than a child should be asked to plunge his arm into the flames of a kitchen fire. Chantry is as much to blame for the horrors of crossing ley lines as is the Unmaker, simply because they ask pilgrims to do it.'

Meldor continued, 'Moreover, Carasma directs the escaping power, using it for evil purposes. He can rearrange the fabric of a man into a monstrosity, create an earthquake or halt the ageing process in his Minions. He uses it to enforce his dominance. He uses it to further Chaos by promoting the unnatural.'

'And you? How do you use it?'

'We have learnt how to absorb a certain amount of ley, just as Minions do. It's easy enough for anyone who is ley-lit. Then it can be used as a weapon – to hit, to cut, to burn, to kill – simply by directing it to do so, as the Minions do. We have had certain success with more pleasant uses, as well. I use it to enhance my senses, to "see" things without vision, as you have guessed. We have had some success with speeding up the healing process in cases of injury. There are probably other uses we have not yet discovered. A close reading of the Holy Books, I might add, indicates that the Maker himself advocates its use – and that in the past it was indeed used by knights and other chantors. We can teach you to use it, if you wish.'

'You think if I have ley in me, it may help me draw a trompleri map.'

'I do.'

'There's a catch,' Davron drawled, ignoring a warning glance from Meldor. 'Ley is somehow addictive. More than that, in fact – once you have started to absorb it, you can't ever do without it. It is my opinion that you would eventually die if you did not have it.'

She stared at him, unravelling the implications of that.

Davron. It meant he could never live away from the Unstable for too long at a time. He had condemned himself to being an Unstabler for ever. And if they won the battle against the Unmaker, if ever the world was restored, he – and Meldor – would die . . .

She felt tears at the back of her eyes. For both men, even victory spelt doom.

With sudden revulsion, she said, 'I'll never mess with ley.'

Meldor said, 'Deverli imbibed lay. It could be important.'

'You think that enabled him to draw trompleri maps?'

'Possibly. We – I – feel it's worth a try.'

You bastard, she thought. You don't care about us, about the people you use: you only care about the end result . . .

'Trompleri could be more important than we thought, Keris,' he continued, imperturbable. 'What are these fixed features that suddenly appeared down south? That is the area Deverli was mapping –'

'You think just mapping a place with trompleri techniques could make it stable?' She shook her head vehemently. 'No.' She knew that wasn't so: the map she had in her possession showed a ley line and all the changes of an Unstable world.

'Well, it's a possibility. However, up until we heard about these new fixed features, we were actually more interested in how ley can be used to *mend* the Unstable.'

In spite of herself, Keris felt a surge of excitement; the immensity of the concept his words suggested staggered her.

'In fact,' Meldor was saying, 'we believe that ley *must* be used if the world is to be mended; we believe that it is ley that has held our world together, that still holds together the stabilities. It is the binding force of Creation. Once it leaks out, Chaos results.'

'Sweet Creation – how Chantry would *hate* to hear that!' She began to smile, then drank the last of the wine and decided it was the most wonderful thing she'd ever tasted. 'I hope you are careful about just who you tell. About using ley, I mean. There's an awful lot of ley-lit fools out there who'd love to have the power of Minions without having to give up their soul and bond themselves to Lord Carasma to get it.'

Meldor glanced at Davron, blind eyes turning towards the black as if they could see. She mistrusted the look; there was a great deal they weren't telling her still. She guessed, with only a smudge of doubt lingering, that there were indeed others out there besides themselves who had been absorbing ley. What in heaven's ordering were they up to?

'Is there anything else I should know?' she asked carefully.

Meldor's reply was bland. 'No, I don't think so.'

She was sure he was lying. She looked across at Davron, only to have him look away. The back of his neck was reddening and she hid the glimmer of a smile. He must find his tendency to blush a terrible nuisance. She tried to be content with the thought that at least he'd warned her against imbibing ley.

'I think I need to have time to consider all this,' she said and stood up.

Neither of them tried to stop her as she said goodnight and left.

Outside the tent she stretched and enjoyed for a moment the luxury of viewing a night sky that blazed with colour. A *normal* sky. At least the Unmaker could not alter that: the heavens remained as they always had, the Blue Necklace swinging its way across the south, the red Sunburst exploding in its motionless glory to the north, the black of the Pitch Tub to the west with its border of Star Sparkles, overhead the milky band of the Moonstones and the eight moons, each not much bigger than the largest of the stars.

'Beautiful, isn't it?' a soft voice asked out of the darkness. It was the courier, Gawen, still sitting by the last glowing turds of the fire. At his feet a pair of black hounds stirred restlessly; they were ugly beasts, with sad red-rimmed eyes, and drooping jowls punctuated by curved canines.

He saw her eyes on the animals and said, 'They are especially restless tonight. I would not be surprised if there was a Minion or two out there somewhere.'

'Are they as formidable as they look?'

'More, probably. In this country, they have to be. I heard once that your father travelled alone, without even animals. Was that true?'

'Not entirely. He hired the excluded from time to time. And he had his horses. Tousson – his packhorse – is as good as a dog any day.' She felt a moment's irritation; she had so much to think about, her mind was churning with ideas – she wanted to be alone. And who had told him she was Piers Kaylen's daughter anyway?

'I never met him, more's the pity. He stayed up north of the Wide, and I always work this territory.' He paused, then said with some bemusement, 'I have just been propositioned by the most extraordinary lady.'

She chuckled. 'I hope it won't upset your pride if I tell

312

you that you are the last in a very long line.'

He grinned. 'No, not really. And I hope you won't take it amiss if I say that I would rather be propositioned by you.' The invitation was so straightforward and without guile that she could not help but smile. He was handsome in a weather-beaten sort of way, a little older than Davron, but she was not tempted.

'Corrian has much more experience,' she said. 'I would be a poor bargain by comparison. Goodnight, Master Gawen.'

'*You* don't look like the back end of my oldest mule,' he said mournfully, but he did not try to delay her further. 'Goodnight, Maid Kaylen.'

Feeling absurdly pleased by his suggestion, even though her more rational self told her that there was hardly much competition in the present company, she turned away to go to her tent.

And there was a sudden caterwaul, a scream – and the sounds of a scuffle, all coming from behind her tent. Without thought, she ran towards the sounds; a second later Davron raced in from her left, recklessly leaping guy ropes, while Scow barrelled in from the right like a bull on the rampage.

'Where?' Davron snapped out the question.

She pointed. 'I think it was Quirk – he was on sentry duty with Portron.'

Then a flare of light blinded them all, arcing through the darkness with throbbing brilliance before vanishing.

'Who's there?' Davron yelled, running on, knife already drawn in one hand, whip clutched in the other. 'Keris, get a proper light –'

But Master Gawen had already plunged a torch prepared for just such an emergency into the heart of the camp fire. He came up bearing it aloft like a banner.

'Watch out! It's a Minion!' The Chameleon's voice came out of the darkness, raw with terror. There was a scrabble of stones and the sounds of running feet somewhere off in the darkness.

Corrian, hauling on clothes, groping about her person for

her pipe, appeared at Keris's side. 'What's all the dither?'

'Quirk?' Davron grabbed the torch from the courier, and moved into the patch of dark beyond Keris's tent.

The Chameleon was lying there on the ground, hands clutched to his knee. 'There was someone trying to get inside Keris's tent,' he said. He rocked himself, trying to overcome the pain of an injured leg.

Davron hesitated, looking off into the darkness. 'Don't be stupid,' Scow told him, with scant politeness as he knelt beside Quirk. 'Whoever it was, he's gone now.'

Davron shrugged and turned his attention back to the Chameleon. 'Did he get you?'

'Yes. With a wretched ley blast. At least, I suppose so – I never saw what hit me. I saw him sneaking around the tents, but nobody sneaks like I do. I came up on him from behind, was about to clobber him one – and then I had to go and stand on the tail of the fellow's Pet.'

Davron looked at him, incredulous. 'You *what?*'

'Well, I didn't see it. It was some slinky black thing –'

'And what were you doing creeping around after a Minion anyway? Are you *mad?*'

'So, I didn't know it was a Minion, did I? I thought it must be another bandit. He was slitting Keris's tent – Ouch! Scow, don't touch that! It hurts like the very devil.'

'We'll get you to Meldor,' Scow said, and hefted the Chameleon into his arms as if he were nothing more than a child, and a half-starved one at that.

Davron glanced around the assembled group. 'Portron, did you see anything?'

'Nothing. I was on the other side.'

'Better get back there, and be especially vigilant. Gawen, you take Quirk's place with your dogs. Keris, did he take anything?'

Keris had walked over to look at the damage. A knife lay on the ground near the tent; she picked it up and gave it to Davron. 'No, he didn't have time to do much. Barely had the knife inserted into the canvas by the look of it.'

He looked at her, face expressionless. 'Odd that it should be your tent he chose, isn't it? Corrian's is closer to the edge of the camp and Quirk's would have been easier to approach without being seen.'

She turned from him, suddenly stiff with fright. Coincidence, surely. Corrian looked at her in sympathy. 'If you feel scared, lass, you can share my tent.'

'I'll be all right, but thanks anyway.'

Inside her tent once more, she lit her only good wax candle with trembling fingers. Coincidence? Or had the Unmaker sent one of his Minions after her, to make sure she did not have the trompleri map? She felt sick.

She sat down for a while, thinking. So much happening all at once, so many ideas . . . She opened up her packs and took out her mapping inks, paints, pens and brushes. Ley was not evil, as Chantry had so long preached. Ley was power – and it could be used. Used to make a trompleri map.

Slowly she reached out and picked up the small bottle in which she had stored the mineral salts she had found in the quiver. She turned it over and over in her hands, wondering if she really wanted to travel down the path her thoughts were taking, wondering if she really wanted to know how to make a trompleri map after all.

Her fingers fumbled over opening the jar. It took a definite effort of will to mix up ink and paints, to add the tannin powder and the dyes to the salts, but finally she had what she wanted: one small amount of black ink and several small amounts of paint of varying shades of brown.

A clean sheet of parchment pinned to the portable mapping board, a tracing of a portion of the Unstable that Piers had mapped on his last journey . . . Just a small part that showed Wedge Hill where the fellowship had stopped on their first night in the Unstable. A large-scale map . . . Then, taking a deep breath, she began inking in the outlines.

It seemed no different from any other map. The hill taking shape under her pen remained flat against the paper. Doggedly, she worked on, waited for the ink to dry, then applied the paint. She had to close her eyes for a minute, so that she could picture the hill, its steep sides of shale and broken earth, the gentler slope to the north, the steep track on the southern side. She mixed and merged the paints on her palette, then on the paper, taking infinite care, until she had achieved what she wanted.

Except that it was not what she had hoped for . . . She heaved a sigh. It looked no different from any other map she had ever created. She pushed the parchment away and washed her brushes, aware now of her fatigue. Perhaps the whole chart had to be completed for it to work, but all she had was browns, and precious little of that. Perhaps all the ingredients of the inks and paints had to come from a ley line, just as she believed the salts had. She dried her brushes and went to put the parchment away – and stopped short. Her colours had become a dark smudge on the paper. Indistinct, without detail or delineation. She stared, not comprehending for a moment. Was there a hint of contour? It did seem to be raised up, she was sure of it. Not as clearly as the hills on Deverli's map, of course –

With an abrupt movement born of her fear, she shoved her map out of sight and took an anxious look around her tent. Belatedly, she pushed her pack in front of the small tear the Minion had made in the canvas.

Deverli's map. For the first time on the journey, she dug into her mapcase and pulled out the trompleri map.

It was dark. Smudged, indistinct.

It took her another minute to understand. *Night. A scene viewed by night.* Of course. She had just never seen the map at night before, but of course it was reflecting the real time of day, as well as the actual conditions of the place it portrayed. If she looked closely she could make out the larger rocks and hills and copses, illuminated by moonlight.

She drew out her own map of Wedge Hill again and knew she had done it. Not very well because she lacked enough of the correct materials, but she had done it.

She had made a trompleri map.

Chapter Twenty-Two

*Alas, that humankind knows not the most precious of its
jewels till it slips from its grasp.*

old saying of the Margravate of Malinawar

'Not asleep, Keris?'

Scow, who had been crossing the camp on his way to
Keris's tent when she had emerged from it, pitched his voice
to a whisper so as not to disturb anyone else. 'I was just
coming to see if you were all right. I saw your candle – I was
worried that you'd gone to sleep with it still burning.'

'No. I – er – couldn't sleep. Are you on guard?'

'Yes. Davron decided to put three on at a time tonight.
You and he and Corrian will take the second shift.'

'How's the Chameleon?'

'Fine. Meldor fixed the worst of it. He'll be a bit sore for
a while, that's all. You'll be tired if you don't sleep.'

'In a moment. First, can I ask you something? Scow, how
well do you know this courier?'

'Gawen? We've come across him from time to time.
Quiet chap, pleasant enough, I think.' He gave her a sharp
look, but did not ask why she was interested.

'A trustworthy courier?'

'All couriers are trustworthy, you know that. Otherwise
they wouldn't *be* couriers.'

'I want to have a few private words with him. Do you
think you could send him to wake me when his stint of guard
duty is finished?'

'As you wish. And really, Keris, you ought to get some sleep —'

'All right, I'm off.'

She ducked back into the tent, knowing Scow was right. She had to get some sleep, but her eyes kept straying to the tear in the canvas of the tent. If the Minion had not been discovered he might have searched her belongings and found her trompleri map. Perhaps that was what he had been after in the first place. She refused even to consider the other possibility: that he had thought she had been in her tent, and had been intent on murder.

She reached out and took up both the trompleri map and her own poor attempt to emulate it. She took one last look at them both, and then — with a cold reluctance — she fed the edge of them both to the candle flame.

'Can't you sleep either?' Scow asked Davron.

The guide, who had just emerged from his tent, regarded Scow with a grimace. 'One of those nights. What do you mean "either"? *You're* not supposed to be sleeping!'

'Not me: Keris.' The Unbound man nodded towards her tent, where the candle still burnt.

'Probably scared stiff. Not that I blame her. Scow, I'm worried about just why that Minion was there. I'd give a day of my life to know if he was aware she wasn't in th— *Holy taint!* What's that?'

A brilliant flash of white light lit up Keris's tent from the inside. Then it burst outward, shrivelling the canvas in an instantaneous flash of heat and incandescence.

For a split second Scow and Davron stood still, momentarily beyond shock, then a blast of air hit them both. Scow, who was larger, was just knocked flat; Davron was lifted and hurled back into his own tent, which then collapsed on top of him, its guy ropes wrenched from the ground as the shockwave filled the canvas like a sail billowing before a gust of wind.

When he crawled out again, it was to find the camp almost completely flattened.

Meldor's tent was still standing – it had been protected by Portron's and Gawen's – but all the others were either collapsed or sagging. Of Keris's tent there was simply no sign.

'Keris,' Davron whispered. He ran to where she had been camped. 'Maker, *Keris*! Damn it – someone get a light.'

There was a babble of questioning voices, of cursing, of running feet. Gawen's hounds were howling. Davron, frantic, knelt in the ruins of Keris's tent, flinging things aside, scrabbling in among the dark huddle of bundles on the ground. 'A light, someone! *Maker damn it, will someone give me a light!*'

In the dark under his hands something stirred and groaned.

Portron strode forward holding the lantern from his tent. Davron snatched it from him and held it up to see better. '*Keris?*'

Another groan and one of the bundles uncurled at Davron's feet. Unbelievably, it was Keris. She said, 'I – I'm all right. I think.' She tried to kneel and staggered, but it was Scow, not Davron, who jumped forward to support her by an arm around her waist, careful not to let his skin brush hers.

'It's not possible,' Davron whispered, scrambling up. 'The heat, your tent – it burnt. Vanished. *You ought to be dead.*'

She touched a weak hand to her hair. 'Almost.'

'*Are you hurt?*'

She seemed to think about that for a moment. Then: 'Singed. I'm all right.'

'By the Creator's holy grace,' Portron exclaimed, 'what happened?'

'You should be dead,' Davron reiterated flatly. 'How is it possible that you survived?'

'The – the blast went upward. Upward and outward. I ducked. Rolled myself into a ball. Dived down behind my packs. It sucked . . . all the air out of . . . me.' She shuddered. 'Oh, midden. I think I've lost most of my hair.'

Meldor frowned. 'I'll take a look at you if you're hurt. The rest of you, get the camp straightened up again, and keep a good watch.'

'I'm all right,' Keris said, still shaking. 'I'm not burnt, just . . . shocked.'

'I don't understand. What happened?' Corrian asked.

'It was ley,' Portron said with certainty. 'Nothing else produces light like that.'

'I think that we can take it that the Minion left something behind,' Meldor said, 'presumably with the intention of killing Keris. Scow, back on duty. Davron, you take Keris to Scow's tent. She can sleep there for the moment. Davron?'

Davron took a deep breath and gathered his wits, aware now that Meldor was doing his job. He made a gesture towards Keris, as if to help her, but she disengaged herself from Scow and stood erect. 'I'm all right.' As the others moved to obey Meldor, she gave a brief glance around her belongings to check them out, but nothing seemed to have been damaged. It was as she had said: the blast had gone upward. Surreptitiously, Davron ran a hand over the nearest of her packs and then rubbed his fingers. There was no ash, nothing. The tent had been completely vaporised.

He picked up her bedroll. 'Are you sure you're not burnt anywhere?' He tried to sound neutral, but had a feeling he was giving more the appearance of a hen fussing over chicks. He waved her towards Scow's tent.

She turned to walk beside him. 'I feel a bit sore on my face, but it's nothing much. My hair – what does my hair look like?'

He held the lamp up, taking the opportunity to study her face. 'Short. A sort of uneven frizz. It'll grow.' His fear was dampening down, to be replaced by an irrational anger. He clutched the bedroll tighter, aware that his hands were shaking. 'What I want to know is what happened.'

'I don't know.'

The denial was all-encompassing, and he did not believe it. He stopped and shoved her bedroll at her. 'Sit down,' he

320

growled and started to re-erect the tent. 'I would like to know just what you've been up to,' he added between blows with a rock to a loosened tent peg. 'Where did that ley come from, Kaylen?'

She was silent.

'You *do* know,' he accused.

'Yes. It's nothing I want to talk about right now.'

'I'm responsible for all that happens to this fellowship. I'm responsible for everyone's safety. I need to know what happened.'

She shook her head. 'It's over. Finished. It won't happen again.'

He hammered the last of the pegs in with unnecessary savagery. He wanted to fling his anger at her, force her to tell him everything she was hiding. And was wise enough to know that, if he did, her stubbornness would increase, not dissipate.

He stood upright and faced her. 'I do have your interests at heart,' he said quietly.

'Yes, I think I believe that now.' Her voice was outwardly calm, with only the tiniest of cracks to show that she was not as steady as she was trying to appear. 'But Meldor does not — and you would go straight to him with whatever I told you.'

He was silent, aware of the truth of that accusation. 'You don't accept my judgement,' he said at last.

'Not in the matter of Meldor. He cares nothing for others, only for what they can offer him. Thank you for fixing the tent.' She picked up her bedroll and opened the tent flap. 'Goodnight.'

He accepted his dismissal.

'She wouldn't tell me anything,' he said to Meldor. 'She distrusts you too much.'

The blind man was sitting on his pack in his tent, sipping water from a mug. 'Ah. You didn't push it.' A statement, not a question. 'You're in love with her, aren't you?'

The denial stuck in his throat. He could not forget the

horror of that moment when he had seen her tent evaporate, disintegrate so thoroughly that not even ashes were left. He had thought her dead and the emotion inside him when he realised she was unhurt was one he had not thought he would ever feel again.

'She's a child,' he said, and knew the remark to be inane. Meldor did not even deign to comment on it.

Davron hung the lantern he had been holding on the central support pole and unhooked the wine skin instead, to pour himself a drink. 'What — what if I am? It's impossible, and we all know it.'

'Don't let it cloud your judgement.'

'Now, just when have I ever allowed love to affect my judgement?' he asked, and the sarcasm lay thick in the air between them. He drank the wine deeply and far too quickly, before he added, 'If you use her badly, Meldor, it will be the end between us.'

The blind man nodded, as if confirming something to himself. 'Love her if you will, Davron — but don't trust her. And don't mention Havenstar. She is far too independent to be trusted. And far too canny.'

Davron did not bother to reply, but he was aware of the irony. Last time it had been he who had been warning Meldor against her.

Keris woke to the feel of a hand on her ankle, shaking her foot. She roused, aware that there was sunlight already touching the peak of the canvas.

'Maid Kaylen?'

'Yes. I'm awake. Master Gawen?'

'That's me. Scow said you wanted to see me.'

He was leaning in the tent flap and she gestured him in all the way. 'It's daylight,' she said, rubbing her eyes. 'I thought I was supposed to be on guard duty last night —'

'The guide thought you had better rest instead. What did you want to talk to me about?'

She regarded him, alert now, the last of sleep gone and all

the memories of the night flooding back. The flame's touch to the maps, the second's warning she'd had as the parchment crackled . . . She had flung the maps upward in an instinctive reaction, and dived behind her packs as the whole world exploded around her. The air had been sucked from her lungs, leaving her curled up and helpless, fighting to draw breath . . . She fingered her hair, remembering.

He sat back on his heels, regarding her speculatively where she sat, still half wrapped in her bedroll. 'I'd like to think that this is an invitation to something more like yon Corrian had in mind – but somehow I think not. So, lass, what is it you want from me? Something to courier, doubtless?'

She nodded. 'Seven letters, to people in different stabs. They are all mapmakers. For some of them I didn't know the full address.' She reached into her bedroll and drew out the letters to show him.

'It doesn't matter – mapmakers are easy enough to find. You do realise I won't be delivering them all myself, though? I'll pass some on to other couriers going in the right direction; it's quicker that way.'

She nodded. 'Pass them on, by all means. And there's something I should tell you, before you accept the letters. They contain knowledge that Carasma and his Minions would kill for.'

Gawen shrugged. 'No reason for them to ever hear about them, is there? I'm a courier, lass. I shan't even tell those who carry them where they came from. Now, let's get down to essentials. It'll cost, you know. Let me see: the Fifth – I'll charge you a silver for that one . . .'

'I don't know why you say you're such a coward,' Keris remarked to the Chameleon. 'Seems to me that jumping a Minion in the dark demonstrates a certain amount of . . . reckless audacity. And as for standing on a Pet's tail . . .!'

Their mounts were walking side by side across a plain of cracked red soil at the time, and Quirk wore an expression of long-suffering fortitude: his knee was hurting him and he did not much mind if everyone knew it. 'Midden,' he said by way of contradiction. 'I thought the fellow was some scrawny bandit. Believe me, it never occurred to me that the apostate bastard would shoot fire from his cheekbones like a spit-lizard shooting its slobber.' He eased his knee against the saddle with his hand. 'The shitty little turd. I may not be able to see it too well, but that stuff *hurt*.'

She nodded. 'Ley moulded to the wishes of the one who wields it. It's said they carry it in all the spaces of the body and can concentrate its exit through the pores of the skin.'

'Like Meldor through his fingers. I don't know what he did, Keris, but it was miraculous. The pain has only just come back. How can ley be used to both hurt and heal?'

She did not answer. She was looking off to the side where a vast tower of red dust swirled upward. 'A whirlwind,' she said, awed. 'Ley fire, look at it!' Its base was twenty paces across; the top disappeared into a red billowing cloud of dust. They had seen many whirlwinds since they had left the Fifth Stability, but this one was by far the largest. It screamed as it moved, sucking up the soil and whisking even rocks into its inverted skirt of whirling power.

'Disintegrating the land,' Portron muttered from behind them. 'The Unmaker at his unholy work again. There won't be much left of the Unstable if he continues to destruct it at this pace, damn his cursed unsoul.'

'We are close to the Deep,' said Scow, riding up to join them. 'You can see the top of the canyon from here.'

The Chameleon grimaced. 'The last bridge. I'll be glad to get this over and done with.'

Keris tore her eyes away from the whirlwind, which was already speeding away into the distance, to see where Scow was pointing. There was a long line of rocky slopes beyond the Deep. The tumbled blocks and pinnacles of rock with ugly patches of slime looked more like a giant's rotting teeth with bits of half-masticated food caught in the gaps. The scree below the blocks was then the giant's gums, wet and slimy with fouled rivulets of moisture, sloping down to the edge of the gullet, the canyon that contained the Deep.

The canyon was the widest they'd had to cross yet and the rope and slat bridge that spanned it had all the fragility of a spider's anchor thread. It swayed and undulated, moved by some invisible draught of air that rose from somewhere below.

'Oh midden,' the Chameleon said, pulling at his ear. 'Keris, I *really* don't have a head for heights.'

Keris, however, was still contemplating the rotting teeth of the landscape ahead. Her expression was one of profound distaste. 'How much was taken away from us!' she murmured. 'Whole cities and communities once lived here. It is said that Malinawar was once the most beautiful of all countries; that its people were the most blessed. Yedron had too much desert; Bellisthron too much water and Pemantra was too flat – but Malinawar was paradise.'

They came to a halt at the edge of the canyon and waited while Meldor and Davron talked to the attendant Unbound. Below, the river of ley coiled its way between pitted walls of purplish stone, and long lines of ley mist cavorted above its surface with an almost sensual abandon.

Scow had managed – as usual – to obtain animal pats for a fire, and was soon serving up char while the fellowship waited.

'Must have been bloody mad,' Corrian muttered as she sipped her char and gazed at the swaying bridge. 'Why the flipping hell didn't I stay in Drumlin's Cess and be damned? Sheesh, but I miss even the smell of that place.'

'The smell?' Keris asked, blinking. She had once accompanied Piers on a trip to Drumlin and had visited the Cess, that tumble of tenements in the heart of the city. There had been a discrepancy between the original cadastral maps of the area and the present configuration of houses – a situation Chantry regarded as grievous more because it involved change than because the cadastral maps were used to calculate taxes. They had called in the mapmaker to check out just what had happened and who was at fault. Keris's memory of the smells involved recollections of urine stink and rat musk, stale pickles and rising damp, dung fires and spreading mildew. It was not anything that she could imagine anyone missing.

'Yep, the smell. Nothing like it. Ever had a whiff of a brothel, lass? Cheap scent and sex, semen and —'

Out of the corner of her eye, Keris saw Portron beginning to puff up, but Corrian was saved from another burst of indignation from the chantor by Davron. 'Everything's set,' he said, as he walked up with Meldor and several of the tainted. 'I'll go first as always. You're next, Chantor. All of you, leave your pack animals for the attendants, as usual, and wait for my signal.'

They had done it all before, but it had not become any easier with practice. Just to watch Davron make the crossing pulling his reluctant mount behind him made Keris feel sick. The bridge jerked and danced like a living thing; the ropes seemed so frail; the canyon so deep . . .

Four ropes, Keris thought. Only four. There was a hand-rope on either side and there were two ropes on to which the slats of the flooring were lashed. A pattern of smaller ropes joined handropes to the base. She tried to convince herself that it was just a path with a fence on either side, nothing to worry about, but she did not believe it, any more than the Chameleon did.

They crossed one by one: Portron after Davron, then Corrian, followed by Quirk (who was interminably slow), and then Scow. Meldor remained behind as well: he regarded it as his job to spend a few minutes talking to each animal, calming it before the crossing.

When Scow had reached the opposite side, Davron gave Keris the signal that it was her turn. She blindfolded Ygraine, nodded to Meldor, and started across.

Don't think about what's below. Difficult, when the slats beneath her feet were each separated by several inches from the next, and there, through the gaps, the roiling of the ley was visible – in ugly purple billows. Purple, the colour of the most violent forces of ley. *Stop thinking about it!*

She was about a third of the way across when something alerted her to trouble behind. She turned her head, glancing back, aware now that the Unbound watching the crossing had raised their voices. They were gazing upward. She followed the line of their pointing fingers.

A bird. No, not a true bird – this was a featherless manta. It had just swooped low over the bridge, between her and the watchers behind. Its spotted wings undulated and as it banked around it passed her overhead, a bare wingspan away. Two close-set eyes positioned at the top of the belly stared down and for one brief second they looked into her own. Intelligence gleamed, and worse – a Wildish malevolence.

She dragged at Ygraine's reins and moved on, more hurriedly this time. The manta ray was a Pet, she was sure of it.

On the next pass, it flew behind her again; but this time it slashed down with its tail as it came over the handrope. The tail, a fleshy poker that trailed out behind it, was edged with sharp bony plates that seemed to discharge searing heat; the slicing edge of it hewed through the rope as if it were straw and left smoking ends.

The bridge bucked under the onslaught. Keris, trying desperately to drag a balking Ygraine at a run, did not see the attack and did not know what had happened. When the bridge lurched, she made a grab for the handrope, missed it completely as it unravelled, and almost toppled over into the canyon. She fell to her knees, slid as the bridge twisted yet again, and snatched at the slats beneath her. Ygraine crashed into her and then – with a scream of fear that tore into Keris's heart – slipped, legs flailing, from the bridge and disappeared into the canyon.

Keris dragged herself back to her knees, clutching the remaining handrope with both hands. Ygraine was gone. The mare that had served Piers Kaylen for fifteen years. The

327

wave of grief she felt submerged her fear. Ygraine had been a link to her father, and now she was gone, just as Piers had gone ... And she was kneeling on a half-wrecked bridge over a canyon, with the Deep beckoning below. She took a deep breath and looked up.

The ray had banked and returned; it was now heading back towards the same part of the bridge. This time it did not have everything its own way: Scow had his bow out on one side of the bridge, and several of the tainted were shooting at it from the other. It slewed, dodging, but came on.

'Keris!' Davron was calling to her from the far end of the bridge. 'Run!'

She picked herself up, staggering as the bridge writhed, and started towards him. She screamed, 'Don't come!' and willed herself not to look behind, not to see what was happening. Willed herself not to notice that there was nothing bordering her on the right now – no side to the bridge, no handrope; nothing to stop her from plunging over the right-hand side should she fall.

And behind her the ray slashed the second handrope, burning and cutting with a single slice.

She was on her knees again, tossed there by the living thing that writhed beneath her feet, clutching hard at the slats. There was no fence on either side now – just a path of slats, still swinging violently, stretching away before her. She stayed on all fours and scrabbled on, unaware that she was sobbing in her terror.

Davron was shouting encouragement, but in her panic she could not hear the words. He had run out on to the bridge, heedless of his own danger.

The next time, the ray came in closer, so close she felt the down draught from its wings, saw the savage slash of its tail as it plunged downward on her right. This time there was no easy target: the two supporting ropes underneath were sheltered by the slats – yet it managed to insert its tail into a gap between the boards to saw at the rope as it dived past. The rope did not snap immediately, but twanged apart, strand by strand. Keris heard it. Felt it, as the bridge shuddered with each breakage.

'Get back!' she screamed at Davron. He dived for the end of the bridge; she clung the best she could to what was left of it. The whole thing was bucking wildly now, alive, possessed, wanting to be rid of her . . .

The rope parted, the right-hand edge of the path tipped down. Keris heard herself screaming. There was nothing under her feet. She was suspended, kicking. Clinging to the one remaining rope, her knees knocking against the slats that now hung vertically . . . Below, the purple ley flowed on.

The ray shrieked out its triumph and dived in once more.

She clamped down hard on her panic. She swung her body, used the momentum to shift herself sideways, sliding her hands one at a time. Once. Twice. *Maker, how long can I hold on?* She had lost sight of Davron; she no longer knew what was happening around her. Her whole being was concentrated on her hands, on holding fast.

She swung and her feet tangled in what had been the handrope. She struggled, but only wound herself tighter into a web of hemp.

The ray struck again.

And again.

It banked for a third attack on the last rope and caught a knife – Davron's – in its eye. It fell tumbling towards the ley, shrieking its pain, but the damage had been done. The last rope was almost severed all the way through.

I'm going to be dashed against the cliff, she thought. Maybe that's a better way to die than to drop into the ley . . .

The final strand parted and she was swinging towards the solid face of the canyon.

There was a vicious jolt on the ropes that entrapped her. If she had not been so tangled she would have lost her hold and fallen free. As it was, the jerk simply pulled everything tighter around her. A split second later she slammed into rock.

The breath was driven from her chest; her shoulder and thigh took the brunt of the blow and pain speared into her body.

For some moments she could see nothing, hear nothing, think nothing. Every rational sense was submerged in pain.

She swung in her cocoon of rope, wrapped tight and paralysed like a spider's hoarded feast, and only slowly did rationality return. She was alive. She was dangling over space on a single anchor strand, free of the cliff that was somehow some distance away. She was bruised from neck to ankle – *but she was alive.*

Tentatively, disbelieving, she looked up.

Some distance above there was an overhang. The bridge had struck that first, and hooked itself there. Her body – entangled further down the rope – must have hit the cliff only at the extremity of its swing from the overhang, thus saving her from the full force of a collision with the canyon wall.

She looked down. The ley line was tens of paces below; if she fell, she would die from the fall alone. Her situation was still hardly encouraging.

Meat on a butcher's hook, she thought. What in the midden do I do now?

Carefully – very carefully – she began to free her arms and hands from the wrapping of rope.

'Keris!'

She choked, acknowledging only then how much she had wanted to hear his voice, to know he was safe: Davron. He was on the overhang, lying flat, poking his head out to look down on her.

'Keris, are you hurt?'

'No,' she lied, ignoring the pain of her bruising. 'Davron, please get me out of here.' *I'm scared.*

'The rope's fraying. Stay very still.'

She froze. She had already freed one arm; the other she left where it was. Her body revolved slowly, showing her the cliff face, then the length of the canyon, then the far side of the gorge wall where the tainted were lined up, watching . . .

'Keris, I don't have any rope I can use here, and I can't haul you up on the one that's supporting you. It will break for sure. I'm going to use my whip – wrap it around your wrist.' The plaited raw hide snaked down. It seemed pathetically thin. The tip of it he had tied around what looked to be his torn-out coat sleeve, giving it more length and something to grab that was not impregnated with glass. It dangled in front of her nose. Cautiously she reached out to take it. Some small stones rattled down and hit her on the head, then there was a cracking sound she could not identify; her rope shivered slightly in sympathy and sent her spinning a little faster.

And another voice bellowed down the canyon. 'Davron! That overhang is breaking away! It can't take your weight . . .' It was Scow's voice from further up, and it was raw with panic. 'Davron – for Creation's sake!'

Keris heard the words with an intense clarity, as if they were outlined in light. Davron's weight. *And her weight.*

'Davron!' Scow's bull-like roar again. 'Take my hand!'

'Wrap it around your wrist, Keris,' Davron said without emotion.

She heard the cracking once more, saw the rock shift beneath him, absorbed the momentary fear on his face.

Scow shouted, in anguish this time, *'Davron!'*

Keris, with a calmness that seemed to belong to someone else, drew her knife from the scabbard at her belt.

Still calm, she reached up to the single line of fraying rope that linked her to the overhang – and cut it through.

She fell in silence.

It was Davron's *'No!'* that echoed from canyon wall to canyon wall, the sound of agony ripped from the soul of a man who had once thought he had no more capacity to feel pain.

Chapter Twenty-Three

Any deep study of the holy texts will tell a diligent student that the Unmaker, while he appears to Humankind most frequently in a human-like guise, is not a Being in any normal sense of the word. He is a god with no form but what he chooses to take. He is, simply, Chaos, just as the Maker is Order. What Carasma cares to show us is illusion . . . and we should never forget this because it is essential to our understanding of his nature.

from the writings of Kt Edion

'Davron — there's no point.' Scow looked at the guide and unaccustomed worry lines furrowed into the large planes of his face. 'She is dead. Even if she survived the fall, she would not have survived the ley. Portron tells me it is still roiling, a bruised purple colour. It is a killing ley.'

'Not necessarily. It is because the Unmaker is down there.'

'How do you know?'

'I know. I felt him. The moment she fell, I felt him. He planned this.'

'Then what the Chaosdamn are you thinking of? He must have wanted her dead very badly to risk a possible violation of the laws that govern his place in this world —'

'She can't be dead. I won't believe it.' Davron pulled on his fingerless riding gloves, then bent to check the lacing on his boots.

'Then will you at least believe that the cliff face you're

intending to descend is dangerous? That overhang broke off, remember. The whole face is friable.'

Davron ignored him.

Scow's worry deepened. 'Ley fire, but I wish Meldor were here. Dav, we have a fellowship that's been split in two, and we're in the half that has no pack animals, no food, very little water and no tents. Somewhere not far away there's a Minion that's just lost his manta ray Pet and he'll be aching for someone's blood. We need your guidance.'

Davron stopped what he was doing and turned to face Scow. He took a deep breath.

'Sammy, *she heard what you said.* She heard *and she cut the rope.* For me. Do you understand that? And so now I'm going to do this for her. And you are perfectly capable of looking after the fellowship for as long as it takes me to do this.'

'Dav, if she hadn't cut it, you'd both be dead. Damn it all, another half-second and you would have plunged down with the overhang when it went. She sacrificed her life for you – and now you want to throw your life away, and it's hardly going to do any good. She's dead, Davron.'

'I would know if she were.'

'What makes you think that? What makes you think you had some sort of rapport with her that would tell you the moment her life snuffed out? You couldn't even tell when she was hurting when she was alive!'

Without warning, Davron's fist shot out and caught Scow in the centre of the chin. Taken by surprise, Scow overbalanced and landed heavily on his rear.

Portron and Quirk, who had been listening with leaden faces, helped him up. Scow, rubbing his jaw, watched as Davron turned away without a word and walked to the cliff edge. The guide stood for a moment, looking down, then he swung himself over the edge.

'Disorder *damn* it!' said Scow.

Portron knelt on one knee and began the ritual of Reverence, hands fluttering and head bobbing in the required gestures to indicate his subservience as a petitioner.

Corrian, who had also been following the whole conversation, gave a snort of disgust. 'You wasted your time there, young man,' she said to Scow. 'Master Davron lost his wits when he lost his heart. There ain't nothing like the idiocy of a man who's thinking with his emotions – or his privates for that matter – instead of his head.'

This statement was greeted with a startled silence. Scow, remembering the beauty and sweetness of Alyss of Tower-and-Fleury, was disbelieving; Quirk, remembering Davron's self-containment, was puzzled; but it was Portron whose reaction was the most extreme. His head jerked around, ritual forgotten, and the expression on his face was one of appalled horror.

Scow finally stirred himself, choosing to ignore Corrian's words altogether. 'Quirk, can you sneak up on to those rocks somewhere and keep guard? I'm worried that the owner of that Pet might decide to wreak some revenge. Chantor, when you've finished your kinesis, would you hobble the horses?' He turned hesitantly towards the canyon's edge. 'I – I want to see how he manages.'

Wordlessly they watched him go.

'Margraf.' Heldiss the Heron scratched the back of one unnaturally long and thin leg with the clawlike toes of the other, as he often did when he was agitated. 'Someone is climbing down the cliff face.'

'Davron,' Meldor said with certainty. 'The poor romantic fool – first Alyss, now her.' He sounded more resigned than annoyed. 'Why, Heldiss, is it that I am surrounded by people who lack vision?' The question was rhetorical and he did not wait for the Unbound man to comment. 'How soon can you have a new bridge across?'

'If we had the materials it could be done in a day. But we don't have enough rope, and we don't have any boards. We'll have to order both. It would be quicker for you to go around rather than wait. There's another bridge to the east as you know. I'll send some of my men with you.' He glanced across to the other side of the canyon. 'They'll need some of their supplies – with some archery and what rope we have we can rig up a pulley system to get necessities over to them. The rest can go with you.'

Meldor nodded his acceptance. 'I'll write a note for Scow that you can send across. I'll leave as soon as your men are ready.'

Heldiss's birdlike eyes widened in surprise. 'You won't wait to see what happens to him?' Forgetting Meldor's sightlessness, he made an explanatory gesture with his hand towards Davron, still inching his way downward.

The blind man shrugged. 'I do not waste my energies on what I cannot change, Heldiss. Davron will either live or die, and I shall find out which soon enough.'

'I thought he was a friend of yours!'

With unerring accuracy, Meldor reached out a hand and laid it on the Heron's bony shoulder. 'Heldiss, you have known me a great many years, yet you still do not know me. I have no time for friendships. You know my vision, I think. You have family in Havenstar, I know. Would you have me linger to weep over a friend, or would you have me turn my back and go on – remembering that there may come a time when I would turn my back on you, if circumstances dictated it?'

Heldiss hesitated before replying, but only briefly. 'I would have you go on, Margraf,' he whispered. 'I have children who need a future.'

Meldor nodded. He had never doubted the answer.

Davron climbed on. The cliff was friable, treacherous; he already knew that. He was not unskilled at rock-climbing; it had been part of his training on the Storre Domain, and he'd had cause to use the skill on occasion in the Unstable. But never before had he climbed with a ley line below, a line that showed itself from time to time through a cloaking mist: turgid purple tangles like the obscene coils of a giant's disembowelled entrails. Never before had he had to climb knowing that the Unmaker was below him, waiting. Never before had he had to climb feeling the way he did now. Ice-cold. With knowledge inside him that he did not want. *Keris.* Scow was right. Why would he know if she lived or died? He felt nothing of her — neither her presence nor her death. Nothing. The knotted agony in him was nothing new: he had felt that the day Alyss had taken his children from him. He felt it every time he returned to Tower-and-Fleury and caught a tantalising glimpse of his daughter at play.

He climbed on and tied the pain deeper into his unconscious. What was the use of letting it surface? Mirrin, his daughter, was lost to him for ever. Staven, his son, would be unknown to him for ever. And Keris — even if she was alive — could never be his, no matter that she loved him enough to come to him in the night, loved him enough to have cut through the rope that tied her to life. His very touch on her skin could only waken pain. He could offer her nothing, except perhaps death in the final call from Lord Carasma.

Despairing thoughts needled him: *What honour have you now, Davron of Storre?* You who once believed that a Trician had a responsibility to serve his stability and his people with rectitude and purity of spirit? A duty to serve the Maker with faith and fortitude? *What price your honour now, Davron of Storre!* A mapmaker's daughter has served with more integrity and more courage, while you remain bondsman to the Unmaker because you haven't the courage to die . . .

He could let go, drop into the ley, meet death and end it all.

He looked down and shuddered. He did not want to die. He did not want to condemn his children to future tainting. And what of Keris? What if she were alive, and Carasma had her?

He climbed on.

And remembered, too, his first few weeks as a bondsman to Carasma. Remembered the times when he had come closest to taking his own life, or ending it in some reckless attack on a Minion or a Minion's Pet. It had been Meldor who had stopped him then. 'No, Davron,' he had said. 'Alive, you will be my advantage against the Unmaker. When Carasma learns who I am, and what I plan, he will decide to use you against me, against Havenstar. You will be his weapon.'

'And how will that be to your advantage?' Davron had asked.

Meldor had smiled, a cold, humourless smile. 'He will not bother to forge another weapon when he thinks he already has one in place. You and I must never be parted, Davron of Storre, for in you I will know my enemy, and an enemy that is known can be defeated. A weapon that is understood can be used against its wielder. One day I shall use you against Carasma of Chaos.'

And now — now Davron no longer knew whether he stayed alive because Meldor decreed it, or because he was selfish enough to want to live, to want his children to live untainted.

He climbed on.

Keris fell silently, but she heard Davron's anguished denial rend the air after her. She heard it and knew that he loved her. It is enough, she thought.

But that was a lie. It wasn't enough. She wanted to live . . .

She hit the first of the ley mists, now drowsily lifting from the boiling below. *And she slowed.* The canyon walls that had been feeding past her so fast they had seemed only a blur now showed their rough details. She was drifting down, a feather on the air. And then the thought hit her: not a feather. A fruit plucked and dropped into the hands of the Unmaker. Only he could have drawn on the power of the ley to slow her fall and save her life. Relief, barely begun, drowned under an even greater fear than that of merely dying.

She landed on her feet and fell, jarred to her knees. The ugly puce of the ley twisted around her feet and thighs, anchoring her there. He had planned it that way, of course, to humiliate her.

He sat on a raised seat — an edifice rather than a chair, with massive feet and arms and back, a throne strewn with animal skins still attached to lifeless heads and clawed feet, all matted with dried blood. Ygraine was among them. Carasma lounged back in his chair, insolently and nakedly at ease, arrogant in his assumed nobility.

'Maid Keris Kaylen,' he purred.

She had to swallow before she could talk. 'Yes.'

'You had Deverli's maps all the time, didn't you?'

She did not answer. In her terror, she could not answer. To gain time she began to unwind what was left of the rope from around her body. Anything to avoid looking at him.

'Now I have had time to consider, I can see that it is the only explanation that makes sense. And you gave yourself away, when you spoke to me of wanting to be trompleri maker. What could make you dream of that, unless you had seen such a map?'

She nodded, knowing herself too frightened to try to deny it. 'There was only one,' she said in a whisper, because that was all she could manage. 'It was delivered to me with my father's things.'

'So Cissi Woodrug missed it, eh? She will be punished for that.' He continued to contemplate her with eyes that were rich with meaning. He enjoyed her fear, no matter how well she contained it, and his smile carried terror into her heart. 'Where is it?'

'I destroyed it.' *He will never believe me!*

But he did believe her. Somehow he burrowed inside her head and lurked there, sorting through her replies for the truth. With a flash of unwelcome intuition — or was it his personal promise? — she knew that, if she lied, she would die.

'Ah,' he said. 'The flash of ley in your tent last night?'

'Yes. I burnt it.'

'Why?'

'Because I was afraid you were sending your Minions to look for it, and it would be found . . . I — I didn't know it would flare up like that.'

'And did you show it to your friends?'

'No.'

He digested that, leaning his chin on a propped hand. He glowed with health and strength and beauty, and all of it was terrible: the health was parasitic, the strength brutal, the beauty merciless. 'So. You have seen a trompleri map. And studied it. And you – foolish child – have told me that you have ached to emulate the mapmakers who made such things . . . I cannot risk that you succeed.'

She knelt motionless at his feet, tasting the bitterness in her mouth. *Get on with it, you sodding monster!*

He smiled as if he had read her thought. 'Joy,' he said with a deliberate malice, 'is in the length of time that suffering lasts. Why else do you think your Master Guide still wanders the Unstable? For the same reason, I shall not kill you. Yet.' He gestured with a hand and a wisp of ley the size of a small melon detached itself from the twists at her feet. He spun his fingers and the ley, obedient, twirled in the air, concentrating as it did so. Its colour changed: it grew darker, more magenta, more tangled with anger. When it was reduced to the size of a large apple, he flicked it over towards her saying, 'Take it in your hands.'

Fear swelled inside her, jagged on the maliciousness of his smile, and threatened to tear her apart.

'Take it,' he said softly.

She could no more have resisted his insistence than she could have spread wings and flown away. She reached out with both hands and plucked the ball from the air.

For one brilliant moment of light she felt nothing. Then her hands gripped convulsively and she began to scream.

She was still screaming when Davron found her, an aeon later.

The screams started when Davron was barely a quarter of the way down the cliff wall.

The depth of their pain painted horrors in his mind. He clung for a minute, gathering himself around with courage, reforging his strength – then climbed on towards the sound. She was alive, and he had thought her dead even as he told himself otherwise, so one part of him rejoiced in the sound of her pain, one part of him wanted it to go on and on, for while it lasted he knew she still lived . . . The rest of him turned inward, refusing to hear, refusing to know because if he accepted the reality of her agony he would be beyond rationality.

And when he finally stepped down into the ley, perhaps he was indeed not wholly sane.

The Unmaker still lounged on his throne, at ease – more so now that he'd had the solace of another's agony so delightfully played before him. Yet he was also weary. Much was drained from him, because he had tampered with one of the Maker's followers. Order always strove to reassert itself; to impose disorder was draining, to impose it on one who worshipped the Maker was doubly draining. When Davron strode through the ley to Keris and knocked the ball from her hands with the stock of his whip, Carasma did nothing but smile lazily.

Davron stared in shock at Keris's hands.

For a moment the rage that welled in him was a bare breath away from madness – but if there was one thing that Davron knew, and knew well, it was control. The slightest of shudders shivered his frame, then he edged his right hand away from the knife at his belt.

Keris no longer screamed. She stood trembling, crying, holding her hands out at arm's length as if to repudiate them. Davron ached to take her in his arms, to hold her, to stroke her hair, to whisper words of comfort in her ears.

He could do none of it. He was untouchable.

Her hands were dried-up claws. Carasma had been unable to taint her because she was ley-lit, unable to unmake her or kill her because she was the Maker's – so he had wrought as he could. He had desiccated her hands. He had drawn all juices from her flesh below each wrist. He had mummified part of a living body.

She could not bend her fingers, nor move any part of her hands. Brown skin stretched over bone, like sun-dried hide on a desert-seared carcass. She stared at the ghastly skeletal things she now carried and then looked at the Unmaker.

'So that you will never draw a trompleri map,' he said.

The pain had ceased even before Davron knocked away the burning ball of ley. There had been nothing left in her fingers to give her pain, yet she had gone on screaming, unable to stop, unable to think, until she was separated from the source of her maiming.

Even then she had stood in shock, unable to deal with the sight of her useless hands, wanting to hide them from Davron, wanting too to throw herself into his arms. She did neither. She stood and looked down at her hands and tried to convince herself that they were hers. They were eroded deadwood at the end of her wrists, artificial things without touch or feeling or movement. She looked up at Davron and swallowed the last of her sobs.

And then Carasma told her he had done it so that she would never draw a trompleri map. And her mind started working again. She thought, incredulous: He doesn't know how the maps are made! Hysteria bubbled through her. He had destroyed her hands, thinking he could stop her – and she had already thwarted him with the letters Gawen carried. She wanted to laugh, but did not; the irony was too painful. She was eternally maimed, hideously deformed, condemned now to live out her life in the Unstable because of her maiming – and all because Carasma had thought she needed her hands to discover how to make a trompleri map. It was her tragedy, and it was unspeakably funny.

Lord Carasma looked past her to Davron. 'You have a remarkable propensity to try my patience, Storre,' he said.

'It's mutual.'

'You may tell Edion that I know who he is now. And what he is doing. And I think perhaps you know what your task will be, don't you, Master Guide?'

341

Davron nodded. 'Doubtless you will tell me the exact moment and the exact details when the time comes, but I have always assumed that I knew what it was to be.' In truth, it had been Meldor's assumption, but Davron wanted to show Carasma strength, not uncertainty.

'I shall include your new lady in with the package.'

Davron's eyes dilated, blackness into blackness. The Unmaker laughed. 'It will add . . . spice to the moment. For us both.' He turned his golden eyes back to Keris. 'It will be his hand that snuffs out your life, lady.'

'I doubt that you can insist on that,' Davron said with a careless shrug. 'She is the Maker's. Besides, there is no need for her to stay by my side. And I am contracted for but one task, remember?'

'Ask her, guide. Ask her where she will be when the time comes. She is no Alyss of Tower-and-Fleury. And what has she to live for now away from you? She will be excluded, yet has been rendered useless by what I have wrought with her flesh. Ask her.' He was laughing – and, laughing, he faded away.

The two of them were left standing in the ley. It was no longer purple, but blue, a soft pleasant blue.

He turned to her, his voice urgent. 'Keris, there is one chance. Just one – but the price comes high.'

She nodded, unnaturally calm. 'Go on.'

'I can teach you to drink in the ley. You know the price, but ley does heal, used in the right way.'

She held up her hands. '*These?*'

He expected bitterness; instead he saw irony mixed with the pain. He had an unwanted vision then: of Alyss. Alyss turning, pity and horror mingled, from a diseased beggar in the rutted streets of Edgeloss, beckoning a servant to dispense coins. *Maker, how could I ever have thought the gilt was gold?*

'It's only a possibility. It may not work. You may take on the ley and achieve nothing –'

'*You* can't . . .?' she began, and stopped.

'We both know what happens when I touch you,' he said gently. 'I could not heal anyone. And I doubt that even Meldor could do much with something so . . . severe. But *you* might – from within. If you tackle it now, before the change hardens with time.' He looked down at her hands without flinching, and then raised dark eyes to her face. 'What you decide, you must decide for yourself . . . I love you, Keris. And I will love you no matter what your hands look like.'

He saw the ache, the longing, in her eyes, and knew they were a reflection of his own. It tore at him, this inability to hold her. To touch her skin. Gently he reached out and pulled her into his arms, careful – so very careful – not to touch her with his bare body, careful not to hold her too tightly because his hands would sear her through her clothing. Gently he allowed his lips to graze her hair. 'I love you,' he repeated, 'but I can offer you nothing. Not home, nor wealth, nor safety, nor a future that has anything in it but death and pain. I can't even offer you myself. All I can say is that I don't care an urchin's curse what your hands look like – I only care that you do what is best for yourself.'

Carefully, she drew away from him. 'One question first, before I decide. Whom does Meldor serve?'

He hesitated slightly before answering. 'His dream,' he said. 'He serves first and foremost his dream. He believes his dream to be Maker-inspired.'

He expected her to ask what the dream was; instead, she said, 'Do you believe it is?'

'I don't know. But I think his dream is better than Chantry's reality. Or this,' he added, waving a hand at their surroundings.

'Then show me,' she said. 'Show me how to take in the ley.'

And so he showed her. He showed her how to tease out the gentle blue, to spiral it upward out of the body of the ley, using just the power of her mind to call it. 'Want it,' he said, 'just want it. Bring it to you, like a tendril of smoke drawn into your lungs when you breathe . . .'

He showed her how to absorb power as a lizard soaks up the warmth of sunlight; he showed her how to drink in ley and fill her body spaces with its pulsing strength; he showed her how to bring it into herself with every breath. 'Feel it,' he said, 'feel it entering you . . .'

And slowly, slowly, she pulled the power into herself, into her body. Slowly she absorbed it. 'Think of yourself as a sponge,' he said, 'full of empty spaces. Think of being able to fill those spaces with ley. Breathe it in, Keris. Absorb it through the skin. Soak it up. Inhale it. Assimilate it. Feel it run in your veins, in your blood. Feel it course through your body . . .'

She pulled the power into herself, and sent it through her body to her hands. Slowly, gradually, her right hand filled out. The fingers swelled and straightened, and responded . . .

It took time, and concentration, and she had to do it alone.

I can't even touch her, he thought, as he watched the agonising process that was giving her back her dexterity. Giving her back her touch and sensitivity . . . As the nerves lived again the agony was renewed. She paled, shook, bit through her lip trying to contain the agony within, hugging it to her, turning it deep, but there was still nothing he could do.

And there was nothing he could do when she collapsed, exhausted. Too much time had passed and she was too weak. He cradled her, carefully, and wept for her courage, and for what she had lost. Her left hand was still an ugly colour; it was wrinkled, gnarled – the hand of an old arthritic woman. The fingers were unnaturally thin, almost clawlike, the knuckles deformed, the hand curled at rest like an eagle's foot – but at least it lived. It was usable. The right hand she had worked at more: it was warm and soft and supple. Normal.

Damn you, Carasma, he thought. You don't have it all your own way. There are some things we *can* win.

Chapter Twenty-Four

*Should we say obey, and expect obedience, if we cannot also
give hope? Perhaps we have cast too many shadows in the
path of the faithful, and framed too few doorways of light.*

from the early writings of Kt Edion

When Meldor rode into the camp three days after the fall of
the bridge, he drew up his horse alongside Keris, singling her
out with unerring accuracy. For a moment he sat absolutely
still, not speaking, then he slid from his horse and said with a
disbelieving murmur. '*Ley*, Keris?' And smiled.

She knew why he smiled. He thought ley would help her
to find the secret of trompleri. Bitterness bubbled up.

A moment later, though, the smile disappeared. 'But there's
something else, isn't there? I smell . . . the Unmaker's touch.'

Wordlessly she held out her left hand to him. He took it
in his, felt its harsh irregularities, its knobbed crenellations,
then dropped it as if it burnt him. He made an imperious
gesture towards her right hand, so she gave him that as well.
His smile returned. 'Ah. Thank the Maker for that at least.'

The bitterness spilt over. All that ever mattered to him
was how effectively those around him could serve his plans
. . . He was glad her right hand was still usable so that she
could draw her maps. He was probably inwardly pleased that
her left was deformed and ugly: it was doubtless enough to
make her one of the excluded — to ensure she would have
nowhere else to go.

'You and I need to talk,' she snapped.

He nodded, as calm as ever. As in control. 'I agree.' He continued to smile. 'But let me settle in first, eh?' He sniffed the air around him and sensed Davron's presence. 'Davron? Everything all right?'

'Yes. We made do. We moved south to the nearest water. This is Garret's Lake.'

'Yes, Heldiss's men said we'd find you here.' He turned back to Keris. 'I brought another tent for you, and a packhorse. You can ride Tousson from now on.'

'What made you think I'd be in any condition to need a mount – or, indeed, be alive?'

'I didn't know for sure. But the Unmaker was in the ley line and, where Carasma is, the unexpected tends to happen.'

Her anger at his casualness saturated her, but then he swept it all away with his next words, uttered with a gentle, sincere conviction in that beautiful voice of his. 'And you: you are a brightly burning star, Keris Kaylen. Your light enters my darkness. You are strong and not easily killed. No, I did not expect you to die when you fell.' He turned smoothly away to greet the others. To Davron he said, 'It was bravely done. But foolish. You never learn, my friend.' Then, for Scow, 'And it was you who finally got them both out of the Deep, I suppose. We all have to rely on you for the practical details.'

Keris could not help her smile. It was true: it had been Scow who had brought first her, then Davron, up the cliff face. He had salvaged sufficient rope from the downed bridge to reach the bottom of the canyon, and had rigged up a winch at the top so they could be safely hauled up. Keris had been puzzled by the wary way that the two men had greeted one another at the top; Davron looking sheepishly embarrassed, had flushed and then mumbled an apology. Scow had been no less discomforted, remarking that there were times when he was delighted to have made a prime ass of himself and this was one of them. Then he too had grinned, rubbed his jaw, and said meaningfully, 'But one of these days, my friend, when *you* are not looking . . .'

'What's all *that* about then?' Keris had asked, but she'd received no satisfactory reply.

The three days that had followed, when they had been waiting for Meldor and the pack animals, were both difficult and joyous for Keris and Davron. Their desire for one another was a throbbing, desperate yearning that they could not satisfy. Normal passion, normal needs had to be denied, buried, ignored. Yet, the deeper they hid what they felt, the greater the tension that bound them. Sometimes Keris felt she wanted to lash out, scream at the world, cry her defiance. She was caught in torment — and there was no solution. There never would be a solution.

During those three days, Portron spent most of the time glowering at them — and would have interrupted their time together if they had tolerated interruption. Davron thought he was jealous, but Keris knew it was not that. The chantor just thought to protect her; why was not so clear to her.

Far more unsettling to them both than the chantor's fussing was the land's upheaval. Numerous whirlwinds danced across the earth, sucking up the loose soil and dust and anything else in their path. They scribbled dust patterns in the sky; they darkened the light with their brown clouds of debris; they spun part of the world into the oblivion of space. They left denuded swaths slashed across the ground wherever they had been, they scoured the land clean or furrowed it deep as they erased the world. 'Chaos hellwinds, in truth,' Portron murmured, and shook his head in sorrow, as if they foretold far worse things to follow.

The disintegration of the land around them frightened Keris, and the constant proximity of Davron made her feel like a street urchin with her nose pressed against the baker's shop window, seeing the wares displayed, but never having enough money to partake of more than a visual feast. She was not sorry when Meldor arrived to put an end to their waiting.

On the evening Meldor arrived, after a supper of stewed dried meat mixed with slices of dried yam and dried riverweed peas that everyone shared, Keris was once more invited into the spaciousness of Meldor's tent. This time Scow stayed as well as Davron.

'I've made some punch,' Scow told her, handing her a mug of spiced wine. 'To celebrate our reunion.'

'And your safe rescue,' Meldor added, raising his own mug in her direction. 'I'm sorry about your maiming, though, Keris. I'd like to know the whole story. What did the Unmaker hope to gain? Did he realise that I had asked you to be my mapmaker to replace Deverli?'

'Yes, I think so. He wanted to stop me being of any use to you. Meldor, I'll tell you everything I know – which is a lot more than you think – in exchange for more truth from you.'

'Ah. And what is it that you know?' he asked, probing.

'How to make a trompleri map, for a start.'

She sat, imperturbable, sipping her wine, enjoying the stir she had prompted. Davron's face flashed with hope; Meldor lost some of his normal regality as he spluttered a little over his warmed wine and Scow sucked in his vast cheeks and then held his hands to the flames of the stove as if he was suddenly feeling the cold.

'And what is it you want to know?' Meldor asked.

'All the things you haven't told me. Where you are bound, what your plans are – in general at least, why you are called Margraf. This has got to be a partnership.'

Meldor glanced at Davron in amusement, and then back at Keris. 'All right – you will have the information you seek; my word on it. And now: how do you make a trompleri map?'

She folded her arms and sat back. 'First, I have a confession – I had one of Deverli's missing trompleri maps. It was delivered to me with Piers's things.' The startled silence that greeted this pronouncement was all she could have hoped for. She added calmly, 'I'm afraid it doesn't exist any

348

more, though — I burnt it. That was what disintegrated my tent.'

Even Meldor, usually so unruffled by events, was horrified. 'You *destroyed* it? But *why*?'

'Because I was afraid. My father died because of that map.'

'But you do know how to reproduce it?' Meldor's tone was sharp.

'As soon as you told me that ley was power, and not innately evil, I guessed. Before that, I made the same mistake that everyone seems to have made — even Carasma: that there must be some sort of mysterious innate skill within the mapmaker, as you find within water diviners, or fortune tellers. Either that or some sort of magic.'

She waved her mug towards Scow. 'This punch is really good.' He acknowledged her compliment with a kinesis of thanks. She continued: 'During our crossing of the Dancer, some mineral salts of the kind I use for making inks were scooped up into my quiver, quite by accident. Not knowing where they came from, I kept them. When I did realise their origins, my first reaction was to throw them out — but by then I had already been carrying them around for several weeks. I decided that, if they hadn't hurt me by then, they were unlikely to do so, so I kept them. Then, when Meldor said ley was power, well, how better to make a trompleri map than to use something impregnated with ley? I thought it was worth a try. And sure enough . . .'

'You drew a trompleri map?' Davron was grinning at her.

'Of sorts. It wasn't a very good effort, because I had to mix the salts with non-ley ingredients, with the result that the contouring was not very obvious. But it was there. Presumably if all the ingredients could be taken from a ley line —'

Scow gaped. 'It's as simple as that?'

'Well, it's hardly a simple matter to dig around in a ley line looking for ochre and sienna and all the other pigments I'd need to make a proper map. To have a full range of colour

– and it would have to be colour, I think – I'd really need things which might be difficult to find in a ley line. Like tannin and madder root and indigo.'

'Deverli must have done it somehow. Or found substitutes within the line,' Davron said thoughtfully. 'Mind you, he was just the sort of devil-may-care fellow who would enjoy digging about in the Wanderer, and laugh about it afterwards.'

'I've another confession,' Keris continued. 'Because I didn't altogether trust you all, I wrote down instructions on how to make a trompleri map and sent it to all the other master mapmakers I knew of. Gawen took the letters for me.'

Once again they all stared at her.

'You *gave* the information away?' Scow asked finally.

'Yes.'

'You could have made a fortune, you know.'

'You mean *sold* them the information?' she asked. 'It never occurred to me! Trompleri maps will save countless lives. Save countless people from tainting. But you've never seen one, have you? Scow, on a trompleri map it is possible to track Minions and their Pets and the Wild. Or study the ley lines. Crossings would be so much easier. You could see what the weather is like. Or the whirlwinds. You could see where other Unstablers were, and what happens to them. The more trompleri maps that are made and sold, the better for us all. It's not something to make us all rich.'

Meldor nodded. 'It was never our intention to make a monetary profit out of trompleri maps. But I don't know that you have done the right thing, though, for all that. Remember that a trompleri map can work both ways. If Unstabler bandits got hold of them, then they would know where the fellowships are, how many people they contain and how best they could be ambushed. If the Minions got hold of them, they would have the same information. A trompleri map would be a weapon against us, against all decent people, when it's in the hands of the wrong person.'

She was crestfallen and said in a small voice, 'I guess I never thought of that.'

'Never mind. I'll write to all the mapmakers myself, warning them of the problem.' His eyes gleamed. 'Perhaps it is time for Kt Edion to be resurrected – they will take more notice of something that is signed by a Knight of Chantry.'

There was an ironic twist to Davron's mouth. 'You would have made a good Hedrin-chantor, Meldor. Cynical.'

'Some of the mapmakers probably won't want to make trompleri maps at all, not when it means searching for the ingredients in ley lines,' Keris mused. 'Anyway, let's get back to my side of our bargain. Why are you called Margraf? Where are we going really? Is there a Havenstar? Do you –'

Meldor held up his hand. 'Do you swear that you will keep the information to yourself?'

'Certainly, as long as no one is injured by my silence.'

Davron gave an amused smile. 'A fair amendment, Meldor.'

'Very well. What was first? The Margraf title? It's not one I claim, but I am the founder of Havenstar and its leader, insofar as it has one. So people call me the Margrave. They like traditions, so I acquiesce, but titles mean little to me. As I have told you, I am not a Trician – and, anyway, in Havenstar Trician blood means nothing. In fact, the only aristocracy in Havenstar are the ley-lit, as you will find out.'

'What is Havenstar? *Where* is it?'

'It's south of the Graven. What is it? It is an enclave for the excluded, including the tainted. That's all. It is stable there, and safe, yet there is no Order, no Rule and no kinesis chain surrounding it.'

It was Keris's turn to stare. 'How is that possible?'

'You will see. We are taking you there. That is where your mapmaker's shop is.'

'Stability without Order? How? *Sorcery?*' The word jerked out of her involuntarily.

Meldor laughed. 'No, no sorcery, I assure you. It is more like – well, the closest thing I can think of are the fixed features, I suppose, although it's not quite the same.'

'If it's safe, yet it doesn't kill the tainted, then why don't all the excluded go there?'

Once again it was Meldor who answered, his mellifluous voice rolling over her like a bank of fog, blanketing any desire she might have had to disbelieve. When Meldor spoke, it was easy to accept. *A dangerous man.* 'Havenstar is small as yet and grows only slowly. One day it will be big enough for all, but not yet. In addition, it remains an exceptionally fragile place — easily sabotaged. We offer a place within its security only to those we trust, and to those who are prepared to pay the price.'

'Which is to fight for the end of the Unmaker,' Scow added.

'Are *you* prepared to pay that price?' Meldor asked.

'Are you going to tell me your plans?' she countered.

He considered. 'I don't suppose it would do any harm. Firstly, we would like every honest Unstabler to have access to trompleri maps. Secondly, we hope to wage war against the Minions and their Pets, to destroy them utterly. Thirdly, we want to enlarge Havenstar so that it does indeed become a home to all excluded. So that no one will ever need to wander the Unstable because they have no other place to go. And finally . . .' He hesitated, as if he was choosing his words carefully. 'Finally, one day soon, there will come the confrontation with the Unmaker himself. A confrontation that we must win.'

Keris felt sick. 'Win? How can you be sure you can win?'

He smiled, but there was no mirth there, only a deep sorrow that tightened Keris's stomach to a ball. 'Sure? I'm not sure. There are predictions in the Holy Books that seem to indicate that we . . . have a chance. Just a chance. Every step I have taken, has been taken because I believe it is what the Maker recommends. But how can I be sure? All I know is that we can't afford to lose.'

It was not what she had wanted to hear.

She sat still, miserable with fear. Someone started yelling

outside: one of the Unbound who had accompanied Meldor from Heldiss's camp, she realised. The shout was taken up by several others, and the sounds were ones of dire urgency. Only one word was clear, but it was enough to freeze her blood: *'Minions!'*

Scow and Davron plunged for the tent opening as one man; she followed them, pulling out her knife as she went. She paused at the tent flap to look about her. The camp was a blur of movement and noise. Something growled off to her left; there was a yapping somewhere in the darkness to her right. In the distance an animal wailed – in pain or anger, she could not tell. A shape loomed up out of the blackness and fell dead at her feet: arrows feathered a matted-fur hide, a serrated tongue lolled out of a boned mouth that gushed fluid in a gurgle. Other sounds nearby made curds of her insides. There were unimaginable creatures there in the darkness, briefly glimpsed when the light from the fire or a lantern glinted in eyes, or on horns, or from the wet sheen of scaled skins. This was not an attack by a few odd Minions and their Pets – this was a full-scale onslaught by tens of beasts and their masters.

Even as that realisation woke in Keris, something leapt at her out of the gloom. She had no time to throw her knife, and would have been flattened under the clawed forefeet of a Wild had not Scow swept his long-handled battle axe between them and half severed a doglike head from the massive shoulders that had been coming her way.

'Get your bow!' Scow yelled at her. 'Keep your distance from them!'

It was good advice. She headed for her tent, stumbling in the dark. She glimpsed Davron fighting a red-haired woman mounted on a tainted animal not unlike Scow's Stockwood: both man and woman were using ley and the clash was like a war between flashes of lightning. A burst of red fire was dissipated against an equal blast of purple force. Flames sprouted and died, sparks fountained at each clash, hiding them both from view. Keris wrenched her eyes away: to watch was more than she could bear.

Behind her, Meldor was now standing calmly outside his tent, his head tilted to better sense what was happening around him. Then, with casual flair, he flicked ley outward from the palms of his hands. He rarely missed his target. Minions, sensing the intensity of his power, flung themselves away from him; animals – not so wise – yelped and jerked as fur or flesh burnt. The brightness of the ley left patterns dancing in front of Keris's eyes.

A burning turd whisked past her ear like a lethal weapon; she had no idea where it came from, but suspected a friend when it hit a Wild that was advancing on her. The creature screamed and veered away out into the night.

Several snarling carnivores appeared out of nowhere and started to herd her away into the dark of the camp perimeter. She swung her knife at them, warding them off. They were almost playing with her, daring her to try to pass them, then darting in with snapping jaws when she did try. Frustrated, aware that her single throwing knife was hardly adequate against such a pair, she was glad to be rescued by Davron, who had apparently rid himself of the redhead's attentions. He slashed at the creatures with his whip. Flayed skin flicked away from their bodies in strips, blood gushed. They turned tail and fled. The smile Davron gave her was grim. 'Don't worry about not killing the bastards this time around,' he said.

'Wouldn't dream of it,' she said and then the battle swirled between them and she lost sight of him. In front of Corrian's tent a bearlike creature backed into her. In a panic she stabbed at it with her knife. It had been edging away from Portron, who – as far as she could see – had been doing nothing more lethal than sprinkling it with water. She pulled the blade out, gratified to find the creature collapsing like a pricked bladder, but then was forced to part company with the knife almost immediately when the Pet's master leapt at her in a rage. Keris had a glimpse of blond hair and a mouth rimmed with blood and threw the weapon, aiming for the man's throat. She misjudged completely — the Minion had been moving towards her and in her hurry she had made no allowance for the diminishing distance. The knife hit his chin and bounced harmlessly to the ground. He jerked away, scarlet lips drawn back in a snarl. Ley flickered out of his fingers, and Keris ducked. Portron flung some more water and the man screamed as it hit his skin.

'What is that stuff?' Keris yelled at the chantor.

'Kinesis dew!' he shouted back, but the words meant nothing to her. The Minion turned his ley on Portron and the chantor emptied his jug at him in total panic. Keris scooped up the knife and hesitated briefly before she could brace her courage enough to slide the blade into the Minion, who was still desperately batting at his arms trying to wipe away the water. The steel caught on bone and grated, making Keris wince, but the man slithered to the ground jerking the knife out of her grasp. 'That's me lass an' all, to be doubtless!' Portron said, slipping almost unintelligibly into his broadest brogue. He smirked with an un-Chantry-like satisfaction and pulled the knife free to hand it back. 'The unsouled bastard of that maggot-ridden Lord of Lies, Carasma — bless me, but ye've snaggled his goings on, once and for evering!'

But there was no time for congratulations, or even to wipe the knife clean. Something came lurching out from behind the tents looking and smelling like a midden heap on the move, with huge maws overflowing with teeth in the middle of a triangular head. Words stirred in Keris's mind: *a pear-shaped dog with too many teeth for its mouth.* And she felt cold prickle her spine.

She edged back, still clutching her bloodied knife. It was useless against such a beast, even if she managed an accurate throw. The Pet had too many layers of fat, too much sheltering flesh . . . It took a step towards her, and she threw the blade anyway. It buried itself hilt-deep just below the creature's eye. It did not even seem to notice.

'Oh ley-life,' Portron muttered, and shook his flask of kinesis dew. It was empty.

'*Midden*,' Keris said, and cast around for someone in a better position to help.

There was only Corrian. She was now standing in the doorway of her tent, swearing — a spate of invective that would have embarrassed a bullock-driver. She was waving what appeared to be an ordinary saucepan about, and when she saw that the Pet was advancing on Keris she threw it. It hit the creature on the back of the head, a blow it scarcely seemed to notice, but this was followed by a volley of missiles pulled haphazardly from Corrian's belongings: a small sack of beans, a packet of dried beef jerky, a boot, a cake of soap, a candle holder, the other boot, her tin of pipeweed (this last representing considerable sacrifice on the old woman's part). The tin caught the Pet between the eyes as it turned its head to investigate the airborne barrage. The animal gave an enraged bleat and flung itself at Corrian.

It snatched at her, and she threw up an arm to ward off the attack, still screaming profanities all the while. And the beast scrunched its many layers of teeth over her forearm.

Teeth stuck out all over the place . . .

When it turned away from Corrian, back towards Keris, it held Corrian's severed arm in its mouth. Blood dripped down its jaws, bone crunched, splintered.

And something had taken a great bite out of his neck . . .

Keris retched.

And remembered, too late for Corrian, her ley. She remembered it only because her rage loosened her hold on it and it danced out of her fingertips, unbidden, to glow there as an aura of wrathful light. The hands of the knights in the mural on the wall of the shrine in Hopen Grat, she thought stupidly. *Ley!* Meldor was right.

And then the Pet, still chewing Corrian's arm, was coming at her. She tilted her fingertips at him, and let her anger and the ley run out like crackling fire, intent and power mingled into force. Her fear vanished. There suddenly seemed to be nothing to fear: perhaps she would die as Piers had died, and maybe that was not such a bad death . . .

She was guilty, she had abandoned her mother, she was drunk on forbidden ley, she loved a man who was bonded to the Unmaker. She had rejected Chantry for a renegade apostate knight, but nothing seemed clear-cut any more.

The ley hit the beast in the middle of his massive brown chest, where wrinkles of skin furrowed into folds. It flared and then spread into lines of burning current. The Pet sizzled. It doubled up, screaming, and began to run. Keris did not watch it go; she looked down at herself, briefly puzzled that she was still alive. Then she remembered Corrian.

She went to follow the old woman, who had dragged herself off into her tent, but Portron prevented her. Around them the noise of the fighting was dying down; the Minions were backing off, calling their Pets to them. They've been repulsed, Keris thought with mild surprise. She looked past Portron to search out Davron. He was unhurt, poking at the mountainous heap of a dead Pet, to make sure it really was dead.

Portron continued to drag at her arm. 'You used ley,' he accused. His face was the colour of white pottery clay. 'Keris – it's a sin! How could you?'

'It saved our lives – yours and mine and Corrian's too, perhaps. Portron, get Meldor. Tell him what happened, quickly. Corrian's hurt –'

She pushed him away and dived into the tent.

It was dark but she could see that the woman was sitting on her bedding, her pipe still in her mouth, and alight at that, her hand gripped tightly around the truncated end of her arm to stop the worst of her bleeding. Keris had expected to find her weak and prostrate with pain. Instead, she was livid with anger. 'Keris, did you *see* what that rotting-livered *bastard* did to me? That pockmarked pox-ridden *sod* of a monster ate my arm! He frigging-well *ate* –'

'Corrian, hold the stump up above your head,' Keris interrupted. 'You don't want to bleed to death.'

'It's all right, Keris,' Meldor said as he entered the tent, Scow behind him. 'We'll take care of it.'

Relieved, Keris ducked out, only to find that she had fallen into Portron's clutches yet again. She tried to divert him. 'Chantor, what, by all that's dark in Chaos, is kinesis dew?'

'It really is dew – dew taken from between the Chantry Houses along the kinesis chain. Dew that's fallen in places that have been soaked with the presence of kinesis devotions for generations. It burns the Chaosdamned like acid. Keris, I want to talk to you about what you have done.'

'Well, I *don't* want to talk about it,' she said rudely. Then, as she glimpsed the anguish on his face, she relented a little. 'Listen, Chantor, I know you're worried about me, but I am of pilgrim age, you know. I make my own decisions, my own mistakes. And the decision I have made is to follow Meldor. With this hand of mine, I probably don't have all that many choices anyway, but I've made this one. And that, Chantor, is that.'

She pulled away and went to look for Davron.

'We lost a man,' Davron said baldly as she came up. 'One of the Unbound who came with Meldor – Kellin Large Ears, poor man. Ley-burnt.'

She shuddered slightly, remembering the sizzling flesh of the Pet. 'Corrian's lost an arm. I left her swearing at Meldor fit to burn the hair from his scalp with her vocabulary. Was anyone else hurt?'

'A few cuts and burns. Nothing that Meldor can't fix. You? I saw you facing up to that Pet.'

'I singed it and it made off.'

'It won't last. I killed its mistress.'

'I'm glad. She was the woman with the red hair, I suppose? I think she may have been Cissie Woodrug, the Minion involved in the death of my father.'

'Then I'm doubly glad I've disposed of her.' There was grim satisfaction in his voice. 'Did you see the Chameleon's trick with the burning turds from the fire? He found it was very effective against furred beasts – burning manure sticks apparently.'

She shivered again. 'Davron, what was it all about? Could it have been . . . me? Carasma said Cissie would be punished for letting the map get to me. Maybe this is her revenge for the punishment.'

He thought that over, then said slowly, 'Or maybe it's just that she sensed from Carasma that he would prefer you dead, especially if it has been reported to him that your hands are not as badly injured as they are supposed to be. Perhaps she thought she'd be in his favour again if she did the deed.'

She closed her eyes for a moment. 'Oh Davron. You've just – just scared the freckles off my nose.'

His lips gave a lopsided twist. 'I have not. I happen to like them.'

'You must be the only person who does.'

'Suits me. Keris, it will be all right. Tomorrow we'll ride like the wind, and we'll leave the bastards behind. Our mounts are rested and the Minions have been sorely battered tonight, I'll swear. We'll sandwich your tent between Meldor's and mine and Scow's from now on. In fact, you are welcome to share my tent if you want, except –' He made a gesture with his hands that spoke volumes.

She shook her head violently. 'I'll be all right.'

I could bear this, she thought. It could even be tantalisingly enjoyable, if I knew that one day we would be together – if I could see some hope, somewhere, sometime. But there's nothing. We have no future together.

Maker help us.

Chapter Twenty-Five

Scorn not any road to salvation if that road be true. When the Lord Carasma uses ley, his evil is manifest, but, should a Knight use ley and his heart be pure, who are we to say that there is not purity in the act?

Knights IV: 9: 5 & 6 (Kt Jorgan)

Keris baffled Portron.

She was just twenty, a maid as yet unwed, and, for all that she had apparently worked with her father, she had no great experience. She should have therefore been biddable, amenable to Chantry strictures, willing to follow the advice of an older and wiser man wearing Chantry colours. Instead she was intractable, stubborn, self-opinionated, recalcitrant and far too curious about things that should not have been of concern to an uncoloured woman of tender years. She ought to have been content to follow a chantor's leadership; instead she had decided to throw in her lot with two Unstablers of dubious morality and motivation who dabbled in the forbidden and kept company with one of the tainted. Scow might be harmless enough, perhaps, but Meldor was clearly an apostate of the worst kind, intent on corrupting the innocent . . . And as for Davron: his influence was diabolical. The man was little better than a satyr, it was obvious.

Could Keris really be interested in such a man, as Corrian had implied? Certainly she had been spending a lot of time in his company lately, and he had rescued her from the Deep, but Portron could not imagine what the attraction was. He thought Davron — for all his presumed lechery — was far too severe a man to appeal to someone as young and as lively as Keris. Why, the fellow hardly ever smiled, and those black eyes of his were like pits filled with coal, showing a soul as cold as a smith's unlit forge.

Portron shook his head in bewilderment and remembered Maylie. Skinny, curious, generous Maylie with her freckled nose and trusting grey eyes. He had loved her — ley-life! How he'd loved her. She'd had red, roughened hands, he remembered, product of a lifetime of hard manual work. He'd thought them a badge of honour. Not like Keris's hands — both of hers had been long and fine and artistic. Had been. *What by all that was holy in Creation had happened to the left one?* She wasn't saying . . .

Sometimes now when he recalled Maylie's face, it was Keris's that he seemed to picture. They were so alike — or was it his memory playing tricks? He had only his memory to rely on: there had never been a picture of Maylie, and his memories of her were twenty years old now. She would remain for ever twenty in his mind. Twenty, and in love.

And so like Keris.

They'd had a daughter, he and Maylie. He knew that much, although the knowledge of the baby's sex was supposed to have been forbidden them. Certainly Maylie had never seen the baby she'd given birth to, but she had bribed a lowly unencoloured worker to tell her whether it had been a girl or a boy and then she had smuggled the information to him. He had been long gone from her chanterie by then, of course, back to his Rule Office.

She would be Keris's age now, wherever she was, his daughter.

Impossible, of course, that Keris was Maylie's child. Keris knew her parents and had been raised by them. Whereas Maylie's child, his child — she'd be a chantora somewhere. She was born into Chantry, would have been raised by Chantry, would now be part of Chantry, encoloured into one of the Orderings.

Yet Chantor Portron could not help but feel that his child, wherever she was, would resemble the pilgrim maid from Kibbleberry. Whether he ached to guard Keris from the twin dangers of her own headstrong nature and ley because she reminded him of Maylie, or because she reminded him of the daughter he had never seen, remained a matter of confusion to Portron. He regarded her with paternal affection and protectiveness, yet there were times when the jealousy he felt was more akin to that of a lover. It shamed him, and he buried it deep. It's just my pastoral duty, he thought. I want to help a girl who is alone in the world, alone and un-supported. It is my duty.

And then he would remember with tearing potency the way Maylie had looked at him the day they had been able to hide her pregnancy no longer and they had known he would be obliged to leave.

When he thought of that moment now, it brought the kind of feelings that made Portron sigh and kneel to perform the kinesis of penance.

Not only did Chantor Portron have trouble understanding Keris, but he was at a loss to explain what had happened to her. He did not know how she could have survived the fall into the canyon; he could not explain the kind of damage that had been done to her hand; he had no idea how she had absorbed ley into her body, or why. He knew only that she was committing a sin of the gravest kind — a sin that was enough to ensure not only automatic exclusion, but also expulsion from Chantry congregations. And she would not listen to him. He had begged her to take heed, he wanted to nag and threaten and cajole, but every time he broached the topic she had brushed him away. 'Not now, Chantor,' she had said. 'I am tired. We have ridden far, and I cannot face an argument.'

It was true that, on the first day after the Minion raid on the camp, she had seemed exhausted. He had noticed with alarmed concern that she had been swaying in the saddle. They had ridden hard and fast, so there was reason to be tired (even Meldor and Davron seemed abnormally fatigued), but Keris had been close to collapse. Still, he did think she ought to have listened. And anyway, that evening, after they had passed through a small ley line, she had seemed much better. Portron had his suspicions about what she had done in the ley line – what all of them had done: Meldor, Davron and Keris – but he did not want to dwell on that.

Several days later, when he tried to bring up the subject again, he was overheard by Corrian and found himself verbally assailed by the old woman. 'Ah, Chantor,' she said after Keris had walked away in irritation, 'what makes you think in that chuckle-skulled head of yours that she'll listen to you sprout such mutton-brained nonsense?' Corrian's tongue was back in form, even if the wild riding they had done had wreaked havoc with her body. She had spent the first two days after losing her arm riding in front of Scow on Stockwood in a semi-sedated state, followed by evenings and nights stretched out in her tent tired and crotchety. Now, on the third day, however, as they sat in the common room of yet another halt, her wits seemed to be as sharp as ever and she was quite capable of berating Portron even as she complained about her aching arm. 'Keris saved our lives, and I don't care if she did shoot invisible whatever out of her fingers to do it. I'm grateful, anyway. I'm mighty attached to this life of mine – it's the only one I've got,' she said. She pointed at her missing forearm. 'See this? See how it's healing? Well, if Meldor's doing that with his ley, why in Creation's Ordering should I – or anyone else – object?'

'Because it's wrong,' Portron mumbled, anxious that Meldor at the next table should not hear. The idea that the charismatic man who had been Knight Edion was now an apostate with the powers of ley within him scared Portron more than he cared to admit. 'It's a sin, Mistress Corrian. Chantry would be within its rights to cut you off from all salvation.'

'Reckon it's not Chantry as does that, Chantor. It's the

Maker, when He comes to decide whether my bits are to be accepted into That Which Was Created, or tossed into Chaos.' She surveyed him shrewdly. 'Seems to me that you got a problem, Chantor. You've been dodging confrontations all your life, and now you've got one right in your own front yard –' she tapped her forehead '– and you got to make up your mind what you're going to do about it.' She cackled. 'Now that's the Maker's justice for you.'

'Don't worry, Chantor,' Quirk interrupted. He was sitting next to them, but they had forgotten he was there. People did that a lot now that he was the Chameleon. 'Doesn't it say something somewhere in the Holy Books about ley being the salvation of humankind?'

'No, it doesn't! Er – well, there is a bit that's saying the act of using ley might possibly be a true act – if the user himself is pure.'

'And that we should not scorn any true route to salvation,' Quirk persisted. 'That's in the Book of Knights somewhere.'

'It's a vague reference,' Portron protested unhappily. 'No one takes any notice of it.'

'Maybe they ought,' Corrian said, and looked smug.

Portron was sure he had never met anyone he had disliked more – unless it was Meldor. Or Davron.

'We'll have to watch him,' Davron said quietly at the next table. 'He is very disturbed by our use of ley.'

Meldor, hands clasped around a mug of something that was misnamed beer, asked, 'Will he take what he knows to Chantry, do you think – once my coercion wears off?'

Scow murmured his assent. Davron said, 'I think so. Although maybe he might feel some reluctance to do so if Keris is with us. He won't want her hurt.' He grimaced. 'Confound the man. Your coercion won't last for ever, and we hardly want Chantry sending Defenders out into the Unstable, chasing after us in righteous indignation.'

'Would they?' Scow asked. 'Why bother with us if we stay within the Unstable?'

'Oh, they'll bother all right,' Meldor said. 'I don't have the slightest doubt of that.' He smiled slightly at Scow. 'Did you know there was a group of Defenders through here only two days back, asking if anyone had seen an elderly blind man with a deep voice? Or so our host informs me.' He did not look particularly worried.

Davron frowned. 'Why, do you think —'

'Maybe they've just heard too many rumours, about Havenstar. About ley. Chantry *fears* ley more than anything else. They believe that anyone who dabbles in ley is akin to being a Minion and for an ordinary person who has access to a stability to do so — well, that's tantamount to declaring war on Order. They fear that such a man could come into a stability and do untold damage.'

Davron sighed. 'Someone like me, for instance.'

'Exactly. Davron, if Portron talks, your life will be in danger whenever you set foot into a stab.'

'So will yours.'

'I'm excluded. I don't venture past border towns. You do.'

'What do you suggest? That we kill him?'

Meldor, to Davron's alarm, seemed to consider this suggestion seriously. 'It would be one solution, but I do have a distaste for acting in a way that makes us no better than those we oppose. No, I think we will let the chantor go his own way. He will have his uses.'

Davron raised an eyebrow. 'When you talk like that, I wonder what you are up to, my sightless friend.'

Meldor smiled again, content. 'Just so long as Chantor Portron doesn't wonder yet a while . . .'

The fellowship avoided the Sixth and Seventh Stabilities. Twice they also deliberately avoided fellowships that were guarded by Defenders. They continued to ride fast. They saw no further signs that they were being observed by Minions on their way — Davron was of the opinion that they had taken the Unmaker's servants by surprise when they had ridden on so quickly after the attack. Their unwanted watchers had been left behind, still licking their wounds. Of course, it was only a matter of time before other Minions spotted them, but that had not happened yet.

They reached the Wanderer and in the crossing of this ley line, renowned for its treachery, Keris absorbed still more ley. She had been shocked at how weak she had been after she had used ley on Cissie Woodrug's Pet; by the time they had reached a small ley line the next day, she had been feeling exhausted and ill. She reflected wryly that she had never thought that she would be glad to plunge into a ley line. Now, several days later at the Wanderer, she was a little uneasy to realise how much she appreciated the possibility of imbibing still more ley. She enjoyed the strength and vitality it gave her.

'Now I know why I was so attracted to the Snarled Fist,' she said to Davron. 'There is something . . . seductive about ley.'

He nodded soberly and they exchanged glances; they knew the price they paid. With ley they felt strong; without it, they would die.

While she was within the Wanderer she searched for more minerals or soils that could be used in inks and paints, but found nothing. It was not until they reached the Graven several days later that she had any luck with discovering something she could use.

The Graven was wide and slow-moving. It presented few dangers to fellowships, being renowned more for its gentle colours and tranquillity than for upheaval. Davron told Keris that no more than a handful of people had ever been tainted in the Graven over the past one hundred years – with which fact she comforted herself while she searched the soil it touched with its flow.

There she managed to find sienna, the earth pigment that would give her varying shades of yellow and brown, including the reddish-brown of burnt sienna once she had done the firing necessary. Nearby she found some ferric oxide that could be used to make brighter reds, so she was well satisfied.

That evening she drew a small portion of a trompleri map using what she had found, but kept it until the morning light before actually showing it to Meldor, Scow and Davron. Meldor, of course, could not see it at all, and it was Davron who described it to him – in a voice that shook with excitement. 'It's a large-scale map of some of the land we passed through yesterday,' he said. 'It shows a brown plain and that rocky gully where we were almost swept aside by that whirlwind.'

'I used a map of Letering's to get the right measurements,' she said. 'And I chose that particular place because I have the right colours for it. I only have browns at the moment, from yellow-brown to red-brown.'

'Oh, ley fire,' Davron said. 'Meldor, there's a whirlwind there. It's spinning across the corner of the map – moving – I can see it. I almost expect it to pick up the paint from the vellum! You'd think you could touch it and feel the wind of it – yet, when I do, there's nothing. I feel nothing, yet it spins away from beneath my fingers . . . And look, what's that? A rider of some sort. Just coming down into the gully. You can see how he's going downhill! It's incredible – the hillside looks so real! A lone person on a – is that a horse? No, I think it's a tainted beast of some sort. Keris, this is *wonderful*.' He looked up and she was disconcerted to see the admiration in his eyes. 'Holy Maker, I wish you could see it, Meldor.'

'I wish I could too.' There was a note of wistfulness in his voice. 'My thanks, Keris. One day you will be honoured in Havenstar.'

She blinked. 'Honoured? I don't want to be honoured. I just want . . .' She paused, trying to think what she did want. 'I guess I just want things to be better. For everyone.'

'Nothing for yourself?' Meldor asked.

'Things being better – that *would* be for myself.'

'They will be better,' Meldor said. 'I promise it.'

She smiled and did not quite believe it.

Scow, as usual, brought them back to practicalities. 'How much difficulty will you have getting the right colours for the maps in ley lines?' he asked.

She frowned. 'Well, I suspect that I shall be able to make all the range from dull red to brown to orange to yellow without any problems because I think the easiest things to find are going to be the ochres, the umbers, the siennas. There won't be any carmine and madder and indigo and gentian and woad, though – they come from plants and animals. Even sepia. That's from the ink of the river squid. And where to find minerals that are usually deep-mined? Copper, for example. If I have copper I can make verdigris to get green. If I have cobalt and aluminium oxides, I can get cobalt blue – that's probably the most important of all. Greens I could mix.' She frowned, thinking. 'Dark green-blues I could probably get from iron pigments . . . And cinnabar. Is that usually mined? I don't even know what it is.'

'Something to do with mercury, I think,' said Davron. 'What about white?'

'I'm bound to find chalk under a ley line somewhere.'

'There will be people to help you in Havenstar,' Meldor said. 'We could probably find an expert in paint-making, I shouldn't wonder. We have just about every artisan you care to name.'

Havenstar . . . To Keris's ears, it did not even sound like a real place. She still had no idea of what it was. She had pestered both Scow and Davron for more information and both of them had been equally vague. 'Oh, you will see,' Davron had said and his voice had softened like that of a man about to describe his lover. 'Havenstar is difficult to explain. It is different. Rare. Perhaps, after seeing it, you would think even an ocean . . . prosaic. Better to wait and see than have me try to explain with words that will only be inadequate. After all, nobody believes in wyverns any more, do they?'

'*Wyverns?* You're joking, right?'

He just laughed.

Scow was even less informative. 'You will see it differently to me,' he had said. 'I am not ley-lit, so I see the shadow, the reflection, the mask. Useless to ask me for a description. And yet Havenstar will never mean as much to you as it does to me, and in that I am luckier. Havenstar speaks to my soul, Keris.'

And that did not help to explain the place, either.

Nor did she feel she knew all the truth about Meldor's plans. There was a kind of suppressed intensity about him now, as if his planning was about to reach its culmination, its finale. He was as an animal poised to spring, with muscles gathered, gaze intent; an animal waiting for just the right moment to surprise an unsuspecting prey. And that frightened her as much as anything else he had ever done.

Often, when they met groups of the excluded, Meldor, Davron and Scow would be involved in long discussions with them, after which camps would sometimes be struck and people would disperse purposefully, or perhaps messengers would hurry off in different directions as if there was no time to be lost. None of the others in the fellowship were ever given an explanation. 'They are Havenbrethren,' was all Keris was told, 'friends to Havenstar.' She could not help but feel that Meldor was stirring the cauldron of his revolution.

'You are *what*?' Portron asked. The chantor stared at Davron across the campfire in shock.

Davron, unperturbed, poured himself a morning cup of char – Scow's Brew, they had come to call it – and repeated what he had just said. 'We are not going to the Eighth Stab after all. I have spoken to my friend Martryn – he's the guide of that fellowship that's camped just over there –' he waved at the small group of tents just down the valley '– and he's more than willing to have you join them. They are on their way from the Seventh to the Eighth, and expect to arrive at the kinesis chain in two days. I have recompensed him; you won't have to pay him anything.'

'But –' The chantor gazed at Davron in bewilderment. 'But where are you going?'

'Our destination does not concern you, Chantor,' Davron said and this time there was a hint of steel in his voice.

Portron turned to Keris, who had been watching the two men uncomfortably. 'Keris . . .?' he asked.

'Chantor,' she said, 'I'm an Unstabler now, and I'm not going to wait to be told I'm also one of the excluded. Besides, I don't want to have Chantry coming after me because I'm drugged up to the ears with ley.'

Portron winced. 'Don't say that –'

'It's true. It's what I am. And you know it's your duty to report it. Just be grateful that Davron is letting you go.'

Portron went several shades paler; it had not occurred to him that he might have been in danger. 'I wouldn't have endangered you,' Portron said quietly to Keris, and thought he meant it.

'Chantor, you have done your best with me, and by your own standards you have failed. Let it remain like that.'

He stared silently for several long minutes. She did not budge, nor did she lower her eyes. He tore his gaze away and looked at Corrian. 'Mistress? Surely you are not going with the Master Guide too?'

She shrugged. 'I hadn't thought to, but what the lass says is dead right. I'm lacking an arm, and I'm no great shakes as a citizen as far as Chantry is concerned at the best of times. What are the odds, think you, that I would be excluded as well?' She turned her gaze to Davron. 'I'm not much use to anyone respectable-like, 'cept maybe as a one-armed cook, and I have only the slimmest notion of where you're bound, Master Guide, but if you'll have me . . .'

He hesitated, glanced at Meldor, who had been standing aloof from the group, received a nod from the blind man, and said with a smile, 'Anyone brave enough to fight a Pet by lobbing cooking pots at it is welcome, Corrian.'

'Not to mention hurling invective,' Keris said with a laugh. 'I believe I learnt more swear words in two minutes than I had in a lifetime before that.'

Portron gave her a grim look of disapproval. 'Then I guess

that means I'm the only one,' he said. 'Very well, I'll go.' He puffed himself up a little. 'I hope you don't all live to regret this.' He stalked away into his tent to pack.

Meldor stirred and the smile he gave was enigmatic. 'I hope so too,' he said softly. 'Havenstar may depend on it.'

Chapter Twenty-Six

*Why must humankind insist on making themselves unequal,
one to another? The soft-spoken man shrinks before the
strong, the proud beauty preens before the plain, and both
accept their place among us as if it were rightful. Havenstar
was built for all men to march as brothers; Havenstar was
created for all women to walk tall — but always there are
some pigeons that strut and others that cringe, for we are all
human after all.*

later writings of Meldor the Blind

Keris's parting with Chantor Portron had not been a happy
one: he was mulishly hurt by her refusal to accompany him
to the Eighth even after he had assured her that he was
certain her maimed hand would not be sufficient reason for
her to be excluded. She had then informed him that she no
longer trusted Chantry to be fair, and was no longer interested in living under the Rule anyway. 'Maylie,' he had cried,
'how can you say that!' He had seemed unaware that he had
called her by the wrong name, and for a moment she had
been sure there had been tears in his eyes. Then his resolution had seemed to harden; he had made a remark about it
being the duty of all chantors to see that the Maker's servants
were dutiful, a comment she did not like the sound of at all.
His final goodbye was cold.

'I'm afraid he might do something foolish,' she said to
Davron as the chantor rode over to Martryn's camp, flicking
his fly switch in agitation as he went. 'Has Meldor coerced

him to make sure he doesn't ride straight to Chantry with news of what you are up to?'

Davron shrugged. 'I don't know, but you can be sure that Meldor has thought of every contingency. Meldor,' he added, 'does not tell me everything.' He flashed her a fleeting smile. 'Perhaps because he knows I wouldn't approve. Or –' the smile was gone '– perhaps because he knows he can't trust me.'

She did not know what to say, and he looked across at her apologetically. 'Sorry. Shouldn't have said that – it was pointless. D'you know, sometimes I wonder if this whole thing is not some sort of divine retribution – the Maker's little joke on me because I was once such a sanctimonious peacock, stuffed up with pride, certain that I would never do anything to be ashamed of, not *me*. And now I have to live with the shame of being Carasma's bondsman. Ley-life, Keris, I *hate* him so much.' He threw up his hands with a laugh. 'There I go again, wallowing in it. Kick me when I get like this.'

'Were you really such an awful prig?' she asked curiously.

'Horrible. So sure I was right. So sure that I knew it all. Now I don't seem to know *anything*. I can't even work out why I am loved by a certain wench who has as many freckles as a wyvern has scales.'

Halfway across to the other camp, Portron looked back and stood stock still. Keris was chasing Davron around the camp, threatening to hit his rump with her blackwood staff, as if they were a couple of children on a picnic. Neither of them noticed him.

They rode for a further five days without seeing anyone. They were heading away from all the pilgrimage and trade routes now; the direction they took went nowhere but Havenstar. They saw no one until the fifth day, when they had stopped for a break in the middle of the day. It was Meldor – as usual – who sensed company before the others had seen or heard anything at all; it was Meldor, too, who first recognised the newcomers as Haveners.

'Favellis and Dita,' he said as soon as the riders came into sight accompanied by a pack of dogs, and turned back to his midday meal. 'I'd know the sound of those undisciplined hounds of theirs anywhere.'

'They work for Meldor,' Scow said by way of explanation to Keris and Quirk. (Corrian had long since dozed off in the shade of a nearby rock, and was now gently snoring.) 'They live in Havenstar. Ley-lit excluded, both of them. I wonder what the Chaos they are doing out here.'

'Women?' Quirk asked, impressed by the idea that two women would venture into the Unstable alone. 'They must be a formidable pair.'

'They are,' Davron agreed, grinning. He walked out a little way to greet them and Keris could not control the stab of irrational jealousy she felt when the two slid off their horses and hugged him with enthusiasm, hugs he returned wholeheartedly – albeit carefully. The dogs milled around sniffing and wagging tails.

Introductions were made and news was swapped back and forth, mostly about people and places unknown to Keris, so she spent the time trying to assess the two women. They were both attractive, in their thirties, Keris guessed, browned by days in the sun, and both muscular and fit enough to suggest they had lived active lives. Favellis was talkative and bright; Dita more serious, slower to think things through and slower to see implications. She allowed Favellis to do most of the talking, inserting only the occasional question, usually about something that had been under discussion a few minutes before. Keris would have thought her a little simple except that the questions were astute, if belated. Both had a good rapport with Davron, and after observing how easy he was with them Keris suspected that they knew of his bonding to Carasma. She tried not to feel jealous. He's had a whole life before you came along, she thought. Other people to share his troubles, to care about him . . .

'— so, when we heard that there were fixed features cropping up like spring mushrooms, and Zeferil asked for someone to go and check it out, we volunteered,' Favellis was saying. 'You know us: can't keep our noses out of trouble.'

'We know *you*,' Davron said to her, and shared a smile with Dita. 'Anyway, what did you find out?'

'Absolutely nothing, really. From what Meldor just said, you've heard pretty much all there was to hear from Rossel when he caught up with you at Pickle's Halt.'

'What has happened to the fixed features since then?' Meldor asked, pushing away a dog that was trying to lay its head on his knee. It trotted off to sniff at the still-sleeping Corrian instead.

'That's what we've just been doing — going back to have a look. Some of them are a little tatty about the edges, as if the Unstable is sort of gnawing away at them, but they are still stable. Green, too. Trees are starting to grow — ley-life, Margraf, if we could only work out how they were made, we could change the face of the Unstable for ever!'

'How many have you found?' Meldor asked.

'Eight.'

'Rossel said there were seven.'

'Yeah. That's the funny thing. The first seven were all found at more or less the same time, and they are in a fairly straight line between Havenstar and the Eighth. As if some-one was travelling that way and changing sections of the route as he went.' She paused to accept the mug of char Scow had just prepared for her before continuing. 'The eighth is along the Writhe. You see, on Zeferil's instructions, we have been looking to see if we could find any more of the fixed features anywhere else — but we never did, until just a month back. That's when we came across the eighth one.'

'The Writhe disappeared there,' Dita said. 'This char of yours is as good as ever, Sammy.'

'Huh?' Davron asked blankly.

Favellis took up the story once more. 'Yes, it's true.

375

About six weeks back we were in that same area and everything was as usual. Then, when we were returning the same way two weeks later, part of the Writhe was missing. Gone. In its place was a fixed feature. Same size as the other seven, with edges as straight as a ruled line. The ley line started to back up at one end and then flowed around it on both sides. The rectangular bit in the middle, the stable part, resists its encroachment like a tortoise with its head pulled in.'

'Weird,' said Scow. 'And we're no closer to knowing just what it was that occurred about four weeks back that did this?'

Dita and Favellis shrugged in unison. Keris gave a strangled sound that brought all eyes to her. 'You – you don't know,' she said, struggling with a concept almost too large for her to handle. 'You – would you possibly know the *name* of the place?'

'I don't imagine it has a name,' Favellis said, and frowned as if she was trying to work out just who Keris was.

'Yes it does,' Dita contradicted. 'It's Draggle Flats West.'

'Oh, Maker.' Colour flooded Keris's face, then drained away, leaving her as white as the chalk in her paintbox.

Davron was quick with concern 'Keris – what is it?'

'Oh, Maker – don't you see? Straight lines, rectangular – Deverli's map. Davron, the map I had *was of Draggle Flats West.*'

'But we ruled out the possibility that you could stabilise something by drawing it into a trompleri map,' Scow protested.

Keris said, impatient, 'Yes, but what happens if you *burn* a trompleri map?'

What Keris said transfixed them all, and they lingered around the fire, reluctant to move on until they had sifted through the ramifications. It did not seem possible – and yet they all finally came to believe it. Everything Keris told them seemed to fit: the stabilisation of Draggle Flats West had happened, as far as they could calculate, around the time Keris had fed the corner of Deverli's map to her candle flame.

Keris was more appalled than delighted. 'What if I *killed* someone?' she whispered. 'Maker help me – what if someone was *there*, at the time?'

'Unlikely,' said Dita. 'It's hardly a well-populated spot.'

'And the other seven patches of stability – I guess we know now what happened to Deverli's missing trompleri maps,' Davron said. 'That area is where he was doing a lot of his mapping, of course. Somebody must have destroyed seven of the maps he had made, either when he was killed – or later, more probably.'

'What's to say anyone who was on the spot at the time would have died anyway?' Dita said, following her own line of thought. 'Just because the map was burnt doesn't say the land and everything in it was, too. We didn't see any signs of scorching, did we, Favellis?'

She shook her head. 'Nothing like that.' She thought back. 'The terrain around the rectangle is very much like it is here. No trees, just a bit of spine grass and the odd prickle bush, and lots of the silver knobs the horses eat. Mostly it's just cracked rocky ground with the whirlwinds and dust storms. Typical unmade sort of place, you know. Inside the rectangle it's quite different, now at least: green grasses, flowers, a stream where the ley line was – a couple of tree saplings starting. Nice place.'

'I'm not sure I know what a trompleri map is, but whatever it is, do you think you could do it again?' Quirk asked Keris. 'Why, with this you might be able to banish the Unstable for ever! Imagine –'

Keris interrupted. 'You're brain-tainted! It's far too dangerous. Imagine if there had been anyone there. Even if he hadn't been rissoled by the upheaval or barbecued by a fire, he would have suddenly found himself in the midst of a stability! He'd have gone mad.'

'There's another possibility,' Meldor said slowly. 'Burning

377

a trompleri map apparently made a ley line disappear and stability appear in its place. If my theories are right, this means the ley was restored to its rightful place in the land and everything became normal again. But just suppose there *had* been one of the Unbound at Draggle Flats West — maybe he would have been *cured,* not killed or driven mad, but cured as the land was cured. Maybe he would have ridden out of there a normal man.'

'Now *there's* a thought,' Davron said with subdued excitement. 'And I wonder what would happen to a Minion. Or to . . . me.'

Keris swallowed back the mixture of horror and hope that surged up from somewhere near her stomach. Davron freed of his sigil; Davron . . . consumed by a blinding white flash of ley; Davron obliterated . . .

'You can't risk it,' she said flatly. 'It's too dangerous —'

He gave a bitter laugh. 'Keris, my love, just living is too dangerous for me. You once agreed on that, remember?'

Quirk blinked, not understanding. Favellis, catching the endearment Davron had used, gave Keris an interested look.

Scow said, 'It's an exciting thought, though, isn't it? Someone will have to volunteer to be — er — fired, so to speak.'

Keris shook her head. 'Fried, more like.'

'I've just this minute become very attached to my Chameleon characteristics,' Quirk said in a hurry. 'I suddenly don't care if I'm never normal. Don't anyone dare go burning the land around *me*, thank you.'

'We could start with a Pet,' Davron suggested.

'Perhaps the first experiment we should do,' Keris said in dry tones, 'is to find out whether we really can stabilise the land. We must make and burn another map, after making absolutely sure no one is there.'

Davron was almost glowing. 'Ah, ley-life! This is the most exciting development we've ever had. I can hardly believe it.' He was having trouble restraining himself from hugging Keris.

Meldor smiled and brought everyone back to the present. 'Keris can't make a proper map out here,' he pointed out, 'so the sooner we get to Havenstar the better. Then we can start investigating all the possibilities. Quirk, go and wake Corrian. Dita, I'd like you two back in Shield too.'

She nodded. 'We'll have to go back and break camp first, so we'll be a bit behind you.' She stood up, calling to the dogs. Favellis followed suit, casually reaching out to brush some dirt from the back of Dita's clothing. Dita turned and gave her friend a fond smile of thanks.

The touch that lingered longer than was needed and the depth of the returned smile momentarily stilled Keris. Her initial reaction, born of her upbringing, was one of shock, but this soon dissolved into an intrigued interest. As she considered what she had seen, she felt a moment's compassion for Baraine. That is what it should be like, she thought as they rode away. No guilt, no Rule. No having to hide what is.

'That's why they were excluded,' Davron said, reading her thoughts again. 'Excluded for loving each other. They deserved better.'

The next day they reached the Riven. They topped a rise and Keris saw the Knuckle – the confluence of the Riven and the Writhe – for the first time. The two ley lines entwined, twisting upward one around the other until they splintered into a shower of colour and fell back into the ley in shivering fingers of light. Brooding treachery and scintillating witchery, glowering malice and eldritch charm – it was all there: the rank nastiness of the Riven and the fey spriteliness of the Writhe in a double spiral.

Once again Keris felt the draw of ley – and feared.

'Power,' Meldor said quietly at her elbow, as if he sensed her emotions. 'Just power, Keris. A vast force, free and wild, mixed with the fickleness of a lesser energy. Both unpredictable. Think of lightning. It can strike a man dead, or it can just knock him off his feet with all his hair standing on end.

Ley's like that too, sometimes. I think one reason why we have been so successful in Havenstar is because we have two such different forms of ley to work with: the truly potent and the charmingly fey.'

'It's beautiful,' she said.

'And downright scary when you can't see a damn thing,' Quirk muttered in a disgruntled way, but his irritation did not last. 'Hey, Keris,' he said, 'what do I look like now?' He placed himself so that she saw him against the background of churning ley.

She had to return his grin: he was suddenly transformed into a twist of colours as he blended into the background of the Knuckle. 'Idiot,' she said fondly. 'You look like a kaleido-scopic sugar-twist covered in fireflies.'

Then she glanced past him and blanched at what she saw coming.

'No,' Davron said in reassurance, before she could call a warning. 'Not Minions. Just Havenguarders. Our Defenders, if you like. See? They have colours tied to their pikes. White and gold: those are the colours of Sunstream, a Havenstar village. And their collars are all tagged green – that denotes a Havenguarder.'

'But those aren't normal dogs that ride with them. They are Pets!' No normal dog had a prehensile nose, and no dog moved with the sort of prancing grace these creatures had.

'There's nothing to say we can't tame the Wild too,' Davron said. His gravel voice was uncharacteristically sooth-ing as he recognised the hint of panic in her tone.

'That's against the Rule!' she protested, aware imme-diately the words were out that what she said was inane. All of Havenstar was against the Rule.

He laughed at her, and the love in his eyes sent her heart galloping towards places she knew it could never wholly reach.

He said, 'Pets are only evil because Minions train them to attack humans and, of course, they usually choose the nastiest animals in the first place. These here are Wildish, certainly, but they are guard animals. We call them sniffers and their job is to home in on strangers in the area. I suppose they might attack if ordered to do so, but it's not their purpose.'

She digested that, trying to discard her preconceived prejudices.

'I want to talk to that Havenguarder patrol,' Meldor said.

Scow grunted. 'They're sending someone across now. Two men. It's Brecon the Sunstream blacksmith, I think, and his son.'

Meldor nodded. 'I remember them. We recruited them five years ago, just out of the Third. The son had become an Unstabler to search for his father who had been tainted twenty years earlier. A fine young man, and a story that had a happy ending when they found one another.'

'How goes it?' Davron asked as the scouts reined in a moment later.

'It goes, with the Maker's grace,' came the not very encouraging reply.

'With the Maker's grace, Brecon,' Meldor returned. 'Good to hear that eastern twang of yours again. But tell me, why aren't you further out? We saw no patrols on the way in.' His voice was carefully neutral, as if he did not want to scold until he knew whether the scouts had a reason for not being where he had thought to find them.

The blacksmith was deferential, but not obsequious. 'Margraf, welcome home.' He was a muscled man riding a tainted six-legged animal. He had purple skin and ears that flopped to his shoulders. His nontainted son, although he wore the dun-coloured clothes of the unencoloured, also wore an ostentatious ring of gold set with a large rough-cut red stone — something more appropriate to a chantor. He inclined his head even though Meldor could not see him. 'Bad news, I fear,' his father was saying. 'We don't ride out too far any more; it's too dangerous. Avian Pets scout for us, and we are subject to Minion attack if we venture too far.'

Meldor's quick frown said it all. 'They've found us.'

'I'm afraid so. None have penetrated our defences so far – but we dare not spread ourselves too thin further out. Their numbers are building up, too.'

Meldor sighed. 'It had to happen sooner or later. I just wish it had been a little later. However, we are getting reinforcements, as you have doubtless noticed, Brecon. I have asked the Havenbrethren to come home. Any sign of the Unmaker?'

'No, thanks be.'

'Ride on, then.' Meldor nodded his thanks, and the two men sketched a kinesis and rode away.

'The son – he was wearing a ring and he's not Chantry,' Quirk said in wonderment. 'Did you see that, Keris?'

'And why should he not?' Scow asked.

'This place is going to take some getting used to,' the Chameleon said, bemused, and the mounds his eyes were mounted on rolled sideways – one to the left and the other to the right – in humorous self-mockery. 'Ley-life, when a blacksmith's son waves a ring with a stone the size of a garlic clove under my nose, I feel weak in the knees – as if the land is going to disintegrate under my feet just with the wicked sin of it all.' He grinned at Keris. 'Isn't it *wonderful*.'

Corrian's grin was even broader and more wicked. 'Aye, that it is. I do believe the place has possibilities.'

'No rings, though, at least not for you two, I'm afraid,' Davron said. 'Although you're welcome to wear any other form of jewellery.'

Corrian was belligerent. 'And why not, when I've always hankered to wear summat on my fingers that could knock the teeth down a snooty Trician's gorge?'

'Because rings are worn in Havenstar as a sign of being ley-lit.'

'And where is Havenstar?' Keris asked, looking around.

'Everything you see sandwiched between the Riven and the Writhe is Havenstar. Look beyond the ley line,' Scow replied.

She stood up in her stirrups to see better, but was

frustrated by the coloured mists drifting over the Writhe.

'Never mind,' said Davron. 'We'll ride on to the bridge not far ahead, and we'll cross the line there. We have twelve bridges in and out of Havenstar because we don't ask the ley-unlit, like Corrian here, to risk tainting unnecessarily.'

'More than that,' Meldor added. 'I came to the conclusion that ley crossings can eventually be felt by the Unmaker. I thought bridges might help us maintain our secrecy.'

Half an hour later, they were greeting the guards at the nearest bridge. Meldor and Davron were quickly recognised and saluted with kinesis gestures of welcome and respect. Then they rode on over the Writhe (Corrian poked her tongue out at it as they passed) and into another world.

Keris stared, speechless.

The land sparkled. Shone. Every particle of soil gleamed with fiery colour; every blade of grass was lambent in its greenness; every bush and every tree seemed to move with opaline life. 'Merciful Maker!' she said at last in appalled disbelief. 'You have soaked the land with ley!'

'That's right,' Meldor agreed with complacent satisfaction.

'How can anyone ever get used to that?' she asked, more to herself than to anyone else. Was it possible to become accustomed to being constantly surrounded by a ley-saturated land, to being constantly aware that colours moved within a solid object?

Quirk halted beside Keris on the other side of the bridge and slid off his horse. 'Tell me what you see,' he begged. 'I don't see anything special. It's just like a stability, any stability, to me – although I'll admit I don't feel sick the way I did when we crossed through the Fifth.'

For a moment Keris was at a loss, aware that they were all listening to her: Quirk, Corrian, Davron, Meldor and Scow. Davron was the only one who would know if she adequately answered the question, for only he could see ley.

She chose her words carefully. 'It is as you see it, a land with copses of trees and meadows and woods – a farm over there with a mosaic of fields – it is all that. But there is more – inlaid into it, woven through it, embroidered on it. Imagine that this world you see is also strewn with iridescent opal dust, that everything is luminescent with effervescent bubbles . . . yet it is not just flashes of colour that I see when I look – it is flashes of *life*. The colour moves, so it is as if Havenstar has a soul, and she has drawn back her veil so that you can glimpse her heart.' She paused. 'When you say that ley is merely power that binds the world together, I have to believe you, Meldor – but what I see tells me that ley is more than that. I used to fear it; here I see that it is the touch of the Maker. It is the – the flash of a kingfisher's blue, the cider-gold sparkle of sun on water, the misty ring around a moon, the dimpled laughter of a baby – it is all those things that make you want to bend your knee and thank the Maker from your heart for all That Which Was Created.' She looked across at the Chameleon. 'I hope that answers your question, Quirk.'

There was silence, then Meldor said – and his voice was torn with grief and pride – 'Thank you, Keris. Thank you for being the first person who has made me see Havenstar.'

'But I still don't understand,' she said. 'You have soaked the land with ley somehow – I can see that – but how does that make it safe? Why is it not just another kind of unstable?'

'The Unstable is unsafe because it has ley on it, but none within it. Ley lines are unsafe because they have too *much* ley. All we did was take some of the ley from the lines and put it back into the land. The result is Havenstar – a safe place, semistable, yet not hostile to the tainted because it is not created with the rigidity of Order, nor constructed with the unforgiving uniformity of the Rule.'

'Do you mean – did Malinawar once look like this?'

'No, no. The Maker is much more skilful at integrating ley than we poor humans! As, apparently, is burning a trompleri map. Our ley keeps leeching out of the soil and we have to keep on putting it back. Perhaps it is this very instability that makes the result acceptable to the Unbound.'

'Come on down,' Davron said, climbing down from his horse. 'I'll show you how it's done.'

They all dismounted and went to look at the complex system of irrigation gates, tanks and sluices next to the bridge. Riven ley – thickly livid and ropelike – was channelled from the line into a buried holding tank. ('Looks like animal guts,' said Corrian, peering in.) Water and ley from the Writhe were then added through irrigation ditches and stirred by means of a giant wooden comb, powered by donkeys that dragged the levers around as they circled the tank on the outside. The mixture was then distributed into Havenstar through irrigation channels.

'There are many such tanks,' Davron said. 'For safety reasons we space them out.'

'The whole of Havenstar is crisscrossed with a complex system of gutters and ditches and trenches,' added Meldor, 'designed by a man, Switchin Lesgon, who was a master bridge-mender in the Fourth until he was excluded for a crime. The ley is held in suspension in the water and is then absorbed into the soil. Separated from the main body of the ley lines and broken up into droplets, it becomes less dangerous and less potent. Eventually it drains out again, along with the water, and is recycled or channelled back into the ley lines.

'It was hard, back-breaking work, I can tell you. There was not one of us, myself included, who did not take their turn with a spade in those early days. At the end of the first year, though, we had a place where the tainted could live and yet where a building was not reabsorbed back into the land within a matter of days, or crumbled by upheavals, or mysteriously changed in nature. When Haveners planted vegetables or crops or fruit trees, they grew – and grew normally. By the end of the first year, I knew we had created something special.' He clapped the Chameleon on the back. 'Tell me, what do you feel, Quirk?'

The Chameleon hesitated. 'Strange. At peace. As if . . . as if I have come home.'

385

'You have. You are an Unbound man in Havenstar. You may not be able to see ley, but the ley that tainted you is still inside you, part of you – and it bonds with the ley of Havenstar. The longer you live here, the more you will love this land. You cannot see its true glory any more than I can, but you can feel it. The ley-lit or the Unbound: who can say who is the luckier?' He moved off to speak to some of the Havenguarders nearby.

Davron said quietly, 'Oh midden, Keris, think: he created Havenstar – yet he has neither seen it nor felt it.' He sounded infinitely sad.

As they walked back towards the horses, Keris eyed the guards and a pile of halberds, pikes and bows outside the door to the bridge guardhouse. 'What is it you fear?' she asked.

It was Scow who replied. 'Minion attack. Or sabotage of the system. If someone were to flood the channels with too much ley – well, we might become one gigantic ley line.' He shook his mane at the thought.

'Someone like me, for example,' Davron said harshly, his flinted voice scraping across Keris's nerves with words she did not want to hear. 'He can't ask me directly to kill any follower of the Maker, remember, but this . . . this he could ask.'

With sickening horror she realised that this was what both Meldor and he thought he was destined to do. She gazed at him and her eyes filled with the pain of knowing.

'There's one disadvantage to Havenstar no one has mentioned to you yet,' Scow said cheerfully to Keris and Quirk and Corrian that night as they sat at the campfire, eating the damper bread Davron had cooked in the coals. They had ridden deeper into Havenstar that afternoon, and had stopped only when the sun was about to set, choosing a camp site beside a stream under some trees. Keris was now delighting in the intensity of the ley glitter – it was brighter in the darkness, providing its own illumination independent of the firelight or the night sky. 'Remember,' Scow continued, 'cockroaches savour the sweetest dishes.'

'Don't tell me,' Quirk groaned, 'the place is riddled with fire-flaming Minions and Pets with bad breath.'

Scow grinned. 'Not quite, but close. It's the Wild that are the problem. They are just as attracted to Havenstar as tainted Haveners like us are. You have to be careful and we'll have to mount guard tonight. As for Minions, well, they could live here just as we do, but up until now there have been none to worry about. They never used to come south of the Riven any more than the ordinary Unstabler did.'

Quirk grimaced. 'Until now. Until I get here. What is it about me, Keris?'

'Can't be you,' she said sleepily and stretched back against her saddle. 'Must be Corrian.'

The old woman sent a stream of acrid smoke in her direction by way of answer. 'What I want to know is: why the Chaos can't I wear a ring in this place and the ley-lit can? It don't make sense, any more than the Rule did, with Chantry dressing up like peonies and us poor whores having to look our best in brown.'

'The rings are for the quick identification of the ley-lit,' Scow said.

'And why is it necessary to know in a hurry who can see ley and who can't?'

It was Meldor who answered and he sounded almost sad. 'We deal with ley every day in Havenstar. The ley-lit are therefore especially valuable here: only they can see what we are doing, literally. Only they can be the irrigation engineers, our master builders, our master planners. And sometimes in an emergency – which event occurs often enough – it is necessary for them to see at a glance just who can see ley and who can't. Hence the rings.' He sighed. 'I thought to make Havenstar a place where there were no Tricians, no Chantry, no Hedrins, no knights. And there aren't. Instead there are the ley-lit. Our new aristocrats.' He gave a smile of pure ironic whimsy. 'Lady Keris, here you are special not only because you make special maps: here you are noble, like it or not, because you are ley-lit.'

Corrian made a noise that sounded distinctly uncomplimentary. 'Wouldn't you know it? I end up on the bottom of the muckheap yet again! Ley-unlit and ringless. Bah!'

'Face it, Corrie,' Quirk said, 'neither you nor I were fated to be noble.' He rolled his eyes upward in comic resignation and then made off towards his tent, too tired to stay awake any longer.

Was *I* so fated? Keris thought. I'm just a mapmaker's daughter! Aloud she asked, 'Where are we bound for tomorrow?'

'Shield,' said Scow. 'That's Havenstar's only city. There are any number of villages, but Shield is the only place of size. We'll be there before nightfall.'

Keris yawned. 'Chaos, I'm tired. Davron, I hope I'm not on guard duty first off because I'll never stay awake.' Yet, even after the others had dispersed, Scow to guard duty, Corrian and Meldor to bed, she lingered with Davron by the fireside, reluctant to say goodnight to him. She sensed a bleakness in him that scored him deep; he was back in Havenstar, and he believed he was doomed to destroy it.

'I love you,' she said quietly. 'And I'll go on loving you.' The additional words, *no matter what*, remained unspoken, but she knew he would hear them anyway.

'I wish I could show you how much you mean to me,' he said evenly. He sounded prosaic, as if he was talking about the dust on his shoes. She was not deceived.

'I know,' she whispered. 'Creation, I know.'

They looked at each other helplessly, and loved all the more, from a distance.

Chapter Twenty-Seven

And out of the darkness of the Unstable will come one who lives in darkness, yet is clad in light. And he shall take up the sword to change the world.

Predictions V: 1: 4 & 5

Edion had been born a wheelwright's son, but perhaps he would not have made a good wheelwright. He was a dreamer, even as a boy, and liked activities that involved his mind rather than his body. He had no skills with his hands and he was content to have it that way. Throughout most of his boyhood he was even glad that Chantry had taken him from his family as a baby – glad because being raised by his true parents would also have meant that he would have been destined to be an artisan. With no understanding of what he had missed, he just appreciated what he had instead: the opportunity to study, to pore over the written word, to learn – even if it also meant the austere life of a chanterie orphanage.

And so it was that Edion the wheelwright's superfluous baby became Edion the novice chantor, later novice knight, a thoughtful, perceptive boy with a strong leaning towards the ascetic; and Novice Edion in turn became Knight Edion of Galman, philosopher and intellectual, seeker after knowledge, a man with little interest in his own comfort or in wealth. The change from Knight Edion, a fervent believer in Chantry and the Rule, to Meldor the Excluded, a rebel against the institution and its creed, was slow in its evolution and might never have reached its logical conclusion had not Edion gone blind.

He had always decried the pain the Rule had inflicted on individuals – it offended both his sense of justice and his idea that Chantry's aim was one of service to humankind. In his early years as a knight he had often spoken out against the more outstanding of the Rule's injustices, and had preached compassion and tolerance against transgressors. He himself lacked an interest in people as individuals: it was more what was *right* that concerned him, rather than what was *kind*. If this was a fault in him it was neither one he recognised nor one that Chantry cavilled over; his superiors thought all compassion should be subordinate to what was better for society, and that meant what was better for Order. Chantry preached the rule because it preserved stability; Edion questioned it because it was unjust.

Such was their respect for the depth of his learning and their healthy regard for his popularity among congregations, that for many years Chantry was loath to criticise Knight Edion for his forthright views. He went among the people and preached his doctrine and generally the Sanhedrin refrained from comment; sometimes his criticisms were even heeded by his superiors. At the same time, his most fervid critics within Chantry – and there were many – bided their time until they had an excuse to strike, which came when it became clear that the knight was losing his vision.

Edion was stripped of his knighthood, although not of a chantor's colours – those he chose to renounce himself, several years later, after he had furthered his travels in the Unstable and discovered the true extent of the suffering there. It was then that he had declared himself a free follower of the Maker, a heresy that was deserving of death, although the Sanhedrin chose not to pursue it for reasons that had a lot to do with their own popularity and very little to do with the Rule. Instead, they had allowed Edion to sever all ties to Chantry, and to change his name. It was in their interests to have Knight Edion of Galman sink into obscurity as quickly as possible.

Although his open rebellion occurred only after his exclusion, the seeds of Havenstar's beginning had been kernelled when he was still a knight, long before he had lost his sight. Driven by a need for an interlude of contemplation and even deprivation, Edion had at one time embarked on a long journey into the Unstable with several fellow chantors. He had thought to travel south in search of the lost lands of Bellisthron and Yedron simply because he wondered if it was possible to find and unite the lost nations against the Unmaker.

He had failed in the attempt – they had been thwarted by the ferocity of the Unstable – but on his journey he had seen a triangle of land caught between the Riven and a ley line he had named the Writhe. It had contained several fixed features that seemed impervious to instability, which was strange since the area was sandwiched between two ley lines of unequalled caprice. It was an exceptionally attractive slice of the Unstable, a green and fertile land, well watered with streams and well endowed with vegetation: a pleasant aberration in an otherwise desolate, barren landscape.

He had remembered the place and years later – after he had gone blind, after he had been excluded, after he had been unencoloured from Chantry, after he had confirmed his own theories with regard to ley – he had gone back, this time carrying with him his dream of creating a home where the excluded could live safely. There he had applied all he had learnt from his wide reading of both holy texts and the unencoloured writings in Chantry libraries. There he had created something unlike any other place, stable or unstable, something unlike anything that had existed before or after the Rending. There he had created Havenstar.

He had not done it alone, of course.

By then he had gathered around him a small core of dedicated Unbound – men and women who believed in his philosophy. Meldor had charisma, and he preached a creed that struck a chord among the dispossessed: Chantry was wrong. There were, he said, other ways to fight the Unmaker, other ways to rebuild what Carasma had taken from them. There was even, he said, a way for the Unbound to live in a stable land. And he had shown them how with Havenstar.

At first the movement and the place were small. In spite of his wish to make it a home for all excluded, Meldor was cautious of incurring Chantry wrath; he therefore kept its size manageably small and its existence and its location shrouded beneath rumour and fairy tale.

Only some years later did he decide that the time was right not only for Havenstar to be substantially expanded, but for it to be actively used as a base in the fight against Lord Carasma and his Minions. He brought in more people, encouraged Havenstar's growth, and actively searched for the kind of men and women who could best help him in his fight against the Unmaker. Some of them, like Davron, he showed how to imbibe ley – a skill he had learnt from his reading of the holy texts. In the past, it had been an accepted practice for knights to use ley, until – after several disastrous instances of misuse – the Sanhedrin had named its use a sin of great evil. Even Meldor could see there was some wisdom in this and was careful in his selection of pupils, and even more careful in what he taught them. Only Scow (who could not use ley anyway) and Davron knew that coercion was possible.

Chantry began to hear of Havenstar, of course. Rumours drifted about for years, facts mixed with fiction, until it was the fiction – abetted by Meldor's agents in the Havenbrethren – that had grown to swamp the fact.

Sorcerers, it was said. Magic, it was said. A sanctuary guarded by dragons and spells, shrouded in mists, where only the Unbound could go and all others were turned into dragonseed (whatever that was) if they dared to venture there. A place of palaces webbed with filigree buttresses, surrounded by swamps where bunyips lurked to eat unwary intruders. A place where there dwelt magicians who – for a price – would turn the tainted into handsome margraves and margravines . . . The stories multiplied until not even the most gullible of chantors could believe them. For many years Chantry heard – and scoffed.

But the rumours persisted and in addition the Sanhedrin was sometimes made uncomfortable by the way in which there seemed to be an increasing number of complaints from within the Unstable about Chantry's leadership. The excluded may have been banished from the stabilities, but they were still considered to be children of the Maker, and subject to Chantry's jurisdiction, their pastoral needs taken care of by itinerant chantors who were themselves Unbound or simply excluded for one reason or another. That was the theory. In practice, the Unbound were increasingly reluctant to accept their maiming as the Maker's punishment for human intransigence; the excluded were no longer prepared to accept that their banishment was a justifiable burden because they were different. They should have gone on obeying the word of the Sanhedrin and worshipping in the same old way; instead they spoke heresy, they talked of a blind holy man – and it all seemed to be connected in some way to a place called Havenstar.

And so it was that when Chantor Portron Bittle – tormented by the thought of Keris being led to damnation – came to the Sanhedrin with his story, in the hope of rescuing her from Meldor's clutches and Davron's arms, he was not received with the ridicule he expected.

'Havenstar? You think they were going to Havenstar?' Anhedrin Rugriss Ruddleby steepled his hands and looked over the top of them at Portron. The rule-chantor did not look like someone who had brought momentous news. Rather Portron seemed pathetic: a worried, fussy little man who had once been plump but who had evidently lost a lot of weight lately. A halo of white flyaway hair which encircled a shiny bald patch only added to the general air of ineffectuality.

For a brief moment Rugriss lost track of the seriousness of the topic under discussion and preened with just a hint of smug satisfaction. He gloried in his sleekness — and the thought that *he* was not bald on top — but then he pulled himself back to what was important. 'And why do you think this fellowship of yours was bound for Havenstar?' he asked.

Portron wriggled uncomfortably. 'Where else would they have been going, Anhedrin Rugriss? They weren't heading for any of the stabs, I'm sure. Yet they were going somewhere settled. I overheard them talking . . . They promised the lass, Keris Kereven, a shop. There are no shops out in the Unstable. There has got to be a place, a settled place. Where else but this Havenstar?'

'What makes you think Havenstar is real? Chantor, I've heard stories about wyverns and witches — it doesn't mean that there are such things.'

Portron, a little desperately, persisted. 'There are too many rumours about Havenstar for it to be a mere fairy tale. I've heard whispers of it in the halts and the travellers' lodges from here to Drumlin. I've heard the Unbound speak of it as though it exists. And that man, Davron, he's Trician, I'm sure. Such a man has made himself a domain somewhere, surely. He may call himself an Unstabler and a guide, but he doesn't work the route on a regular basis. I checked that out. Nor has he lived on the Storre domain in years.'

'Very well, Chantor. You've made your point. You can safely leave the matter in our hands now.' The Anhedrin stood, his scarlet silk robes rustling against the nacre sewn to the gold satin of his stole of office. He shook the stole to sound the bells.

The doors swung open in answer to the ringing and Portron was being ushered out by the novice on door duty before he realised what was happening. Then, at the last moment, he balked and Rugriss hid a sigh. He watched as the chantor — all his instincts telling him to go quietly — battled the temptation to take the easy way out, and won.

'Er . . . ,' he started, sounding as wretched as he looked,

'the lass —' Rugriss raised an eyebrow. 'She has been subverted by these men. A good lass, only needing the guidance of Chantry, you understand —'

'You can leave the matter in our hands, Chantor.'

'But —'

'You are not saying, surely, that we do not do what is best for our faithful?'

'Oh — er — no, of course not.' Flustered, Portron went down on one knee in the posture of subservience and then left the room looking miserable.

Rugriss was no longer even looking at him.

The moment the outer door closed behind the chantor, another opened on the opposite side of the room and Cylrie Mannertee stepped in, her elegant slippers making no noise on the plushness of the carpeting. Rugriss, unsurprised by her entrance, waved a hand at the padded chair just vacated by Portron.

'So Edion has surfaced again,' she said. She leant back and crossed her legs, arranging her robes carefully about her as she settled.

'I'm afraid so. Maker, if I'd known he was going to cause us problems like this, I'd have had him dumped on his head from the knighten wind-chime tower instead of just seeing him excluded.' He looked at her half hopefully. 'I don't suppose it could be anyone else, could it?'

'Hardly. Portron recognised him. Who's the other?'

'The Trician? Davron of Storre. I asked around after the first time I talked to our worthy rule-chantor. Storre — there's an odd story there too. He was a Defender, had a promising career — then suddenly threw it all up, walked out on his wife and children and disappeared into the Unstable. As Portron said, he occasionally turns up doing a spot of guiding — competent fellow, I understand. Which makes this particular crossing all the harder to comprehend.' He began to count off the fellowship's disasters on his fingers: 'The tainting of a courier's son, the corruption of a Trician youth, the maiming of a raddled old whore, the subversion of a young woman, a Minion discovered in their ranks, numerous attacks, the destruction of a bridge beneath the girl and her subsequent fall and maiming – what does all that tell us?'

She raised a languid eyebrow. 'That it was a rough crossing?'

He ignored her flippancy. 'That the Unmaker took an amazingly close interest in that particular fellowship.'

'Or in one particular member of it.' She began to buff her fingernails on her stole.

'Exactly. But which one? Edion? Davron? Kereven? And why?'

'Possibly Edion. Or what about the Kereven girl? A tent that vaporises, a fall from a great height that ends up not being fatal, a hand maimed in a peculiar way . . . all very mysterious. What's Portron's interest there, anyway?'

'Besotted old fool. Hankering after what he thinks of as prime virtue, I suppose. The girl's obviously as guilty as Chaos – she's thrown her lot in with ley-users. That worries me, Cylrie. That they use ley, I mean.'

She frowned, and a new set of wrinkles appeared on her face. 'Why?'

He was angry, knowing that she was asking the question for some devious reason of her own. 'You know perfectly well why! Because it is an abomination. Because using it gives people certain – certain powers that are evil. We've all seen how Minions use it and Portron just told us that Edion managed to stop him talking about what he saw – for a time anyway. And using ley weakens Order. Holy taint, just think of the damage one ley-user could do if he started splashing it around inside a stab!'

A tiny smile played around the corners of her lips. 'Specifically, you're just afraid of what Edion might do with ley.'

'Damn it, yes!'

'You've always been in awe of him.'

'You're needling me again, Cylrie. I'll say it out loud if you want: *Edion scares me*. I don't know what he is after. I can't imagine that he would ever turn to Carasma, but he's also not on our side and he is dangerous.' His shoulders slumped. 'I just wish I knew what he is up to right now.'

'He's on his way to Havenstar,' she said calmly. 'Friend Portron just told you.'

He banged a frustrated hand down on the arm of his chair. 'How can Havenstar exist, Cylrie? How is it possible to have a settlement in the Unstable?'

'People build halts.' She swung her leg, admiring the arch of her foot and the elegant heel of her slipper.

'Yes, but only bang on top of a fixed feature. Which is always a very small area. And which gets smaller with every passing year. And even then they have to hope a ley line doesn't come their way. Did you know that the halt between the Fourth and the Seventh disappeared overnight last month, with fourteen people in it? It simply vanished into a new ley line that had not existed the day before. Disorder be damned, Cylrie, *how can anyone build anything large that lasts out there*?'

'Surely what matters right now is not how, but why – and where. We must find it. All the resources of Chantry must be turned to this problem.' Her casualness was suddenly gone; now the woman who sat opposite him was poised steel honed on years of intrigue. 'We've been letting this man Meldor-Edion make a mockery of us, Rugriss. Somewhere out there, under our very noses, he has built a place called Havenstar, and we have ignored it far too long. It is my belief that his plan is to use it as a base to attack us. I can tell you what he wants – he wants power, he wants nothing less than Chantry itself.'

'How can you possibly know that?'

'I know Edion.'

'I doubt it,' he said nastily. 'If you'd known Edion, you wouldn't have thought you could seduce him.' The look she gave him flashed fire. 'Oh yes,' he said, 'I know why you hate him – he hurt your pride. You were a fool, Cylrie. Edion is – was, anyway – an ascetic. He took his vows seriously and he didn't bed women. Or men for that matter. But, then, I suppose that was what attracted you in the first place. It always was the excitement of the forbidden, wasn't it?'

'That's all last night's dreams, Rugriss. Keep your mind on the present problem. What do we do about Edion and Havenstar? Not to mention whosit of Storre, this Kereven woman – and who knows how many others?'

'I've called a meeting of all the available Sanhedrin for immediately after Reverence. I want your vote, Cylrie. That's why I asked you to listen in on Portron just now. I want to ask for the power to lead out the Defenders of our Stability – and of the Sixth and the Seventh as well – to find and destroy Havenstar. I want Edion dead, and Storre with him. The Kereven lass I want brought here in restraints. I want to find out what it is that enables a woman to drop from a bridge into the Deep and remain unharmed.'

'Perhaps she's a Minion. And so probably is the man Davron. He rejected his family because he became a Minion and a Minion can't go around hugging and kissing his children and bedding a normal wife.'

'Then how do you explain the fact that he goes deep into stabilities? Once again, I think you show just how little you know Edion. He would not throw in his lot with Minions.'

She shrugged. 'Perhaps he doesn't know what they are. Surely it's a simple thing to – er – pull the wool over the eyes of a man who can't see a damn thing.'

Rugriss shook his head, unconvinced.

'You'll have my vote,' she said. She had relaxed again, and was examining her rings as she spoke. They were ostentatiously large. 'Of course you will. But where will you lead your Defenders *to*, if you don't know where Havenstar is?'

'I have an inkling,' he admitted. 'There have been so many reports coming in just lately, and they seem to be saying the same thing: that excluded people – Unbound mainly – are heading southeast in both small and large groups. They talk of a final battle, of being needed by Havenstar. There's been careless talk in halts and around campfires. A number of chantors and concerned members of our congregations have reported the essence of such talk. Of a ley line called the Writhe, of a place bordered by the Riven — there are clues. We know enough to know where to look.'

'Clues?' she looked doubtful. 'Clues make me think of traps.'

He was dismissive. 'That's just your convoluted mind, my dear. What trap could there be? Edion is not about to launch an attack on Chantry. His followers wouldn't stand for it, for a start. Being critical of Chantry is one thing; waging war against us is another. And how could a few maimed and tainted people entrap the forces of Chantry? Besides, for all Edion's deviousness, it's not in his nature to attack. He wasn't a *physical* person.' He smiled in memory. 'Edion. Edion. Who would have thought he'd walk this road?'

She inclined her head as if she shared the memory that had prompted his sudden amusement. 'Do you know?' she said softly. 'I have a strong desire to see this Havenstar before you destroy it. May I come with you, Rugriss?'

He stared at her, and then started to laugh. 'Tell me another, Cylrie. What you want to see is the end of Edion, not the marvels of Havenstar.'

She smoothed down the satin of her stole. 'So?' she looked at him steadily. 'Take me with you, Ru — and you'll have your vote.'

'Bitch,' he said softly. But he was smiling.

It was only later that he stirred uneasily in his chair, as he remembered another aspect of Edion's character that he had almost forgotten. The man had been subtle . . .

Chapter Twenty-Eight

True tragedy comes not from dying, nor yet from living, but from loving; 'tis loving that grinds the soul.

old saying of the Margravate of Malinawar

Keris halted her horse and sat, transfixed. Before her was Shield, the main settlement of Havenstar. She had thought she had come to an end of the surprises, but Shield was far beyond anything she had ever expected.

Shield was a celestial city.

Shield floated in the sky.

Shield was anchored to the earth by a group of central pillars, slim elegant pillars, pillars that soared impossibly high, pillars that widened out at the top to support the base of the city, like a tray balanced on the palm of a hand. A tray that was stacked with buildings.

They had been riding through the rain, becoming thoroughly wet and uncomfortable and depressed, hoping to see Shield and the end of their journey ahead of them any moment – but all there had been was endless grey cloud and misty drizzle.

And then, suddenly, the rain stopped. Ahead the cloud lifted, there were patches of blue sky – and there was Shield above them. Floating in the sunshine, high above a lakeside. A shining, sparkling city of ley – in the sky.

And blue water underneath. Blue water that went on and on. *Blue.*

Keris felt her heart miss its beat under the impact of the

sight. *What an expanse of water!* There were lakes in the First, but they were just village ponds compared with this. Here it was only just possible to see the opposite shore, and the lake was large enough to contain islands. It had boats with sails. *Sails.* She had never seen those before, either.

But her gaze kept drifting back to Shield. It was not just an optical illusion: it really was up in the air, balanced on the pillars.

Speechless with wonder, she urged her horse closer. There were whole streets and squares up there, as well as buildings, buildings that shone with living ley, that glowed in the sunlight.

Impossible, she thought. It can't be true.

There were also buildings on the ground by the lakeside — port buildings, she guessed. There was a quayside, with ships tied up. Ships larger than anything she had seen in her life, their flapping sails luminescent with shifting ley.

She did not know which way to look.

'How?' she asked, suddenly aware that she had been gaping.

'*Why?*' asked the Chameleon, beside her, craning his neck.

'Forget the how and the why,' Corrian grumbled, refusing to be impressed. 'Just don't tell me that we have to go up there.'

Meldor answered Quirk with offhand casualness: 'Why scar the land with a town if one can build it in the air?'

'But *how?*' Keris repeated.

'Switchin and his fellow builders extended the possibilities of building with ley-impregnated brick to the limits.' He smiled at them. 'Here a pedestrian bridge-mender has learnt to soar. He found that whole streets could be supported by a single column — so why not?'

'It was as if, once the restraints of the Rule were removed, there was a whole lifetime of experimentation to be crammed into a few years of construction,' Davron added. 'And, when using ley-impregnated brick and stone, there are few limits to what can be done.'

'I trust ley doesn't leech out of the brickwork,' Keris said.

Meldor laughed. 'Fortunately, no. Just out of the soil because of Carasma's past unmaking of the earth. And, if it's any comfort, a city that sounds very much like Shield is mentioned in Predictions as lasting a thousand years.'

'I'll be tainted,' Corrian muttered. 'But how do we get up there? I don't see any stairs, and it'd be quite a walk up anyways. Too much for my old bones.'

'Stunning, isn't it?' Davron said. 'It never fails to take my breath away, and I've seen it all before. And as for getting up there – well, let's ride on to the port. We take the transport from there.'

'Oh, Chaos,' said Keris. Her thoughts were taking her in directions she did not want to pursue. 'Davron, tell me you were joking about the wyverns.'

'I was joking about the wyverns,' he said obediently.

'Then *what?*'

'Something called a wildbell. We used them for the building of the towers, for transporting materials to build the city – and now they are our transport. You'll see.'

He urged his horse onward towards the cluster of buildings at the quayside, and the rest of them followed. As they rode under the edge of the town, Keris, Corrian and Quirk automatically looked upward and flinched as they crossed from sunlight into shade. 'Unnatural,' Corrian said, still muttering. 'Humankind weren't supposed to live up in the air like a turkey perched in a tree.'

'I've got a bad feeling about this wildbell,' Quirk added in a mutter of his own. 'I'm not sure that I'm going to like anything that's capable of getting me from *here* to *there*. Oh, Keris, I really wasn't born to have adventures.'

There was a notice on the wall of one of the buildings that read, WILDBELL TRANSPORT, TWO COPPERS PER HEAD. A sleepy-eyed man was sitting on an upturned fishpot underneath the notice. He was untainted and wore silver rings. Next to him there was a huge wicker basket big enough to hold a dozen people, strongly built, with several handles. Keris could not guess its purpose or see how it could be used to transport people upward, but a couple of wooden steps next to it seemed to indicate that it was meant for people to occupy.

'Lamri,' Davron said. 'How's business?'

The man jumped up and made a stiff bow. 'Margraf, milord, welcome back. How's my business, milor'? Excellent! Lots of newcomers been coming to gawp. Your animals going upside too?' He waved at a row of paired horse stalls. They too were made of closely woven wicker.

Davron nodded. Lamri called out to someone inside the building and soon there were people bustling about, blindfolding the horses and leading them into the stalls. Lamri waved a hand at the steps. 'Would you be so good as to board the basket?'

Corrian looked dubious, the Chameleon was horrified. 'Tell me you're joking,' he said.

'Tell *me* what it is that picks this thing up,' Corrian said, and balked, until Scow approached her as if he was going to lift her over the edge of the wickerwork. She hurriedly scrambled up the steps and stepped down into the inside. The others followed.

Davron tried to hand over some money to Lamri; it was firmly refused. The man would not accept money from the Margrave and his party.

Once inside the basket, Quirk was openly nervous; Keris and Corrian contained themselves better, but only just. 'Now what?' the old woman growled.

'Hold on to the rope looped around the side,' Davron advised, 'and watch Lamri.'

The man had turned to face the water and was now letting ley drift out of his hands in a ribbon-like band, towards the surface of the lake. 'I know I'm not going to like this,' Quirk moaned.

The surface of the lake erupted. A round hump pushed out from underneath the water; it was grey and smooth and glistening. It was also huge – the size of a room. Water poured off it as it pushed upward like a mushroom pushing through soil.

'I *knew* I wouldn't like this,' Quirk said, and closed his eyes.

The creature broke free of the water and hovered above it. It was round and fringed with hundreds of white tentacles, each the length of a man's arm. The grey canopy rhythmically contracted and expanded, keeping the creature otherwise stationary in the air. Jets of air, expelled with an almost subliminal hum, churned the water below its undulating edges. From the centre of the underside hung twelve or so long trailing feelers, purple and tuberculated, that tangled and untangled like writhing worms. Lamri's twisting line of blue ley now connected these feelers to his palms.

The Chameleon, peeping through his fingers, groaned again and then managed to stutter, 'What – what does it eat?' He sounded hoarse.

'Fish,' said Davron. 'Don't worry, Quirk. Lamri has it under control with that ley of his. And here come his brothers to call up some more to transport for our horses. Wildbells – like most Pets – are very attracted to ley, and they can be pushed and pulled and directed with it. Perhaps they are open to suggestion from the mind as well; we really don't know how it works. It just does. Anyway, Lamri and the other members of his family know how to handle wildbells just as skilfully as Minions handle their Pets. They haven't had a single fatality yet, or even a bad accident, and remember: we had these creatures help us with the building of Shield – a much more complex task than just lifting us up to the city.'

The creature shivered, still humming, and a shower of water droplets pattered down into the lake. When Lamri deemed the beast sufficiently dry, he directed it to a position above the basket, and he himself stepped in with his customers. 'Hold tight,' he advised. Quirk went one better: he slid down on to the floor of the basket and put his arms over his head.

Keris looked upward at the underside of the wildbell. It was not an attractive sight, nor a reassuring one. In the middle of the ring of central tentacles there was a beak-shaped mouth and its edges were razor-sharp. 'Do you think it ordinarily uses these tentacles to lift things into its gut?' Corrian enquired.

Keris had an idea that that might have been the case, but she did not want to think about it.

With surprising gentleness, the creature looped its tentacles around the basket handles, then — in apparent answer to some change in Lamri's ley — it squeezed its canopy and jetted upward, the hum becoming a louder whoosh. A few drops of water trickled down to splash on to the wickerwork and the basket floated away from the land. Keris's heart lurched in sympathy. She felt like a hapless rabbit seized by a hungry eagle. The analogy appalled her, but then she looked over the edge and saw the tops of port buildings below and the lake spread out before her — as if it was one of her own maps — and she forgot her fear. Further out, over the lake, she could see several other wildbells. These seemed smaller and they carried no baskets. Instead, a single man stood within the cradle of central tentacles. One of them lifted a hand and casually waved. Possibilities began to flood her mind.

She turned towards Davron, face glowing, the question hovering. He grinned at her, and answered before she could ask, 'Don't get too carried away, Keris. Wildbells can survive out of the water only half an hour or so. Therefore, they can't be ridden too far from the lake. But there's no reason why you couldn't ride them to map the lake edges.'

She changed her question. 'How do you know what I'm going to say?'

'Oh, I know,' he said, very softly.

The basket lifted over a waist-height wall and was lowered down to a patch of grass. They had arrived in Shield.

'You can open your eyes now, Quinling,' Corrian said.

'Won't the horses be terrified?' Keris said to Scow.

'Not half as terrified as you were,' he said cheerfully. 'What they can't see they don't worry about. Besides, they rather like the smell of wildbells for some reason or another.'

While they waited for the other horses to arrive, she looked around, almost overwhelmed with a simultaneous desire to laugh with joy at the sheer light-heartedness of it all, and to cringe with fear at what Chantry would think. As she absorbed the details of what she had only grasped in general from the ground, she decided that, even for the ley-unlit, Shield would be pure magic. Humble houses were buttressed with flying filigree; arches thrust skyward in impossible shapes to decorate ordinary shopfronts; domes and towers and vaulted roofs flaunted themselves across the skyline. Everywhere there were oddities and ornamentation: external staircases up to upper floors, cowled pots over ornate chimneys, oriel windows, stained glass, carved tracery, copper roofing, architraves, pargeting, pilasters . . . Nothing was overly large or high; the emphasis was more on the delicate than the grandiose. It was a joyous place of absurdities and delight, as if the people of Havenstar, freed from Chantry's strictures, had gone mad.

Yet, to Corrian, Quirk and Keris, seeing it for the first time, it was also shocking. They had been brought up in a world where architecture was austere and utilitarian – and never changed. Where nothing was ever new, or different. Where, although the occasional sod-roof of a house may sprout spring flowers in season, most buildings were old and crumbling, lichen-covered or dirt-grey. In the stabilities only Chantry buildings had colour and decorations, only Chantry Houses had carvings, only Chantry shrines had murals, only Chantry devotion halls had towers. Here everything was new, everything was different, everything was decorated. And everything was lambent with ley.

'Well,' Corrian remarked in a satisfied way, as they mounted up, 'Chantry prigs wouldn't like this very much, would they?'

'I can't even *imagine* what Portron would say,' Keris said, 'let alone the devotions-chantor back home.' She turned to Davron. 'Is that a windmill up on the roof there?'

'It is indeed. There are quite a few. They supply power for the mills, and they draw water up from the lake. Come, follow me − it's getting late and we're all tired.' He turned his horse up into the nearest cobbled street. Keris followed and tried not to remember that she was suspended several hundred feet above the lakeside.

'Hmph,' said Corrian, looking around. 'If they do this to mere buildings, I wonder what the whores look like.'

Quirk craned to look upward at a spiralled tower. 'Do you think it will all still be here when I wake up tomorrow?'

'You may not believe this,' Davron said, 'but Meldor actually insisted on considerable restraint. You should have seen some of the things Switchin wanted to build. Places with doors twelve feet high, towers that would snag passing clouds, onion domes piled one on top of the other, glass windows the size of a bean field −'

'I was in two minds,' Meldor said. 'I still am, if it comes to that. This is undeniably pretty and joyful, and of course it's obvious that everything has to be built new − but the Rule wasn't all bad, you know. To dig the clay for the bricks, to quarry the stone for the blocks, to cut down trees for beams, to mine the copper for the roofs − all this marks the landscape in horrible ways. Not all change is good, I find. I did insist that everything should be on a small scale. No unnecessarily high roofs or huge rooms, for example. Every tree cut must be replaced − just as the Rule decrees. But even so . . .' He shook his head. 'Some awful things were done to Havenstar to build all this. Perhaps I should have been more severe with the rules.'

'Why weren't you?' Keris asked, knowing that Meldor never did anything without a reason.

'Because somehow it seemed to be important for the human spirit to seek beauty. We have been too long under the Rule; too long constrained to conform. It has made people petty and mean-minded. I don't need frills in my life – I didn't need them before I was blind and I certainly don't need them now – but I don't like what the lack of frills and fripperies does to other men's souls. We had become a bleak race of people, Keris, always thinking to punish and restrict, hating our neighbour if he dared to be different. I didn't want Havenstar to be like that. Here people can spread their wings – we just have to be sure that in so doing we don't destroy with the claws of our greed.'

Keris turned her attention to the people they passed in the street, many of whom gave kineses of respect when they saw the Margrave. Did they look happier than people of the stabilities? She was not sure. They certainly appeared brighter: there was no restraint on apparel here. Any colour, any fashion, and any decoration was possible. She was not sure she entirely enjoyed the result.

'Doubtless they will tone themselves down eventually,' Davron remarked. He had been reading her mind again. 'It's just reaction to the narrow austerity that was forced on them under the Rule.'

'I suppose so.' Keris sounded doubtful. A man hurried by; he had shoes that curled up at the toes so outrageously they had to be tied to his breeches at the knee. A woman struggled through a doorway sideways because her skirts were too wide to enter any other way.

'Maybe there's an answer to your question about what whores wear,' Quirk said to Corrian, indicating a woman standing in a doorway. She wore surprisingly little.

'Those children –' Keris said suddenly, staring to where a group of very young children played. 'Ley. There's ley – and I've noticed so many children too! But the ley. Are they . . .?'

Scow nodded. 'As far as we can tell, children are born normal here, even to tainted parents, except that they contain noticeable amounts of ley. Noticeable, that is, to the ley-lit. We don't know yet whether it affects their development. So far, it doesn't seem to. They can be ley-lit or not, just like anywhere else. And this isn't the Unstable, thank the Maker – the children don't appear to have in any way degenerated, and none of them are tainted. And you're right, of course. There are a lot of them. People are not restricted to just two any more. Not yet, anyhow. They can choose how many to have.'

Keris turned to Davron to remark how wonderful that was, and caught a look on his face that left her breathless with pain for him. He had been staring at the children – and aching. She left unspoken the words she had been about to utter.

Further on down the road, they pulled up outside a shop. Keris looked up. There was a sign dangling above the door, and her heart leapt as she saw the symbol: a map scroll. This was a mapmaker's shop.

'This was Kereven Deverli's,' Meldor said. 'It is now yours, Keris, with all its contents. Kereven had no family, and we bought most of what it contains for him anyway. There is everything you will need for mapmaking. I hope you do not mind taking hold of a dead man's pen.'

'I think I would be honoured. Deverli was a fine mapmaker, if the map I had was any indication.'

Davron dismounted and pulled the bell. 'His manservant should still be here. If it suits you, then keep him on. His name is Colibran, but he is known as the Cricket. His wife acted as Deverli's housekeeper, I believe.'

'I suggest Corrian and Quirk stay with you, Keris, until they decide what they want to do,' Meldor added. Keris nodded, a little intimidated. There were times now when something about Meldor made her want to sink down on one knee in obeisance. She was becoming reluctant to address him by name.

Davron looked up at her. 'Come on,' he said. 'Get off that animal and come and have a look at your house.'

'Of course.' Keris was in a daze. A house of her own. A shop. Mapmaking equipment. Servants. *Keris Kaylen of Kibbleberry?*

The door opened and they saw why Colibran was called the Cricket. He was one of the Unbound, and his tainting had resulted in stick-thin legs and arms – two pairs of arms – and an elongated head that sprouted rudimentary feelers. Two large oval eyes set perpendicularly on the sides of his face stared up at Davron out of a long mournful face. 'It's late,' he said. 'The shop is closed – oh, it's *you*, milor'! And *Margraf* – my apologies.' His twelve-inch feelers waved in a flustered fashion as he performed a kinesis of respect. 'Do come in.'

Meldor shook his head. 'Not I, I think. Scow and I will go on to the Hall.'

Davron nodded, and as the two men rode away he indicated the mounts belonging to Corrian, Keris and Quirk. 'Take the horses, would you please, Colibran? And spoil them a bit, if you wouldn't mind. They've come a long way and they need a bit of coddling.'

'I'll get my two boys to do it,' the Cricket said. '*Nothing* they like better than coddling horses. Will you be staying the night, then, milor'?'

'No, but you do have guests, Colibran.' Davron introduced the three others and added, 'In fact, maid Keris Kaylen here is your new mistress and mapmaker.'

The feelers danced. 'Kaylen? Kaylen? Would that be Piers Kaylen's daughter, milady?'

Davron answered for her. 'It would.'

'Then I am doubly honoured. Fine maps he makes. Fine indeed.' The man called for his sons and led the horses away; Keris muttered to Davron, 'Milor'? *Milady?* You might be entitled, but I certainly am not.'

'That's the way all ley-lit are addressed here, Keris. You are going to have to get used to it, I'm afraid.'

She wrinkled her nose and Corrian snorted.

Inside the house Colibran's wife, who was also tainted,

made them welcome, showed them the bedrooms, then bustled around talking of meals and baths. She was a large woman with whiskers and kitten's ears.

'Come,' said Davron. 'Before you get plied with food and such, I shall show you the shop.' Which was exactly what Keris most wanted to see, of course, and he knew it.

It was all she could have hoped for, and more. There was a theodolite in the corner, complete with a telescope – worth a small fortune, she knew. She fingered some of the parchment on the workbench and itched to delve into the pile of maps on the shelf next to her. Davron saw the way her eyes lingered on them and said, 'We did look through everything here, of course, looking for a clue about trompleri maps – but the shop had been robbed by then, by the Mantis. And, apart from the maps, we didn't know what to look for. Inks are just inks to us.' He nodded at the corked bottles on the bench. 'Who knows? They may be made of ley-drenched pigments.'

'I'll check first thing in the morning.' She shivered slightly, aware that she was stepping into a dead man's shoes.

'He wasn't killed here, you know. He died out in the Unstable. The Mantis was with him, but managed to escape. We don't think the Mantis betrayed him; we think he just thought he'd take advantage of the situation. He came back here, telling no one what had happened, and stole the maps. Probably he intended to sell them. Silly fool – the moment he tried to sell one, both Havenbrethren and the Minions were on to him and he had to flee. That's probably when the first lot of maps were destroyed – exactly how, we'll never know.'

He came and stood close to her. 'Keris, I have something for you.' He fumbled in his jerkin pocket. 'I bought it in the Fifth. I knew you'd need it here if you came.' He produced a ring and held it up.

'You bought me a ring?' The enormity of that left her breathless. She was to wear jewellery. How Sheyli would have loved to have done that! Instead she'd had to embroider lace on her underwear in secret . . .

The ring was gold and set all around with tiny ruby, emerald and sapphire chips. She stared, disbelieving. 'It's beautiful!' She was not sure how she could come to terms with wearing such a thing. It seemed sacrilegious.

'Your finger, milady?'

She held up both hands, still bemused. She had no idea which finger to use.

'Let's try this one for size.' Careful not to touch her, he slipped it on to the middle finger of her left hand. For a moment she stood admiring it, then a single tear slid down her cheek. He reached out and collected the drop on his fingertip. Still not touching her, he placed it on his tongue, an act of such tenderness that her hands went to her face in a gesture of distress. She covered the nose and mouth with steepled fingers, watching him.

'Don't cry,' he said gently. They were standing so close that the buttons on his coat brushed her breast. 'You know, I used to feel perhaps you had the right of it when you first found out what I was: you said it would be better for us all if I died. But now, what you have found out about the trompleri map has given me hope. It makes things . . . easier, when you hope.'

'I want – I want –' She choked.

'I know. So do I. Keris, perhaps it is better we do not see each other too much.'

She shuddered. 'I can't bear it either way.'

'I know.'

They looked at each other helplessly.

She said, 'I am so afraid for you.'

'I know that too.'

'Promise . . . promise me –'

'I can't make any promises. When the time comes, I must do what I think is right, and who can say now what that will be?' He rushed on, changing the subject. 'I am going to the Hall now. That's the City Hall. Meldor and Scow and I have rooms there – it's where all the administration of Havenstar is done. I — I can't afford ever to be far from Meldor, you know. Not in Havenstar.'

She nodded and dropped her hands away from her face. 'I love you, Davron of Storre,' she said and walked away from him, back into the main rooms of the house.

Chapter Twenty-Nine

*He of darkness who offers light; she of talent who bestows
colour; he of betrayal who shows courage; he of cowardice
who is inconstant: apart they are nothing; together they offer
hope. Pray that they prevail, for, if not, Chaos shall.*

Predictions XXII: 5: 1

On her first morning in Deverli's shop – her shop – Keris
discovered that all the inks and paints that he kept under his
counter out of sight were made with ley-soaked earths and
pigments and minerals. They were all the colours she could
have wished for: not only the earth tints, but cobalt blue,
greens of all descriptions, reds, sun-gold and moon-cream,
shadow purples, sepia, devil's black and chalk white . . .
There was a faint lambency to them that told her they were
probably infected with some kind of ley, but that was not
unusual in Havenstar. So many things – children included –
had visible ley.

So, without too much hope, she tried out all the colours,
tracing an outline in the ley ink from one of her own maps,
then colouring it with the paints. No sooner had she filled in
the lines than the hills and trees and rocks leapt up out of
the vellum at her. She stared, gripped tight with emotion.
Trompleri, in all its perfection. An immediate three-dimen-
sional map. But where had Deverli obtained such a range of
trompleri hues? Surely he could not have found all the
ingredients conveniently situated under ley lines.

She called Colibran into the workroom of the shop to ask

how much he knew about where the inks and colours had come from.

One of his feelers moved around to scratch the back of his head. 'I don't *really* know, milady,' he said, apologetic. 'Milord Deverli was *very* secretive and always, always out, you understand. He'd bring back the ingredients for the paints and the Mantis'd mix them up here – but he *never* said where they came from in the first place. Except for the verdigris – he used to get that from old Graynix at the metalmakers. Oh, and the chalk he used for white – I used to get that from the herbalist in Solidarity Street. I *think* she uses it in her medicines.' Every time he emphasised a word, his feelers would flick backwards in harmony. Keris had to concentrate to prevent herself from nodding in rhythm.

'Tell me about him, about Kereven Deverli. What sort of things did he do? Where did he go?'

'Well, he was *always* messing about in ley lines. There was such a big argument about it, because we aren't supposed to go into ley lines any more, you know. That's what the bridges are for.'

'Why did he keep some of the colours under the counter, separate from the others on the shelf?'

'Oh, he said they were his special ones. We weren't *ever* to touch them. He mixed them himself. I never even saw him use them – but, then, he often used to lock the door. It's a very secretive business, making maps, you know.'

'So they weren't made special somehow, *after* they were made? They were special from the moment he mixed them?'

'Oh, well . . .' The feeler scratched some more as he pondered; Colibran wanted very badly to help. 'I *think* so.'

She continued to pester him with questions and gradually began to build up a picture of Deverli and his mapmaking. 'I think – and this is all conjecture, mind,' she said to Davron and Meldor when they came to see her that afternoon '– I think that Deverli took ordinary ingredients and left them in a ley line. He then brought them back and mixed up his colours. I don't think he actually had to dig in a ley line for

415

his pigments, or anything like that. I'll need to go to a ley line to prove it.'

While Meldor considered what she had said, she studied him. He was dressed in something that was halfway between the flamboyant garb of a knight-prophet of Chantry and the plain austerity of a margrave. It was a white robe, both simple yet rich (it was embroidered around the neck and hem with gold thread), that fell to his ankles. It made him seem noble, yet there was a touch of the ascetic as well. She wondered who had chosen it for him; it did not seem to be the kind of thing that either Scow or Davron would approve of overmuch, but she could not help feeling that it was exactly right for Meldor the Blind, one-time knight and now Margrave of Havenstar. She knew that he would never be just Meldor to her again.

'Keris,' he said finally, 'you are very valuable to us. We want to use your time to the best advantage. I think experiments like this can best be left to others. I will send someone I trust to assist you – you just tell him what the problem is, and what experiments to do. After all,' he said with a smile, 'the more people who know, the safer you are.'

'What *do* you want me to do with my time, then? Experiment with burning trompleri maps?'

'No,' he said, faintly impatient. 'Not that either. Favellis and Dita can work on that, once you've done some maps for them to experiment with. I want you to do what you do best: make maps. Let me explain. Eventually I want maps of all Havenstar and all the surrounding areas, but more importantly for now I want maps of our borders. How better to protect our land than to watch the enemy approach on a map, and thus know when and where to thwart him with our Havenguard?'

'Large-scale maps . . .' She nodded, thinking. 'You have to have that to be able to tell friend from foe. That's going to require an enormous amount of parchment. And inks.'

'And labour,' Davron added. 'She'll need help, Meldor.'

He nodded. 'You'll have everything you need. I'll put

people on to making the paper for you — there's no way we can get hold of enough parchment in such a short time. You'll need more staff — train people to do the tedious unskilled work. Confine yourself to what others can't do: the surveying and the actual mapping.'

'It's not as much as it sounds, I suppose,' she said, half to herself. 'Deverli had already done a lot of maps of the Havenstar area before he died. I can transfer that work over into trompleri — or have other people do it.'

'Davron and Scow will go with you when you are out surveying.'

She nodded and felt her heart lift. Surveying, mapmaking — and Davron. Davron . . . almost. She looked across at him to share her pleasure, only to see that he was gazing at Meldor in consternation. At first she thought it might just be concern that they would both find it too much of a strain, then she realised the real reason: he was afraid — afraid of being separated from Meldor because the Margrave was the only one who might be able to thwart the Unmaker when he came to claim the service Davron owed him. She waited for Davron's protest, but he shrugged in resignation and grunted his acquiescence. She did not know whether the acceptance came from his trust in his friend, or from his innate fatalism. He looked across at her and smiled, but all her joy of anticipation had drained away.

'There's one other thing I came to talk to you about, Keris,' Meldor was saying. 'I want nobody to know what happens when a trompleri map is burnt. It is to be kept absolutely confidential — I can't stress that enough. And I want you to write to each of the mapmakers who had letters from you about trompleri. I want you to tell them that on *no* account should a trompleri map be burnt or, in fact, destroyed in any way whatsoever. Put the fear of the Maker into them — tell them anything: that it will give off poisonous fumes, that it will unmake stability — anything except the truth.'

'But why?'

'Trust me.'

She subsided reluctantly. 'I'll do it today.'

'I'll send a courier to collect them. And now I want to see the Chameleon. May I go through into the house, Keris?' He was asking *her* permission? She was embarrassed and called for Colibran to show him the way.

She and Davron were left looking at each other. 'How bad is it, Davron?' she asked. 'Why does he fear attack after all these years of peace? Why is he calling all the Havenbrethren home?'

He was sombre. 'The Unmaker knows about us now, knows where we are. He knows we search for the secret of trompleri. Minions may have already told him that we have found a way to stabilise the Unstable. We are too dangerous to him, too dangerous to be allowed to live here in peace.' He toyed with the edge of one of her maps where it lay on the table in front of him. 'It won't be long before he attacks. He is moving his Minions through the Unstable already – and we are doing the same thing with our Havenbrethren. We have to reinforce our Havenguarders, train more men and women – we have a number of Unbound Tricians helping us.'

She listened, and watched him. He was clad in clean clothes of a finer material than she had been used to seeing him wearing, and he now wore a chunky red-gold ring on his right hand. 'You aren't wearing your knives!' she said suddenly. He wasn't carrying his whip, either. It was the first time she had ever seen him unarmed.

'I don't wear them in Havenstar.' He sounded casual, but the telltale red flush spread from the back of his neck up to his ears. He said hurriedly, 'You do realise, don't you, that Portron might bring Chantry down on our heads?'

She would not be diverted. 'Not wear them? Why not? It's not *that* safe here, surely? I'm told the Wild can be very bold –'

'Not inside the city.' He sighed, seeing that she was not about to be sidetracked. 'Keris, *I'm* the danger here. *Me*. It's

418

better I carry no weapons. It evens up the chances that I can be stopped when the time comes.'

She was silenced, feeling sick, wishing she'd had the sense not to ask.

Suddenly he laughed, sounding almost light-hearted. 'It's that damned blush of mine, isn't it? I just can't seem to do anything about it and it gives me away every time. I feel an awful fool, colouring up like a torchlight all the time.'

'Don't denigrate it. I may never have spared you a thought if you hadn't lit up like a flame the day we first met.'

'Really? That almost might make it worth it. But no — maybe not. You try impressing a troop of ley-scarred Defenders under your leadership — or a fellowship of wily sinners on a pilgrimage — when you blush like a lass at her first kiss! It's been the bane of my life.'

'Well, I like it,' she said.

'Ah,' he said. 'Just as I happen to like a certain spattering of freckles across an otherwise very ordinary nose . . .'

She pulled a face at him and felt her sorrow dissipate.

'When do you want to leave for the borders?' he asked.

She dragged her mind back to business, forgetting in the meantime what he had said about Portron. 'I have to write those letters, go through the rest of Deverli's maps to see exactly what areas he has surveyed. I'll have to make some decisions about just what I want done with regards to the production of more inks and paints. Organise whoever it is that Meldor sends me, start training people, prepare a number of trompleri maps for Favellis and Dita —' She looked up at him, suddenly appalled by the amount of work involved. 'Shall we say six days?'

'Fine. I'll get the paper organised for you and do what else I can to help. Make me a list of paint ingredients you may need.'

'And the Chameleon? Why does Meldor want to speak to him? He's not going to send him back into the Unstable, is he?'

'Everyone who comes to Havenstar knows they can be

called upon to fight, Quirk included. Meldor wants him to embark on a career of Minion-watching.'

She sighed. 'An impressive profession for someone who vows and declares that, of all the world's lily-livered cowards, he has the lilyest liver!'

Davron looked resigned. 'The Unstable makes cowards of us all. And none of us get what we want when he plays with us.'

It was surprising how quickly Keris slipped into routine. She would spend a week or more at a time out on the borders doing the surveying with Davron and Scow, then return to Shield to stock up on supplies, to check how her team of helpers were coping with the work she gave them, and to draw up maps of those areas she had just surveyed. She enjoyed the work and felt much more at home in the Unstable than she had ever felt before. She may have retained a healthy respect for its vagaries, but she no longer feared it. She had grown more sure of herself and her abilities. She was even – under Davron's tutelage – becoming an expert with the throwing knife.

Her one complaint was that sometimes she felt as if she was swamped under heaps of vellum and parchment and charts. She worked all day, every day, and nights as well, mapping by lamplight in her tent or in the bustle of her shop workroom in Shield. She surveyed for maps, planned maps, drew maps, altered maps. She talked about maps, thought about maps, dreamt about maps. She had become a map-maker with a vengeance.

She found out that maps that deviated too far from the true aspect of the land simply refused ever to become trompleri maps, no matter how much ley ink was applied. She found out that maps with too small a scale also could never be made into a trompleri map. Her assistants, experimenting in ley lines, soon found that ten hours in a ley line was enough to turn almost all of the components for inks and colours into ingredients so ley-soaked that the final mixture, when she made it up, was as good as any Deverli had made.

'As simple as that!' she laughed, sharing her pleasure with Davron.

In spite of the long hours she worked, she and Davron spent a lot of time together. It was he who obtained the things she needed for mapmaking and the people to help her; it was he who discussed everything with her before decisions were made and he who invariably contributed some of the best ideas; it was he who planned their trips with meticulous care; and he who – together with Scow – guarded her as she surveyed the Unstable bordering Havenstar. They slipped into an easy friendship that contained as much laughter as pain. He could be cheerful, romantic and humorous – it was all there, even though he walked a knife blade: on one side death at the hands of his friends, on the other the death of his friends at his hands – with Carasma already reaching to twist the knife handle.

That he could often close all that off behind a steel gate of pain and let his eyes gleam with love, or humour, was to Keris nothing short of a miracle.

At these times when she felt the saddest, when she felt at her most pensive, she liked to go up to her bedroom and look out of the window there. She had never seen a window with such a large expanse of thick glass (made possible by ley, she supposed) and the view was something that never failed to make her catch her breath in awe. To the right and left there were the rooftops of Shield – ornate flamboyance and a mixture of styles made them look like a playground for faerie – and then directly in front of her was a view over the lake. Perhaps she would never glimpse the ocean as she had dreamt, but here there was more water than she had ever hoped to see all at once. The sea, she decided, must be blue like this. She loved its many moods, the way it reflected the sky and the clouds, the way it could sparkle with sunshine and ley, or brood in slatey darkness with bad weather. She loved to watch the fishing boats go out with their triangular sails filled, bouncing on the breeze.

She knew she would never tire of it. If she could not have the ocean, at least she could have the lake.

Corrian still stayed in the house, and so did the Chameleon when he was in Shield. Most of the time, though, Quirk was out in the Unstable, spying on Minion camps. Keris feared for his life, but he seemed to lead a charmed existence, shielded by his camouflage abilities. He travelled alone, and on foot. In spite of his constant protestations about his basic faint-heartedness — worthy, he said, of the most abject of invertebrates — he seemed almost to enjoy his dangerous forays into the Unstable. He was fond of maintaining that his worst enemy was sheer grinding boredom. 'Minions,' he said, 'are the dullest creatures on earth. Left to themselves, all they ever seem to do is pick on one another and tease their Pets into mouth-frothing rages. And watching hour after hour of *that* is about exciting as gawping at spiders having sex.'

His periodic protest to the Margrave about mind-numbing tedium were ignored; Meldor insisted the information he obtained was invaluable. Thanks to Quirk, they were able to position Havenguarders according to the concentrations of Minions outside Havenstar borders. 'To know your enemy is to have won the first battle,' Meldor told him.

In the meantime, Corrian had opted for a much quieter life. She seemed content not to move elsewhere. She earned her keep by helping with the cooking, doing the best she was able with one arm. She took up with a one-legged street-sweeper, and regaled anyone who would listen with a discourse on the variations possible in bed when you had only six limbs between you. Most of her time, however, seemed to be directed at becoming the neighbourhood herbalist for women's ailments. She seemed to be able to dispense remedies for everything from cramps to infertility, apparently with some success as there was a constant stream of women coming to the kitchen door and she seemed to be buying the best of pipeweed (which was a horrendous price in Havenstar). Missie, Colibran's wife, whiskers twitching in indignation, complained about the house becoming a medicine shop, but only when Corrian was not around.

The only time that Keris met Meldor was when he came to the shop to meet Favellis and Dita to discuss what they were doing with regard to the burning of trompleri maps. These discussions always took place late at night when everyone else had gone to bed, and, other than the two women and Meldor, they involved only herself, Scow and Davron. Meldor, it seemed, was determined to keep the whole matter a close secret. Dita and Favellis performed their experiments on an area Keris first surveyed and mapped to the south of Havenstar, far from Minion eyes, and reported back their findings only to the select group.

They had found out that the burning of any trompleri map brought about the same result: an instant and possibly lasting stability. The only limitations were in the limitations of trompleri maps themselves: small-scale maps and poorly executed maps could never become trompleri maps and were therefore of no use in creating stability.

'So, that means the transposing of the Unstable is going to be a very slow and piecemeal process,' Davron lamented once, 'one small area at a time.'

Meldor smiled an enigmatic smile, leaving everyone with the impression that that thought pleased him. It was Scow who remarked, 'Which is probably just as well for the likes of the untainted. Need I remind you that we would all eventually die in stability? And we know that the Unbound are all reporting that they find the new stabilities – the ones created by the burning of Deverli's maps – inimical to them, unlike the old fixed features.'

Sobered, Keris thought about the irony of that. They were the ones who had brought the possible end of instability to within the bounds of possibility – and they were among the ones who could never benefit. Even Favellis and Dita were doomed, because they also had imbibed ley. 'Nonetheless,' Keris said, 'I think this is how the old fixed features were created. I suspect the tainted can live in them now because their stability has been compromisd by time and the Unstable. I think that once they were a lot bigger, and a lot more stable — a thousand years ago.'

'A thousand years is rather a long time for us to wait for a stability we can live in,' Scow said mournfully.

'Havenstar will never be stabilised,' Meldor said, and his voice was the closest she had ever heard to harshness. '*Never*. We will always have Havenstar.'

The other experiments done by Favellis and Dita had shown that there was no other way out for the tainted. When the two women had stabilised an area containing six tainted animals captured by Havenguarders, three had died in agony with frightening rapidity and the other three lived but appeared to have gone mad. They had tested one of their own untainted dogs (Favellis had drugged it first): that animal had not died but it had woken up very ill indeed and it was days before Favellis could forgive herself. After that, nobody suggested any more experiments with living things.

Favellis and Dita continued to keep a close eye on the stabilised areas, watching for any signs of change, and had come to the conclusion that Keris had been right: they were very much like the old fixed features. Left alone, their edges would gradually be eaten away by instability and they could be more immediately threatened by the vagaries of a capricious ley line, but they would probably have the capacity to last hundreds of years. 'We can make them large,' Favellis said. 'Keris gave us contiguous maps and we have successfully enlarged the first area we did.'

'Good,' said Meldor. 'But that's enough for now. Trompleri maps are going to be too precious to waste burning them. We know all we need to know for the time being.'

It was true that trompleri maps were invaluable. People were coming to Havenstar, more and more each day, and each day guides left with some of Keris's maps to show the newcomers the safest routes into the enclave. If they had blundered into a Minion camp people would have died. Instead they came in safely: the Unbound and the excluded, the tainted and the ley-lit, the Unbred who had somehow escaped execution at birth; and all the variety of Unstablers: traders, Tricians, couriers, tinkers, pedlars, guides. There were good men and rogues, the cast-offs of Chantry and the rebels from Order, men and women, all with one thing in common: they were Havenbrethren, and had served Havenstar – even though in many cases they had not yet seen the place. They came because Meldor asked them; they came because they knew him or knew of him; they came because they trusted him. They came safely because of Keris's maps.

He's bringing them to war, Keris thought, and still they trust him.

War. There had not been a war in what remained of Malinawar since just after the Rending, a thousand years past. Nobody waged wars when there was nothing to be gained, and everything to be lost – until now. Yet even she could see it was coming. Each time she drew a map that portrayed an area close to Havenstar, Minions could be seen on it. Just as Havenbrethren moved in, so did Carasma move in his forces. They did not approach Havenstar territory too closely – yet. They camped where they thought they could remain unseen. 'Waiting for the right moment,' Meldor remarked with cold calm. 'Waiting for a gathering big enough to form an army. Never mind, we grow stronger with very passing day, too. Keris, we need as many maps as you can possibly make.'

'Davron!'

Davron jumped, spilt his char and cursed heartily. 'Quirk – damn it, you misbegotten lizard, you frightened ten years' growth out of me!'

'Sorry,' Quirk said cheerfully, lowering his small pack to the ground. 'But I can't help it if you people are all as blind as moles in a hole.'

Scow's voice drifted across the camp from the darkness.

'Disorder be damned – I could have sworn that he wouldn't make it in tonight without me seeing. Unmaker take you, Quirk.' They had known he was coming – their meeting was by arrangement – but still the Chameleon could arrive unseen by either Scow on guard duty, or Keris, perusing her trompleri maps of the area.

Keris stuck her head out of her tent and laughed. 'Quirk – how are you? Don't take any notice of these sulky menfolk; it's good to see you. We've brought you your new supplies, as promised.'

Scow came in to join them around the fire. 'Anything to worry about out there, Keris, or can I take a break?'

She glanced at the map she had been working on. It was hard to see much at night, of course, but there had not been anyone around at dusk. 'Nothing as far as I can see. The nearest Minions were a couple of hours away, beyond those hills. I've seen quite a few,' she added, faintly worried.

'I know,' Quirk said. 'I've just come from that direction. There's a big camp there.'

'We thought as much,' Davron said. 'Keris has been mapping the foot of the valley between them and Havenstar. That way, if ever they move out, we'll be able to see.'

'Can I get you a meal, Quirk?' she asked.

'Whatever you have left over from supper will be fine. And a cup of your brew, Scow. You do make a good drink, for all that you're as short-sighted as a blindworm.'

'Watch it – or the char won't taste as good,' Scow told him.

'You mean you would dare to *sabotage* the Brew?' Quirk asked, aghast.

Scow said loftily, 'I merely meant that an artist like me needs to be free from strife, dissension and insults before I can produce a true blend of the ingredients that make up the smooth perfection of –' Quirk threw a pebble at him.

The banter went on, followed by a more serious discussion of the Minion movements Quirk had noted, but Keris sat remote from it, letting the talk roll over her. She

426

watched as Davron joked with Scow and Quirk, and was glad that he could appear light-hearted, but her mood was sombre. Somehow Davron appeared so very much alone, sitting there. He could laugh and talk and swap tales, but at the end of it all he was still a lonely man. He had not touched another human being, skin to skin, in over five years. He had not held a woman or played with his daughter or known his son. He was truly alone. She could love him, and go on loving him, but she could not change his loneliness. She sighed, said goodnight and went to bed.

And in the morning he was gone.

Chapter Thirty

*There will come a Betrayer to your new land. Beware this
man, for he will wreak destruction in Lord Carasma's name.
Yet pity him, for he will destroy that which he loves. Hold to
hope, you people of the shining land, for even as he cuts a
swath through your aspirations, even as your children drown
in the flood he will loose behind him, yet has he the power to
cast the Unmaker into Chaos.*

Predictions 24: 5: 12—13

Keris woke to sunlight streaming through her tent walls,
bright and warm. Too warm. She crawled out of her bedroll
and stretched, a little puzzled. Why had no one woken her
earlier than this? They had many things to do; time was
precious as war came closer. She poked her head out of the
tent. There was no one up. Quirk was still lying out in the
open in his bedroll; he had a blanket pulled up over his nose.
The sun was already high in the sky.

She stood up and looked for Davron, who had been on the
dawn shift, and could not see him. She woke Quirk and went
to wake Scow, to find him snoring, but of Davron there was
no sign. His tent was still up, his packs were still there, but
he was gone.

So was his crossings-mount.

At first they were more puzzled than worried, but nonetheless Keris turned to her trompleri maps of the area. There
were mounted figures moving right at the edge of one of
them, about to move out of range of the chart – and there

did not seem to be anything else moving anywhere.

'That can't be him, surely,' Scow said in shock. 'He wouldn't have ridden off with someone without telling us.'

Keris wrenched her enlarging glass out of her pack. What she saw through it left her stunned. She sat back on her heels and gazed at Scow in dismay.

'What is it?' he asked, shaken just by the agony in her expression.

'A Minion,' she said in a strangled whisper. 'He's with a Minion.'

'How can you tell?' Quirk asked. 'Minions often don't look any different from most untainted people.'

Wordlessly she handed him the enlarging glass. 'It's him — I'd know that horse of his anywhere, and the way he rides.' She swallowed. 'There's just one other person with him, riding some sort of tainted animal, and there's a Pet. It's a Minion's Pet — no ordinary person would ride with a creature like that.'

Quirk looked and then handed the glass to Scow. 'I'm afraid she's right. It's a monstrous six-legged thing with a horn in front and spines down the back.' He looked at Keris and Scow in shock. 'He's been taken prisoner.'

Scow looked through the glass in turn. 'No. I can see nothing to indicate that he is a prisoner. Besides, what single Minion — no matter how hideous his Pet — could take Davron Storre a prisoner? He went willingly.'

'But *why*?'

It was Keris who told him, choking back her tears.

'You mean,' Quirk said, when he finally understood, 'that he can't help himself? He has to serve the Unmaker? *Davron Storre?*'

'Yes. From the moment the Unmaker calls him until the moment he completes the task he is given, he is as much a Minion as the man he now rides with.'

'No,' Quirk said flatly.

Tears slid down her cheeks, but her weeping was silent.

'He has become our enemy. And, should we meet him, we are bound to stop him.'

'Kill him? But you *love* him,' Quirk cried in anguish.

'And I failed to stop him,' Scow said, bitterness seeping out of every word. 'Great help I was . . . Meldor would have felt *something*. I just slept.' He slammed one massive hand into the palm of another and turned away.

'Can we catch up with them?' Quirk asked, gesturing at the tiny figures on the map.

Scow shook his head, visibly upset. 'They have at least two hours' start and they'll be off the map soon. And we don't have a chart showing the area they are riding towards. Useless to follow – we'd never find them. Besides, he'll join up with other Minions soon – or meet the Unmaker somewhere in the Writhe. Chaosdamn, poor Davron.'

Quirk looked shocked. 'But we should stop him – he knows so much! About trompleri maps, about the defences of Havenstar, about everything! If the Unmaker questions him –'

'– he won't say anything,' Scow said quietly. 'Quirk, all the Unmaker can do is to give him a task. One task. Which will probably be to destroy Havenstar somehow. He can't force Davron to answer questions, unless he gets his Minions to torture him.' Keris shuddered. 'But he won't want Davron hurt, I think,' he added quickly. 'He will want him in good health to perform his mission, whatever it is. One mission, that's all.'

Quirk continued to look appalled. Scow was trying to be encouraging, but it was clear to them all that it made very little difference if Davron answered questions or not.

'How long to Shield?' Keris asked Scow.

'If we leave the packs, if we change horses at the border, we can be there tonight.'

'Then we ride now. We must warn Meldor, warn everyone – warn them that Davron is . . .' But she could not finish. She could not name him their enemy. She stopped, gathering herself together with conscious physical effort. She

430

felt cold, frozen, as if ice were working through her body from the inside out. Dead, she thought. Maker, I feel as if something inside me is dead . . . and I grow cold. 'Strike the tents,' she said.

That same morning Meldor was woken by his scribe, Nablon, also known as the Ant. Like Colibran the Cricket, Nablon had feelers, but the resemblance ended there. His feelers were short and pointed forward; his eyes were round and glossy black; his cheeks were marred by external mandibles, appendages ideally suitable for cracking nuts and marrow bones, that met in front of his human mouth. The rest of Nablon was wholly human. It was unfortunate that when he was agitated the mandibles clacked together of their own accord, and, that morning at dawn, that was exactly what they were doing.

'Margraf (*clack*),' he said, shaking Meldor. 'Margraf (*clack*), wake up. An emergency —'

Meldor woke and was immediately alert. He was used to early rising, although he was usually awoken in a more pleasant way: with a cup of char and the sounds of hot water splashing into the basin on his washstand. Clacking mandibles were quite another thing. 'What is it?' he asked and groped around his bedpost for his dressing gown. Nablon thrust it at him.

'An attack,' the scribe said. 'It's started. There are hundreds of Minions (*clack*) coming with their Pets. They are pouring out of the hills and gullies, on all the maps we have. It is much worse (*clack*) than we feared. Margraf, there are *thousands* of them.'

Meldor remained quietly calm. 'Have they got to the border yet anywhere?'

'No, not yet, but —'

'Did you look at the maps of the route from the Eighth?'

'Yes, of course (*clack*).'

'And?'

'There are forces there. A large army it looks like.'

'Ah. So Portron did go to the Sanhedrin, eh? Now that is the news you should have given me first, Nablon. Davron's not back yet, I suppose?'

Under the tranquil questioning Nablon began to calm. 'No, Margraf.'

'As I expected. It had to happen this way,' Meldor said and bent to wash his face. The water was cold. When he lifted his head again and held out his hand for his towel, he added, 'And no point in sending after him — what's done is done by now. Go and tell my valet to come in, will you Nablon? And arrange for my breakfast to be taken in the map room.'

Nablon handed him the towel and went, his clacking beginning all over again.

Meldor's valet helped him to dress while a string of flustered officials came and went and Meldor gathered information and issued orders. It seemed that the vast number of the Minions and Pets were approaching from the east, that side of Havenstar bordered by an irrigation ditch filled with a mixture of water and ley to make a dyke they had named the Channel.

When Meldor arrived ten minutes later in the huge map room of the Hall, he went unerringly to the area where the channel maps were mounted. The room had been built as an audience hall; now three long rows of sloping boards had been erected to make a triangle that approximated in proportion to the borders of Havenstar. On these, a set of Keris's border maps had been mounted in a continuous line. As Meldor approached, Nablon turned away from where he had been studying the maps, his feelers stiff and his mandibles clacking unceasingly. 'Margraf — it's getting worse with every passing minute!'

Next to him stood the man in charge, a one-time Trician called Zeferil of Overton. He had been excluded for blasphemy and was now Meldor's ley-lit commander, in charge of Havenstar defences. Right then there was a glazed look of shock to his eyes, but he'd held himself under rigid control.

'A major invasion, Margraf,' he said. 'On all fronts, but it seems to be concentrated on the Channel. Elsewhere there are smaller numbers. I suspect they aim to have a number of skirmishes along the Writhe border and even south of the Riven – just to keep the guard there busy enough so that we can't bring them to support our forces at the Channel. I've ordered a full alert,' he added, 'as we agreed must be done if something like this happened. All trained men are to report for duty, with mounts where possible. Couriers have been sent to warn all the border corps, although I imagine they'll all know by now. Margraf, I'd like your permission to go to the Channel area.'

'No. You stay here with the maps. Here you will have an eagle's view of what is happening; what more could a commander ask for?'

'The opportunity to fight, damn it,' he said bad-temperedly. 'We are half a day's bloody ride from the Channel here: how can I give orders that can't be carried out for six or eight whole blasted hours?' For all his courage, Zeferil was a frightened man. He had not expected his command to be challenged on such a scale; he had never expected to have his forces in danger of being swamped so overwhelmingly. Nablon looked scandalised at his language, but Zeferil had been a Trician, and he did not perceive of himself as being innately inferior to a Margrave who was not Trician-born, so he saw no need to moderate his language – or did not until Meldor said, in the kind of voice that did not invite discussion, 'You stay here. If you were at the middle of the Channel, it would be three or four hours to either end of it. And what about other places along the borders? Here you can see what is happening everywhere and send orders everywhere. And it is not half a day's ride to the Channel if you make use of relays of runners with good tainted mounts to take those orders – as I know you have long since arranged. Right now I want instructions sent out that no one is to go beyond the borders of Havenstar for any reason whatsoever, not by as much as a footfall, and that includes Havenguarders.' He nodded dismissively and

Zeferil drew himself up smartly, made the kinesis symbol of obedience and subordination, and turned away to bark out instructions.

Meldor grasped Nablon by the elbow. 'And now, Nablon, I want you to describe to me exactly what it is you see on the maps, and without too much excitement, please.'

Davron, on guard duty that morning, had heard something just before dawn. A faint scrabbling in the darkness, somewhere on the slope below him. He had slipped one of his throwing knives out of its sheath (outside of Havenstar he went armed again) and crouched, trying to see what – or who – it was that was approaching. He did not immediately think that there was any danger: whatever was approaching was not using stealth. Its advance was steady and far from noiseless. He stirred restlessly as he peered into the darkness; the sigil on his arm seemed tight. He scratched at it absently. Something gleamed; he caught a glimpse of starlight on armour – a man's breastplate perhaps, or even the shiny hide of an animal. Only one; nothing he couldn't deal with. He scratched again. He could have sworn he felt his sigil move – which should have been impossible. It was merged with his flesh, after all. He stared at it, suddenly stilled with fear.

A purple gleam came out of the darkness, a single beam of light. It stabbed fitfully, then seemed to *bend* – and homed in on him. It hit his arm even as he moved, and pain flared under his sigil. He knew then, and half turned to yell into the camp, but stopped with the gesture half made and the words frozen. He could not do it. He could not call for help, he could not retreat, he could not resist. The purple light drew him.

He started to walk towards it, ensnared by whatever was at the other end of the beam; he was being reeled in like a fish on a string. Yet he could still think, still feel. He knew exactly what was happening to him, and why – and there was not a thing in the world he could do about it.

434

His mind screamed its rejection of what was happening. *No! Not now — not yet.*

But he knew it was useless to rail against what must happen. This fate was all he had, and he had chosen it when he had elected to save his wife and child from the curse of tainting. He was heading towards a destiny that was so terrible it was beyond his comprehension, and there was not a thing he could do about it. For five years he had lived knowing that this moment would arrive; he had hoped to die when it did, killed by his friends. Instead he was walking coolly out into the night, unable to raise the knife in his hand to defend himself — or to kill himself.

He reached deep inside his being, into his reserve of courage, and tightened his barrier to any feeling of regret. He prayed as blind Meldor prayed, without kinesis. He sent words — not symbols that had lost their depth of meaning — out into the night, knowing that the Maker probably could not hear, yet saying them anyway. He smothered the shame he felt and tried to stand tall even as he attempted to cast around for any other solution that would redeem Havenstar from his obliterating hand. In the face of crushing despair, he still looked for a sliver of hope, because it was not in Davron Storre to surrender. When he prayed it was not for help or forgiveness, or even for death — but for victory. I will not give up, he told himself. If Keris has found a way to make the Unstable stable, cannot I find a way to defeat the Unmaker? I know him better than any man alive, and Meldor has always believed that it is possible . . .

And so it was that in that short walk into the darkness he confronted his fate with a courage that marked him as a man beyond the ordinary.

The Minion who waited for him had the appearance of a middle-aged man, a tough and wiry fighter with flat eyes that held no mercy and no compassion — or even interest. The Pet that slobbered at his side was a horror of scales and spines, with a face like a greedy fat boy and a horn in the middle of its forehead. It had a rudimentary intelligence and

435

he heard it say hopefully, 'Eat, Master. Sogol want eat man.'

The beam of purple shone from a ball of ley the Minion grasped in his hand. When Davron confronted him, he asked, uninterested, 'Are you Storre?'

'I am.'

'Lord Carasma the Unmaker wishes to see you. He says to tell you that your time has come.'

The words dried out the inside of Davron's mouth, so that he had to lick his lips before he could reply. 'Yes, I guessed as much.'

'My name is Galbar. You are to go back and get your horse and saddle — quietly, without waking the camp — then return to me and we will ride for the Writhe.'

'My packs?'

'You won't be needing anything where you're going.' The Minion's lack of interest in his captive was as chilling as inhumanity would have been. 'Go,' he said, and Davron went. He could do nothing else.

He could not arouse the camp, could not leave a message, could do nothing except what he had been told: get his horse and saddle and return to the Minion. His helplessness was infuriating, but he quelled the feeling of frustration. He refused to expend his energies on useless regret.

When he returned with his horse, Galbar was already seated on his tainted mount, waiting. He indicated that Davron should saddle his horse and mount up.

'Eat,' said the Pet and eyed Davron hungrily. As he strapped on his saddle, it sharpened its horn on a nearby rock. 'Master — Sogol want eat man,' it said. 'Want *now*!' It sounded petulant, like a spoilt child.

Galbar ignored it. 'Follow me,' he said and turned his mount without bothering to see if Davron followed. The purple light still shone from the ball he carried; it was still attached to Davron's sigil, bending around corners if necessary — like a leash of leather. Davron thought of lunging for the ball that generated the light, but the thought was all he could manage. Action was denied him.

They rode in silence. Galbar set a swift pace and Davron followed. He still had his knives and his whip, but that served only to remind him of his helplessness. It seemed Galbar was so confident of his mastery that he had not even bothered to disarm him.

Davron tried to shut his mind to the numbing despair that washed over him.

Across on the Channel side of the triangle that made up Havenstar, Heldiss the Heron was the first to see the Minions coming, which was not surprising considering he was two feet taller than anyone else, thanks to his elongated stick-thin legs. Heldiss, one-time Havenbrother and guardian of a rope bridge in the wilds of the Unstable, was now a Havener like his two sons. One of them was a baker in Shield; the other now stood beside his father, watching the Minions stream towards them. The long horizontal line of attackers was continuous, as far as the eye could see in either direction, and it was five or six deep. Worse even than the Minions were the Pets that accompanied their masters: they ranged from human-like fauns and satyrs with horns, to lumbering monsters the size of a small hut on legs. The number of teeth, fangs, talons, claws and other needle-sharp prongs they had between them would have supplied enough cutting and chiselling and slicing power for all the carpentry shops of the stabilities.

'Middenshit,' Heldiss muttered. 'We're dead unless the Margrave comes up with something new.'

He and his men were standing behind an earthen barrier; in front of these ramparts the Channel flowed, full of ley and water. It would provide some sort of obstacle to the invasion, especially as most of the attacking force would not be expecting the water. They would think it was just a small ley line. They would not know, either, that it was seeded with sharpened caltrops – newly seeded caltrops – which, with luck, would last long enough, in spite of the ley, to do some damage.

Heldiss surveyed the enemy forces, and wondered why the midden he had listened to the Margrave when the blind man had suggested that it was time for all Havenbrethren to come to Havenstar. They had been standing by the canyon that contained the Deep at the time, just before that girl had been attacked by the manta ray, and the Margrave's deep sonorous voice had been hypnotic. It had not occurred to the Heron to refuse – and now here he was standing waiting to be slaughtered. He glanced at his son. Well, there was one good reason for returning, right there, he supposed. His sons, his grandchildren – they had a home here, a future, if only these corrupted bastards could be defeated.

'Pass the word,' he said to his son. 'Hold arrow fire until you're sure you can hit the target, then fire at will.' As the words went down the line of defenders, he wondered just how it was he had ended up giving orders. He had a sneaking suspicion his officer status had a lot to do with his towering height. He knew damned little about arms and fighting a war, nor was he ley-lit and primed with ley like most of the officers – but he was rather imposing to look at. Damn it.

'Holy taint, Pa,' his son said, his eyes fixed on the advancing lines, 'have we any hope at all against that lot?'

'Steady, lad. Remember, arrows have a better range than ley. And those bastards are so used to hiding behind their Pets and their ley, they'll have forgotten a well-aimed shaft can feather you before you say midden-heap. And, then again, their ley doesn't last for ever. They have to renew it. We have a hope,' he concluded. A hope, but not much else.

His son eyed the advance, raised his bow, nocked the first arrow . . .

And the battle began.

'Minions behind us!' Scow shouted. '*Ride!*'

Automatically Keris kicked Tousson into a gallop – without glancing behind. When someone shouted in the kind of voice Scow had used, you acted first and looked afterwards. She grabbed the pommel when she did turn, and it was just as well because what she saw jolted her with shock. There was a flood of Minions and Pets pouring out of a side valley, and they rode as if they were intent on obliterating the three of them beneath the thundering of their countless hooves.

Beside her Quirk swore. 'Middenshit. That looks like every Minion that's ever been corrupted in the past three hundred years.' He ducked his head low and rode as he had never ridden before, blessing the fact that it was Keris's new packhorse – another crossings-mount – beneath him.

Keris also hunkered down as a dozen contradictory thoughts crowded her mind: this was the threatened invasion at last; she was going to die soon; did it matter, anyway, with Davron gone? (Dear heaven, was it only this morning that he had vanished?) Davron was probably already performing his task for Carasma; when the Chaos was Meldor going to start burning trompleri maps and fry these corrupted sods to cinders? Chaosdamn, what would happen to us if he did it *now*?

She glanced back at Scow. He was concentrating on chivvying the two horses to run faster. Whenever one of them began to flag he brought Stockwood up on its flank; one glimpse of the swinging horns on the tainted beast was enough to frighten any horse to renewed effort.

The border to Havenstar lay half an hour ahead. If they were lucky they would get there before the Minions caught up. Keris looked back again, and decided they were unlikely to be lucky. Although the Minions on horses were not gaining, those who rode tainted beasts were steadily over-hauling their quarry, while several low-slung Pets with loping legs had outstripped their masters and were coming up even faster. Keris gave a low moan. A shaft of ley slamming into her back might not have been a bad death, but she dreaded the idea of being torn to pieces by a beast that had teeth like axe blades and claws like curved upholstery needles.

As the lopers approached she gestured to Quirk and Scow to go ahead. Quirk did not need a second invitation; Scow hesitated momentarily, but then realised what she was going to do and nodded. He made a kinesis in her direction: forefinger and thumb held in a circle against his cheek – Victory to the Maker, it meant. She assumed he meant it more personally: Good luck, Keris. She nodded, and turned her eyes to the half-dozen lopers approaching. She waited until the last possible moment and then let fly with ley, ripping it out of her fingers, feeling it slip through the spaces of her body to flow wild and free in a coloured blast. The ley hit the first of the lopers and sent it spinning away into the second. They were downed in a tangle of legs and torn flesh. The third received the ley in the eye, and curled up, screaming, into a ball. The rest dropped back a little, more circumspect now.

Keris urged her horse on. Ahead of her, Quirk – unarmed and deciding discretion and speed were better than any heroic gestures that would help no one – was still racing for the Writhe while Scow had swung Stockwood back to face her. He sent a couple of arrows into the lopers, causing more confusion, then he wheeled his mount again to follow her as she raced past. 'Good work!' he shouted. 'That gave 'em something to think about!'

But Keris had seen the host behind her and there was no way she could tackle them: Minion after Minion on their tainted beasts, still more Pets. Worse, the Unmaker's servants also had ley and probably a great deal more experience with its use – and the thoughts that directed the ley would be more malicious, increasing its destructive power. They were a bare few minutes behind, and gaining all the time.

She heard a bellow ahead and turned her attention that way, to see Quirk waving with such enthusiasm that he endangered his seat on his horse. She looked to the left and saw a patrol riding in: Haveners. Nine or ten of them, all armed. They had seen the chase and were cutting across to intercept. Still not enough, of course, but it would mean they could make a fight of it . . .

She raced on, neck to neck with Stockwood.

And then the two of them were in the midst of friends, ploughing through them and then wheeling back to shoot arrows and ley at oncoming Pets. It seemed so confused: she could get no overall view of what was happening — just shots and screams and her own blasts of colour in showers of sparks, the smell of burning flesh, the animal yaps and yelps of rage and pain. People milling around, the first of the Minions arriving, Haveners burning, bloodied, screaming; more ley, Haveners with pikes, Minions with ley — it did not seem a fair fight, and they were so outnumbered . . .

And suddenly there seemed to be more arrows than ley, more Minions falling than Haveners.

She looked around, to see that they had been reinforced by Havenguarders from across the bridge over the Writhe, tens of them, and at least two officers, who had also evidently imbibed ley. Relieved, she disengaged and rode on towards the bridge, now only ten minutes away. She was drained of ley, exhausted. Her bow was still on her back, untouched, but the palms of her hands were raw and aching. Her whole body was aching, reacting against the sudden emptiness within. She scorned the bridge, and dismounted to walk instead into the ley line, drinking in the ley to restore herself, imbibing it the way Davron had taught her, absorbing it, replenishing it. It felt good, refreshing. A drug, she knew. Maker only knew what harm it did her, but she could no longer live without it.

Then, still tired but more in control, she led her horse up on to the bridge. Quirk was there and together they surveyed what was happening. The Minions were pulling back; the Haveners were collecting their dead and wounded and withdrawing as well. A skirmish rather than an invasion, but a nasty one. There would be homes that would be in mourning tonight because of this.

'I'm sorry I rode off and left you,' Quirk said. He sounded only mildly contrite; it was no longer in his nature to be abject.

'Just good sense,' she said. 'I never did think a dead hero was much use to anyone.'

'Just as well,' he replied with a grin. 'I'll never be a hero, and I intend to take good care that I'm not a dead anything. Are you all right?'

'Fine. Here comes Scow.'

The Unbound man seemed in one piece; his large face was lit with a grin like a happy mastiff. 'Nice bit of battle, that,' he said. 'If this is what war is like, I think I might find I have a taste for it.' He wiped his axe casually across his boot and hooked it on to his belt.

Speaking to the Havenguarders a few minutes later, they discovered the officers had kept a close watch on the trompleri map in the guardhouse and, as soon as they had seen three people riding for the border pursued by what looked like a horde of animals, they had sent men to the rescue – just ten minutes before Meldor's order arrived forbidding anyone to cross the border. Scow grinned when he heard that. 'Why, Keris, you saved yourself with one of your own maps!' The thought appealed to his sense of humour: his tongue lolled out in appreciation.

Keris, remembering the lopers, was less amused, if just as appreciative of the result. 'Only just, it seems. Let's get some fresh mounts,' she said, her weariness coming through in her voice. 'We still have to get our news to Meldor.'

Briefly she closed her eyes, and – as she had been doing all day – she thought silently: Oh Davron, love, where are you now?

Chapter Thirty-One

And it shall be said of them that they had courage beyond the usual.

the later writings of Meldor the Blind

Early that afternoon the Margrave stood in the hall that was now a map room, felt the weight of his responsibilities pressing in on him, and curbed a useless urge to curse his blindness. 'Go on,' he said calmly.

'On all fronts,' Nablon the Ant said, trying to subdue his clacking as he and Zeferil studied the maps in front of them. 'On all fronts. The numbers along the Channel are . . . frightening. The barrage of our arrows is continuing to keep them at bay and has inflicted heavy losses, but —' He clacked desperately.

Impatient, Zeferil took over and gave a more concise picture as he saw it in the maps. He included the latest casualty figures and an update estimate of the numbers involved in the various sectors.

'Would you say that there is a maximum number of the attackers within sight of our borders?' Meldor asked.

Zeferil looked puzzled.

Meldor was patient. 'Later today — will there be more Minions?'

'No, I don't think so. They've been arriving all morning, as I told you earlier, but I think this is about it. As far as we can tell from the maps.'

Meldor nodded, making his mind up about something.

'Nablon, would you be so good as to give me that file of maps I asked for — the duplicates of the Havenstar borders?' As the Ant went off to find the folder, Meldor added, 'Carasma must have dragged every old Minion out of his ley mire to get those sorts of numbers, all the old half-crazy men and women.'

'Old?' Zeferil asked.

'Yes, old. Don't doubt it, Zeferil. Minions may be immortal where illness and ageing are concerned, but, just as they can be slain, so can they grow old and tired in mind. Many of them will just be stuffed targets for our archers, rather than fighters.'

'They outnumber us at least ten to one. And every single one of them has a Pet. We can't hold them off indefinitely. The dark is the Minion's world — there is no way we will last the night.'

'We will, with the Maker's grace,' Meldor said. 'What about the other approaching forces?'

'Hard to say how many there are, because we only see those that happen to cross one of the trompleri-mapped areas. I have seen the standards of the Sixth, Seventh and Eighth Stabilities, though, and an impressive number of domain symbols. It looks as if Chantry has sent the entire Defender forces from all three stabs.'

Meldor gave the faintest of ironical smiles. 'We should be complimented, Zeferil. It seems that the Sanhedrin holds our strength in considerable esteem, if they feel so many are needed to bring us down. When will they reach us?'

'My estimation is that they will camp two hours out tonight. Margraf, what will they do when they see us under siege?'

'You mean: which is greater — Chantry's hatred of Rule-breakers, or their hatred of Minions?' *Rugriss's hatred of me or his hatred of Carasma?* 'I don't know, Zeferil. I have gambled on the latter. Maker help us all if I am wrong. No word of Davron yet?'

The commander shook his head.

Meldor raised an eyebrow. 'There are many things I can do, Zeferil; tell the difference between a nod and a shake of the head is not one of them.'

'Oh. Sorry, Margraf. No, Davron's not back yet and we have been unable to see him on any of the maps. The Mapmaker Kaylen and Scow have been spotted, though. They crossed the border some time ago. They are riding in on tainted beasts and should be here about nightfall.'

Meldor took the news with outward calm, saying, 'I am going to meditate for a while. I wish to be alone.'

Zeferil nodded, surprised. He knew that, although the Margrave might have done away with kinesis devotions, he still liked to give time to the Maker — what surprised Zeferil was the timing. Havenstar was under attack, and Meldor wanted to pray?

Nablon returned with the folder of maps Meldor had asked for. 'You have checked them personally?' Meldor asked.

'Yes. All the border maps are there.'

'And none that show the ley lines or the Havenstar side of the ley lines?'

'No, Margraf.'

Meldor nodded his thanks, and with a surety of long familiarity, he made his way not to his room but up to the flat roof of the Hall. For a moment he stood, enjoying the cool freshness of the air, the scent of water drifting in from the lake. Then he walked to the centre of the roof where a large open brazier was filled with wood and coals ready for burning. Carefully he rolled up the first of the maps and pushed it deep into the piled wood, taking care not to crumple it. Then, sheet by sheet, he did the same with every other map in the folder. When he had finished, he stepped back away from the brazier.

He hesitated the barest of moments, breathed deeply to catch the scent of old woodsmoke and fresh-cut wood from the brazier, then sent out a line of ley unerringly towards it.

Maker grant that this works, he thought, because if it

doesn't we'll all be Minions or Unbound before the day is out . . .

Cylrie Mannertee, Hedrina-Chantor, looked at Anhedrin Rugriss Ruddleby in horror. 'You're jesting,' she said. She sat up on her camp bed where she had been resting after her mid-afternoon repast, her face crinkling in her consternation. 'How do you know?'

'The scouts just rode back with the news. There is not the slightest doubt about it – Havenstar is only a couple of hours away. At least, we *assume* the place is Havenstar – and it is being besieged by an army of Minions and Pets.'

'Who's winning?' she asked and began to fluff up her hair. Not even news of a battle could distract Cylrie long enough to make her neglect her appearance.

'Neither, it seems – yet. Meldor's people are holding them off with arrows and other missiles. Once they run out of arrows it will doubtless be a different story.'

'Well, then, maybe we can pack up and go home. Let the Minions deal with the rebels.'

'Cylrie, that is hardly an observation worthy of a hedrina. It is the duty of all Defenders to defend humankind against the Unmaker's forces. It is the duty of Chantry to order all Minions to be killed wherever possible. The death of any Minion is a blow struck for the Maker and for Order.'

'Sweet Maker – you mean to attack? To attack *Minions*? Rugriss, tell me you are joking.'

'Cylrie, it seems that just about every Minion in the Unstable is right here, pounding on Edion's gate. Now *why*, do you think? The stakes must be *very* high for Carasma to risk inflaming Minions to the point that they will attack humans – he risks breaking the law that governs his very presence in our world! Now think, Cylrie, do we *really* want Carasma to win? To gain whatever it is he wants so very, very badly?'

She thought about that and paled. 'But we came here to

446

fight Edion and his followers, not Carasma and his.' She sounded petulant. And more than a little frightened.

'I know. But I'm still sending the Defenders on. Tomorrow morning they will attack. You and I and the other chantors will wait here and perform a kinesis for victory.'

She sighed and fingered the embroidery on her stole. The bells tinkled. 'And after the victory? What then for Edion?'

He gave an unpleasant smile. 'I don't think there will be too much left of Edion's forces after tonight. He will be in the mood to compromise – if he still lives.'

She said flatly, 'He planned this. For us to be here, I mean. That silly rule-chantor, Portron something-or-other – Edion used him to hook us.'

'I'm afraid you are right.' Rugriss's bitterness at his own gullibility smothered his admiration. 'He wanted the Chantry forces and we have obliged him – he has played us for fools. Never mind, we fools will prevail in the end, with the Maker's grace. Come, it is time for kinesis.' He held out his hand to help her up.

'Oh! What was that?' Cylrie asked, looking beyond him, out towards where he had said Havenstar was.

He turned, too late to see the sheet of light that had lit the sky to the east. 'What was what? I don't see anything.'

Cylric looked for a moment longer, then shrugged. 'Just a lightning storm, I suppose.' She took his hand and smothered another sigh as she stood. She may have been a hedrina, but she did so hate the bother of kinesis devotions.

Heldiss the Heron made a snappy kinesis; he had learnt that much since he had joined the Havenguarders. If you saw an officer who had more colours on his collar than you had, you made a kinesis of subordination: two hands crossed with the back of the right one pressed to your forehead. It all seemed rather ridiculous to Heldiss, but officers liked it and said it helped corps morale, whatever that was.

The officer was too harassed to make a kinesis in return. 'Report!' he snapped.

'Low on arrows, milor'! And there's another wave of 'em coming down the slope now.'

The officer opened his mouth to reply, but, whatever he was going to say, Heldiss never found out. There was a flash of bright light – too bright. And Heldiss found himself flat on his back trying to suck air into his lungs, wondering if he was dead or not.

Baraine of Valmair smiled fondly at his Pet, Carve. The creature was so midden-blamed beautiful. Sleek, like a wet otter. Silky-haired, with hair finer than any woman's. Its animal characteristics – the furred back, the tail, the ridge on the spine, the spurred calves and taloned feet – these things only made Carve so much more desirable in Baraine's eyes. Maybe his need of it was, well, twisted, but who cared? Carve was everything another man could be, and more. He could talk and think and reason, after a fashion; he was loyal and adoring – and he had a penis that made Baraine shiver just to *think* about. Gone were the days when even to speak of such things was to risk the shame of society, to ensure Chantry's punishment. Now he was *free*, and he did not care what the price had been.

His caressing eyes glanced away from Carve towards the Channel. *Havener peasants!* They had withdrawn behind their ramparts and then shot off enough arrows to make kindling for every one of Drumlin's fireplaces, all for very little effect. Brainless churls. How long did they think they could keep that up? When the Unmaker's army attacked this time, they'd have scarcely an arrow left between them.

Baraine flexed the muscles of his arms, enjoying the feel of his strength. The strength that would be his for ever. The thought was still intoxicating, even though he'd had some months to grow used to the idea of immortality. Immortality, that is, as long as one of those damn Haveners didn't get off a lucky arrow. He wasn't afraid of wounds: he'd found out that Minions healed fast, even when the wounds seemed grave.

Still, an arrow could end a Minion's life just as easily as a normal man's.

Even so, Baraine was enjoying this fight. He found he had a taste for battle, for pitting his skills against another's, for the kill at the end of it all – because he always won, of course. He even enjoyed watching his Pet rip a man to pieces with its talons and spurs . . .

A Minion – one of Lord Carasma's specials – was organising another attack on the Haveners and Baraine found himself grinning. How could these puny ploughmen and unwashed off-scourings withstand such a force as this for long? They had fought well so far, it was true. But it was desperation that had given them determination, and it could not last. They were just too outnumbered.

Uncomprehending, he saw the light begin along the edge of the channel and travel like flame inward towards him. He had time only to turn his head, to realise the light was coming at him from all directions, and then the blaze swathed him and Carve, so bright that it was the light of it that burnt, not the heat. There was no heat. He closed his eyes against it, flung up an arm to protect his face, and felt himself lifted through the air – flung like a dried autumn leaf in a winter tempest. He landed heavily, but it was not the pain of landing he felt: it was the pain of the tear that was made inside him. Something was ripped from his being, torn out of his body like a public bill ripped down from a wall in the marketplace when the show advertising it was done. Leaving him gasping in appalling anguish. Leaving him crying against the emptiness left behind. Weeping for the desolation of knowing –

Knowing –

Knowing what he had lost.

His immortality.

A moment later stability hit him. Terrible rigid stability, the Law of the Universe, all that was ordered and true through all eternity, all the regularity of even the most idiosyncratic of Nature's wonders . . . It ran counter to what

449

Baraine had become. He no longer belonged to that world: he was part of Chaos. He was one of the Unmaker's get, an irregularity of the universe, something that did not fit into the symmetry of That Which Was Created. And now he, the aberration, was being slotted into the stability where he no longer fitted.

Baraine raised his face from the earth and quietly went mad.

Next to him another Minion lurched upward on one elbow and watched in disbelief as his own skin disintegrated, desiccated . . . Watched until his heart stopped beating and he collapsed, nothing more than a dried-out skeleton of bones over two hundred years old.

Lord Carasma the Unmaker was in the Writhe; not where it bordered Havenstar but further out, towards the Graven. Davron and his escort arrived there at nightfall. The ride had been long and arduous; they had stopped only once, to water their mounts, and Davron was beginning to feel increasingly aware that he had not eaten all day. The Minion's Pet was apparently feeling equally ill-used; its litany of woes had expanded to include, 'Sogol tired, Master. Want sleep.' Galbar continued to ignore it, which worried Davron a little. The hungry gleam in the animal's eye was alarming.

The Writhe did not look its usual fey self when they finally drew rein beside it; the presence of the Unmaker within haunted it as storm clouds haunt mountain peaks. Its colour had deepened to damson and the particles within boiled like angry cumulus. Davron grimaced but he dismounted as asked.

'He's in there,' Galbar said. This time there was some slight emotion in the flatness of his eyes: the beginnings of a sneer perhaps. It was chilling.

Davron took a deep breath and shrugged off his fear. 'Hey, Galbar,' he drawled, 'do all Minions get henpecked by their Pets? Or is it just you?' He was rewarded by a flash of hate and rage and felt a moment's pointless satisfaction.

He faced the ley line and prepared himself. What's done is done, he thought. This is the penalty I have to pay. But I will never give up.

Keris, may the Maker keep you safe.

Carasma had chosen to seat himself on his fur-strewn throne. He seemed at ease, sprawled and comfortable in his human guise.

'Storre. At last.' His smile was pure poison. 'The moment of payment has arrived, as you see.'

Davron inclined his head in polite acknowledgement.

His lack of overt emotion seemed to offend the Unmaker. Carasma frowned deeply. 'Have you nothing to say?'

Davron shrugged. 'What so you want: that I grovel?'

Carasma's face hardened with noticeable rage. Grovelling was exactly what he wanted: wanted and expected he would have.

'My task?' Davron asked evenly.

Carasma controlled himself. 'Do you think to thwart me, Storre?' he asked. 'It is not possible.'

Davron did not reply.

Carasma leant forward on his throne. 'Let me show you what I am, so that you fully comprehend the magnitude of my power.' His voice was almost a snarl. Davron blinked; he had not thought his outward calm would so enrage the Unmaker.

And then the world about him changed. One moment he was standing in the purple shadows of ley, the next he was standing in space, in the sky itself. There was nothing beneath his feet, nothing tangible anywhere within reach. He could feel the emptiness, the nothingness around him. Carasma was nowhere to be seen. In spite of himself, Davron began to sweat with fear. Illusion, he tried to tell himself. Only illusion.

Trails of ley swirled past in the distance, chaotic in their movement, like sand whipped up in a gale to stream across the dry surface of a dune. Behind these ley streamers was the black emptiness of an infinity that terrified simply by its existence. Somewhere off to his left an exploding star was caught in mid-cataclysm; its matter was being tossed into a void, each particle spinning away from the next in nihilistic dispersal. Below his feet a burning comet had been thrown across the firmament, dragging destruction in its wake, searing the planets that impinged on its path, destroying, obliterating. Beyond it, still further away, a black hole seemed to have eaten the stars out of the sky . . .

'I am Chaos,' Carasma's disembodied voice said. Its resonance rolled around Davron like thunder, not of the world, but of the universe. 'What you see, guide, is my work. Look on it, you puny human, and despair. What are you, to stand against me without quaking? I am all you see before you: destruction . . . death . . . extinction . . . annihilation . . . nullity.

'I am the end of the universe.'

And Davron, terrified, managed to think: And yet, if you need to prove your greatness to me, you have a weakness, Lord Carasma . . .

He was back facing Carasma on his throne, grateful for the feel of solid ground beneath his feet.

Carasma continued, 'What you see before you here and now is mere illusion, a tiny particle of what I am. I take human form because that is all your finite mind can understand. How can you possibly comprehend the extent of my being?'

'I don't particularly care to,' Davron conceded. 'But, for all that, why do you have the need to tell me? By your standards, I am nothing, and yet what I think or do seems to worry you. I find that . . . intriguing, my Lord Carasma.'

If Carasma felt the edge of his irony, he did not show it. He replied, 'Because, Davron of Storre, there is only one thing that gives me pleasure. I have no sensory organs to feel anything. I have no pleasure or pain centres – yet I can feel and gain pleasure. Human agony brings me pleasure – my only pleasure. I am Chaos, and I must deliver utter destruction to whatever I touch — but only human pain gives me the thrill of pleasure. I crave it. Not just physical pain — that is nothing. No, I speak of the agony of a woman betrayed, or of a man watching loved ones die — or of a man who loves being forced to destroy what he most cares for. Do you understand?'

Davron flicked an imaginary speck of dust from his coat and tried not to show how his fingers shook. 'You've made it clear enough, I think.' He raised his black eyes to stare at the Unmaker, a flat depthless look. 'Let us dispense with these childish games, Carasma. What is my task?'

'You will go to the Knuckle,' the Unmaker snapped. 'You will enter it, and you will seize the ley from it and take it to this place you call Havenstar.' He smiled. 'You will drown your promised haven in a purple ley that will taint the untainted, a destructive ley that will despoil the land, a relentless ley that will destroy the hopes of all Unbound, of all excluded. That, Davron of Storre, is your task.'

'Impossible. Seize hold of ley? I am a man, not some sort of god.'

Carasma pointed a finger at him. 'It is more than possible, Davron Storre. *It is certain*. You will indeed be able to take ley from the Knuckle and drag it into Havenstar.'

'Why don't you do it yourself?' Davron asked. He was tired and the fatigue was pulling at him, clouding his mind even as it tugged him down.

Carasma shrugged, with an all too human gesture. 'Because I cannot directly kill humans who have given themselves to the Maker — you know that. And it is undoubted that there will be people of his within Havenstar who will die. I can break the world, I can order ley or Minions to do my bidding — but I cannot drain ley into Havenstar without coming perilously close to breaking the Law of the Universe.'

Davron sighed. 'The distinction is beyond me. You tell Minions to kill —'

Carasma held up his hand to halt him. 'Never. I can incite

their rage perhaps, no more than that. Of course, I don't actually *object* too much when a death is the result . . .'

'Naturally not.'

'Just as I won't object too much if Maker-worshippers are killed in the invasion of Havenstar.'

'Invasion?'

'I have given orders that every building in Havenstar be razed to the ground, every tree cut, every crop burnt, every drop of water fouled. I did not mention the people – but presumably my Minions will defend themselves.'

'Splitting hairs, Carasma. Do you think that is fulfilling the letter of the Law?'

He shrugged again, carelessly. 'Certainly. And who cares about the spirit of it?' He stood up. 'Come with me, Storre, through the ley. Come with me and fetch the ley to Havenstar. You will find it amenable; I can do that much. That is your task. That's all.'

That's all. To taint the untainted, to destroy the land, to swallow up all that was built . . . Davron thought of the untainted children born to the Unbound, children who believed themselves safe. To destroy the hope of the Unbound, Carasma had said. Their hope, their children.

And there was nothing, nothing, he could do to stop himself. Already he felt the urge within him, the need to do as Carasma asked . . . 'Yes,' he said bitterly. 'Yes, of course. I will go and do your bidding. Perform my task.' *Alyss, Mirrin, Staven – for this, I bought your untainting –*

'What will your mapmaker think of her beloved guide when she sees what it is he has done?' Carasma asked. 'Ah, Storre, the pain, the pain. I can already feel it.'

Davron turned and stumbled after the Unmaker.

Feel the pain? So could he, and he had not even started.

'We've made good time.' Scow tried to smile across at Keris. 'There are the lights of Lamri's lift station. We'll be having dinner in the Hall in minutes – I'll get Lamri to take us all the way there on a wildbell.'

'I don't care about eating,' Quirk growled back at him as their tainted mounts jogged the last stretch down to the lakeside. 'I just have to get off this beast while I still have any skin whatsoever on my backside. Creation, Scow, I've never been so sore in my whole life.'

'I know,' Keris said in commiseration. 'I haven't found a comfortable saddle since I lost that one into the Deep with Ygraine. I'll swear this one is stuffed with clover burrs.'

'Hullo, there's someone else in a hurry,' Quirk said peering through the gathering dusk. Two mounts were thundering in from their right, also heading for the wildbell station.

Scow followed his line of sight. 'Isn't that Favellis and Dita?' he asked.

He was right, as moments later the two women rode up on sweating mounts. 'Keris! Scow! Good to see you again!' Favellis shouted. 'Keris, all your maps — they worked! Oh, hullo, Quirk, I didn't see you there.'

'What do you mean?' Keris asked.

'The Margrave must have fired them. We were at the border — Maker, it was wonderful! I thought we were dead, all of us, and then — wham. A light —'

'Come on,' Dita interrupted. 'Let's get to the Margrave. We can tell everybody what happened at one and the same time.'

Keris, desperately tired and sore, nodded and urged her mount down the final slope. Even the sight of Havenstar by night, seen from the wildbell basket a few minutes later, failed to cheer her. She had ridden out with Davron; she was returning without him . . .

They found Meldor in the sitting room of his private apartments, having his evening meal with Nablon in attendance. He looked up as they entered, sniffed the air, and, before anyone could speak, said, 'Davron's not with you.' The flatness of his tone caught at her, choking her, and she could not reply.

'No,' said Scow. 'Favellis and Dita are here, though. They have news from the border.'

Meldor nodded and turned to Nablon. 'Have food brought for everyone. Then get some baths organised, clean clothes, whatever is needed.' He waited until the door had closed behind the scribe before he added, 'Davron first. The Unmaker came for him?'

Scow exchanged a look with Keris and then explained what had happened. Meldor looked grim, but made no comment. 'Were you near the border when I burnt the maps?' he asked.

'No, but we were,' Favellis said, unable to contain herself any longer. 'It worked, Margraf! It was unbelievable — you should have seen it! I just couldn't believe my eyes —'

Dita laid a hand on Favellis's arm. 'I think perhaps I'd better tell it,' she said gently. 'Margraf, Favellis and I were standing on the bridge at Greenwell. There was a horde of Minions and Pets attacking us — Havenguarders there had run out of arrows and things were looking pretty bleak. The Minions got an order to attack and were advancing at a run towards the ley line. On the bridge it was already hand-to-hand. Then, just when I thought it was all up with us, there was this blinding light and I found myself half draped over the bridge railing with Favellis beside me on her hands and knees.

'But we weren't the only ones flattened. When I got to my feet it was to see that all the Minions seemed to be lying on the ground too, as far as the eye could see. And everything beyond the ley line was stable . . .' She smiled wryly at Scow. 'Sorry. You are going to have to cross a league or so of stability every time you want to leave Havenstar.'

'I'll live.'

'It was . . . weird, Margraf,' Favellis said, unable to keep silent. 'A lot of the Minions seemed to have disintegrated like . . . like old clothes left in the sun and rain for season upon season. They had . . . shrunk. Crumbled. What on earth *happened* to them?'

'I suspect that they merely became their real age,' Meldor said. He sounded pleasantly satisfied at the thought. 'Stability has been re-established, and with it the Law of the Universe. The Law has no place for what is unnatural – and eternal life is unnatural.'

Dita nodded, understanding. 'Many of those still alive *have* aged. The one I had been fighting a while before was suddenly as decrepit as my grannie back home. I don't remember ever seeing an old Minion before.' She grinned, as if the idea amused her.

'Have we won, then?' Quirk dared to ask.

'I don't think it will be quite that easy,' Dita replied. 'Lots were still alive and sort of . . . well, crazy, I suppose. They came at us like they were berserk, not caring if they lived or died. And the Pets! Not all of them died, either. Maybe only about half. Margraf, there are hundreds – no, *thousands* – of masterless Pets milling around out there, and every darned one of them is hopping mad.'

'You should have heard the *noise*,' Favellis said. 'The wailing.' She shuddered, remembering. A great ululation of grief and rage and madness had gathered in volume, picking up the echo of similar lamentations further away. 'It was horrible, like hearing all the grief in the world, all at once.'

'They were going mad, too,' Meldor said. 'Stability rejects them even as it wrenches away the immortality of their masters. It is not going to be a pleasant night for those on the borders. Some are bound to get through, as well. Ah, here's Nablon back with some food, by the smell of it. Nablon, send Zeferil in to me, will you? People must be warned.'

'Do you mean to tell me burning the maps might have made things *worse*?' Dita asked after Nablon and the servants had left.

'Yes – and no,' Meldor said. 'Before, we could never have won, or even have held out. Not even if Chantry came to our aid. Not against those numbers. They would have broken through our lines and overrun us sooner or later, probably sooner. We have no kinesis chain to protect us, and no normal stability or Order. We were doomed. Now – well there are many fewer of them.'

'Fewer in number, but insane,' Scow said. He sounded grim.

'It won't be easy. We'll just have to hope that Chantry comes to our aid tomorrow morning,' Meldor told him calmly.

They all stared at him. 'Chantry's *here*?' Keris asked, incredulous.

'Approaching our borders with Defender forces.'

'And you think they'll come to our aid?'

'I think they have a powerful dislike of Minions,' Meldor said carefully. 'And I think the Anhedrin is wise enough to know that Defenders would not take kindly to seeing Unstablers massacred by Minions and Pets while they stood by and did nothing. We'll see in the morning. Dita, Favellis, go and get some rest. And then get back to the border. Everyone will be needed there. The rest of you, eat – while I explain what I want you to do.'

Dita and Favellis both stood up in silence. No one said anything. Meldor's words, calmly spoken, had somehow managed to chill them all. It's not finished yet, Keris thought. Dita made a kinesis of farewell, followed by a *Maker be with you,* and Favellis followed suit.

'You knew Carasma had taken Davron before we told you,' Keris said to Meldor after the two women had left. She had not meant to sound accusatory, but that was the way the words came out.

'Yes. It was inevitable once the invasion started. Carasma would attack on all fronts – and Davron is one of his weapons. I want you all to go to the Knuckle, leaving as soon as you can. Keris, do eat. You will need the strength.'

'The Knuckle? Why?' She picked at the food without appetite.

'Because that is where Davron is. When Zeferil comes I shall give orders for fresh tainted mounts to be sent out towards the Knuckle immediately. Later you can go after them – by wildbell. That will give you a chance to eat and wash and you can even rest while you are flying back to catch up with your mounts. Ah, here he is now, if I am not mistaken.'

It was indeed Zeferil who entered, hard on the heels of Nablon, and the next few minutes were given over to numerous orders from Meldor and a few grunts from Zeferil. In the meantime, Quirk – in spite of having said he wasn't interested in eating – managed to demolish almost as much food as Scow, an impressive achievement. Even Keris managed to force some of it down, but she pushed her plate away the moment Zeferil and Nablon had left.

'How do you know that's where Davron is?' she asked, as if they had not been interrupted.

'I read the Holy Books,' he said complacently. 'If you had spent any time at all studying the Book of Predictions, you'd know all I do, instead of looking at me as if I was mad. Keris, why do you think I have worked so hard to keep Davron from killing himself – when I knew that he could be asked to destroy everything I have done here in Havenstar?'

'I don't know. Do you mean to tell me that *Davron*'s mentioned in the Holy Books?'

'Oh, not by name, but I believe both of you are there – you and Davron.'

He could not have said anything that astounded her more. She gaped at him. *'Me?'*

'You.'

'Maker and midden, how can that be true?' Creation, she thought, will I ever have to dip into the Holy Books after this . . . I should have taken more notice of that dolt, Devotions-chantor Nebuthnar of Kibbleberry. Aloud she said, 'You're crazy. I suppose it's too dark now to see Davron on the map I did of the Knuckle . . .?'

'Nablon's been keeping an eye on it for me all day. The ley there is troubled: there is nothing visible in its depths.'

'But . . . what is going to happen?' Scow asked. 'I mean, what do the predictions *say*?'

Meldor shrugged. 'Well, that's the problem, as it usually is with foretellings of any kind. They are always couched

459

in such convoluted language that one can never be sure what they mean until after it has happened. But Davron is described as the Betrayer. Keris is mentioned as the bringer of salvation with magic in her colours – the maps, of course – and as having death in her hands. Presumably what happens when her maps are burnt.'

'And Davron's fate?' she asked, the catch in her voice giving her away.

'Unknown. Predictions are only possibilities, after all. It does seem to indicate that he will be the cause of many deaths of Haveners. It hints that he could be the instrument of the Unmaker's ultimate victory. Possibly he will be the instrument of the Unmaker's defeat. It could go either way, but, if I read it correctly, the Book of Predictions mentions him as dragging ley into the land from the fist of colour – where else would that be but the Knuckle?'

He looked at Scow. 'Your job will be to stop him if it looks like he is dooming Havenstar. But I rather think it might be better if you didn't kill him.'

'And how by all that's dark in Chaos do I do that? Go up to him and say, "Do stop it, Davron, there's a good fellow"?'

'Try. Our lives – our land – may depend on your success.'

Keris shot an unpleasant look at the Margrave, which – quite naturally – he missed entirely. 'I'll be with you, Scow,' she said.

'And me too,' Quirk added. 'Sometimes a Chameleon can creep up on a body and do things – like bop him over the head – when he least expects it.'

Scow regarded him gravely. 'For a coward, Quirk, you do behave in the most extraordinarily brave way.'

'Well, I haven't actually *done* it yet,' he pointed out.

'Be ready to move in an hour,' the Margrave said.

Obedient, Scow and Quirk immediately stood to go. Keris stood as well, but it was to say, 'I'd like to talk to you alone, if I may, Margraf.' Meldor nodded his acquiescence, and, as soon as the others had left the room, she said unhappily, 'You deliberately let this happen, didn't you?'

He did not pretend to misunderstand. 'You mean – did I order Davron to ride out with you all the time, knowing Carasma would call him and I wouldn't be there to stop it? Yes, I did.'

'Why?' The word was torn from her, her agony real. 'You made a promise to him, and you *betrayed* him.'

'Davron had faith in me. Can't you also take it on trust, Keris?'

'No! No, I can't. You wanted him to go to the Unmaker – *why*?'

'Years ago, I promised I would have him killed when the Unmaker called, if I could. But things have changed since then. You came along, with your maps, the Chameleon appeared, Chantor Portron, we found out how to stabilise the Unstable – all these things changed the face of the future. I could reinterpret the Book of Predictions. I came to believe that our hope lay in Davron going to Carasma. After all, one passage says he has hope in his hand, while another suggests that he is both the betrayer and the salvation of us all. It says something about his casting the Unmaker into Chaos.' He turned his eyes towards Keris. Though blind, they were filled with compassion. 'My dear, Davron accepted it. He accepted that he is fated to kill innocent people. If he lives, then he will have to come to terms with that – but I suspect he does not think he will live long enough to have to worry about it. He knows that he could doom us all, or save us all. For the first time since the Unmaker came to our benighted land we have a *chance*. And *Davron* is that chance. There is no easy road for Davron, but the Maker does not choose the weak to be the keys to the future. Hold to that – that he is strong enough in resources to find a way to save us all.'

'You let it happen,' she accused again.

'Yes, and he acquiesced. We are all in the Maker's hands.'

'Chaos – I wish we were! But the Maker probably can't even see us here! And maybe He doesn't care –'

'He cares. Never doubt that. Keris, over the centuries He sent us word, and He gave *me* the wisdom to see which were his words. We have a chance because of what He has done. Have faith. Never despair — never. Everything may depend on that. Just as I believe everything will depend on Davron never giving up. It is my belief, my hope, that he won't, that it is not in his nature to give up, no matter how terrible his fate. If he was a different sort of man, he would have killed himself long since, and we would all be doomed as a consequence.'

She blinked away tears. 'It will devastate him —'

Meldor was implacable. 'Yes, it will. Go to him, Keris. Help him to be strong.'

She stood, without replying. There seemed to be no more words she could say. Even words of farewell seemed super-fluous. With his usual unerring instinct, he reached out and touched her hand, no more than that. She allowed the touch, knowing it said all that could be said, and then left him.

Chapter Thirty-Two

*And of those who hold our hope and stand before Lord
Carasma in the final hour of battle: even in victory shall one
fall; in defeat all shall die.*

Predictions XXIV: 6: 1

With the dawn, Keris, Scow and Quirk saw for the first time
the rampant, turbulent ley now loose within the bounds of
Havenstar. A flood, Keris thought, shocked. Storm ley turgid
within the very heart of Havenstar . . . And she felt something clench right in the middle of her chest. Fear, pure fear.
It screwed up her insides like ruthless hands wringing out a
cloth.

It was only ley, she knew, but such ley.

Purple — not clear magenta-purple, but an angry colour,
slashed through with bulging skeins of puce and plum. Ugly,
threatening. It rolled inexorably across the landscape before
them, from right to left, head-high and moving.

I can't be tainted, she thought. I have no need to fear this.
But fear she did.

'Is it very bad?' Quirk asked.

'Yes,' she said shortly.

'And *he* did this?'

She nodded miserably. 'It must be killing him.' It was an
unfortunate choice of words. Scow blanched, aware that the
killing of Davron was exactly what might result from a
confrontation between them.

A rider, a stranger, came plunging out of the ley. He was

463

whipping his horse, and did not slow even though he must have seen them. They drew up and waited, but he galloped past, unheeding. Wild eyes stared unseeing out of a blanched face and there was a trickle of blood down his cheek.

'What is there up ahead?' Keris asked Scow. Her voice was thin and unnaturally high.

Scow answered, equally shaken. 'A village. Dawnbreak. About half an hour's ride from here. Fifteen houses or so, maybe sixty or seventy people. It's the only village between us and the Knuckle. A farming community. There are a couple of additional isolated farms as well, over to the east. That's all. The other villages are behind us, outside of the ley still, I would say.' He sounded matter-of-fact, but there was none of his usual good humour lurking in his voice.

'This is scaring my eyelashes off,' the Chameleon said. 'Do we ride on?' He meant: do we ride on into *that*?

Keris nodded and resolutely dug her heels into the sides of the tainted beast she was riding. They stopped again just before they entered the ley, not because they hesitated to enter, but because they saw shapes coming towards them out of it: people, refugees – the inhabitants of Dawnbreak, fleeing on foot or leading carts loaded with their families and their most precious belongings. They emerged from the thick tangle of ley, coughing and retching as if they had been walking in particle-laden smoke, the pitiful human remnants of what had been a prosperous village.

The first man staggered past dazed and unheeding. It seemed doubtful that he even realised he had emerged from the ley. He was middle-aged; he wore the rough working clothes of a farmer and he led a tainted ox and wagon. The rest of his family were piled on to the wagon: an old woman, a younger woman with furred ears, and three children, all tainted. Every one of them was bloodied, dirty, exhausted. One of the children was hideously maimed, twisted into something that scarcely seemed human. The younger woman held the girl and rocked to and fro, crooning in a monotone that set Keris's teeth on edge. The child looked out of idiot eyes and drooled.

Keris felt the tears coming and bit them back. *Davron! Oh, Maker, Davron my love . . .*

Another woman stepped out of the ley behind the first group. There was more sense in her gaze, although she limped and reeled as she walked. 'Don't go that way, milady,' she said to Keris and shuddered. 'Don't go that way.' Scow dismounted and reached out to stop her, but she eluded his grasp and waded on. 'The ley is coming!' she shouted at him. 'I don't have time to stop.'

Scow let her pass and clutched at one of the refugees in the next group instead. 'What happened?' he asked. 'Tell us!'

The man, wearing the collar tags of the Havenguard, looked fearfully back over his shoulder. He wore the ring of the ley-lit and had a child on his back and another in his arms. 'The Lord Betrayer,' he said. 'The Lord Betrayer came, riding on the Beast. And he pulled the ley behind him. Such ley! I've never seen such ley. Red ley, red as blood. The colour of fresh-spilt blood.' The eyes that turned back to meet Scow's were wild with pain and shock. 'I had three untainted children.' He held out the child he carried so they could see her. She was more animal than human, with the furred face of a weasel and the sharp teeth of a carnivore. 'See?' he asked. He sounded half mad. 'She's wildish now. Look at her. She can't even talk. Her mother went mad and killed herself. Yesterday I had a wife and three fine children and a farm and a house and a life.' He started crying. 'Then the Beast came. The Beast and the Betrayer.'

Davron, love, how will you ever forgive yourself?

The child standing silently at the man's side clutched a kitten and sucked her thumb. She was nine or ten years old and she had ley-lit eyes that were too large: terror-filled.

No child ought to look like that, Keris thought.

'Poor Havenstar,' the man said. 'My poor children.' He turned away and walked on with his burden.

'The Beast?' Quirk asked finally.

Keris shook her head. She knew no more than he did.

They stood, numbed, waiting for nothing in particular, while that pathetic stream of people passed with their jumbled belongings, things chosen unwisely in their hurry. This one had saved the wind chimes from the doorway, but had forgotten to bring food for the children; that one had bundled his daughters on to a cart wearing only thin shifts. Almost all the children were tainted or deformed. At least one Keris saw was dead.

And as they streamed by, those uprooted people, Scow's normal ebullience dulled and the Chameleon looked away, refusing to do more than glance at the refugees.

Both Scow and Quirk were Haveners now, and the spirit of the land had entered their blood. Now they felt its demise like molten metal eating through their skin to their hearts. Even Keris – who was not bonded as they were – ached in her heart with a pain that seemed almost beyond bearing: dead children, tainted human beings, a village lost, broken hopes and dreams; it all hurt so.

And then one last desperate scatter of people passed by in silence, heads down, and Quirk said in a flat, un-emotional voice, 'There were only forty people, counting the children.'

'How will he live with himself afterwards?' Scow murmured.

Nobody said that he might not be alive afterwards. Nobody said that it might be up to them to kill him if that was the only way it could be stopped. Nobody mentioned his name.

'Let's move on,' Keris said.

'Where to?' Quirk asked.

'Meldor said the Knuckle – so I suppose that's where we'll look first,' she said.

She urged her reluctant mount forward and then she was into the purple skeins. Even Scow and Quirk, who could see nothing more than mist, were subdued by it. It clung, wet and cloying and somehow evil. Only power, Keris tried to convince herself, and failed. This was more than just ley. It had been tainted by the Unmaker as well — it *was* evil.

They saw then that not all the people had managed to escape. Some were still running inside the ley, almost aimlessly, no longer sure of direction or where safety lay. They were fleeing in panic, beyond rationale — and the children they carried with them were screaming in terror, their bodies newly twisted with brutal tainting.

'Oh Maker preserve us,' Quirk whispered.

They tried to offer assistance, to point the way out of the ley, but these people were beyond assistance, beyond reason.

'We must stop him.' It was Scow who said the words, and there was a new hardness in his voice. Scow would kill his friend if he had to, if he could.

Keris drew out her compass; it was needed now to keep a correct heading towards the Knuckle. There was no way they could work out the direction any more. It almost seemed that all recognisable landmarks around them were being dissolved. The trees they passed were melting down into slime, the grass beneath the feet of their mounts was slick with foulness, already decomposing. The smell of putrefaction was all around them.

When they reached Dawnbreak, it was to find that the houses were already half dissolved into rotting heaps. Farm animals lay piled together in yards, flesh liquefying, smelling vile. There was nothing in the fields that resembled growing crops, and it took considerable imagination to resurrect the lines of rotten stumps into fences or hedgerows. The village and its surroundings were all disintegrating into foulness.

The ley was thick around it, and dark. It was almost as if it was *feeding* on the ruins.

'Let's go on,' said Scow quietly.

Keris and Quirk turned their mounts after Scow without a word.

'I'm going back,' Keris said.

'But why?' Scow asked, reining in beside her.

'He's not there,' Keris said flatly. 'He won't be in the Knuckle.'

Scow eyed her dubiously. 'How can you tell?'

'The ley — the ley is growing weaker the further we go into it. The damage here was done hours ago, whereas back at the edge it was recent . . .'

He did not understand.

'Scow, when we first rode into it, the ley was travelling from right to left and it was *strong*. Then we went further in and it was flowing from left to right. Further on still, right to left. And now look: ahead of us it's left to right again, but behind us it's still right to left. And ahead of us it's weaker. Don't you see what that means?'

He shook his massive head, troubled.

'That man said he was mounted on the Beast, pulling ley behind him. Davron is going methodically through Havenstar, destroying it piece by piece, line by line. Snaking his way. North to the Writhe, south to the Riven, north to the Writhe, south to the Riven — slightly further east after each turn, dragging ley behind him — destroying great swaths of the land as he goes.'

'That's impossible!' Scow gasped. 'Keris, think of the distances involved. He can't possibly cover all of Havenstar!'

'The Beast. That's the Beast's doing,' she replied grimly. 'Whatever it is. He's riding some supernatural beast — some anti-creation of Carasma's: tireless, fast beyond belief . . .'

Quirk drew in a shuddering breath. 'What do you want to do?'

'Go back. Wait for him outside the ley, in that part of Havenstar that is still . . . untainted.' She used the word deliberately; that was how she viewed what was being done to the land. It was being unmade, unbound, *tainted*.

'And then?' Scow asked.

'Burn a map, I suppose. To destroy the ley.' And maybe Davron as well.

He was silent, thinking. Then he said slowly, 'Keris, where is the ley coming from?'

'Out of the Knuckle,' she replied.

'Would it help if we cut off the source, do you think? You did bring the map of the Knuckle, didn't you?'

She drew in a sharp breath. 'Yes. Yes, of course I did. I brought everything we could possibly need.' She slipped down from her mount and unpacked her maps from the saddlebags. Scow and Quirk dismounted to look over her shoulder. There was no sign of any people anywhere in the area portrayed. It did not include the bridge and the guardhouse or the irrigation works to the east of the Knuckle, so the lack of human activity was not unexpected. People did not frequent the areas around ley confluences too closely.

The Knuckle itself seethed like a stew pot on the boil, but the stew was as red as newly shed blood and as thick as glue. It seemed to pour over into Havenstar, a broad red ribbon of liquid.

'If you stabilise it, what will happen to the ley supply for Havenstar?' Quirk asked.

'I *think* it will be all right after a day or two,' Keris said. 'Remember the map I burnt? The ley from further up just flowed around the edges of the stabilised bit. But dare we do it? What if I'm wrong and Davron is still there? We might kill him. Or worse.'

By way of answer Scow reached for his flint and steel.

'No,' Keris said, assailed with doubt, fighting back panic. 'No — don't.' *I can't. Not like that —*

'Then I'll go on to the Knuckle,' he said. 'I'll take the map with me. If Davron's not there, I'll go ahead.'

She nodded, breathing more freely. 'Yes. Good idea. If the ley stops pouring over into Havenstar, then you'll know that, somehow or other, I have managed to stop Davron and you won't have to burn the map. You go with him, Quirk. I'll go back to ley-free Havenstar, and I'll wait there.'

'It's a pity we don't have maps of Havenstar proper,' Quirk said. 'Then we could see exactly where he is.'

'He'll turn up.' As if I were talking about a latecomer to a festival dinner, she thought, and winced. 'You take the compass, Scow. I can get back simply by putting myself at right angles to the flow of ley.'

'And what if — what if I am needed where you are?' Scow asked lamely. Needed to kill Davron.

She stared him down. 'You heard what Meldor said. There are other chances. And hear what I say — if Davron dies, it will be by my hand, no one else's.' *If I can —*

He looked at her, considering, then nodded, took the compass from her and looked away. She stepped forward, and very deliberately kissed his cheek, ignoring the pain it caused her. Then she did the same for Quirk, mounted her tainted hack — careful as always not to touch the beast — and rode away without looking back.

Behind her Scow and Quirk exchanged glances.

Quirk raised a questioning eyebrow. 'Shall I come with you, do you think?'

'No, I think not,' Scow said, with a hint of his usual humour. 'I think we'd both be much happier if you did not.'

'Someone has to be around to bop him over the head,' Quirk agreed. 'Although just how I could do that when he charges past on the back of a rampaging beast, I'm not sure.'

'Just do your best to look after them both,' Scow said. The depth of sadness in his voice said it all.

Keris rode a little way out into the untainted part of Havenstar, away from the throbbing ugly line of contaminating ley. She needed time, and she did not want to meet Davron and the Beast before she was ready.

When she decided she was far enough away from the ley, she unpacked her mapping things and set to work to make a map of her immediate surroundings. She measured the distance between some rocks and the top of a small hill to give herself a fixed distance for one side of the triangle, and took angles from both ends of the line for triangulation of the area she wanted to cover. It was not large — she did not want a small-scale map — and once she had been able to fix the main features on it (a clump of trees, the hill, the rocks) she drew them in on a blank piece of parchment using ley inks. By that time several hours had passed.

Before she could start colouring the map she became aware of a rumbling noise. For a moment she was not sure whether she heard it, or felt it. She sensed vibrations through the earth, then a tingling in the air. She looked up from her work to see a cloud of dust approaching along the edge of ley — fast.

With a cold rein on her feelings she readied her telescope and prepared to look.

Distant movement enlarged, clarified . . .

Davron rode the Beast.

He stood on its massive shoulders, a man tormented beyond reason. His whole body shuddered. Sweat poured from him. He had stripped off his shirt, and his upper body was racked by the pain of his terrible journey. The sigil he wore seemed too big for him now; he had shrunk. Lost weight in a matter of hours . . . His ribs and veins showed beneath his shivering skin — there was a living map traced beneath a fragile covering, and it showed a man who was touched with death. His skull was a death's head, his cheeks sunken, his lips pulled back into an unnatural rictus smile.

His eyes, dear Maker, his eyes. They burnt deep into himself, with a pain that was beyond comprehension.

And the Beast he rode . . .

It was huge. Larger than anything that had ever lived naturally in the world, surely. At the shoulder it already stood taller than a man, and the shoulders were immense. They gave way into a solid neck and a head like a battering ram. The distance between its red eyes was as wide as the span of a man's arms, and the malevolent gleam there was pure evil. There was a single spiralled prong projecting from its forehead, and it glowed red-hot — it steamed in the cool air of the cloudy day. Powerful legs thundered the Beast on its way; they churned up the ground with their power and scorched the soil as the creature passed. Flecks of molten heat flaked scarlet from its flanks as it ran . . .

Davron drove the Beast. He stood on its shoulders, holding twisting black reins. Guiding it on its terrible path, a man tormented beyond reason. And behind the Beast, attached by streamers of molten fire, came the ley. A long red ribbon scraping blood from the land with its raw evil, dragging its destruction through Havenstar, contaminating with its scarifying touch.

Keris could watch no longer. She dropped her face to her mapboard and touched the nadir of existence in her despair. The Beast and its rider passed her at a distance without seeing her where she knelt, huddled on the ground.

She pulled herself back up to life, willed her spirit back to wanting to live, forced herself to pick up her brushes once more. And made her map. She made it as well as she knew how, and was gratified to see how quickly it took on dimension, came to life. She shrank her memory of Davron and the Beast to a tiny pinpoint in the back of her mind, for only then could she work. Only then could she *live*.

And, when she had finished, then there was nothing she could do but wait. And perhaps that was the most terrible time of all. The Beast and Davron had been travelling towards the Writhe, which was not far from where she stood. At that pace, in just an hour or two they would be back . . .

She stood in their path, map in her hand.

He saw her, and stopped, as she had known he must. Though he was driven by his need to complete his task, she knew in her heart that she still had the power to halt his wild ride. For a moment.

He drew back on the reins. Leant against them in his effort to drag the creature he rode to a reluctant halt. It propped, skidded — and came to a heaving, steaming stop just before it ploughed into her.

She whispered, 'Davron . . .'

He answered, and the answer shivered her with horror.

'Keris, if you come any closer, if you let loose your ley, I will be forced to kill you. I am charged to finish the task and I must do whatever it takes . . . And don't doubt that I can do it. I have enough ley in me to blast you from here to Drumlin.' His voice was strung out with pain, thinned with it, utterly unlike his normal gravelly tones. 'Don't make me kill you,' he said softly, pain upon pain. 'Not you too. Don't attack me, Keris – I will be so much faster than you.' She believed him even though he never actually looked at her. And yet she heard the pleading in his tone, she heard the words he dared not speak: *Stop me. Do whatever it takes to stop me. Please.* His spoken words were said not for her, but for Carasma.

'Davron –' She did not know what to say. There was nothing she could say. His pain unmanned her, dissolved her resolution, shattered her determination.

The Beast pawed the ground, and its fire licked out in her direction. She could feel the heat. It was impatient. Davron's hold on it was slipping. Within seconds the beast would be out of control, running once more.

She could not bear Davron's pain. His hands were lacerated on the reins and dripped blood. His chest heaved. His skin was scarred with burns. She turned her head away, unable to watch him, wishing that she had not heard the agony in his voice.

'I trust you,' he whispered. 'You will always do what is right.' He turned to look ahead and flicked the reins.

In that split second of movement, while his gaze was not upon her and his hands were busy with manipulating the reins, she held up the map above her head and touched her ley to its edge. He started to look back at her. His arm started to move in her direction with its weapon of ley, but was snagged by the reins wrapped around his hands. His devastated eyes radiated their approval, their love – and their fear.

There were many words she could have said to Davron; she spoke none of them. They both knew they could die, and die horribly. They both knew that there could be worse things, perhaps, than death. They both knew how they loved. Words would not have added anything.

The flame flared at the edge of the map and moved inward . . .

Keris smiled through a blur of tears. At least they would be together as they went forward into an unknown instant. Davron's hand untangled from the reins, and swung towards her, even as he fought it. Keris twisted the map so that the flames snatched the map's centre.

The world exploded into burning incandescence.

A second became an eternity, stretching out without foreseeable end. Keris felt herself to be transparent, to be without solidity. All around there was only a white light, a brightness that precluded all thought, all feeling. Davron vanished, the Beast vanished, there was no background, nothing to be seen but light.

A feeling of joy, so intense it burnt, touched Keris's mind. Love engulfed her, heavy with power and weight, frightening in its hugeness – and then vanished. She thought she was dead. She thought she was being absorbed into That Which Was Created.

Then the light disappeared.

She opened her eyes, but for a moment still could not see anything while her eyes adjusted.

'Keris?' The word was tentative, yet pregnant with caring.

She felt a hand slip into hers and hold hard.

'Davron?'

'Mm.'

'Maker –' Her vision cleared. Davron was kneeling at her side, still holding her hand – *and she felt no pain*. Her eyes went to his upper arm: the sigil was gone. Her first wave of joy was so intense she almost fainted with it. Then she saw that he glowed with ley, a sick ley, heavy with Carasma's influence.

She scrambled up on to her knees and looked about them. The ley had vanished from the area she had mapped. They were in a small rectangle of stability – not Havenstar stability but real stability. There was normal meadow grass beneath her feet, tangled through with flowers and thistles. To her left she could see the Beast, lying on the ground under some trees. It was not moving.

Stretching off in that direction, the landscape seemed stable, normal, until it met the band of purple that bordered it like a wall. A few scattered patches of ley did remain, where perhaps it had been at its most virulent. In one of the patches the Unmaker stood, marooned. He was reeling, and his figure was no longer quite human. His face seemed flattened and deformed; his body kept shifting in size and shape, as if he was having trouble maintaining a human form. As if he could not quite decide what he was supposed to look like. She said, more to herself than to Davron, 'Of course! He would have had to have been there in the ley the Beast was dragging: otherwise it wouldn't have been so evil.' And then the truth of what she was seeing really hit her. 'Maker and midden,' she whispered, clutching hard at Davron. '*I stabilised the Unmaker.*'

She turned to him, appalled at the enormity of what she had done. And felt his anger at Carasma. The rage in him was deep-rooted wrath, the product of his five years of pain. Every muscle tensed.

'No –' she said, fearing what he would do. He mustn't die now, not when he was free of his sigil.

And then someone screamed at them, tearing her out of one fear and into another. '*Look out!* Keris, Davron, look out –'

They both turned in shock. It was the Chameleon.

Hidden, watching all that had happened, driven half mad by the shock of being suddenly stabilised, Quirk had staggered to his feet because he had seen what Keris and Davron had not: the Beast lived. It had dragged itself up and was lumbering towards them, insane with fear and rage and stability, intent on the destruction of the man it blamed. It lowered its fiery prong and began to gather speed.

'Oh Chaos,' Keris whispered.

Davron stood, his body straightening, to find poise and courage where moments before he had seemed beyond both.

And Quirk flung himself across the intervening space towards the Beast, waving and shouting, attracting its attention. It hesitated and turned towards him. And charged.

It was all the time Keris and Davron needed. Ley fled from their hands, fast and true and searing. The Beast shook its gigantic head in pain. Quirk danced nimbly out of the way.

The ley bounced across the burning hide of the Beast, annoying but not destroying it.

'Its eyes, go for its eyes,' Davron said.

The beast turned back towards its tormentors. This time the ley pierced its eyes and it bellowed with rage and pain, but still it came on.

'Do you have your knife, Keris?' Davron asked, almost casually. His hand reached to his waist where the whip handle was thrust through his belt. The plaited rawhide with its impregnated glass lay curled against his thigh. He shook it free and held out his left hand to Keris. She pressed her knife into his palm.

As the Beast snorted up towards Davron, the whip snaked out and wrapped itself around the base of its red-hot prong. Davron dodged to run alongside the creature, brushing against it, shoulder to shoulder as it swung around. Then, hauling himself up on the whip, he plunged the knife deep into its eye. The great animal sagged, its run ending. Its prong snapped, sawn through as Davron wrenched on the whip handle. Davron fell free, tumbling. Ichor pumped out of the hole left in the Beast's forehead as the body toppled, missing Davron by inches.

And it changed. It had been animal-like; now it became something else. A blackness, a nothingness that yet had

476

dimension, like a dark furriness. The earth beneath it crumbled as if eaten away. Davron scrambled back from the edge of the hollow in shock.

Keris winced, realising that the smell of scorched meat in her nostrils was Davron's own flesh, crisped where he had brushed against the Beast. He must have been in agony, yet he did not seem even to acknowledge that he had been hurt. He stared down at the blackness that had been the Beast and watched it melt away until there was nothing left but a hole with charred edges, and the still-smoking horn lying nearby on the ground. Then he turned towards the Unmaker.

Carasma stood where he had been, in the midst of the small patch of ley. His human form had further disintegrated. It was blurred now, its shape only vaguely human. A string of ley snaked out from him and before any of them could react it had encircled Quirk's neck. Quirk stood rigid with terror within the razor-sharp light of it. It was as slick as a honed knife blade, as dangerous as a garrotter's wire, and it was clear from the expression on his face that the Chameleon had been made to see it even though it was made of ley. One false move and he would decapitate himself.

'Don't touch me,' Carasma said to Davron, 'or I'll kill this man.'

Keris flicked a glance at Davron in which horror and amazement were equally mixed. *Carasma was frightened.*

'I belong to the Maker,' the Chameleon pointed out, his voice squeaky with fright. 'You cannot touch me, or you break the Law of the Universe, and condemn yourself.'

'Quirk will cut his own head off if he moves as much as an inch,' Davron muttered, despairing, 'and Carasma won't have done a thing.' Sooner or later Quirk would tire and fall against the garrotte . . .

'Do nothing,' the Unmaker warned Davron, 'or I shall never let him loose.' His mouth was a mouth no longer, yet he spoke.

'Coward,' Quirk said, still squeaking. 'Pick on someone your own size. What are you, anyway, some bully in the schoolroom? Is this the great Lord Carasma? Why, you're a nothing! Scared shitless, you are, with only your feet damped by ley. Put you in a stability, and you're gutless!'

He's right, Keris thought in wonder. Carasma's afraid, because he can only survive on this world within ley. And all he has about him is that little mud puddle ... She watched his wavering form and wondered if he felt pain. He had indicated once that he could not, yet obviously being marooned in such a small patch of ley caused him an anguish he could not hide. Perhaps he fears extinction, she thought. Or madness.

And then she saw what he was doing. He was sending out another string of ley, this time towards the band of ley that edged the area of stability. He intended to hook on to it, to pull it to himself, to make himself safe again in a haven of ley. All he needed was a little time.

'You worm,' Quirk told Carasma. Keris signed a kinesis of silence, but the Chameleon took no notice of the gesture; he seemed unable to keep his mouth sensibly shut. He continued, 'How are you going to crawl out of this one, eh? That's stability all around you. And let me tell you something else that you don't know, you oh, so clever fellow – burning a trompleri map brings instant stability. That's what happened here, in case you didn't notice. And yesterday Meldor the Blind burnt trompleri maps up and down the borders of Havenstar, sizzling your Minions to a blister, or sending them mad –'

'*You're* mad!' the Unmaker rasped, but his shock was obvious.

'Yes, of course I am. Flinging me from unstable Havenstar to stability like this has sent me out of my mind!' Quirk laughed, *giggled*. 'I'm the biggest coward in the world – ask anyone – and here I am telling the great Lord Carasma the unpalatable truths he doesn't want to hear. Hasn't the guts to hear! I'm as mad as a water-beetle. But I'm just an Unbound man – imagine what has happened to your Corrupted Ones. Your Minions and their Pets are dropping dead all around the borders to Havenstar, raving mad and foaming at the mouth.'

'It's true,' Davron agreed. 'My word on it as a Trician of Storre, honour of a Master Guide. Your attack on Havenstar has failed. And don't think that killing Keris here will stop the output of trompleri maps – the secret of their making is no secret any longer. Anyone can make a trompleri map now, thanks to us.'

Through the ley, Carasma tested the truth of Quirk's words and darted a desperate look around.

'You've failed, you miserable cur,' Quirk said. 'Your Minions are dying and the Unstable will soon be ours – what then, Lord Muck of nowhere?'

And Carasma, in a burst of uncontrolled rage, jerked on the line of ley that ringed the Chameleon's neck.

'*No!*' Keris screamed.

The Unmaker blanched, realising too late what he had done.

For a moment Quirk still stood, face expressionless, as if nothing had happened. Then his head rolled from his shoulders, the severing cut so fine that at first there did not seem to be even any blood. For one horrifying moment his body still stood where it was. Then, silently, it fountained blood and crumpled.

And the anger in Davron sought its balm.

He pulled the ley surrounding the Unmaker into himself: all its savage colour, all its corruption and contamination. It unwound from the ley mire like string from a ball and twisted its way across the intervening space towards the guide.

Carasma battled its loss, but he was weakened by the nearness of stability, driven to the edge of madness by its encirclement, fundamentally damaged because of his crime against the Law. He had killed one of the Maker's own.

Yet he tried. For a moment there was a tug of war. The ley twisted between the two like strung-out animal guts. It was a combat between an entity who was being called to account for his offence against the Law and a man fuelled by his anger at what had been taken from him. The weapon was not brute force, but will. '*Maker!*' Davron cried, the cry of a man too long denied solace. And the ley moved — towards Davron.

The age-old battle between Chaos and Creation had been replayed yet again, and this time Chaos lost.

Lord Carasma the Unmaker took the only way out. He reached upward to the other parts of himself, to the Chaos of the universe beyond the world, and pulled himself free.

The force of his going rent the air and ground. The earth was split deep beneath his feet, hurtling the Chameleon's body into the rift. The air was ripped apart from ground to sky by a band of black lightning, the bitter tang of it lingering long after it was gone. Carasma vanished with it, gone in a flash of Chaos back to the beginnings of the universe to lick his wounds, leaving the world to the Maker.

The sun shone and the grass was crisply green. It crushed beneath Keris's feet — and stayed crushed even after she had passed across it to Davron's side.

She gathered him into her arms, his skin to her skin, feeling his body against hers for the first time.

'Davron?'

'I'm here. Weak, but I'm here.'

'I think you have to rid yourself of the ley you have in you. It's too contaminated.'

'Maker, yes. It'll kill me else. Let me rest a minute and then we'll go to the Writhe. I'll replace it there.'

'Are you sure you're all right? Those burns —'

'Try a spot of healing, love. It would help. It hurts.'

'I don't know how.'

'Give me your ley. Think of it as a balm, turn it towards healing, and tease it out to me.'

She did as he asked, doing her best to soothe away his hurts, but the depth of the anguish she saw in his eyes — she was not sure she could ever cure that. She bent over him and her tears came. Tears of grief, of relief, of sorrow. For Davron, for Quirk. For what they both had lost.

'I'm sorry,' Davron said, thinking of Quirk. 'It was . . . quick. Was he truly mad, do you think – or did he goad Carasma deliberately? Knowing what he might achieve?'

'He – he knew I was going to burn a map. He must have known he could burn with it, and yet he stayed; he was that brave. Was he mad after that? Perhaps. But I think he knew what he was doing nonetheless.' She choked on the words, remembering, and had to stop.

He held her close, cradling her, burying his face into her neck. 'I don't know that I can go on living,' he whispered at last. 'Keris, the village, Dawnbreak – what I did –'

'You did nothing except act with honour,' she said firmly. 'The crime was Carasma's. And you – you and Quirk between you – you have sent the Unmaker back to the beginnings of time. How many will not die young because of that? How many will never be tainted? What you have done this day will set the balance right. As for any idea of not living: do you think I will let you go so easily? Davron – *we have a future*. For the first time I can hold you! And you can see your daughter, look after her, love her. And perhaps we can even look for your son – don't speak to me of not being able to live!'

She smiled down at him, and entwined her hand with his. Then she held the interlocked hands up for him to see. 'Look,' she whispered. 'Look at that, and tell me you want to die.'

She looked so smugly pleased that he could not help himself: he laughed.

And Davron of Storre began to heal.

Chapter Thirty-Three

*And why should we stop there? Once there were other lands:
Yedron and Yefron, Bellisthron and Brazis. Once there was a
sea that stretched beyond the horizon. Should we not seek to
find these places again?*

from the later writings of Meldor the Blind

Meldor leant against the railing of the balcony that over-
looked the audience room of the Hall. The map tables had
been long since cleared away. Now there were rows of chairs
for the dignitaries who would be taking part in the ceremony
to come, and at the head of the room there were ten
thrones side by side. Meldor could not see what was happening below, but his other senses told him that some of
the middle-ranking Tricians and clerics had already arrived.
Conversation drifted upward and with a little effort he
could separate one voice from the another. '– colour everywhere,' someone was muttering venomously. 'Shouldn't be
allowed –' Mingled in with the voices was the faint tinkling
of chantor bells sewn to stoles of office, and, when Meldor
listened very carefully and used his ley to filter out other
noise, he could even hear someone – a servant presumably –
brushing the velvet that covered the thrones. Shortly Rugriss
Ruddleby's reluctant backside would be gracing one of those
chairs next to the Margrave of Havenstar. Meldor felt a very
unregal satisfaction.

A moment later the door behind him opened. He had not
known that anyone had seen him up on the balcony and he

turned, senses alert. Pleasure arrived hard on the heels of his surprise. 'Keris!' he said. 'My dear, I am delighted you came. Is Davron here too?'

'Yes, indeed.' She walked to stand at his side, and looked down into the Hall. 'He's down there now. And don't tell me you didn't know.'

He gave a wry smile. 'Yes, I knew. I can feel his ley at five hundred paces. But tell me – how is he? How does he look?'

He sensed her softening. 'He is well. Today, in fact, he is rather magnificent, if I may say so. He is dressed in scarlet and black and he wears enough gold jewellery to sink a wildbell.'

'Ah. Then I gather he intends that to be a slap in the face to Chantry.'

She laughed. 'Of course! He – he is finding it hard to accept what you are doing, Margraf. As you know, his feelings towards Chantry are decidedly . . . mixed.'

'I can hardly blame him. But I have my reasons.'

She turned towards him, seeking something in his face. 'Then tell me. Why must you deal with them? I know they came to our aid when the Minions attacked. I know they helped us defeat those who survived the burning of the maps – but that was their choice. We both know they initially came to wipe us off the face of the land. Why must we deal with men and women who would rather see us dead than see us free?'

'I would not deal with them at all, except that we are in the position to dictate terms. Keris, no mapmaker outside Havenstar has discovered how easy it is to make trompleri maps. They all still think that you have to dig in ley lines to find the ingredients and, even with the Unmaker gone, they are chary of the vagaries of ley. They would rather buy their trompleri paints and inks from us. And none of them knows how we use maps to stabilise the Unstable. The Margraves do not know. *Chantry* does not know. They all have to come to us, to ask us to make their stabilities bigger, to convert the Unstable for them. As the old saying goes, we own the quarry for the stone to make the house.'

'Then why make concessions to Chantry? Why are you allowing them and their sanctimonious encoloured inside Havenstar to set up their chanteries?'

'Because it means they will acquiesce to what I want — what *we* want in return.'

'Which is?'

'All land south of the Writhe and the Riven, all the way to the borders of Yedron, if the place still exists. To do with what we want — to impregnate with ley to make a land suitable for people like you and me and Scow. I build for the future, Keris. With this treaty, signed by the Anhedrin and every single Margrave, we become a separate nation, not part of what will be New Malinawar. We will truly be Havenstar, separate and free.'

'And Chantry-guided.'

He laughed. 'I doubt it. Keris, think. Chantry has based its power on keeping Order, on the necessity of the Rule and maintaining kinesis chains. Now none of those things are necessary! As a consequence, Chantry is desperately scheming for power and losing out to the Margraves, and at the same time they are having to fight a battle for ascendancy over the hearts and minds of people who don't need them any more.' He shook his head in mock sympathy. 'Let them come. If they want any credibility then they must cater to the people's need for spiritual guidance. As a temporal power they are finished. But I am not so foolish as to think they can be ignored for ever. People need them.'

She was silent for such a long time he wondered if she accepted what he said.

Finally she said in a voice that was barely a whisper, 'He touched us both, out there. That day when I burnt the map.'

'Pardon?'

'The Maker.'

He absorbed the implications of that and felt a pang of painful jealousy begin behind his breastbone. With effort he pushed it back down. 'What do you mean?'

'We both felt Him. And I can tell you one thing: He

doesn't need to be worshipped. He doesn't even need to be thanked. Why should He? He is the Creator! All He wants of us is that we take care of That Which Was Created – nothing more.'

Lord Maker, he thought, his bitterness almost overwhelming. Why did You come to her? Why not me? He took a deep breath and subdued the pain. 'Keris, it has never been *He* who needs *us*. But that's a subject for a long philosophical discussion, not something we have time for now! We will talk of it another time. Did you have a particular reason for seeking me out just now?'

'No. Just to – to say congratulations, I guess.'

He heard the dryness in her tone and matched it with his own. 'You think I'm inhuman, don't you?' He blocked off the sounds from the hall and concentrated wholly on her, making her the total focus of his being. Others called it charisma; Meldor knew that it was nothing more than a trick of calculated concentration, turned on and off at will. He said, his candour deliberate, 'Keris, the larger picture has always seemed . . . more important to me than the players. If that is a crime, then I am guilty.'

'Yes, you are,' she said, forthright as usual. 'When we got back from our trip, for example, you could at least have asked us about . . . well, the more personal aspects. Instead of just wanting to know how many trompleri maps I'd made and whether Rugriss Ruddleby had listened to what Davron had to say.'

'Ah.' So that was what rankled, was it?

Once the last of the maddened Minions and Pets had been dispatched or scattered, he had sent Davron, Keris and Scow out to all the stabilities of Old Malinawar, carrying Havenstar's message: for the price of a treaty, Havenstar would sell them stability. Keris had mapped some of the crucial regions of the Unstable as they went, making the first of the trompleri maps they would one day burn – in secret – to fulfil their side of the treaty. Davron, playing the part of the Trician negotiator, had spoken with the Margraves and (reluctantly) with Rugriss Ruddleby. Eventually, he'd promised, all the Unstable north of the Riven and Writhe would be stable. He had not told them that it was something that Meldor had no intention of doing *too* quickly – Havenstar intended to make the stabilities pay, well into the future, for every bit of land that was claimed back from the Unstable.

The trip had been a long one: it had been a year before Keris and Davron and Scow had ridden back into Havenstar. 'Not as bad a journey as it used to be,' Davron had said laconically when he had greeted Meldor. 'With no Carasma lurking in the ley lines, or unmaking the landscape, with far fewer Minions or Pets than there used to be, things seem a lot tamer out there.'

'Don't believe him,' Keris had contradicted. 'Make him tell you about the Minions that attacked us near the Fourth, or the Pet that ate one of our horses as we crossed the Wide, or the whirlwind that came through our camp up near Bartle's Halt.'

In time, Meldor had indeed heard about those incidents, and he'd read Davron's official report, but he had never bothered to ask whether Davron had gone to see his daughter, or if Keris had seen her brother. It hadn't seemed important. 'Remiss of me,' he admitted now. 'I do know that you went to the Fifth twice during your trip, but Davron's daughter has not returned with you to Havenstar. And I can hear the pain in him still.' He hesitated. 'Is it now too late to ask what happened?'

Once again she was silent so long that he wondered if she was going to reply at all. Then she said carefully, 'Yes, we went to the Fifth twice. In the stabs he is a hero, you know. The man who banished the Unmaker. It is a little hard to take, but at least it opens doors. Tower-and-Fleury had to welcome him. But it was . . . difficult for Mirrin. She has such conflicting memories of what happened the day she met Carasma. And her mother poured all sorts of nonsense into her ears before she vanished off into Chantry. They are not barriers you can break down in a day or two. However, she is a bright, kind-hearted little girl — and time mends most things.' She smiled. 'And she has a lively curiosity. I write to her, you know, telling her about the magic of Havenstar, and she is gradually developing a desire to see for herself. Unfortunately, she cannot bring herself to cross a ley line. So we will have to wait until we have made the stability roads between all the stabs and Havenstar.'

He nodded, amused. 'You are not going to give up.'

He felt her slow smile. 'Me? No.' And then she sighed. 'He still does not find it easy, Meldor. They who remember Dawnbreak call him the Betrayer. In the streets of Shield there are those who spit on him. There is still . . . a darkness in him. She could take that away.'

He nodded. 'I know.' He turned away from the Hall and faced her once more. 'And what of you? Did you see your brother?'

'Yes. He runs a successful tavern now, where Kaylen the Mapmaker's used to be.' There was another long pause. 'My mother died about three weeks after I left Kibbleberry.'

'Ah.' Aware that an expression of sympathy would have been suspect, he switched the topic back to Thirl Kaylen. 'Did your brother give you any problems?'

'He might have done, except that he's scared silly of Davron. And Davron paid for the things I stole.' He heard laughter in her voice as she added, 'Except for the dowry money. Davron just fixed him with one of those black stares of his and growled, "That was intended as a dowry, and that's what it was. If you want it back, ask *me* for it." Thirl didn't say another word.'

'Is there anything else I should ask to redeem myself? Perhaps I should ask after Scow. Where is he? Why didn't he come today?'

She smiled, aware that he was gently mocking her as well as his own failings. 'I believe he is visiting Corrian. He said to tell you that not even the promise of the most lavish repast in all the history of Havenstar could get him to sit through eight

Margraves and Rugriss Ruddleby making speeches first.'

Meldor laughed. 'Something hasn't changed, at least! Still, I do wish he was here. The Chameleon too.' There, another sign of concern.

Her voice softened. 'Yes.' She had trouble getting the words out. 'Maker, how I – how I *miss* him!'

They fell silent for a moment, remembering. There had been so many who would not be present at the signing ceremony. So many who had died battling Minions and Pets. So many who had simply vanished – eaten perhaps. The pang Meldor felt was suddenly genuine. He said, 'He will never be forgotten. He is already part of Havenstar legend.'

'Yes,' she whispered. 'But he's not *here.*'

He nodded, knowing what she meant, and with a touch of smugness, played his winning piece. 'One more thing, Keris. I added a codicil to the treaty we are signing with Chantry. One more requirement I have demanded of them. Perhaps it will help to – er – appease Davron when he learns of it.'

She looked at him in enquiry. 'Oh?'

He nodded towards the closed door of an anteroom in front of them. 'Why don't you take a look?'

Mystified, she went to open the door. She expected to find some sort of document; instead Nablon was there, watching over a small boy who was seated on the floor, engrossed in the movement on a trompleri map in front of him.

Nablon's mandibles clacked in embarrassment. 'Oh, Mistress Storre – one of your maps – I'm sorry. It was the only thing I had that would amuse a six-year-old.'

She stared long and hard before turning back to Meldor. 'Six-year-old?'

He nodded. 'It's amazing what you can prise away from Chantry if you have the right price.'

'Oh. Oh, *Meldor*!'

It was just as well that no one in the Hall below looked up just then. Otherwise they would have seen the Margrave of Havenstar being soundly kissed by another man's wife.

* * *

Davron was suffering the attentions of Cylrie Mannertee when a servant appeared at his side to tell him that his wife would like to see him in the anteroom. Gratefully, he turned back to Cylrie. 'Hedrina, you must excuse me.'

She smiled coyly. 'Of course, Milor'. One must always obey the summons of one's spouse. But we shall meet again, I hope? And soon . . . perhaps?'

Gracefully he kissed her fingertips in a very Trician gesture, and smiled charmingly. 'Not if I can help it,' he said.

He was already out of the hall before the import of his words had sunk in.

The servant, half awed and half fearful just at being in his presence, ushered him to the anteroom and bowed reverently before leaving. With a smothered sigh Davron opened the door. He had not expected to find Keris alone, but neither had he expected to find her in the company of a child.

'What have we here?' he asked. Black eyes looked up at him solemnly from under a shock of equally black hair and he found himself smiling under the critical scrutiny.

'This is someone I'd like you to meet,' Keris said, her voice husky. 'Sent by Meldor.'

'Oh?' Mildly curious, he came over to the lad and knelt beside him. 'My name's Davron Storre. What's yours?'

The child regarded him solemnly. 'In the chanterie they called me Avred. But this lady says my daddy called me Staven. She says I'll know my daddy 'cos he's got black eyes just like mine.' His features rearranged themselves into a picture of childish concentration. 'You've got black eyes. Does that make you my daddy?'

He caught his breath, the pain of memory and hope inextricably mixed as they spasmed his insides. It seemed an aeon before he could clear his throat and say with a semblance of calm, 'Yes, I rather think it must. If you'll have me.' He reached out to slide the boy on to his knee and two chubby arms responded by wrapping themselves around his neck. Davron, unable to say anything more, raised his gaze

489

to Keris over the top of the dark curls and reached for her hand.

Outside, trumpets blared to mark the arrival of the Margraves of the Eight Stabilities and the Anhedrin, but neither Keris nor Davron even heard them.

In a nearby anteroom, the Margrave of Havenstar, waiting for the time to make his own grand entrance, schemed while his valet fussed about the set of his sleeves.

Yedron, he was thinking. We really must find out what happened to Yedron . . .